D0794516

Canto XXVI
Canto XXVII
Canto XXVIII
Canto XXIX
Canto XXX
Canto XXXI

THE PARADISO

Canto I
Canto II
Canto III
Canto IV
Canto V
Canto VI
Canto VII
Canto VIII
Canto IX
Canto X
Canto XI
Canto XII
Canto XIII
Canto XIV
Canto XV
Canto XVI
Canto XVII
Canto XVIII
Canto XIX
Canto XX
Canto XXI
Canto XXII
Canto XXIII
Canto XXIV
Canto XXV
Canto XXVI
Canto XXVII
Canto
XXVIII
Canto XXIX
Canto XXX

Canto I

THE DARK WOOD OF ERROR

Midway in his allotted threescore years and ten, Dante comes to himself with a start and realizes that he has strayed from the True Way into the Dark Wood of Error (Worldliness). As soon as he has realized his loss, Dante lifts his eyes and sees the first light of the sunrise (the Sun is the Symbol of Divine Illumination) lighting the shoulders of a little hill (The Mount of Joy). It is the Easter Season, the time of resurrection, and the sun is in its equinoctial rebirth. This juxtaposition of joyous symbols fills Dante with hope and he sets out at once to climb directly up the Mount of Joy, but almost immediately his way is blocked by the Three Beasts of Worldliness: THE LEOPARD OF MALICE AND FRAUD, THE LION OF VIOLENCE AND AMBITION, and THE SHE-WOLF OF INCONTINENCE. These beasts, and especially the She-Wolf, drive him back despairing into the darkness of error. But just as all seems lost, a figure appears to him. It is the shade of VIRGIL, Dante's symbol of HUMAN REASON.

Virgil explains that he has been sent to lead Dante from error. There can, however, be no direct ascent past the beasts: the man who would escape them must go a longer and harder way. First he must descend through Hell (The Recognition of Sin), then he must ascend through Purgatory (The Renunciation of Sin), and only then may he reach the pinnacle of joy and come to the Light of God. Virgil offers to guide Dante, but only as far as Human Reason can go. Another guide (BEATRICE, symbol of DIVINE LOVE) must take over for the final ascent, for Human Reason is self-limited. Dante submits himself joyously to Virgil's guidance and they move off.

Midway in our life's journey, I went astray
from the straight road and woke to find myself
alone in a dark wood. How shall I say

what wood that was! I never saw so drear,
so rank, so arduous a wilderness!
Its very memory gives a shape to fear.

Death could scarce be more bitter than that place!
But since it came to good, I will recount

all that I found revealed there by God's grace.

How I came to it I cannot rightly say,
so drugged and loose with sleep had I become
when I first wandered there from the True Way.

But at the far end of that valley of evil
whose maze had sapped my very heart with fear!
I found myself before a little hill

and lifted up my eyes. Its shoulders glowed
already with the sweet rays of that planet
whose virtue leads men straight on every road,

and the shining strengthened me against the fright
whose agony had wracked the lake of my heart
through all the terrors of that piteous night.

Just as a swimmer, who with his last breath
flounders ashore from perilous seas, might turn
to memorize the wide water of his death—

so did I turn, my soul still fugitive
from death's surviving image, to stare down
that pass that none had ever left alive.

And there I lay to rest from my heart's race
till calm and breath returned to me. Then rose
and pushed up that dead slope at such a pace

each footfall rose above the last. And lo!
almost at the beginning of the rise
I faced a spotted Leopard, all tremor and flow

and gaudy pelt. And it would not pass, but stood
so blocking my every turn that time and again
I was on the verge of turning back to the wood.

This fell at the first widening of the dawn
as the sun was climbing Aries with those stars
that rode with him to light the new creation.

Thus the holy hour and the sweet season
of commemoration did much to arm my fear
of that bright murderous beast with their good omen.

Yet not so much but what I shook with dread
at sight of a great Lion that broke upon me
raging with hunger, its enormous head

held high as if to strike a mortal terror
into the very air. And down his track,
a She-Wolf drove upon me, a starved horror

ravening and wasted beyond all belief.
She seemed a rack for avarice, gaunt and craving.
Oh many the souls she has brought to endless grief!

She brought such heaviness upon my spirit
at sight of her savagery and desperation,
I died from every hope of that high summit.

And like a miser—eager in acquisition
but desperate in self-reproach when Fortune's wheel
turns to the hour of his loss—all tears and attrition

I wavered back; and still the beast pursued,
forcing herself against me bit by bit
till I slid back into the sunless wood.

And as I fell to my soul's ruin, a presence
gathered before me on the discolored air,
the figure of one who seemed hoarse from long silence.

At sight of him in that friendless waste I cried:

"Have pity on me, whatever thing you are,
whether shade or living man." And it replied:

"Not man, though man I once was, and my blood
was Lombard, both my parents Mantuan.
I was born, though late, *sub Julio*, and bred

in Rome under Augustus in the noon
of the false and lying gods. I was a poet
and sang of old Anchises' noble son

who came to Rome after the burning of Troy.
But you—why do *you* return to these distresses
instead of climbing that shining Mount of Joy

which is the seat and first cause of man's bliss?"
"And are you then that Virgil and that fountain
of purest speech?" My voice grew tremulous:

"Glory and light of poets! now may that zeal
and love's apprenticeship that I poured out
on your heroic verses serve me well!

For you are my true master and first author,
the sole maker from whom I drew the breath
of that sweet style whose measures have brought me honor.

See there, immortal sage, the beast I flee.
For my soul's salvation, I beg you, guard me from her,
for she has struck a mortal tremor through me."

And he replied, seeing my soul in tears:
"He must go by another way who would escape
this wilderness, for that mad beast that fleers

before you there, suffers no man to pass.
She tracks down all, kills all, and knows no glut,

but, feeding, she grows hungrier than she was.

She mates with any beast, and will mate with more
before the Greyhound comes to hunt her down.
He will not feed on lands nor loot, but honor
and love and wisdom will make straight his way.
He will rise between Feltro and Feltro, and in him
shall be the resurrection and new day

of that sad Italy for which Nisus died,
and Turnus, and Euryalus, and the maid Camilla.
He shall hunt her through every nation of sick pride

till she is driven back forever to Hell
whence Envy first released her on the world.
Therefore, for your own good, I think it well

you follow me and I will be your guide
and lead you forth through an eternal place.
There you shall see the ancient spirits tried

in endless pain, and hear their lamentation
as each bemoans the second death of souls.
Next you shall see upon a burning mountain

souls in fire and yet content in fire,
knowing that whensoever it may be
they yet will mount into the blessed choir.

To which, if it is still your wish to climb,
a worthier spirit shall be sent to guide you.
With her shall I leave you, for the King of Time,

who reigns on high, forbids me to come there
since, living, I rebelled against his law.
He rules the waters and the land and air

and there holds court, his city and his throne.
Oh blessed are they he chooses!" And I to him:
"Poet, by that God to you unknown,

lead me this way. Beyond this present ill
and worse to dread, lead me to Peter's gate
and be my guide through the sad halls of Hell."

And he then: "Follow." And he moved ahead
in silence, and I followed where he led.

Canto II

The Descent

It is evening of the first day (Friday). Dante is following Virgil and finds himself tired and despairing. How can he be worthy of such a vision as Virgil has described? He hesitates and seems about to abandon his first purpose.

To comfort him Virgil explains how Beatrice descended to him in Limbo and told him of her concern for Dante. It is she, the symbol of Divine Love, who sends Virgil to lead Dante from error. She has come into Hell itself on this errand, for Dante cannot come to Divine Love unaided; Reason must lead him. Moreover Beatrice has been sent with the prayers of the Virgin Mary (COMPASSION), and of Saint Lucia (DIVINE LIGHT). Rachel (THE CONTEMPLATIVE LIFE) also figures in the heavenly scene which Virgil recounts.

Virgil explains all this and reproaches Dante: how can he hesitate longer when such heavenly powers are concerned for him, and Virgil himself has promised to lead him safely?

Dante understands at once that such forces cannot fail him, and his spirits rise in joyous anticipation.

The light was departing. The brown air drew down
all the earth's creatures, calling them to rest
from their day-roving, as I, one man alone,

prepared myself to face the double war
of the journey and the pity, which memory
shall here set down, nor hesitate, nor err.

O Muses! O High Genius! Be my aid!
O Memory, recorder of the vision,
here shall your true nobility be displayed!

Thus I began: "Poet, you who must guide me,
before you trust me to that arduous passage,
look to me and look through me—can I be worthy?

You sang how the father of Sylvius, while still
in corruptible flesh won to that other world,
crossing with mortal sense the immortal sill.

But if the Adversary of all Evil
weighing his consequence and who and what
should issue from him, treated him so well—

that cannot seem unfitting to thinking men,
since he was chosen father of Mother Rome
and of her Empire by God's will and token.

Both, to speak strictly, were founded and foreknown
as the established Seat of Holiness
for the successors of Great Peter's throne.

In that quest, which your verses celebrate,
he learned those mysteries from which arose
his victory and Rome's apostolate.

There later came the chosen vessel, Paul,
bearing the confirmation of that Faith
which is the one true door to life eternal.

But I—how should I dare? By whose permission?
I am not Aeneas. *I* am not Paul.
Who could believe me worthy of the vision?

How, then, may I presume to this high quest
and not fear my own brashness? You are wise
and will grasp what my poor words can but suggest."

As one who unwills what he wills, will stay
strong purposes with feeble second thoughts
until he spells all his first zeal away—

so I hung back and balked on that dim coast

till thinking had worn out my enterprise,
so stout at starting and so early lost.

"I understand from your words and the look in your eyes,"
that shadow of magnificence answered me,
"your soul is sunken in that cowardice

that bears down many men, turning their course
and resolution by imagined perils,
as his own shadow turns the frightened horse.

To free you of this dread I will tell you all
of why I came to you and what I heard
when first I pitied you. I was a soul

among the souls of Limbo, when a Lady
so blessed and so beautiful, I prayed her
to order and command my will, called to me.

Her eyes were kindled from the lamps of Heaven.
Her voice reached through me, tender, sweet, and low.
An angel's voice, a music of its own:

'O gracious Mantuan whose melodies
live in earth's memory and shall live on
till the last motion ceases in the skies,

my dearest friend, and fortune's foe, has strayed
onto a friendless shore and stands beset
by such distresses that he turns afraid

from the True Way, and news of him in Heaven
rumors my dread he is already lost.
I come, afraid that I am too-late risen.

Fly to him and with your high counsel, pity,
and with whatever need be for his good

and soul's salvation, help him, and solace me.

It is I, Beatrice, who send you to him.
I come from the blessed height for which I yearn.
Love called me here. When amid Seraphim

I stand again before my Lord, your praises
shall sound in Heaven.' She paused, and I began:
'O Lady of that only grace that raises

feeble mankind within its mortal cycle
above all other works God's will has placed
within the heaven of the smallest circle;

so welcome is your command that to my sense,
were it already fulfilled, it would yet seem tardy.
I understand, and am all obedience.

But tell me how you dare to venture thus
so far from the wide heaven of your joy
to which your thoughts yearn back from this abyss.'

'Since what you ask,' she answered me, 'probes near
the root of all, I will say briefly only
how I have come through Hell's pit without fear.

Know then, O waiting and compassionate soul,
that is to fear which has the power to harm,
and nothing else is fearful even in Hell.

I am so made by God's all-seeing mercy
your anguish does not touch me, and the flame
of this great burning has no power upon me.

There is a Lady in Heaven so concerned
for him I send you to, that for her sake
the strict decree is broken. She has turned

and called Lucia to her wish and mercy
saying: "Thy faithful one is sorely pressed;
in his distresses I commend him to thee."

Lucia, that soul of light and foe of all
cruelty, rose and came to me at once
where I was sitting with the ancient Rachel,

saying to me: "Beatrice, true praise of God,
why dost thou not help him who loved thee so
that for thy sake he left the vulgar crowd?

Dost thou not hear his cries? Canst thou not see
the death he wrestles with beside that river
no ocean can surpass for rage and fury?"

No soul of earth was ever as rapt to seek
its good or flee its injury as I was—
when I had heard my sweet Lucia speak—

to descend from Heaven and my blessed seat
to you, laying my trust in that high speech
that honors you and all who honor it.'

She spoke and turned away to hide a tear
that, shining, urged me faster. So I came
and freed you from the beast that drove you there,

blocking the near way to the Heavenly Height.
And now what ails you? Why do you lag? Why
this heartsick hesitation and pale fright

when three such blessed Ladies lean from Heaven
in their concern for you and my own pledge
of the great good that waits you has been given?"

As flowerlets drooped and puckered in the night
turn up to the returning sun and spread
their petals wide on his new warmth and light—

just so my wilted spirits rose again
and such a heat of zeal surged through my veins
that I was born anew. Thus I began:

"Blesséd be that Lady of infinite pity,
and blesséd be thy taxed and courteous spirit
that came so promptly on the word she gave thee.

Thy words have moved my heart to its first purpose.
My Guide! My Lord! My Master! Now lead on:
one will shall serve the two of us in this."

He turned when I had spoken, and at his back
I entered on that hard and perilous track.

Canto III

The Poets pass the Gate of Hell and are immediately assailed by cries of anguish. Dante sees the first of the souls in torment. They are THE OPPORTUNISTS, those souls who in life were neither for good nor evil but only for themselves. Mixed with them are those outcasts who took no sides in the Rebellion of the Angels. They are neither in Hell nor out of it. Eternally unclassified, they race round and round pursuing a wavering banner that runs forever before them through the dirty air; and as they run they are pursued by swarms of wasps and hornets, who sting them and produce a constant flow of blood and putrid matter which trickles down the bodies of the sinners and is feasted upon by loathsome worms and maggots who coat the ground.

The law of Dante's Hell is the law of symbolic retribution. As they sinned so are they punished. They took no sides, therefore they are given no place. As they pursued the ever-shifting illusion of their own advantage, changing their courses with every changing wind, so they pursue eternally an elusive, ever-shifting banner. As their sin was a darkness, so they move in darkness. As their own guilty conscience pursued them, so they are pursued by swarms of wasps and hornets. And as their actions were a moral filth, so they run eternally through the filth of worms and maggots which they themselves feed.

Dante recognizes several, among them POPE CELESTINE V, but without delaying to speak to any of these souls, the Poets move on to ACHERON, the first of the rivers of Hell. Here the newly-arrived souls of the damned gather and wait for monstrous CHARON to ferry them over to punishment. Charon recognizes Dante as a living man and angrily refuses him passage. Virgil forces Charon to serve them, but Dante swoons with terror, and does not reawaken until he is on the other side.

I AM THE WAY INTO THE CITY OF WOE.
I AM THE WAY TO A FORSAKEN PEOPLE.
I AM THE WAY INTO ETERNAL SORROW.

SACRED JUSTICE MOVED MY ARCHITECT.

I WAS RAISED HERE BY DIVINE OMNIPOTENCE,
PRIMORDIAL LOVE AND ULTIMATE INTELLECT.

ONLY THOSE ELEMENTS TIME CANNOT WEAR
WERE MADE BEFORE ME, AND BEYOND TIME I STAND.
ABANDON ALL HOPE YE WHO ENTER HERE.

These mysteries I read cut into stone
above a gate. And turning I said: "Master,
what is the meaning of this harsh inscription?"

And he then as initiate to novice:
"Here must you put by all division of spirit
and gather your soul against all cowardice.

This is the place I told you to expect.
Here you shall pass among the fallen people,
souls who have lost the good of intellect."

So saying, he put forth his hand to me,
and with a gentle and encouraging smile
he led me through the gate of mystery.

Here sighs and cries and wails coiled and recoiled
on the starless air, spilling my soul to tears.
A confusion of tongues and monstrous accents toiled

in pain and anger. Voices hoarse and shrill
and sounds of blows, all intermingled, raised
tumult and pandemonium that still

whirls on the air forever dirty with it
as if a whirlwind sucked at sand. And I,
holding my head in horror, cried:
"Sweet Spirit,

what souls are these who run through this black haze?"

And he to me: "These are the nearly soulless
whose lives concluded neither blame nor praise.

They are mixed here with that despicable corps
of angels who were neither for God nor Satan,
but only for themselves. The High Creator

scourged them from Heaven for its perfect beauty,
and Hell will not receive them since the wicked
might feel some glory over them." And I:

"Master, what gnaws at them so hideously
their lamentation stuns the very air?"
"They have no hope of death," he answered me,

"and in their blind and unattaining state
their miserable lives have sunk so low
that they must envy every other fate.

No word of them survives their living season.
Mercy and Justice deny them even a name.
Let us not speak of them: look, and pass on."

I saw a banner there upon the mist.
Circling and circling, it seemed to scorn all pause.
So it ran on, and still behind it pressed

a never-ending rout of souls in pain.
I had not thought death had undone so many
as passed before me in that mournful train.

And some I knew among them; last of all
I recognized the shadow of that soul
who, in his cowardice, made the Great Denial.

At once I understood for certain: these were of that retrograde and faithless crew
hateful to God and to His enemies.

These wretches never born and never dead
ran naked in a swarm of wasps and hornets
that goaded them the more the more they fled,

and made their faces stream with bloody gouts
of pus and tears that dribbled to their feet
to be swallowed there by loathsome worms and maggots.

Then looking onward I made out a throng
assembled on the beach of a wide river,
whereupon I turned to him: "Master, I long

to know what souls these are, and what strange usage
makes them as eager to cross as they seem to be
in this infected light." At which the Sage:

"All this shall be made known to you when we stand
on the joyless beach of Acheron." And I
cast down my eyes, sensing a reprimand

in what he said, and so walked at his side
in silence and ashamed until we came
through the dead cavern to that sunless tide.

There, steering toward us in an ancient ferry
came an old man with a white bush of hair,
bellowing: "Woe to you depraved souls! Bury

here and forever all hope of Paradise:
I come to lead you to the other shore,
into eternal dark, into fire and ice.

And you who are living yet, I say begone
from these who are dead." But when he saw me stand
against his violence he began again:

"By other windings and by other steerage
shall you cross to that other shore. Not here! Not here!
A lighter craft than mine must give you passage."

And my Guide to him: "Charon, bite back your spleen:
this has been willed where what is willed must be,
and is not yours to ask what it may mean."

The steersman of that marsh of ruined souls,
who wore a wheel of flame around each eye,
stifled the rage that shook his woolly jowls.

But those unmanned and naked spirits there
turned pale with fear and their teeth began to chatter
at sound of his crude bellow. In despair

they blasphemed God, their parents, their time on earth,
the race of Adam, and the day and the hour
and the place and the seed and the womb that gave them birth.

But all together they drew to that grim shore
where all must come who lose the fear of God.
Weeping and cursing they come for evermore,
and demon Charon with eyes like burning coals
herds them in, and with a whistling oar
flails on the stragglers to his wake of souls.

As leaves in autumn loosen and stream down
until the branch stands bare above its tatters
spread on the rustling ground, so one by one

the evil seed of Adam in its Fall
cast themselves, at his signal, from the shore
and streamed away like birds who hear their call.

So they are gone over that shadowy water,
and always before they reach the other shore

a new noise stirs on this, and new throngs gather.

"My son," the courteous Master said to me,
"all who die in the shadow of God's wrath
converge to this from every clime and country.
And all pass over eagerly, for here
Divine Justice transforms and spurs them so
their dread turns wish: they yearn for what they fear.

No soul in Grace comes ever to this crossing;
therefore if Charon rages at your presence
you will understand the reason for his cursing."

When he had spoken, all the twilight country
shook so violently, the terror of it
bathes me with sweat even in memory:

the tear-soaked ground gave out a sigh of wind
that spewed itself in flame on a red sky,
and all my shattered senses left me. Blind,

like one whom sleep comes over in a swoon,
I stumbled into darkness and went down.

Canto IV

CIRCLE ONE: LIMBO
The Virtuous Pagans

Dante wakes to find himself across Acheron. The Poets are now on the brink of Hell itself, which Dante conceives as a great funnel-shaped cave lying below the northern hemisphere with its bottom point at the earth's center. Around this great circular depression runs a series of ledges, each of which Dante calls a CIRCLE. Each circle is assigned to the punishment of one category of sin.

As soon as Dante's strength returns, the Poets begin to cross the FIRST CIRCLE. Here they find the VIRTUOUS PAGANS. They were born without the light of Christ's revelation, and, therefore, they cannot come into the light of God, but they are not tormented. Their only pain is that they have no hope.

Ahead of them Dante sights a great dome of light, and a voice trumpets through the darkness welcoming Virgil back, for this is his eternal place in Hell. Immediately the great Poets of all time appear—HOMER, HORACE, OVID, and LUCAN. They greet Virgil, and they make Dante a sixth in their company.

With them Dante enters the Citadel of Human Reason and sees before his eyes the Master Souls of Pagan Antiquity gathered on a green, and illuminated by the radiance of Human Reason. This is the highest state man can achieve without God, and the glory of it dazzles Dante, but he knows also that it is nothing compared to the glory of God.

A monstrous clap of thunder broke apart
the swoon that stuffed my head; like one awakened
by violent hands, I leaped up with a start.

And having risen; rested and renewed,
I studied out the landmarks of the gloom
to find my bearings there as best I could.

And I found I stood on the very brink of the valley
called the Dolorous Abyss, the desolate chasm
where rolls the thunder of Hell's eternal cry, so depthless-deep and nebulous and dim

that stare as I might into its frightful pit
it gave me back no feature and no bottom.

Death-pale, the Poet spoke: "Now let us go
into the blind world waiting here below us.
I will lead the way and you shall follow."

And I, sick with alarm at his new pallor,
cried out, "How can I go this way when you
who are my strength in doubt turn pale with terror?"

And he: "The pain of these below us here,
drains the color from my face for pity,
and leaves this pallor you mistake for fear.

Now let us go, for a long road awaits us."
So he entered and so he led me in
to the first circle and ledge of the abyss.

No tortured wailing rose to greet us here
but sounds of sighing rose from every side,
sending a tremor through the timeless air,

a grief breathed out of untormented sadness,
the passive state of those who dwelled apart,
men, women, children—a dim and endless congress.

And the Master said to me: "You do not question
what souls these are that suffer here before you?
I wish you to know before you travel on

that these were sinless. And still their merits fail,
for they lacked Baptism's grace, which is the door
of the true faith *you* were born to. Their birth fell

before the age of the Christian mysteries,
and so they did not worship God's Trinity

in fullest duty. I am one of these.

For such defects are we lost, though spared the fire
and suffering Hell in one affliction only:
that without hope we live on in desire."

I thought how many worthy souls there were
suspended in that Limbo, and a weight
closed on my heart for what the noblest suffer.

"Instruct me, Master and most noble Sir,"
I prayed him then, "better to understand
the perfect creed that conquers every error:

has any, by his own or another's merit,
gone ever from this place to blessedness?"
He sensed my inner question and answered it:

"I was still new to this estate of tears
when a Mighty One descended here among us,
crowned with the sign of His victorious years.

He took from us the shade of our first parent,
of Abel, his pure son, of ancient Noah,
of Moses, the bringer of law, the obedient.

Father Abraham, David the King,
Israel with his father and his children,
Rachel, the holy vessel of His blessing,

and many more He chose for elevation
among the elect. And before these, you must know,
no human soul had ever won salvation."

We had not paused as he spoke, but held our road
and passed meanwhile beyond a press of souls
crowded about like trees in a thick wood.

And we had not traveled far from where I woke
when I made out a radiance before us
that struck away a hemisphere of dark.

We were still some distance back in the long night,
yet near enough that I half-saw, half-sensed,
what quality of souls lived in that light.

"O ornament of wisdom and of art,
what souls are these whose merit lights their way
even in Hell. What joy sets them apart?"

And he to me: "The signature of honor
they left on earth is recognized in Heaven
and wins them ease in Hell out of God's favor."

And as he spoke a voice rang on the air:
"Honor the Prince of Poets; the soul and glory
that went from us returns. He is here! He is here!"

The cry ceased and the echo passed from hearing;
I saw four mighty presences come toward us
with neither joy nor sorrow in their bearing.

"Note well," my Master said as they came on,
"that soul that leads the rest with sword in hand
as if he were their captain and champion.

It is Homer, singing master of the earth.
Next after him is Horace, the satirist,
Ovid is third, and Lucan is the fourth.

Since all of these have part in the high name
the voice proclaimed, calling me Prince of Poets,
the honor that they do me honors them."

So I saw gathered at the edge of light
the masters of that highest school whose song
outsoars all others like an eagle's flight.

And after they had talked together a while,
they turned and welcomed me most graciously,
at which I saw my approving Master smile.

And they honored me far beyond courtesy,
for they included me in their own number,
making me sixth in that high company.

So we moved toward the light, and as we passed
we spoke of things as well omitted here
as it was sweet to touch on there. At last

we reached the base of a great Citadel
circled by seven towering battlements
and by a sweet brook flowing round them all.

This we passed over as if it were firm ground.
Through seven gates I entered with those sages
and came to a green meadow blooming round.

There with a solemn and majestic poise
stood many people gathered in the light,
speaking infrequently and with muted voice.

Past that enameled green we six withdrew
into a luminous and open height
from which each soul among them stood in view.

And there directly before me on the green
the master souls of time were shown to me.
I glory in the glory I have seen!

Electra stood in a great company

among whom I saw Hector and Aeneas
and Caesar in armor with his falcon's eye.

I saw Camilla, and the Queen Amazon
across the field. I saw the Latian King
seated there with his daughter by his throne.

And the good Brutus who overthrew the Tarquin:
Lucrezia, Julia, Marcia, and Cornelia;
and, by himself apart, the Saladin.

And raising my eyes a little I saw on high
Aristotle, the master of those who know,
ringed by the great souls of philosophy.

All wait upon him for their honor and his.
I saw Socrates and Plato at his side
before all others there. Democritus

who ascribes the world to chance, Diogenes,
and with him there Thales, Anaxagoras,
Zeno, Heraclitus, Empedocles.

And I saw the wise collector and analyst—
Dioscorides I mean. I saw Orpheus there,
Tully, Linus, Seneca the moralist,

Euclid the geometer, and Ptolemy,
Hippocrates, Galen, Avicenna,
and Averroës of the Great Commentary.

I cannot count so much nobility;
my longer theme pursues me so that often
the word falls short of the reality.

The company of six is reduced by four.
My Master leads me by another road

Canto V

CIRCLE TWO
The Carnal

The Poets leave Limbo and enter the SECOND CIRCLE. Here begin the torments of Hell proper, and here, blocking the way, sits MINOS, the dread and semi-bestial judge of the damned who assigns to each soul its eternal torment. He orders the Poets back; but Virgil silences him as he earlier silenced Charon, and the Poets move on.

    They find themselves on a dark ledge swept by a great whirlwind, which spins within it the souls of the CARNAL, those who betrayed reason to their appetites. Their sin was to abandon themselves to the tempest of their passions: so they are swept forever in the tempest of Hell, forever denied the light of reason and of God. Virgil identifies many among them. SEMIRAMIS is there, and DIDO, CLEOPATRA, HELEN, ACHILLES, PARIS, and TRISTAN. Dante sees PAOLO and FRANCESCA swept together, and in the name of love he calls to them to tell their sad story. They pause from their eternal flight to come to him, and Francesca tells their history while Paolo weeps at her side. Dante is so stricken by compassion at their tragic tale that he swoons once again.

So we went down to the second ledge alone;
a smaller circle of so much greater pain
the voice of the damned rose in a bestial moan.

There Minos sits, grinning, grotesque, and hale.
He examines each lost soul as it arrives
and delivers his verdict with his coiling tail.

That is to say, when the ill-fated soul
appears before him it confesses all,
and that grim sorter of the dark and foul

decides which place in Hell shall be its end,
then wraps his twitching tail about himself
one coil for each degree it must descend.

The soul descends and others take its place:
each crowds in its turn to judgment, each confesses,
each hears its doom and falls away through space.

"O you who come into this camp of woe,"
cried Minos when he saw me turn away
without awaiting his judgment, "watch where you go

once you have entered here, and to whom you turn!
Do not be misled by that wide and easy passage!"
And my Guide to him: "That is not your concern;

it is his fate to enter every door.
This has been willed where what is willed must be,
and is not yours to question. Say no more."

Now the choir of anguish, like a wound,
strikes through the tortured air. Now I have come
to Hell's full lamentation, sound beyond sound.

I came to a place stripped bare of every light
and roaring on the naked dark like seas
wracked by a war of winds. Their hellish flight

of storm and counterstorm through time foregone,
sweeps the souls of the damned before its charge.
Whirling and battering it drives them on,

and when they pass the ruined gap of Hell
through which we had come, their shrieks begin anew.
There they blaspheme the power of God eternal.

And this, I learned, was the never-ending flight
of those who sinned in the flesh, the carnal and lusty
who betrayed reason to their appetite.

As the wings of wintering starlings bear them on
in their great wheeling flights, just so the blast
wherries these evil souls through time foregone.

Here, there, up, down, they whirl and, whirling, strain
with never a hope of hope to comfort them,
not of release, but even of less pain.

As cranes go over sounding their harsh cry,
leaving the long streak of their flight in air,
so come these spirits, wailing as they fly.

And watching their shadows lashed by wind, I cried:
"Master, what souls are these the very air
lashes with its black whips from side to side?"

"The first of these whose history you would know,"
he answered me, "was Empress of many tongues.
Mad sensuality corrupted her so

that to hide the guilt of her debauchery
she licensed all depravity alike,
and lust and law were one in her decree.

She is Semiramis of whom the tale is told
how she married Ninus and succeeded him
to the throne of that wide land the Sultans hold.

The other is Dido; faithless to the ashes
of Sichaeus, she killed herself for love.
The next whom the eternal tempest lashes

is sense-drugged Cleopatra. See Helen there,
from whom such ill arose. And great Achilles,
who fought at last with love in the house of prayer.

And Paris. And Tristan." As they whirled above

he pointed out more than a thousand shades
of those torn from the mortal life by love.

I stood there while my Teacher one by one
named the great knights and ladies of dim time;
and I was swept by pity and confusion.

At last I spoke: "Poet, I should be glad
to speak a word with those two swept together
so lightly on the wind and still so sad."

And he to me: "Watch them. When next they pass,
call to them in the name of love that drives
and damns them here. In that name they will pause."

Thus, as soon as the wind in its wild course
brought them around, I called: "O wearied souls!
if none forbid it, pause and speak to us."

As mating doves that love calls to their nest
glide through the air with motionless raised wings,
borne by the sweet desire that fills each breast—

Just so those spirits turned on the torn sky
from the band where Dido whirls across the air;
such was the power of pity in my cry.

"O living creature, gracious, kind, and good,
going this pilgrimage through the sick night,
visiting us who stained the earth with blood,

were the King of Time our friend, we would pray His peace
on you who have pitied us. As long as the wind
will let us pause, ask of us what you please.

The town where I was born lies by the shore
where the Po descends into its ocean rest

with its attendant streams in one long murmur.

Love, which in gentlest hearts will soonest bloom
seized my lover with passion for that sweet body
from which I was torn unshriven to my doom.

Love, which permits no loved one not to love,
took me so strongly with delight in him
that we are one in Hell, as we were above.

Love led us to one death. In the depths of Hell
Caïna waits for him who took our lives."
This was the piteous tale they stopped to tell.

And when I had heard those world-offended lovers
I bowed my head. At last the Poet spoke:
"What painful thoughts are these your lowered brow covers?"

When at length I answered, I began: "Alas!
What sweetest thoughts, what green and young desire
led these two lovers to this sorry pass."

Then turning to those spirits once again,
I said: "Francesca, what you suffer here
melts me to tears of pity and of pain.

But tell me: in the time of your sweet sighs
by what appearances found love the way
to lure you to his perilous paradise?"

And she: "The double grief of a lost bliss
is to recall its happy hour in pain.
Your Guide and Teacher knows the truth of this.

But if there is indeed a soul in Hell
to ask of the beginning of our love
out of his pity, I will weep and tell:

On a day for dalliance we read the rhyme
of Lancelot, how love had mastered him.
We were alone with innocence and dim time.

Pause after pause that high old story drew
our eyes together while we blushed and paled;
but it was one soft passage overthrew

our caution and our hearts. For when we read
how her fond smile was kissed by such a lover,
he who is one with me alive and dead

breathed on my lips the tremor of his kiss.
That book, and he who wrote it, was a pander.
That day we read no further." As she said this,

the other spirit, who stood by her, wept
so piteously, I felt my senses reel
and faint away with anguish. I was swept

by such a swoon as death is, and I fell,
as a corpse might fall, to the dead floor of Hell.

Canto VI

Dante recovers from his swoon and finds himself in the THIRD CIRCLE. A great storm of putrefaction falls incessantly, a mixture of stinking snow and freezing rain, which forms into a vile slush underfoot. Everything about this Circle suggests a gigantic garbage dump. The souls of the damned lie in the icy paste, swollen and obscene, and CERBERUS, the ravenous three-headed dog of Hell, stands guard over them, ripping and tearing them with his claws and teeth.

These are the GLUTTONS. In life they made no higher use of the gifts of God than to wallow in food and drink, producers of nothing but garbage and offal. Here they lie through all eternity, themselves like garbage, half-buried in fetid slush, while Cerberus slavers over them as they in life slavered over their food.

As the Poets pass, one of the speakers sits up and addresses Dante. He is CIACCO, THE HOG, a citizen of Dante's own Florence. He recognizes Dante and asks eagerly for news of what is happening there. With the foreknowledge of the damned, Ciacco then utters the first of the political prophecies that are to become a recurring theme of the Inferno. The Poets then move on toward the next Circle, at the edge of which they encounter the monster Plutus.

My senses had reeled from me out of pity
for the sorrow of those kinsmen and lost lovers.
Now they return, and waking gradually,

I see new torments and new souls in pain
about me everywhere. Wherever I turn
away from grief I turn to grief again.

I am in the Third Circle of the torments.
Here to all time with neither pause nor change
the frozen rain of Hell descends in torrents.

Huge hailstones, dirty water, and black snow
pour from the dismal air to putrefy

the putrid slush that waits for them below.

Here monstrous Cerberus, the ravening beast,
howls through his triple throats like a mad dog
over the spirits sunk in that foul paste.

His eyes are red, his beard is greased with phlegm,
his belly is swollen, and his hands are claws
to rip the wretches and flay and mangle them.

And they, too, howl like dogs in the freezing storm,
turning and turning from it as if they thought
one naked side could keep the other warm.

When Cerberus discovered us in that swill
his dragon-jaws yawed wide, his lips drew back
in a grin of fangs. No limb of him was still.

My Guide bent down and seized in either fist
a clod of the stinking dirt that festered there
and flung them down the gullet of the beast.

As a hungry cur will set the echoes raving
and then fall still when he is thrown a bone,
all of his clamor being in his craving,

so the three ugly heads of Cerberus,
whose yowling at those wretches deafened them,
choked on their putrid sops and stopped their fuss.

We made our way across the sodden mess
of souls the rain beat down, and when our steps
fell on a body, they sank through emptiness.

All those illusions of being seemed to lie
drowned in the slush; until one wraith among them
sat up abruptly and called as I passed by:

"O you who are led this journey through the shade
of Hell's abyss, do you recall this face?
You had been made before I was unmade."

And I: "Perhaps the pain you suffer here
distorts your image from my recollection.
I do not know you as you now appear."

And he to me: "Your own city, so rife
with hatred that the bitter cup flows over
was mine too in that other, clearer life.

Your citizens nicknamed me Ciacco, The Hog:
gluttony was my offense, and for it
I lie here rotting like a swollen log.

Nor am I lost in this alone; all these
you see about you in this painful death
have wallowed in the same indecencies."

I answered him: "Ciacco, your agony
weighs on my heart and calls my soul to tears;
but tell me, if you can, what is to be

for the citizens of that divided state,
and whether there are honest men among them,
and for what reasons we are torn by hate."

And he then: "After many words given and taken
it shall come to blood; White shall rise over Black
and rout the dark lord's force, battered and shaken.

Then it shall come to pass within three suns
that the fallen shall arise, and by the power
of one now gripped by many hesitations

Black shall ride on White for many years,
loading it down with burdens and oppressions
and humbling of proud names and helpless tears.

Two are honest, but none will heed them. There,
pride, avarice, and envy are the tongues
men know and heed, a Babel of despair."

Here he broke off his mournful prophecy.
And I to him: "Still let me urge you on
to speak a little further and instruct me:

Farinata and Tegghiaio, men of good blood,
Jacopo Rusticucci, Arrigo, Mosca,
and the others who set their hearts on doing good—

where are they now whose high deeds might be-gem
the crown of kings? I long to know their fate.
Does Heaven soothe or Hell envenom them?"

And he: "They lie below in a blacker lair.
A heavier guilt draws them to greater pain.
If you descend so far you may see them there.

But when you move again among the living,
oh speak my name to the memory of men!
Having answered all, I say no more." And giving

his head a shake, he looked up at my face
cross-eyed, then bowed his head and fell away
among the other blind souls of that place.

And my Guide to me: "He will not wake again
until the angel trumpet sounds the day
on which the host shall come to judge all men.

Then shall each soul before the seat of Mercy

return to its sad grave and flesh and form
to hear the edict of Eternity."

So we picked our slow way among the shades
and the filthy rain, speaking of life to come.
"Master," I said, "when the great clarion fades

into the voice of thundering Omniscience,
what of these agonies? Will they be the same,
or more, or less, after the final sentence?"

And he to me: "Look to your science again
where it is written: the more a thing is perfect
the more it feels of pleasure and of pain.

As for these souls, though they can never soar
to true perfection, still in the new time
they will be nearer it than they were before."

And so we walked the rim of the great ledge
speaking of pain and joy, and of much more
that I will not repeat, and reached the edge
where the descent begins. There, suddenly,
we came on Plutus, the great enemy.

Canto VII

CIRCLE FOUR
CIRCLE FIVE
The Hoarders and the Wasters
The Wrathful and the Sullen

PLUTUS menaces the Poets, but once more Virgil shows himself more powerful than the rages of Hell's monsters. The Poets enter the FOURTH CIRCLE and find what seems to be a war in progress.

The sinners are divided into two raging mobs, each soul among them straining madly at a great boulder-like weight. The two mobs meet, clashing their weights against one another, after which they separate, pushing the great weights apart, and begin over again.

One mob is made up of the HOARDERS, the other of the WASTERS. In life, they lacked all moderation in regulating their expenses; they destroyed the light of God within themselves by thinking of nothing but money. Thus in death, their souls are encumbered by dead weights (mundanity) and one excess serves to punish the other. Their souls, moreover, have become so dimmed and awry in their fruitless rages that there is no hope of recognizing any among them.

The Poets pass on while Virgil explains the function of DAME FORTUNE in the Divine Scheme. As he finishes (it is past midnight now of Good Friday) they reach the inner edge of the ledge and come to a Black Spring which bubbles murkily over the rocks to form the MARSH OF STYX, which is the FIFTH CIRCLE, the last station of the UPPER HELL.

Across the marsh they see countless souls attacking one another in the foul slime. These are the WRATHFUL and the symbolism of their punishment is obvious. Virgil also points out to Dante certain bubbles rising from the slime and informs him that below that mud lie entombed the souls of the SULLEN. In life they refused to welcome the sweet light of the Sun (Divine Illumination) and in death they are buried forever below the stinking waters of the Styx, gargling the words of an endless chant in a grotesque parody of singing a hymn.

"Papa Satán, Papa Satán, aleppy,"
Plutus clucked and stuttered in his rage;
and my all-knowing Guide, to comfort me:

"Do not be startled, for no power of his,
however he may lord it over the damned,
may hinder your descent through this abyss."

And turning to that carnival of bloat
cried: "Peace, you Wolf of Hell. Choke back your bile
and let its venom blister your own throat.

Our passage through this pit is willed on high
by that same Throne that loosed the angel wrath
of Michael on ambition and mutiny."

As puffed out sails fall when the mast gives way
and flutter to a self-convulsing heap—
so collapsed Plutus into that dead clay.

Thus we descended the dark scarp of Hell
to which all the evil of the Universe
comes home at last, into the Fourth Great Circle

and ledge of the abyss. O Holy Justice,
who could relate the agonies I saw!
What guilt is man that he can come to this?

Just as the surge Charybdis hurls to sea
crashes and breaks upon its countersurge,
so these shades dance and crash eternally.

Here, too, I saw a nation of lost souls,
far more than were above: they strained their chests
against enormous weights, and with mad howls

rolled them at one another. Then in haste
they rolled them back, one party shouting out:
"Why do you hoard?" and the other: "Why do you waste?"

So back around that ring they puff and blow,
each faction to its course, until they reach
opposite sides, and screaming as they go

the madmen turn and start their weights again
to crash against the maniacs. And I,
watching, felt my heart contract with pain.

"Master," I said, "what people can these be?
And all those tonsured ones there on our left—
is it possible they *all* were of the clergy?"

And he: "In the first life beneath the sun
they were so skewed and squint-eyed in their minds
their misering or extravagance mocked all reason.

The voice of each clamors its own excess
when lust meets lust at the two points of the circle
where opposite guilts meet in their wretchedness.

These tonsured wraiths of greed were priests indeed,
and popes and cardinals, for it is in these
the weed of avarice sows its rankest seed."

And I to him: "Master, among this crew
surely I should be able to make out
the fallen image of some soul I knew."

And he to me: "This is a lost ambition.
In their sordid lives they labored to be blind,
and now their souls have dimmed past recognition.

All their eternity is to butt and bray:
one crew will stand tight-fisted, the other stripped
of its very hair at the bar of Judgment Day.

Hoarding and squandering wasted all their light

and brought them screaming to this brawl of wraiths.
You need no words of mine to grasp their plight.

Now may you see the fleeting vanity
of the goods of Fortune for which men tear down
all that they are, to build a mockery.

Not all the gold that is or ever was
under the sky could buy for one of these
exhausted souls the fraction of a pause."

"Master," I said, "tell me—now that you touch
on this Dame Fortune—what *is* she, that she holds
the good things of the world within her clutch?"

And he to me: "O credulous mankind,
is there one error that has wooed and lost you?
Now listen, and strike error from your mind:

That king whose perfect wisdom transcends all,
made the heavens and posted angels on them
to guide the eternal light that it might fall

from every sphere to every sphere the same.
He made earth's splendors by a like decree
and posted as their minister this high Dame,

the Lady of Permutations. All earth's gear
she changes from nation to nation, from house to house,
in changeless change through every turning year.

No mortal power may stay her spinning wheel.
The nations rise and fall by her decree.
None may foresee where she will set her heel:

she passes, and things pass. Man's mortal reason
cannot encompass her. She rules her sphere

as the other gods rule theirs. Season by season

her changes change her changes endlessly,
and those whose turn has come press on her so,
she must be swift by hard necessity.

And this is she so railed at and reviled
that even her debtors in the joys of time
blaspheme her name. Their oaths are bitter and wild,

but she in her beatitude does not hear.
Among the Primal Beings of God's joy
she breathes her blessedness and wheels her sphere.

But the stars that marked our starting fall away.
We must go deeper into greater pain,
for it is not permitted that we stay."

And crossing over to the chasm's edge
we came to a spring that boiled and overflowed
through a great crevice worn into the ledge.

By that foul water, black from its very source,
we found a nightmare path among the rocks
and followed the dark stream along its course.

Beyond its rocky race and wild descent
the river floods and forms a marsh called Styx,
a dreary swampland, vaporous and malignant.

And I, intent on all our passage touched,
made out a swarm of spirits in that bog
savage with anger, naked, slime-besmutched.

They thumped at one another in that slime
with hands and feet, and they butted, and they bit
as if each would tear the other limb from limb.

And my kind Sage: "My son, behold the souls
of those who lived in wrath. And do you see
the broken surfaces of those water-holes

on every hand, boiling as if in pain?
There are souls beneath that water. Fixed in slime
they speak their piece, end it, and start again:

'Sullen were we in the air made sweet by the Sun;
in the glory of his shining our hearts poured
a bitter smoke. Sullen were we begun;

sullen we lie forever in this ditch.'
This litany they gargle in their throats
as if they sang, but lacked the words and pitch."

Then circling on along that filthy wallow,
we picked our way between the bank and fen,
keeping our eyes on those foul souls that swallow

the slime of Hell. And so at last we came
to the foot of a Great Tower that has no name.

Canto VIII

The Poets stand at the edge of the swamp, and a mysterious signal flames from the great tower. It is answered from the darkness of the other side, and almost immediately the Poets see PHLEGYAS, the Boatman of Styx, racing toward them across the water, fast as a flying arrow He comes avidly, thinking to find new souls for torment, and he howls with rage when he discovers the Poets. Once again, however, Virgil conquers wrath with a word and Phlegyas reluctantly gives them passage.

As they are crossing, a muddy soul rises before them. It is FILIPPO ARGENTI, one of the Wrathful. Dante recognizes him despite the filth with which he is covered, and he berates him soundly, even wishing to see him tormented further. Virgil approves Dante's disdain and, as if in answer to Dante's wrath, Argenti is suddenly set upon by all the other sinners present, who fall upon him and rip him to pieces.

The boat meanwhile has sped on, and before Argenti's screams have died away, Dante sees the flaming red towers of Dis, the Capital of Hell. The great walls of the iron city block the way to the Lower Hell. Properly speaking, all the rest of Hell lies within the city walls, which separate the Upper and the Lower Hell.

Phlegyas deposits them at a great Iron Gate which they find to be guarded by the REBELLIOUS ANGELS. These creatures of Ultimate Evil, rebels against God Himself, refuse to let the Poets pass. Even Virgil is powerless against them, for Human Reason by itself cannot cope with the essence of Evil. Only Divine Aid can bring hope. Virgil accordingly sends up a prayer for assistance and waits anxiously for a Heavenly Messenger to appear.

Returning to my theme, I say we came
to the foot of a Great Tower; but long before
we reached it through the marsh, two horns of flame

flared from the summit, one from either side,
and then, far off, so far we scarce could see it
across the mist, another flame replied.

I turned to that sea of all intelligence
saying: "What is this signal and counter-signal?
Who is it speaks with fire across this distance?"

And he then: "Look across the filthy slew:
you may already see the one they summon,
if the swamp vapors do not hide him from you."

No twanging bowspring ever shot an arrow
that bored the air it rode dead to the mark
more swiftly than the flying skiff whose prow

shot toward us over the polluted channel
with a single steersman at the helm who called:
"So, do I have you at last, you whelp of Hell?"

"Phlegyas, Phlegyas," said my Lord and Guide,
"this time you waste your breath: you have us only
for the time it takes to cross to the other side."

Phlegyas, the madman, blew his rage among
those muddy marshes like a cheat deceived,
or like a fool at some imagined wrong.

My Guide, whom all the fiend's noise could not nettle,
boarded the skiff, motioning me to follow:
and not till I stepped aboard did it seem to settle

into the water. At once we left the shore,
that ancient hull riding more heavily
than it had ridden in all of time before.

And as we ran on that dead swamp, the slime

rose before me, and from it a voice cried:
"Who are you that come here before your time?"

And I replied: "If I come, I do not remain.
But you, who are *you*, so fallen and so foul?"
And he: "I am one who weeps." And I then:

"May you weep and wail to all eternity,
for I know you, hell-dog, filthy as you are."
Then he stretched both hands to the boat, but warily

the Master shoved him back, crying, "Down! Down!
with the other dogs!" Then he embraced me saying:
"Indignant spirit, I kiss you as you frown.

Blessed be she who bore you. In world and time
this one was haughtier yet. Not one unbending
graces his memory. Here is his shadow in slime.

How many living now, chancellors of wrath,
shall come to lie here yet in this pigmire,
leaving a curse to be their aftermath!"

And I: "Master, it would suit my whim
to see the wretch scrubbed down into the swill
before we leave this stinking sink and him."

And he to me: "Before the other side
shows through the mist, you shall have all you ask.
This is a wish that should be gratified."

And shortly after, I saw the loathsome spirit
so mangled by a swarm of muddy wraiths
that to this day I praise and thank God for it.

"After Filippo Argenti!" all cried together.
The maddog Florentine wheeled at their cry

and bit himself for rage. I saw them gather.

And there we left him. And I say no more.
But such a wailing beat upon my ears,
I strained my eyes ahead to the far shore.

"My son," the Master said, "the City called Dis
lies just ahead, the heavy citizens,
the swarming crowds of Hell's metropolis."

And I then: "Master, I already see
the glow of its red mosques, as if they came
hot from the forge to smolder in this valley."

And my all-knowing Guide: "They are eternal
flues to eternal fire that rages in them
and makes them glow across this lower Hell."

And as he spoke we entered the vast moat
of the sepulchre. Its wall seemed made of iron
and towered above us in our little boat.

We circled through what seemed an endless distance
before the boatman ran his prow ashore
crying: "Out! Out! Get out! This is the entrance."

Above the gates more than a thousand shades
of spirits purged from Heaven for its glory
cried angrily: "Who is it that invades

Death's Kingdom in his life?" My Lord and Guide
advanced a step before me with a sign
that he wished to speak to some of them aside.

They quieted somewhat, and one called, "Come,
but come alone. And tell that other one,
who thought to walk so blithely through death's kingdom,

he may go back along the same fool's way
he came by. Let him try his living luck.
You who are dead can come only to stay."

Reader, judge for yourself, how each black word
fell on my ears to sink into my heart:
I lost hope of returning to the world.

"O my beloved Master, my Guide in peril,
who time and time again have seen me safely
along this way, and turned the power of evil,

stand by me now," I cried, "in my heart's fright.
And if the dead forbid our journey to them,
let us go back together toward the light."

My Guide then, in the greatness of his spirit:
"Take heart. Nothing can take our passage from us
when such a power has given warrant for it.

Wait here and feed your soul while I am gone
on comfort and good hope; I will not leave you
to wander in this underworld alone."

So the sweet Guide and Father leaves me here,
and I stay on in doubt with yes and no
dividing all my heart to hope and fear.

I could not hear my Lord's words, but the pack
that gathered round him suddenly broke away
howling and jostling and went pouring back,

slamming the towering gate hard in his face.
That great Soul stood alone outside the wall.
Then he came back; his pain showed in his pace.

His eyes were fixed upon the ground, his brow
had sagged from its assurance. He sighed aloud:
"Who has forbidden me the halls of sorrow?"

And to me he said: "You need not be cast down
by my vexation, for whatever plot
these fiends may lay against us, we will go on.

This insolence of theirs is nothing new:
they showed it once at a less secret gate
that still stands open for all that they could do—

the same gate where you read the dead inscription;
and through it at this moment a Great One comes.
Already he has passed it and moves down

ledge by dark ledge. He is one who needs no guide,
and at his touch all gates must spring aside."

Canto IX

At the Gate of Dis the Poets wait in dread. Virgil tries to hide his anxiety from Dante, but both realize that without Divine Aid they will surely be lost. To add to their terrors THREE INFERNAL FURIES, symbols of Eternal Remorse, appear on a nearby tower, from which they threaten the Poets and call for MEDUSA to come and change them to stone. Virgil at once commands Dante to turn and shut his eyes. To make doubly sure, Virgil himself places his hands over Dante's eyes, for there is an Evil upon which man must not look if he is to be saved.

But at the moment of greatest anxiety a storm shakes the dirty air of Hell and the sinners in the marsh begin to scatter like frightened Frogs. THE HEAVENLY MESSENGER is approaching. He appears walking majestically through Hell, looking neither to right nor to left. With a touch he throws open the Gate of Dis while his words scatter the Rebellious Angels. Then he returns as he came.

The Poets now enter the gate unopposed and find themselves in the Sixth Circle. Here they find a countryside like a vast cemetery. Tombs of every size stretch out before them, each with its lid lying beside it, and each wrapped in flames. Cries of anguish sound endlessly from the entombed dead.

This is the torment of the HERETICS of every cult. By Heretic, Dante means specifically those who did violence to God by denying immortality. Since they taught that the soul dies with the body, so their punishment is an eternal grave in the fiery morgue of God's wrath.

My face had paled to a mask of cowardice
when I saw my Guide turn back. The sight of it
the sooner brought the color back to his.

He stood apart like one who strains to hear
what he cannot see, for the eye could not reach far
across the vapors of that midnight air.

"Yet surely we were meant to pass these tombs,"
he said aloud. "If not . . . so much was promised . . .

Oh how time hangs and drags till our aid comes!"

I saw too well how the words with which he ended
covered his start, and even perhaps I drew
a worse conclusion from that than he intended.

"Tell me, Master, does anyone ever come
from the first ledge, whose only punishment
is hope cut off, into this dreary bottom?"

I put this question to him, still in fear
of what his broken speech might mean; and he:
"Rarely do any of us enter here.

Once before, it is true, I crossed through Hell
conjured by cruel Erichtho who recalled
the spirits to their bodies. Her dark spell

forced me, newly stripped of my mortal part,
to enter through this gate and summon out
a spirit from Judaïca. Take heart,

that is the last depth and the darkest lair
and the farthest from Heaven which encircles all,
and at that time I came back even from there.

The marsh from which the stinking gases bubble
lies all about this capital of sorrow
whose gates we may not pass now without trouble."

All this and more he expounded; but the rest
was lost on me, for suddenly my attention
was drawn to the turret with the fiery crest

where all at once three hellish and inhuman
Furies sprang to view, bloodstained and wild.
Their limbs and gestures hinted they were women.

Belts of greenest hydras wound and wound
about their waists, and snakes and horned serpents
grew from their heads like matted hair and bound

their horrid brows. My Master, who well knew
the handmaids of the Queen of Woe, cried: "Look:
the terrible Erinyes of Hecate's crew.

That is Megaera to the left of the tower.
Alecto is the one who raves on the right.
Tisiphone stands between." And he said no more.

With their palms they beat their brows, with their
nails they clawed
their bleeding breasts. And such mad wails broke
from them
that I drew close to the Poet, overawed.

And all together screamed, looking down at me:
"Call Medusa that we may change him to stone!
Too lightly we let Theseus go free."

"Turn your back and keep your eyes shut tight;
for should the Gorgon come and you look at her,
never again would you return to the light."

This was my Guide's command. And he turned me about
himself, and would not trust my hands alone,
but, with his placed on mine, held my eyes shut.

Men of sound intellect and probity,
weigh with good understanding what lies hidden
behind the veil of my strange allegory!

Suddenly there broke on the dirty swell
of the dark marsh a squall of terrible sound

that sent a tremor through both shores of Hell;

a sound as if two continents of air,
one frigid and one scorching, clashed head on
in a war of winds that stripped the forests bare,

ripped off whole boughs and blew them helter-skelter
along the range of dust it raised before it
making the beasts and shepherds run for shelter.

The Master freed my eyes. "Now turn," he said,
"and fix your nerve of vision on the foam
there where the smoke is thickest and most acrid."

As frogs before the snake that hunts them down
churn up their pond in flight, until the last
squats on the bottom as if turned to stone—

so I saw more than a thousand ruined souls
scatter away from one who crossed dry-shod
the Stygian marsh into Hell's burning bowels.

With his left hand he fanned away the dreary
vapors of that sink as he approached;
and only of that annoyance did he seem weary.

Clearly he was a Messenger from God's Throne,
and I turned to my Guide; but he made me a sign
that I should keep my silence and bow down.

Ah, what scorn breathed from that Angel-presence!
He reached the gate of Dis and with a wand
he waved it open, for there was no resistance.

"Outcasts of Heaven, you twice-loathsome crew,"
he cried upon that terrible sill of Hell,
"how does this insolence still live in you?

Why do you set yourselves against that Throne
whose Will none can deny, and which, times past,
has added to your pain for each rebellion?

Why do you butt against Fate's ordinance?
Your Cerberus, if you recall, still wears
his throat and chin peeled for such arrogance."

Then he turned back through the same filthy tide
by which he had come. He did not speak to us,
but went his way like one preoccupied

by other presences than those before him.
And we moved toward the city, fearing nothing
after his holy words. Straight through the dim

and open gate we entered unopposed.
And I, eager to learn what new estate
of Hell those burning fortress walls enclosed,

began to look about the very moment
we were inside, and I saw on every hand
a countryside of sorrow and new torment.

As at Arles where the Rhone sinks into stagnant marshes,
as at Pola by the Quarnaro Gulf, whose waters
close Italy and wash her farthest reaches,

the uneven tombs cover the even plain
such fields I saw here, spread in all directions,
except that here the tombs were chests of pain:

for, in a ring around each tomb, great fires
raised every wall to a red heat. No smith
works hotter iron in his forge. The biers

stood with their lids upraised, and from their pits
an anguished moaning rose on the dead air
from the desolation of tormented spirits.

And I: "Master, what shades are these who lie
buried in these chests and fill the air
with such a painful and unending cry?"

"These are the arch-heretics of all cults,
with all their followers," he replied. "Far more
than you would think lie stuffed into these vaults.

Like lies with like in every heresy,
and the monuments are fired, some more, some less;
to each depravity its own degree."

He turned then, and I followed through that night
between the wall and the torments, bearing right.

Canto X

*As the Poets pass on, one of the damned hears Dante speaking, recognizes him
as a Tuscan, and calls to him from one of the fiery tombs. A moment later he
appears. He is FARINATA DEGLI UBERTI, a great war-chief of the Tuscan
Ghibellines. The majesty and power of his bearing seem to diminish Hell itself.
He asks Dante's lineage and recognizes him as an enemy. They begin to talk
politics, but are interrupted by another shade, who rises from the same tomb.*

*This one is CAVALCANTE DEI CAVALCANTI, father of Guido Cavalcanti, a
contemporary poet. If it is genius that leads Dante on his great journey, the
shade asks, why is Guido not with him? Can Dante presume to a greater genius
than Guido's? Dante replies that he comes this way only with the aid of powers
Guido has not sought. His reply is a classic example of many-leveled symbolism
as well as an overt criticism of a rival poet. The senior Cavalcanti mistakenly
infers from Dante's reply that Guido is dead, and swoons back into the flames.*

*Farinata, who has not deigned to notice his fellow-sinner, continues from the
exact point at which he had been interrupted. It is as if he refuses to recognize
the flames in which he is shrouded. He proceeds to prophesy Dante's
banishment from Florence, he defends his part in Florentine politics, and then,
in answer to Dante's question, he explains how it is that the damned can foresee
the future but have no knowledge of the present. He then names others who
share his tomb, and Dante takes his leave with considerable respect for his great
enemy, pausing only long enough to leave word for Cavalcanti that Guido is still
alive.*

We go by a secret path along the rim
of the dark city, between the wall and the torments.
My Master leads me and I follow him.

"Supreme Virtue, who through this impious land
wheel me at will down these dark gyres," I said,
"speak to me, for I wish to understand.

Tell me, Master, is it permitted to see
the souls within these tombs? The lids are raised,
and no one stands on guard." And he to me:

"All shall be sealed forever on the day
these souls return here from Jehosaphat
with the bodies they have given once to clay.

In this dark corner of the morgue of wrath
lie Epicurus and his followers,
who make the soul share in the body's death.

And here you shall be granted presently
not only your spoken wish, but that other as well,
which you had thought perhaps to hide from me."

And I: "Except to speak my thoughts in few
and modest words, as I learned from your example,
dear Guide, I do not hide my heart from you."

"O Tuscan, who go living through this place
speaking so decorously, may it please you pause
a moment on your way, for by the grace

of that high speech in which I hear your birth,
I know you for a son of that noble city
which perhaps I vexed too much in my time on earth."

These words broke without warning from inside
one of the burning arks. Caught by surprise,
I turned in fear and drew close to my Guide.

And he: "Turn around. What are you doing? Look there:
it is Farinata rising from the flames.
From the waist up his shade will be made clear."

My eyes were fixed on him already. Erect,

he rose above the flame, great chest, great brow;
he seemed to hold all Hell in disrespect.

My Guide's prompt hands urged me among the dim
and smoking sepulchres to that great figure,
and he said to me: "Mind how you speak to him."

And when I stood alone at the foot of the tomb,
the great soul stared almost contemptuously,
before he asked: "Of what line do you come?"

Because I wished to obey, I did not hide
anything from him: whereupon, as he listened,
he raised his brows a little, then replied:

"Bitter enemies were they to me,
to my fathers, and to my party, so that twice
I sent them scattering from high Italy."

"If they were scattered, still from every part
they formed again and returned both times," I answered,
"but yours have not yet wholly learned that art."

At this another shade rose gradually,
visible to the chin. It had raised itself,
I think, upon its knees, and it looked around me

as if it expected to find through that black air
that blew about me, another traveler.
And weeping when it found no other there,

turned back. "And if," it cried, "you travel through
this dungeon of the blind by power of genius,
where is my son? why is he not with you?"

And I to him: "Not by myself am I borne
this terrible way. I am led by him who waits there,

and whom perhaps your Guido held in scorn."

For by his words and the manner of his torment
I knew his name already, and could, therefore,
answer both what he asked and what he meant.
Instantly he rose to his full height:
"He *held*? What is it you say? Is he dead, then?
Do his eyes no longer fill with that sweet light?"

And when he saw that I delayed a bit
in answering his question, he fell backwards
into the flame, and rose no more from it.

But that majestic spirit at whose call
I had first paused there, did not change expression,
nor so much as turn his face to watch him fall.

"And if," going on from his last words, he said,
"men of my line have yet to learn that art,
that burns me deeper than this flaming bed.

But the face of her who reigns in Hell shall not
be fifty times rekindled in its course
before you learn what griefs attend that art.

And as you hope to find the world again,
tell me: why is that populace so savage
in the edicts they pronounce against my strain?"

And I to him: "The havoc and the carnage
that dyed the Arbia red at Montaperti
have caused these angry cries in our assemblage."

He sighed and shook his head. "I was not alone
in that affair," he said, "nor certainly
would I have joined the rest without good reason.

But I *was* alone at that time when every other
consented to the death of Florence; I
alone with open face defended her."

"Ah, so may your soul sometime have rest,"
I begged him, "solve the riddle that pursues me
through this dark place and leaves my mind perplexed:

you seem to see in advance all time's intent,
if I have heard and understood correctly;
but you seem to lack all knowledge of the present."

"We see asquint, like those whose twisted sight
can make out only the far-off," he said,
"for the King of All still grants us that much light.

When things draw near, or happen, we perceive
nothing of them. Except what others bring us
we have no news of those who are alive.

So may you understand that all we know
will be dead forever from that day and hour
when the Portal of the Future is swung to."

Then, as if stricken by regret, I said:
"Now, therefore, will you tell that fallen one
who asked about his son, that he is not dead,

and that, if I did not reply more quickly,
it was because my mind was occupied
with this confusion you have solved for me."

And now my Guide was calling me. In haste,
therefore, I begged that mighty shade to name
the others who lay with him in that chest.

And he: "More than a thousand cram this tomb.

The second Frederick is here, and the Cardinal
of the Ubaldini. Of the rest let us be dumb."

And he disappeared without more said, and I
turned back and made my way to the ancient Poet,
pondering the words of the dark prophecy.

He moved along, and then, when we had started,
he turned and said to me, "What troubles you?
Why do you look so vacant and downhearted?"

And I told him. And he replied: "Well may you bear
those words in mind." Then, pausing, raised a finger:
"Now pay attention to what I tell you here:

when finally you stand before the ray
of that Sweet Lady whose bright eye sees all,
from her you will learn the turnings of your way."

So saying, he bore left, turning his back
on the flaming walls, and we passed deeper yet
into the city of pain, along a track

that plunged down like a scar into a sink
which sickened us already with its stink.

Canto XI

CIRCLE SIX
The Heretics

The Poets reach the inner edge of the SIXTH CIRCLE and find a great jumble of rocks that had once been a cliff, but which has fallen into rubble as the result of the great earthquake that shook Hell when Christ died. Below them lies the SEVENTH CIRCLE, and so fetid is the air that arises from it that the Poets cower for shelter behind a great tomb until their breaths can grow accustomed to the stench.

Dante finds an inscription on the lid of the tomb labeling it as the place in Hell of POPE ANASTASIUS.

Virgil takes advantage of the delay to outline in detail THE DIVISION OF THE LOWER HELL, a theological discourse based on The Ethics *and* The Physics *of Aristotle with subsequent medieval interpretations. Virgil explains also why it is that the Incontinent are not punished within the walls of Dis, and rather ingeniously sets forth the reasons why Usury is an act of Violence against Art, which is the child of Nature and hence the Grandchild of God. (By "Art," Dante means the arts and crafts by which man draws from nature, i.e., Industry.)*

As he concludes he rises and urges Dante on. By means known only to Virgil, he is aware of the motion of the stars and from them he sees that it is about two hours before Sunrise of Holy Saturday.

We came to the edge of an enormous sink
rimmed by a circle of great broken boulders.
Here we found ghastlier gangs. And here the stink

thrown up by the abyss so overpowered us
that we drew back, cowering behind the wall
of one of the great tombs; and standing thus,

I saw an inscription in the stone, and read:
"I guard Anastasius, once Pope,
he whom Photinus led from the straight road."

"Before we travel on to that blind pit
we must delay until our sense grows used
to its foul breath, and then we will not mind it,"

my Master said. And I then: "Let us find
some compensation for the time of waiting."
And he: "You shall see I have just that in mind.

My son," he began, "there are below this wall
three smaller circles, each in its degree
like those you are about to leave, and all

are crammed with God's accurst. Accordingly,
that you may understand their sins at sight,
I will explain how each is prisoned, and why.

Malice is the sin most hated by God.
And the aim of malice is to injure others
whether by fraud or violence. But since fraud

is the vice of which man alone is capable,
God loathes it most. Therefore, the fraudulent
are placed below, and their torment is more painful.

The first below are the violent. But as violence
sins in three persons, so is that circle formed
of three descending rounds of crueler torments.

Against God, self, and neighbor is violence shown.
Against their persons and their goods, I say,
as you shall hear set forth with open reason.

Murder and mayhem are the violation
of the person of one's neighbor: and of his goods;
harassment, plunder, arson, and extortion.

Therefore, homicides, and those who strike

in malice—destroyers and plunderers—all lie
in that first round, and like suffers with like.

A man may lay violent hands upon his own
person and substance; so in that second round
eternally in vain repentance moan

the suicides and all who gamble away
and waste the good and substance of their lives
and weep in that sweet time when they should be gay.

Violence may be offered the deity
in the heart that blasphemes and refuses Him
and scorns the gifts of Nature, her beauty and bounty.

Therefore, the smallest round brands with its mark
both Sodom and Cahors, and all who rail
at God and His commands in their hearts' dark.

Fraud, which is a canker to every conscience,
may be practiced by a man on those who trust him,
and on those who have reposed no confidence.

The latter mode seems only to deny
the bond of love which all men have from Nature;
therefore within the second circle lie

simoniacs, sycophants, and hypocrites,
falsifiers, thieves, and sorcerers,
grafters, pimps, and all such filthy cheats.

The former mode of fraud not only denies
the bond of Nature, but the special trust
added by bonds of friendship or blood-ties.

Hence, at the center point of all creation,
in the smallest circle, on which Dis is founded,

the traitors lie in endless expiation."

"Master," I said, "the clarity of your mind
impresses all you touch; I see quite clearly
the orders of this dark pit of the blind.

But tell me: those who lie in the swamp's bowels,
those the wind blows about, those the rain beats,
and those who meet and clash with such mad howls—

why are *they* not punished in the rust-red city
if God's wrath be upon them? and if it is not,
why must they grieve through all eternity?"

And he: "Why does your understanding stray
so far from its own habit? or can it be
your thoughts are turned along some other way?

Have you forgotten that your *Ethics* states
the three main dispositions of the soul
that lead to those offenses Heaven hates—

incontinence, malice, and bestiality?
and how incontinence offends God least
and earns least blame from Justice and Charity?

Now if you weigh this doctrine and recall
exactly who they are whose punishment
lies in that upper Hell outside the wall,

you will understand at once why they are confined
apart from these fierce wraiths, and why less anger
beats down on them from the Eternal Mind."

"O sun which clears all mists from troubled sight,
such joy attends your rising that I feel
as grateful to the dark as to the light.

Go back a little further," I said, "to where
you spoke of usury as an offense
against God's goodness. How is that made clear?"

"Philosophy makes plain by many reasons,"
he answered me, "to those who heed her teachings,
how all of Nature,—her laws, her fruits, her seasons,—

springs from the Ultimate Intellect and Its art:
and if you read your *Physics* with due care,
you will note, not many pages from the start,

that Art strives after her by imitation,
as the disciple imitates the master;
Art, as it were, is the Grandchild of Creation.

By this, recalling the Old Testament
near the beginning of Genesis, you will see
that in the will of Providence, man was meant

to labor and to prosper. But usurers,
by seeking their increase in other ways,
scorn Nature in herself and her followers.

But come, for it is my wish now to go on:
the wheel turns and the Wain lies over Caurus,
the Fish are quivering low on the horizon,

and there beyond us runs the road we go
down the dark scarp into the depths below."

Canto XII

The Poets begin the descent of the fallen rock wall, having first to evade the MINOTAUR, who menaces them. Virgil tricks him and the Poets hurry by.

Below them they see the RIVER OF BLOOD, which marks the First Round of the Seventh Circle as detailed in the previous Canto. Here are punished the VIOLENT AGAINST THEIR NEIGHBORS, great war-makers, cruel tyrants, highwaymen—all who shed the blood of their fellowmen. As they wallowed in blood during their lives, so they are immersed in the boiling blood forever, each according to the degree of his guilt, while fierce Centaurs patrol the banks, ready to shoot with their arrows any sinner who raises himself out of the boiling blood beyond the limits permitted him. ALEXANDER THE GREAT is here, up to his lashes in the blood, and with him ATTILA, THE SCOURGE OF GOD. They are immersed in the deepest part of the river, which grows shallower as it circles to the other side of the ledge, then deepens again.

The Poets are challenged by the Centaurs, but Virgil wins a safe conduct from CHIRON, their chief, who assigns NESSUS to guide them and to bear them across the shallows of the boiling blood. Nessus carries them across at the point where it is only ankle deep and immediately leaves them and returns to his patrol.

The scene that opened from the edge of the pit
was mountainous, and such a desolation
that every eye would shun the sight of it:

a ruin like the Slides of Mark near Trent
on the bank of the Adige, the result of an earthquake
or of some massive fault in the escarpment—

for, from the point on the peak where the mountain split
to the plain below, the rock is so badly shattered
a man at the top might make a rough stair of it.

Such was the passage down the steep, and there
at the very top, at the edge of the broken cleft,
lay spread the Infamy of Crete, the heir

of bestiality and the lecherous queen
who hid in a wooden cow. And when he saw us,
he gnawed his own flesh in a fit of spleen.

And my Master mocked: "How you do pump your breath!
Do you think, perhaps, it is the Duke of Athens,
who in the world above served up your death?

Off with you, monster; this one does not come instructed by your sister, but of
himself to observe your punishment in the lost kingdom."

As a bull that breaks its chains just when the knife
has struck its death-blow, cannot stand nor run
but leaps from side to side with its last life—

so danced the Minotaur, and my shrewd Guide
cried out: "Run now! While he is blind with rage!
Into the pass, quick, and get over the side!"

So we went down across the shale and slate
of that ruined rock, which often slid and shifted
under me at the touch of living weight.

I moved on, deep in thought; and my Guide to me:
"You are wondering perhaps about this ruin
which is guarded by that beast upon whose fury

I played just now. I should tell you that when last
I came this dark way to the depths of Hell,
this rock had not yet felt the ruinous blast.

But certainly, if I am not mistaken,
it was just before the coming of Him who took

the souls from Limbo, that all Hell was shaken

so that I thought the universe felt love
and all its elements moved toward harmony,
whereby the world of matter, as some believe,

has often plunged to chaos. It was then,
that here and elsewhere in the pits of Hell,
the ancient rock was stricken and broke open.

But turn your eyes to the valley; there we shall find
the river of boiling blood in which are steeped
all who struck down their fellow men." Oh blind!

Oh ignorant, self-seeking cupidity
which spurs us so in the short mortal life
and steeps us so through all eternity!

I saw an arching fosse that was the bed
of a winding river circling through the plain
exactly as my Guide and Lord had said.

A file of Centaurs galloped in the space
between the bank and the cliff, well armed with arrows,
riding as once on earth they rode to the chase.

And seeing us descend, that straggling band
halted, and three of them moved out toward us,
their long bows and their shafts already in hand.

And one of them cried out while still below:
"To what pain are you sent down that dark coast?
Answer from where you stand, or I draw the bow!"

"Chiron is standing there hard by your side;
our answer will be to him. This wrath of yours
was always your own worst fate," my Guide replied.

And to me he said: "That is Nessus, who died in the wood
for insulting Dejanira. At his death
he plotted his revenge in his own blood.

The one in the middle staring at his chest
is the mighty Chiron, he who nursed Achilles:
the other is Pholus, fiercer than all the rest.

They run by that stream in thousands, snapping their bows
at any wraith who dares to raise himself
out of the blood more than his guilt allows."

We drew near those swift beasts. In a thoughtful pause
Chiron drew an arrow, and with its notch
he pushed his great beard back along his jaws.

And when he had thus uncovered the huge pouches
of his lips, he said to his fellows: "Have you noticed
how the one who walks behind moves what he touches?

That is not how the dead go." My good Guide,
already standing by the monstrous breast
in which the two mixed natures joined, replied:

"It is true he lives; in his necessity
I alone must lead him through this valley.
Fate brings him here, not curiosity.

From singing Alleluia the sublime
spirit who sends me came. He is no bandit.
Nor am I one who ever stooped to crime.

But in the name of the Power by which I go
this sunken way across the floor of Hell,
assign us one of your troop whom we may follow,

that he may guide us to the ford, and there
carry across on his back the one I lead,
for he is not a spirit to move through air."

Chiron turned his head on his right breast
and said to Nessus: "Go with them, and guide them,
and turn back any others that would contest

their passage." So we moved beside our guide
along the bank of the scalding purple river
in which the shrieking wraiths were boiled and dyed.

Some stood up to their lashes in that torrent,
and as we passed them the huge Centaur said:
"These were the kings of bloodshed and despoilment.

Here they pay for their ferocity.
Here is Alexander. And Dionysius,
who brought long years of grief to Sicily.

That brow you see with the hair as black as night
is Azzolino; and that beside him, the blonde,
is Opizzo da Esti, who had his mortal light

blown out by his own stepson." I turned then
to speak to the Poet but he raised a hand:
"Let him be the teacher now, and I will listen."

Further on, the Centaur stopped beside
a group of spirits steeped as far as the throat
in the race of boiling blood, and there our guide

pointed out a sinner who stood alone:
"That one before God's altar pierced a heart
still honored on the Thames." And he passed on.

We came in sight of some who were allowed

to raise the head and all the chest from the river,
and I recognized many there. Thus, as we followed

along the stream of blood, its level fell
until it cooked no more than the feet of the damned.
And here we crossed the ford to deeper Hell.

"Just as you see the boiling stream grow shallow
along this side," the Centaur said to us
when we stood on the other bank, "I would have you know

that on the other, the bottom sinks anew
more and more, until it comes again
full circle to the place where the tyrants stew.

It is there that Holy Justice spends its wrath
on Sextus and Pyrrhus through eternity,
and on Attila, who was a scourge on earth:

and everlastingly milks out the tears
of Rinier da Corneto and Rinier Pazzo,
those two assassins who for many years

stalked the highways, bloody and abhorred."
And with that he started back across the ford.

Canto XIII

Nessus carries the Poets across the river of boiling blood and leaves them in the Second Round of the Seventh Circle, THE WOOD OF THE SUICIDES. Here are punished those who destroyed their own lives and those who destroyed their substance.

The souls of the Suicides are encased in thorny trees whose leaves are eaten by the odious HARPIES, the overseers of these damned. When the Harpies feed upon them, damaging their leaves and limbs, the wound bleeds. Only as long as the blood flows are the souls of the trees able to speak. Thus, they who destroyed their own bodies are denied a human form; and just as the supreme expression of their lives was self-destruction, so they are permitted to speak only through that which tears and destroys them. Only through their own blood do they find voice. And to add one more dimension to the symbolism, it is the Harpies— defilers of all they touch—who give them their eternally recurring wounds.

The Poets pause before one tree and speak with the soul of PIER DELLE VIGNE. In the same wood they see JACOMO DA SANT' ANDREA, and LANO DA SIENA, two famous SQUANDERERS and DESTROYERS OF GOODS pursued by a pack of savage hounds. The hounds overtake SANT' ANDREA, tear him to pieces and go off carrying his limbs in their teeth, a self-evident symbolic retribution for the violence with which these sinners destroyed their substance in the world. After this scene of horror, Dante speaks to an UNKNOWN FLORENTINE SUICIDE whose soul is inside the bush which was torn by the hound pack when it leaped upon Sant' Andrea.

Nessus had not yet reached the other shore
when we moved on into a pathless wood
that twisted upward from Hell's broken floor.

Its foliage was not verdant, but nearly black.
The unhealthy branches, gnarled and warped and tangled,
bore poison thorns instead of fruit. The track

of those wild beasts that shun the open spaces
men till between Cecina and Corneto
runs through no rougher nor more tangled places.

Here nest the odious Harpies of whom my Master
wrote how they drove Aeneas and his companions
from the Strophades with prophecies of disaster.

Their wings are wide, their feet clawed, their huge bellies
covered with feathers, their necks and faces human.
They croak eternally in the unnatural trees.

"Before going on, I would have you understand,"
my Guide began, "we are in the second round
and shall be till we reach the burning sand.

Therefore look carefully and you will see
things in this wood, which, if I told them to you
would shake the confidence you have placed in me."

I heard cries of lamentation rise and spill
on every hand, but saw no souls in pain
in all that waste; and, puzzled, I stood still.

I think perhaps he thought that I was thinking
those cries rose from among the twisted roots
through which the spirits of the damned were slinking

to hide from us. Therefore my Master said:
"If you break off a twig, what you will learn
will drive what you are thinking from your head."

Puzzled, I raised my hand a bit and slowly
broke off a branchlet from an enormous thorn:
and the great trunk of it cried: "Why do you break me?"

And after blood had darkened all the bowl

of the wound, it cried again: "Why do you tear me?
Is there no pity left in any soul?

Men we were, and now we are changed to sticks;
well might your hand have been more merciful
were we no more than souls of lice and ticks."

As a green branch with one end all aflame
will hiss and sputter sap out of the other
as the air escapes—so from that trunk there came
words and blood together, gout by gout.
Startled, I dropped the branch that I was holding
and stood transfixed by fear, half turned about
to my Master, who replied: "O wounded soul,
could he have believed before what he has seen
in my verses only, you would yet be whole,

for his hand would never have been raised against you.
But knowing this truth could never be believed
till it was seen, I urged him on to do

what grieves me now; and I beg to know your name,
that to make you some amends in the sweet world
when he returns, he may refresh your fame."

And the trunk: "So sweet those words to me that I
cannot be still, and may it not annoy you
if I seem somewhat lengthy in reply.

I am he who held both keys to Frederick's heart,
locking, unlocking with so deft a touch
that scarce another soul had any part

in his most secret thoughts. Through every strife
I was so faithful to my glorious office
that for it I gave up both sleep and life.

That harlot, Envy, who on Caesar's face
keeps fixed forever her adulterous stare,
the common plague and vice of court and palace,

inflamed all minds against me. These inflamed
so inflamed him that all my happy honors
were changed to mourning. Then, unjustly blamed,

my soul, in scorn, and thinking to be free
of scorn in death, made me at last, though just,
unjust to myself. By the new roots of this tree

I swear to you that never in word or spirit
did I break faith to my lord and emperor
who was so worthy of honor in his merit.

If either of you return to the world, speak for me,
to vindicate in the memory of men
one who lies prostrate from the blows of Envy."

The Poet stood. Then turned. "Since he is silent,"
he said to me, "do not you waste this hour,
if you wish to ask about his life or torment."

And I replied: "Question him for my part,
on whatever you think I would do well to hear;
I could not, such compassion chokes my heart."

The Poet began again: "That this man may
with all his heart do for you what your words
entreat him to, imprisoned spirit, I pray,

tell us how the soul is bound and bent
into these knots, and whether any ever
frees itself from such imprisonment."

At that the trunk blew powerfully, and then

the wind became a voice that spoke these words:
"Briefly is the answer given: when

out of the flesh from which it tore itself,
the violent spirit comes to punishment,
Minos assigns it to the seventh shelf.

It falls into the wood, and landing there,
wherever fortune flings it, it strikes root,
and there it sprouts, lusty as any tare,

shoots up a sapling, and becomes a tree.
The Harpies, feeding on its leaves then, give it
pain and pain's outlet simultaneously.

Like the rest, we shall go for our husks on Judgment Day,
but not that we may wear them, for it is not just
that a man be given what he throws away.

Here shall we drag them and in this mournful glade
our bodies will dangle to the end of time,
each on the thorns of its tormented shade."

We waited by the trunk, but it said no more;
and waiting, we were startled by a noise
that grew through all the wood. Just such a roar

and trembling as one feels when the boar and chase
approach his stand, the beasts and branches crashing
and clashing in the heat of the fierce race.

And there on the left, running so violently
they broke off every twig in the dark wood,
two torn and naked wraiths went plunging by me.

The leader cried, "Come now, O Death! Come now!"
And the other, seeing that he was outrun

cried out: "Your legs were not so ready, Lano,

in the jousts at the Toppo." And suddenly in his rush,
perhaps because his breath was failing him,
he hid himself inside a thorny bush

and cowered among its leaves. Then at his back,
the wood leaped with black bitches, swift as greyhounds
escaping from their leash, and all the pack

sprang on him; with their fangs they opened him
and tore him savagely, and then withdrew,
carrying his body with them, limb by limb.

Then, taking me by the hand across the wood,
my Master led me toward the bush. Lamenting,
all its fractures blew out words and blood:

"O Jacomo da Sant' Andrea!" it said,
"what have you gained in making me your screen?
What part had I in the foul life you led?"

And when my Master had drawn up to it
he said: "Who were you, who through all your wounds
blow out your blood with your lament, sad spirit?"

And he to us: "You who have come to see
how the outrageous mangling of these hounds
has torn my boughs and stripped my leaves from me,

O heap them round my ruin! I was born
in the city that tore down Mars and raised the Baptist.
On that account the God of War has sworn

her sorrow shall not end. And were it not
that something of his image still survives
on the bridge across the Arno, some have thought

those citizens who of their love and pain
afterwards rebuilt it from the ashes
left by Attila, would have worked in vain.

I am one who has no tale to tell:
I made myself a gibbet of my own lintel."

48. *In my verses only:* The *Aeneid*, Book III, describes a similar bleeding plant.

Canto XIV

Dante, in pity, restores the torn leaves to the soul of his countryman and the Poets move on to the next round, a great PLAIN OF BURNING SAND upon which there descends an eternal slow RAIN OF FIRE. Here, scorched by fire from above and below, are three classes of sinners suffering differing degrees of exposure to the fire. The BLASPHEMERS (The Violent against God) are stretched supine upon the sand, the SODOMITES (The Violent against Nature) run in endless circles, and the USURERS (The Violent against Art, which is the Grandchild of God) huddle on the sands.

The Poets find CAPANEUS stretched out on the sands, the chief sinner of that place. He is still blaspheming God. They continue along the edge of the Wood of the Suicides and come to a blood-red rill which flows boiling from the Wood and crosses the burning plain. Virgil explains the miraculous power of its waters and discourses on the OLD MAN OF CRETE and the origin of all the rivers of Hell.

The symbolism of the burning plain is obviously centered in sterility (the desert image) and wrath (the fire image). Blasphemy, sodomy, and usury are all unnatural and sterile actions: thus the unbearing desert is the eternity of these sinners; and thus the rain, which in nature should be fertile and cool, descends as fire. Capaneus, moreover, is subjected not only to the wrath of nature (the sands below) and the wrath of God (the fire from above), but is tortured most by his own inner violence, which is the root of blasphemy.

Love of that land that was our common source
moved me to tears; I gathered up the leaves
and gave them back. He was already hoarse.

We came to the edge of the forest where one goes
from the second round to the third, and there we saw
what fearful arts the hand of Justice knows.

To make these new things wholly clear, I say

we came to a plain whose soil repels all roots.
The wood of misery rings it the same way

the wood itself is ringed by the red fosse.
We paused at its edge: the ground was burning sand,
just such a waste as Cato marched across.

O endless wrath of God: how utterly
thou shouldst become a terror to all men
who read the frightful truths revealed to me!

Enormous herds of naked souls I saw,
lamenting till their eyes were burned of tears;
they seemed condemned by an unequal law,

for some were stretched supine upon the ground,
some squatted with their arms about themselves,
and others without pause roamed round and round.

Most numerous were those that roamed the plain.
Far fewer were the souls stretched on the sand,
but moved to louder cries by greater pain.

And over all that sand on which they lay
or crouched or roamed, great flakes of flame fell slowly
as snow falls in the Alps on a windless day.

Like those Alexander met in the hot regions
of India, flames raining from the sky
to fall still unextinguished on his legions:

whereat he formed his ranks, and at their head
set the example, trampling the hot ground
for fear the tongues of fire might join and spread—

just so in Hell descended the long rain
upon the damned, kindling the sand like tinder

under a flint and steel, doubling the pain.

In a never-ending fit upon those sands,
the arms of the damned twitched all about their bodies,
now here, now there, brushing away the brands.

"Poet," I said, "master of every dread
we have encountered, other than those fiends
who sallied from the last gate of the dead—

who is that wraith who lies along the rim
and sets his face against the fire in scorn,
so that the rain seems not to mellow him?"

And he himself, hearing what I had said
to my Guide and Lord concerning him, replied:
"What I was living, the same am I now, dead.

Though Jupiter wear out his sooty smith
from whom on my last day he snatched in anger
the jagged thunderbolt he pierced me with;

though he wear out the others one by one
who labor at the forge at Mongibello
crying again 'Help! Help! Help me, good Vulcan!'

as he did at Phlegra; and hurl down endlessly
with all the power of Heaven in his arm,
small satisfaction would he win from me."

At this my Guide spoke with such vehemence
as I had not heard from him in all of Hell:
"O Capaneus, by your insolence

you are made to suffer as much fire inside
as falls upon you. Only your own rage
could be fit torment for your sullen pride."

Then he turned to me more gently. "That," he said,
"was one of the Seven who laid siege to Thebes.
Living, he scorned God, and among the dead

he scorns Him yet. He thinks he may detest
God's power too easily, but as I told him,
his slobber is a fit badge for his breast.

Now follow me; and mind for your own good
you do not step upon the burning sand,
but keep well back along the edge of the wood."

We walked in silence then till we reached a rill
that gushes from the wood; it ran so red
the memory sends a shudder through me still.

As from the Bulicame springs the stream
the sinful women keep to their own use;
so down the sand the rill flowed out in steam.

The bed and both its banks were petrified,
as were its margins; thus I knew at once
our passage through the sand lay by its side.

"Among all other wonders I have shown you
since we came through the gate denied to none,
nothing your eyes have seen is equal to

the marvel of the rill by which we stand,
for it stifles all the flames above its course
as it flows out across the burning sand."

So spoke my Guide across the flickering light,
and I begged him to bestow on me the food
for which he had given me the appetite.

"In the middle of the sea, and gone to waste,
there lies a country known as Crete," he said,
"under whose king the ancient world was chaste.

Once Rhea chose it as the secret crypt
and cradle of her son; and better to hide him,
her Corybantes raised a din when he wept.

An ancient giant stands in the mountain's core.
He keeps his shoulder turned toward Damietta,
and looks toward Rome as if it were his mirror.

His head is made of gold; of silverwork
his breast and both his arms, of polished brass
the rest of his great torso to the fork.

He is of chosen iron from there down,
except that his right foot is terra cotta;
it is this foot he rests more weight upon.

Every part except the gold is split
by a great fissure from which endless tears
drip down and hollow out the mountain's pit.

Their course sinks to this pit from stone to stone,
becoming Acheron, Phlegethon, and Styx.
Then by this narrow sluice they hurtle down

to the end of all descent, and disappear
into Cocytus. You shall see what sink that is
with your own eyes. I pass it in silence here."

And I to him: "But if these waters flow
from the world above, why is this rill met only
along this shelf?" And he to me: "You know

the place is round, and though you have come deep

into the valley through the many circles,
always bearing left along the steep,

you have not traveled any circle through
its total round; hence when new things appear
from time to time, that hardly should surprise you."

And I: "Where shall we find Phlegethon's course?
And Lethe's? One you omit, and of the other
you only say the tear-flood is its source."

"In all you ask of me you please me truly,"
he answered, "but the red and boiling water
should answer the first question you put to me,

and you shall stand by Lethe, but far hence:
there, where the spirits go to wash themselves
when their guilt has been removed by penitence."

And then he said: "Now it is time to quit
this edge of shade: follow close after me
along the rill, and do not stray from it;

for the unburning margins form a lane,
and by them we may cross the burning plain."

Canto XV

The Violent Against Nature

Protected by the marvelous powers of the boiling rill, the Poets walk along its banks across the burning plain. The WOOD OF THE SUICIDES is behind them; the GREAT CLIFF at whose foot lies the EIGHTH CIRCLE is before them.

They pass one of the roving bands of SODOMITES. One of the sinners stops Dante, and with great difficulty the Poet recognizes him under his baked features as SER BRUNETTO LATINO This is a reunion with a dearly-loved man and writer, one who had considerably influenced Dante's own development, and Dante addresses him with great and sorrowful affection, paying him the highest tribute offered to any sinner in the Inferno. *BRUNETTO prophesies Dante's sufferings at the hands of the Florentines, gives an account of the souls that move with him through the fire, and finally, under Divine Compulsion, races off across the plain.*

We go by one of the stone margins now
and the steam of the rivulet makes a shade above it,
guarding the stream and banks from the flaming snow.
As the Flemings in the lowland between Bruges
and Wissant, under constant threat of the sea,
erect their great dikes to hold back the deluge;
as the Paduans along the shores of the Brent
build levees to protect their towns and castles
lest Chiarentana drown in the spring torrent—
to the same plan, though not so wide nor high,
did the engineer, whoever he may have been,
design the margin we were crossing by.
Already we were so far from the wood
that even had I turned to look at it,
I could not have made it out from where I stood,

when a company of shades came into sight
walking beside the bank. They stared at us

as men at evening by the new moon's light

stare at one another when they pass by
on a dark road, pointing their eyebrows toward us
as an old tailor squints at his needle's eye.

Stared at so closely by that ghostly crew,
I was recognized by one who seized the hem
of my skirt and said: "Wonder of wonders! You?"

And I, when he stretched out his arm to me,
searched his baked features closely, till at last
I traced his image from my memory

in spite of the burnt crust, and bending near
to put my face closer to his, at last
I answered: "Ser Brunetto, are *you* here?"

"O my son! may it not displease you," he cried,
"if Brunetto Latino leave his company
and turn and walk a little by your side."

And I to him: "With all my soul I ask it.
Or let us sit together, if it please him
who is my Guide and leads me through this pit."

"My son!" he said, "whoever of this train
pauses a moment, must lie a hundred years
forbidden to brush off the burning rain.

Therefore, go on; I will walk at your hem,
and then rejoin my company, which goes
mourning eternal loss in eternal flame."

I did not dare descend to his own level
but kept my head inclined, as one who walks
in reverence meditating good and evil.

"What brings you here before your own last day?
What fortune or what destiny?" he began.
"And who is he that leads you this dark way?"

"Up there in the happy life I went astray
in a valley," I replied, "before I had reached
the fullness of my years. Only yesterday

at dawn I turned from it. This spirit showed
himself to me as I was turning back,
and guides me home again along this road."

And he: "Follow your star, for if in all
of the sweet life I saw one truth shine clearly,
you cannot miss your glorious arrival.

And had I lived to do what I meant to do,
I would have cheered and seconded your work,
observing Heaven so well disposed toward you.

But that ungrateful and malignant stock
that came down from Fiesole of old
and still smacks of the mountain and the rock,

for your good works will be your enemy.
And there is cause: the sweet fig is not meant
to bear its fruit beside the bitter sorb-tree.

Even the old adage calls them blind,
an envious, proud, and avaricious people:
see that you root their customs from your mind.

It is written in your stars, and will come to pass,
that your honours shall make both sides hunger for
you:
but the goat shall never reach to crop that grass.

Let the beasts of Fiesole devour their get
like sows, but never let them touch the plant,
if among their rankness any springs up yet,

in which is born again the holy seed
of the Romans who remained among their rabble
when Florence made a new nest for their greed."

"Ah, had I all my wish," I answered then,
"you would not yet be banished from the world
in which you were a radiance among men,

for that sweet image, gentle and paternal,
you were to me in the world when hour by hour
you taught me how man makes himself eternal,

lives in my mind, and now strikes to my heart;
and while I live, the gratitude I owe it
will speak to men out of my life and art.

What you have told me of my course, I write
by another text I save to show a Lady
who will judge these matters, if I reach her height.

This much I would have you know: so long, I say,
as nothing in my conscience troubles me
I am prepared for Fortune, come what may.

Twice already in the eternal shade
I have heard this prophecy; but let Fortune turn
her wheel as she please, and the countryman his spade."

My guiding spirit paused at my last word
and, turning right about, stood eye to eye
to say to me: "Well heeded is well heard."

But I did not reply to him, going on
with Ser Brunetto to ask him who was with him
in the hot sands, the best-born and best known.

And he to me: "Of some who share this walk
it is good to know; of the rest let us say nothing,
for the time would be too short for so much talk.

In brief, we all were clerks and men of worth,
great men of letters, scholars of renown;
all by the one same crime defiled on earth.

Priscian moves there along the wearisome
sad way, and Francesco d'Accorso, and also there,
if you had any longing for such scum,

you might have seen that one the Servant of Servants
sent from the Arno to the Bacchiglione
where he left his unnatural organ wrapped in cerements.

I would say more, but there across the sand
a new smoke rises and new people come,
and I must run to be with my own band.

Remember my *Treasure*, in which I shall live on:
I ask no more." He turned then, and he seemed,
across that plain, like one of those who run

for the green cloth at Verona; and of those,
more like the one who wins, than those who lose.

Canto XVI

The Poets arrive within hearing of the waterfall that plunges over the GREAT
CLIFF into the EIGHTH CIRCLE. The sound is still a distant throbbing when
three wraiths, recognizing Dante's Florentine dress, detach themselves from
their band and come running toward him. They are JACOPO RUSTICUCCI,
GUIDO GUERRA, and TEGGHIAIO ALDOBRANDI, all of them Florentines
whose policies and personalities Dante admired. Rusticucci and Tegghiaio have
already been mentioned in a highly complimentary way in Dante's talk with
Ciacco (Canto VI).

The sinners ask for news of Florence, and Dante replies with a passionate
lament for her present degradation. The three wraiths return to their band and
the Poets continue to the top of the falls. Here, at Virgil's command, Dante
removes a CORD from about his waist and Virgil drops it over the edge of the
abyss. As if in answer to a signal, a great distorted shape comes swimming up
through the dirty air of the pit.

We could already hear the rumbling drive
of the waterfall in its plunge to the next circle,
a murmur like the throbbing of a hive,

when three shades turned together on the plain,
breaking toward us from a company
that went its way to torture in that rain.

They cried with one voice as they ran toward me:
"Wait, oh wait, for by your dress you seem
a voyager from our own tainted country."

Ah! what wounds I saw, some new, some old,
branded upon their bodies! Even now
the pain of it in memory turns me cold.

My Teacher heard their cries, and turning-to,
stood face to face. "Do as they ask," he said,
"for these are souls to whom respect is due;

and were it not for the darting flames that hem
our narrow passage in, I should have said
it were more fitting you ran after them."

We paused, and they began their ancient wail
over again, and when they stood below us
they formed themselves into a moving wheel.

As naked and anointed champions do
in feeling out their grasp and their advantage
before they close in for the thrust or blow—

so circling, each one stared up at my height,
and as their feet moved left around the circle,
their necks kept turning backward to the right.

"If the misery of this place, and our unkempt
and scorched appearance," one of them began,
"bring us and what we pray into contempt,

still may our earthly fame move you to tell
who and what you are, who so securely
set your live feet to the dead dusts of Hell.

This peeled and naked soul, who runs before me
around this wheel, was higher than you think
there in the world, in honor and degree.

Guido Guerra was the name he bore,
the good Gualdrada's grandson. In his life
he won great fame in counsel and in war.

The other who behind me treads this sand
was Tegghiaio Aldobrandi, whose good counsels
the world would have done well to understand.

And I who share their torment, in my life
was Jacopo Rusticucci; above all
I owe my sorrows to a savage wife."

I would have thrown myself to the plain below
had I been sheltered from the falling fire;
and I think my Teacher would have let me go.

But seeing I should be burned and cooked, my fear
overcame the first impulse of my heart
to leap down and embrace them then and there.

"Not contempt," I said, "but the compassion
that seizes on my soul and memory
at the thought of you tormented in this fashion—

it was grief that choked my speech when through the
scorching
air of this pit my Lord announced to me
that such men as you are might be approaching.

I am of your own land, and I have always
heard with affection and rehearsed with honor
your name and the good deeds of your happier days.

Led by my Guide and his truth, I leave the gall
and go for the sweet apples of delight.
But first I must descend to the center of all."

"So may your soul and body long continue
together on the way you go," he answered,
"and the honor of your days shine after you—

tell me if courtesy and valor raise
their banners in our city as of old,
or has the glory faded from its days?

For Borsiere, who is newly come among us
and yonder goes with our companions in pain,
taunts us with such reports, and his words have stung us."

"O Florence! your sudden wealth and your upstart
rabble, dissolute and overweening,
already set you weeping in your heart!"

I cried with face upraised, and on the sand
those three sad spirits looked at one another
like men who hear the truth and understand.

"If this be your manner of speaking, and if you can
satisfy others with such ease and grace,"
they said as one, "we hail a happy man.

Therefore, if you win through this gloomy pass
and climb again to see the heaven of stars;
when it rejoices you to say 'I was',

speak of us to the living." They parted then,
breaking their turning wheel, and as they vanished
over the plain, their legs seemed wings. "Amen"

could not have been pronounced between their start
and their disappearance over the rim of sand.
And then it pleased my Master to depart.

A little way beyond we felt the quiver
and roar of the cascade, so close that speech
would have been drowned in thunder. As that river—

the first one on the left of the Apennines

to have a path of its own from Monte Veso
to the Adriatic Sea—which, as it twines

is called the Acquacheta from its source
until it nears Forlì, and then is known
as the Montone in its further course—

resounds from the mountain in a single leap
there above San Benedetto dell'Alpe
where a thousand falls might fit into the steep;

so down from a sheer bank, in one enormous
plunge, the tainted water roared so loud
a little longer there would have deafened us.

I had a cord bound round me like a belt
which I had once thought I might put to use
to snare the leopard with the gaudy pelt.

When at my Guide's command I had unbound
its loops from about my habit, I gathered it
and held it out to him all coiled and wound.

He bent far back to his right, and throwing it
out from the edge, sent it in a long arc
into the bottomless darkness of the pit.

"Now surely some unusual event,"
I said to myself, "must follow this new signal
upon which my good Guide is so intent."

Ah, how cautiously a man should breathe
near those who see not only what we do,
but have the sense which reads the mind beneath!

He said to me: "You will soon see arise
what I await, and what you wonder at;

soon you will see the thing before your eyes."

To the truth which will seem falsehood every man
who would not be called a liar while speaking fact
should learn to seal his lips as best he can.

But here I cannot be still: Reader, I swear
by the lines of my Comedy—so may it live—
that I saw swimming up through that foul air

a shape to astonish the most doughty soul,
a shape like one returning through the sea
from working loose an anchor run afoul
of something on the bottom—so it rose,
its arms spread upward and its feet drawn close.

Canto XVII

The monstrous shape lands on the brink and Virgil salutes it ironically. It is GERYON, the MONSTER OF FRAUD. Virgil announces that they must fly down from the cliff on the back of this monster. While Virgil negotiates for their passage, Dante is sent to examine the USURERS (The Violent against Art).

These sinners sit in a crouch along the edge of the burning plain that approaches the cliff. Each of them has a leather purse around his neck, and each purse is blazoned with a coat of arms. Their eyes, gushing with tears, are forever fixed on these purses. Dante recognizes none of these sinners, but their coats of arms are unmistakably those of well-known Florentine families.

Having understood who they are and the reason for their present condition, Dante cuts short his excursion and returns to find Virgil mounted on the back of Geryon. Dante joins his Master and they fly down from the great cliff.

Their flight carries them from the Hell of the VIOLENT AND THE BESTIAL (The Sins of the Lion) into the Hell of the FRAUDULENT AND MALICIOUS (The Sins of the Leopard).

"Now see the sharp-tailed beast that mounts the brink.
He passes mountains, breaks through walls and weapons.
Behold the beast that makes the whole world stink."

These were the words my Master spoke to me;
then signaled the weird beast to come to ground
close to the sheer end of our rocky levee.

The filthy prototype of Fraud drew near
and settled his head and breast upon the edge
of the dark cliff, but let his tail hang clear.

His face was innocent of every guile,
benign and just in feature and expression;
and under it his body was half reptile.

His two great paws were hairy to the armpits;
all his back and breast and both his flanks
were figured with bright knots and subtle circlets:

never was such a tapestry of bloom
woven on earth by Tartar or by Turk,
nor by Arachne at her flowering loom.

As a ferry sometimes lies along the strand,
part beached and part afloat; and as the beaver,
up yonder in the guzzling Germans' land,

squats halfway up the bank when a fight is on—
just so lay that most ravenous of beasts
on the rim which bounds the burning sand with stone.

His tail twitched in the void beyond that lip,
thrashing, and twisting up the envenomed fork
which, like a scorpion's stinger, armed the tip.

My Guide said: "It is time now we drew near
that monster." And descending on the right
we moved ten paces outward to be clear

of sand and flames. And when we were beside him,
I saw upon the sand a bit beyond us
some people crouching close beside the brim.

The Master paused "That you may take with you
the full experience of this round," he said,
"go now and see the last state of that crew.

But let your talk be brief, and I will stay
and reason with this beast till you return,
that his strong back may serve us on our way."

So further yet along the outer edge
of the seventh circle I moved on alone.
And came to the sad people of the ledge.

Their eyes burst with their grief; their smoking hands
jerked about their bodies, warding off
now the flames and now the burning sands.

Dogs in summer bit by fleas and gadflies,
jerking their snouts about, twitching their paws
now here, now there, behave no otherwise.

I examined several faces there among
that sooty throng, and I saw none I knew;
but I observed that from each neck there hung

an enormous purse, each marked with its own beast
and its own colors like a coat of arms.
On these their streaming eyes appeared to feast.

Looking about, I saw one purse display
azure on or, a kind of lion; another,
on a blood red field, a goose whiter than whey.

And one that bore a huge and swollen sow
azure on field argent said to me:
"What are you doing in this pit of sorrow?

Leave us alone! And since you have not yet died,
I'll have you know my neighbor Vitaliano
has a place reserved for him here at my side.

A Paduan among Florentines, I sit here
while hour by hour they nearly deafen me
shouting: 'Send us the sovereign cavalier

with the purse of the three goats!' " He half arose,

twisted his mouth, and darted out his tongue
for all the world like an ox licking its nose.

And I, afraid that any longer stay
would anger him who had warned me to be brief,
left those exhausted souls without delay.

Returned, I found my Guide already mounted
upon the rump of that monstrosity.
He said to me: "Now must you be undaunted:

this beast must be our stairway to the pit:
mount it in front, and I will ride between
you and the tail, lest you be poisoned by it."

Like one so close to the quartanary chill
that his nails are already pale and his flesh trembles
at the very sight of shade or a cool rill—

so did I tremble at each frightful word.
But his scolding filled me with that shame that makes
the servant brave in the presence of his lord.

I mounted the great shoulders of that freak
and tried to say "Now help me to hold on!"
But my voice clicked in my throat and I could not speak.

But no sooner had I settled where he placed me
than he, my stay, my comfort, and my courage
in other perils, gathered and embraced me.

Then he called out: "Now, Geryon, we are ready:
bear well in mind that his is living weight
and make your circles wide and your flight steady."

As a small ship slides from a beaching or its pier,
backward, backward—so that monster slipped

back from the rim. And when he had drawn clear

he swung about, and stretching out his tail
he worked it like an eel, and with his paws
he gathered in the air, while I turned pale.

I think there was no greater fear the day
Phaëthon let loose the reins and burned the sky
along the great scar of the Milky Way,

nor when Icarus, too close to the sun's track
felt the wax melt, unfeathering his loins,
and heard his father cry, "Turn back! Turn back!"—

than I felt when I found myself in air,
afloat in space with nothing visible
but the enormous beast that bore me there.

Slowly, slowly, he swims on through space,
wheels and descends, but I can sense it only
by the way the wind blows upward past my face.

Already on the right I heard the swell
and thunder of the whirlpool. Looking down
I leaned my head out and stared into Hell.

I trembled again at the prospect of dismounting
and cowered in on myself, for I saw fires
on every hand, and I heard a long lamenting.

And then I saw—till then I had but felt it—
the course of our down-spiral to the horrors
that rose to us from all sides of the pit.

As a flight-worn falcon sinks down wearily
though neither bird nor lure has signalled it,
the falconer crying out: "What! spent already!"—

then turns and in a hundred spinning gyres
sulks from her master's call, sullen and proud—
so to that bottom lit by endless fires

the monster Geryon circled and fell,
setting us down at the foot of the precipice
of ragged rock on the eighth shelf of Hell.

And once freed of our weight, he shot from there
into the dark like an arrow into air.

Canto XVIII

CIRCLE EIGHT (MALEBOLGE)
BOLGIA ONE
BOLGIA TWO
The Fraudulent and Malicious
The Panderers and Seducers
The Flatterers

Dismounted from Geryon, the Poets find themselves in the EIGHTH CIRCLE, called MALEBOLGE (The Evil Ditches). This is the upper half of the HELL OF THE FRAUDULENT AND MALICIOUS. Malebolge is a great circle of stone that slopes like an amphitheater. The slopes are divided into ten concentric ditches; and within these ditches, each with his own kind, are punished those guilty of SIMPLE FRAUD.

A series of stone dikes runs like spokes from the edge of the great cliff face to the center of the place, and these serve as bridges.

The Poets bear left toward the first ditch, and Dante observes below him and to his right the sinners of the first bolgia, *The PANDERERS and SEDUCERS. These make two files, one along either bank of the ditch, and are driven at an endless fast walk by horned demons who hurry them along with great lashes. In life these sinners goaded others on to serve their own foul purposes; so in Hell are they driven in their turn. The horned demons who drive them symbolize the sinners' own vicious natures, embodiments of their own guilty consciences. Dante may or may not have intended the horns of the demons to symbolize cuckoldry and adultery.*

The Poets see VENEDICO CACCIANEMICO and JASON in the first pit, and pass on to the second, where they find the souls of the FLATTERERS sunk in excrement, the true equivalent of their false flatteries on earth. They observe ALESSIO INTERMINELLI and THAIS, and pass on.

There is in Hell a vast and sloping ground
called Malebolge, a lost place of stone
as black as the great cliff that seals it round.

Precisely in the center of that space

there yawns a well extremely wide and deep.
I shall discuss it in its proper place.

The border that remains between the well-pit
and the great cliff forms an enormous circle,
and ten descending troughs are cut in it,

offering a general prospect like the ground
that lies around one of those ancient castles
whose walls are girded many times around

by concentric moats. And just as, from the portal,
the castle's bridges run from moat to moat
to the last bank; so from the great rock wall

across the embankments and the ditches, high
and narrow cliffs run to the central well,
which cuts and gathers them like radii.

Here, shaken from the back of Geryon,
we found ourselves. My Guide kept to the left
and I walked after him. So we moved on.

Below, on my right, and filling the first ditch
along both banks, new souls in pain appeared,
new torments, and new devils black as pitch.

All of these sinners were naked; on our side
of the middle they walked toward us; on the other,
in our direction, but with swifter stride.

Just so the Romans, because of the great throng
in the year of the Jubilee, divide the bridge
in order that the crowds may pass along,

so that all face the Castle as they go
on one side toward St. Peter's, while on the other,

all move along facing toward Mount Giordano.

And everywhere along that hideous track
I saw horned demons with enormous lashes
move through those souls, scourging them on the back.

Ah, how the stragglers of that long rout stirred
their legs quick-march at the first crack of the lash!
Certainly no one waited a second, or third!

As we went on, one face in that procession
caught my eye and I said: "That sinner there:
It is certainly not the first time I've seen that one."

I stopped, therefore, to study him, and my Guide
out of his kindness waited, and even allowed me
to walk back a few steps at the sinner's side.

And that flayed spirit, seeing me turn around,
thought to hide his face, but I called to him:
"You there, that walk along with your eyes on the ground—

if those are not false features, then I know you
as Venedico Caccianemico of Bologna:
what brings you here among this pretty crew?"

And he replied: "I speak unwillingly,
but something in your living voice, in which
I hear the world again, stirs and compels me.

It was I who brought the fair Ghisola 'round
to serve the will and lust of the Marquis,
however sordid that old tale may sound.

There are many more from Bologna who weep away
eternity in this ditch; we fill it so
there are not as many tongues that are taught to say

'sipa' in all the land that lies between
the Reno and the Saveno, as you must know
from the many tales of our avarice and spleen."

And as he spoke, one of those lashes fell
across his back, and a demon cried, "Move on,
you pimp, there are no women here to sell."
Turning away then, I rejoined my Guide.
We came in a few steps to a raised ridge
that made a passage to the other side.

This we climbed easily, and turning right
along the jagged crest, we left behind
the eternal circling of those souls in flight.

And when we reached the part at which the stone
was tunneled for the passage of the scourged,
my Guide said, "Stop a minute and look down

on these other misbegotten wraiths of sin.
You have not seen their faces, for they moved
in the same direction we were headed in."

So from that bridge we looked down on the throng
that hurried toward us on the other side.
Here, too, the whiplash hurried them along.

And the good Master, studying that train,
said: "Look there, at that great soul that approaches
and seems to shed no tears for all his pain—

what kingliness moves with him even in Hell!
It is Jason, who by courage and good advice
made off with the Colchian Ram. Later it fell

that he passed Lemnos, where the women of wrath,

enraged by Venus' curse that drove their lovers
out of their arms, put all their males to death.

There with his honeyed tongue and his dishonest
lover's wiles, he gulled Hypsipyle,
who, in the slaughter, had gulled all the rest.

And there he left her, pregnant and forsaken.
Such guilt condemns him to such punishment;
and also for Medea is vengeance taken.

All seducers march here to the whip.
And let us say no more about this valley
and those it closes in its stony grip."

We had already come to where the walk
crosses the second bank, from which it lifts
another arch, spanning from rock to rock.

Here we heard people whine in the next chasm,
and knock and thump themselves with open palms,
and blubber through their snouts as if in a spasm.

Steaming from that pit, a vapour rose
over the banks, crusting them with a slime
that sickened my eyes and hammered at my nose.

That chasm sinks so deep we could not sight
its bottom anywhere until we climbed
along the rock arch to its greatest height.

Once there, I peered down; and I saw long lines
of people in a river of excrement
that seemed the overflow of the world's latrines.

I saw among the felons of that pit
one wraith who might or might not have been tonsured—

one could not tell, he was so smeared with shit.

He bellowed: "You there, why do you stare at me
more than at all the others in this stew?"
And I to him: "Because if memory

serves me, I knew you when your hair was dry.
You are Alessio Interminelli da Lucca.
That's why I pick you from this filthy fry."

And he then, beating himself on his clown's head:
"Down to this have the flatteries I sold
the living sunk me here among the dead."

And my Guide prompted then: "Lean forward a bit
and look beyond him, there—do you see that one
scratching herself with dungy nails, the strumpet

who fidgets to her feet, then to a crouch?
It is the whore Thaïs who told her lover
when he sent to ask her, 'Do you thank me much?'

'Much? Nay, past all believing!' And with this
let us turn from the sight of this abyss."

Canto XIX

CIRCLE EIGHT: BOLGIA THREE
The Simoniacs

Dante comes upon the SIMONIACS (sellers of ecclesiastic favors and offices) and his heart overflows with the wrath he feels against those who corrupt the things of God. This bolgia *is lined with round tubelike holes and the sinners are placed in them upside down with the soles of their feet ablaze. The heat of the blaze is proportioned to their guilt.*

The holes in which these sinners are placed are debased equivalents of the baptismal fonts common in the cities of Northern Italy and the sinners' confinement in them is temporary: as new sinners arrive, the souls drop through the bottoms of their holes and disappear eternally into the crevices of the rock.

As always, the punishment is a symbolic retribution. Just as the Simoniacs made a mock of holy office, so are they turned upside down in a mockery of the baptismal font. Just as they made a mockery of the holy water of baptism, so is their hellish baptism by fire, after which they are wholly immersed in the crevices below. The oily fire that licks at their soles may also suggest a travesty on the oil used in Extreme Unction (last rites for the dying).

Virgil carries Dante down an almost sheer ledge and lets him speak to one who is the chief sinner of that place, POPE NICHOLAS III. Dante delivers himself of another stirring denunciation of those who have corrupted church office, and Virgil carries him back up the steep ledge toward the FOURTH BOLGIA.

O Simon Magus! O you wretched crew
who follow him, pandering for silver and gold
the things of God which should be wedded to

love and righteousness! O thieves for hire,
now must the trump of judgment sound your doom
here in the third fosse of the rim of fire!

We had already made our way across
to the next grave, and to that part of the bridge

which hangs above the mid-point of the fosse.

O Sovereign Wisdom, how Thine art doth shine
in Heaven, on Earth, and in the Evil World!
How justly doth Thy power judge and assign!

I saw along the walls and on the ground
long rows of holes cut in the livid stone;
all were cut to a size, and all were round.

They seemed to be exactly the same size
as those in the font of my beautiful San Giovanni,
built to protect the priests who come to baptize;

(one of which, not so long since, I broke open
to rescue a boy who was wedged and drowning in it.
Be this enough to undeceive all men).

From every mouth a sinner's legs stuck out
as far as the calf. The soles were all ablaze
and the joints of the legs quivered and writhed about.

Withes and tethers would have snapped in their throes.
As oiled things blaze upon the surface only,
so did they burn from the heels to the points of their toes.

"Master," I said, "who is that one in the fire
who writhes and quivers more than all the others?
From him the ruddy flames seem to leap higher."

And he to me: "If you wish me to carry you down
along that lower bank, you may learn from him
who he is, and the evil he has done."

And I: "What you will, I will. You are my lord
and know I depart in nothing from your wish;
and you know my mind beyond my spoken word."

We moved to the fourth ridge, and turning left
my Guide descended by a jagged path
into the strait and perforated cleft.

Thus the good Master bore me down the dim
and rocky slope, and did not put me down
till we reached the one whose legs did penance for him.

"Whoever you are, sad spirit," I began,
"who lie here with your head below your heels
and planted like a stake—speak if you can."

I stood like a friar who gives the sacrament
to a hired assassin, who, fixed in the hole,
recalls him, and delays his death a moment.

"Are you there already, Boniface? Are you there
already?" he cried. "By several years the writ
has lied. And all that gold, and all that care—

are you already sated with the treasure
for which you dared to turn on the Sweet Lady
and trick and pluck and bleed her at your pleasure?"

I stood like one caught in some raillery,
not understanding what is said to him,
lost for an answer to such mockery.

Then Virgil said, "Say to him: 'I am not he,
I am not who you think.' " And I replied
as my good Master had instructed me.

The sinner's feet jerked madly; then again
his voice rose, this time choked with sighs and tears,
and said at last: "What do you want of me then?

If to know who I am drives you so fearfully

that you descend the bank to ask it, know
that the Great Mantle was once hung upon me.

And in truth I was a son of the She-Bear,
so sly and eager to push my whelps ahead,
that I pursed wealth above, and myself here.

Beneath my head are dragged all who have gone
before me in buying and selling holy office;
there they cower in fissures of the stone.

I too shall be plunged down when that great cheat
for whom I took you comes here in his turn.
Longer already have I baked my feet

and been planted upside-down, than he shall be
before the west sends down a lawless Shepherd
of uglier deeds to cover him and me.

He will be a new Jason of the Maccabees;
and just as that king bent to his high priests' will,
so shall the French king do as this one please."

Maybe—I cannot say—I grew too brash
at this point, for when he had finished speaking
I said: "Indeed! Now tell me how much cash

our Lord required of Peter in guarantee
before he put the keys into his keeping?
Surely he asked nothing but 'Follow me!'

Nor did Peter, nor the others, ask silver or gold
of Matthias when they chose him for the place
the despicable and damned apostle sold.

Therefore stay as you are; this hole well fits you—
and keep a good guard on the ill-won wealth

that once made you so bold toward Charles of Anjou.

And were it not that I am still constrained
by the reverence I owe to the Great Keys
you held in life, I should not have refrained
from using other words and sharper still;
for this avarice of yours grieves all the world,
tramples the virtuous, and exalts the evil.

Of such as you was the Evangelist's vision
when he saw She Who Sits upon the Waters
locked with the Kings of earth in fornication.

She was born with seven heads, and ten enormous
and shining horns strengthened and made her glad
as long as love and virtue pleased her spouse.

Gold and silver are the gods you adore!
In what are you different from the idolator,
save that he worships one, and you a score?

Ah Constantine, what evil marked the hour—
not of your conversion, but of the fee
the first rich Father took from you in dower!"

And as I sang him this tune, he began to twitch
and kick both feet out wildly, as if in rage
or gnawed by conscience—little matter which.

And I think, indeed, it pleased my Guide: his look
was all approval as he stood beside me
intent upon each word of truth I spoke.

He approached, and with both arms he lifted me,
and when he had gathered me against his breast,
remounted the rocky path out of the valley,

nor did he tire of holding me clasped to him,
until we reached the topmost point of the arch
which crosses from the fourth to the fifth rim

of the pits of woe. Arrived upon the bridge,
he tenderly set down the heavy burden
he had been pleased to carry up that ledge
which would have been hard climbing for a goat.
Here I looked down on still another moat.

46-47. *like a friar, etc.:* Persons convicted of murdering for hire were

Canto XX

*Dante stands in the middle of the bridge over the FOURTH BOLGIA and looks
down at the souls of the FORTUNE TELLERS and DIVINERS. Here are the
souls of all those who attempted by forbidden arts to look into the future. Among
these damned are: AMPHIAREUS, TIRESIAS, ARUNS, MANTO, EURYPYLUS,
MICHAEL SCOTT, GUIDO BONATTI, and ASDENTE.*

*Characteristically, the sin of these wretches is reversed upon them: their
punishment is to have their heads turned backwards on their bodies and to be
compelled to walk backwards through all eternity, their eyes blinded with tears.
Thus, those who sought to penetrate the future cannot even see in front of
themselves; they attempted to move themselves forward in time, so must they go
backwards through all eternity; and as the arts of sorcery are a distortion of
God's law, so are their bodies distorted in Hell.*

*No more need be said of them: Dante names them, and passes on to fill the
Canto with a lengthy account of the founding of Virgil's native city of Mantua.*

Now must I sing new griefs, and my verses strain
to form the matter of the Twentieth Canto
of Canticle One, the Canticle of Pain.

My vantage point permitted a clear view
of the depths of the pit below: a desolation
bathed with the tears of its tormented crew,

who moved about the circle of the pit
at about the pace of a litany procession.
Silent and weeping, they wound round and round it.

And when I looked down from their faces, I saw
that each of them was hideously distorted
between the top of the chest and the lines of the jaw;
for the face was reversed on the neck, and they came on

backwards, staring backwards at their loins,
for to look before them was forbidden. Someone,

sometime, in the grip of a palsy may have been
distorted so, but never to my knowledge;
nor do I believe the like was ever seen.

Reader, so may God grant you to understand
my poem and profit from it, ask yourself
how I could check my tears, when near at hand

I saw the image of our humanity
distorted so that the tears that burst from their eyes
ran down the cleft of their buttocks. Certainly

I wept. I leaned against the jagged face
of a rock and wept so that my Guide said: "Still?
Still like the other fools? There is no place

for pity here. Who is more arrogant
within his soul, who is more impious
than one who dares to sorrow at God's judgment?

Lift up your eyes, lift up your eyes and see
him the earth swallowed before all the Thebans,
at which they cried out: 'Whither do you flee,

Amphiareus? Why do you leave the field?'
And he fell headlong through the gaping earth
to the feet of Minos, where all sin must yield.

Observe how he has made a breast of his back.
In life he wished to see too far before him,
and now he must crab backwards round this track.

And see Tiresias, who by his arts
succeeded in changing himself from man to woman,

transforming all his limbs and all his parts;
later he had to strike the two twined serpents
once again with his conjurer's wand before
he could resume his manly lineaments.

And there is Aruns, his back to that one's belly,
the same who in the mountains of the Luni
tilled by the people of Carrara's valley,

made a white marble cave his den, and there
with unobstructed view observed the sea
and the turning constellations year by year.

And she whose unbound hair flows back to hide
her breasts—which you cannot see—and who also wears
all of her hairy parts on that other side,

was Manto, who searched countries far and near,
then settled where I was born. In that connection
there is a story I would have you hear.

Tiresias was her sire. After his death,
Thebes, the city of Bacchus, became enslaved,
and for many years she roamed about the earth.

High in sweet Italy, under the Alps that shut
the Tyrolean gate of Germany, there lies
a lake known as Benacus roundabout.

Through endless falls, more than a thousand and one,
Mount Apennine from Garda to Val Cammonica
is freshened by the waters that flow down

into that lake. At its center is a place
where the Bishops of Brescia, Trentine, and Verona
might all give benediction with equal grace.

Peschiera, the beautiful fortress, strong in war
against the Brescians and the Bergamese,
sits at the lowest point along that shore.
There, the waters Benacus cannot hold within its bosom, spill and form a river
that winds away through pastures green and gold.

But once the water gathers its full flow,
it is called Mincius rather than Benacus
from there to Governo, where it joins the Po.

Still near its source, it strikes a plain, and there
it slows and spreads, forming an ancient marsh
which in the summer heats pollutes the air.

The terrible virgin, passing there by chance,
saw dry land at the center of the mire,
untilled, devoid of all inhabitants.

There, shunning all communion with mankind,
she settled with the ministers of her arts,
and there she lived, and there she left behind

her vacant corpse. Later the scattered men
who lived nearby assembled on that spot
since it was well defended by the fen.

Over those whited bones they raised the city,
and for her who had chosen the place before all others
they named it—with no further augury—

Mantua. Far more people lived there once—
before sheer madness prompted Casalodi
to let Pinamonte play him for a dunce.

Therefore, I charge you, should you ever hear
other accounts of this, to let no falsehood
confuse the truth which I have just made clear."

And I to him: "Master, within my soul
your word is certainty, and any other
would seem like the dead lumps of burned out coal.

But tell me of those people moving down
to join the rest. Are any worth my noting?
For my mind keeps coming back to that alone."

And he: "That one whose beard spreads like a fleece
over his swarthy shoulders, was an augur
in the days when so few males remained in Greece

that even the cradles were all but empty of sons.
He chose the time for cutting the cable at Aulis,
and Calchas joined him in those divinations.

He is Eurypylus. I sing him somewhere
in my High Tragedy; you will know the place
who know the whole of it. The other there,

the one beside him with the skinny shanks
was Michael Scott, who mastered every trick
of magic fraud, a prince of mountebanks.

See Guido Bonatti there; and see Asdente,
who now would be wishing he had stuck to his last,
but repents too late, though he repents aplenty.

And see on every hand the wretched hags
who left their spinning and sewing for soothsaying
and casting of spells with herbs, and dolls, and rags.

But come: Cain with his bush of thorns appears
already on the wave below Seville,
above the boundary of the hemispheres;

and the moon was full already yesternight,
as you must well remember from the wood,
for it certainly did not harm you when its light

shone down upon your way before the dawn."
And as he spoke to me, we traveled on.

Canto XXI

CIRCLE EIGHT: BOLGIA FIVE
The Grafters

*The Poets move on, talking as they go, and arrive at the FIFTH BOLGIA. Here
the GRAFTERS are sunk in boiling pitch and guarded by DEMONS, who tear
them to pieces with claws and grappling hooks if they catch them above the
surface of the pitch.*

*The sticky pitch is symbolic of the sticky fingers of the Grafters. It serves also
to hide them from sight, as their sinful dealings on earth were hidden from men's
eyes. The demons, too, suggest symbolic possibilities, for they are armed with
grappling hooks and are forever ready to rend and tear all they can get their
hands on.*

*The Poets watch a demon arrive with a grafting SENATOR of LUCCA and
fling him into the pitch where the demons set upon him.*

*To protect Dante from their wrath, Virgil hides him behind some jagged rocks
and goes ahead alone to negotiate with the demons. They set upon him like a
pack of mastiffs, but Virgil secures a safe-conduct from their leader,
MALACODA. Thereupon Virgil calls Dante from hiding, and they are about to
set off when they discover that the BRIDGE ACROSS THE SIXTH BOLGIA lies
shattered. Malacoda tells them there is another further on and sends a squad of
demons to escort them. Their adventures with the demons continue through the
next Canto.*

*These two Cantos may conveniently be remembered as the GARGOYLE
CANTOS. If the total* Commedia *is built like a cathedral (as so many critics have
suggested), it is here certainly that Dante attaches his grotesqueries. At no other
point in the* Commedia *does Dante give such free rein to his coarsest style.*

Thus talking of things which my Comedy does not care
to sing, we passed from one arch to the next
until we stood upon its summit. There

we checked our steps to study the next fosse
and the next vain lamentations of Malebolge;
awesomely dark and desolate it was.

As in the Venetian arsenal, the winter through
there boils the sticky pitch to caulk the seams
of the sea-battered bottoms when no crew

can put to sea—instead of which, one starts
to build its ship anew, one plugs the planks
which have been sprung in many foreign parts;

some hammer at a mast, some at a rib;
some make new oars, some braid and coil new lines;
one patches up the mainsail, one the jib—

so, but by Art Divine and not by fire,
a viscid pitch boiled in the fosse below
and coated all the bank with gluey mire.

I saw the pitch; but I saw nothing in it
except the enormous bubbles of its boiling,
which swelled and sank, like breathing, through all the pit.

And as I stood and stared into that sink,
my Master cried, "Take care!" and drew me back
from my exposed position on the brink.

I turned like one who cannot wait to see
the thing he dreads, and who, in sudden fright,
runs while he looks, his curiosity

competing with his terror—and at my back
I saw a figure that came running toward us
across the ridge, a Demon huge and black.

Ah what a face he had, all hate and wildness!
Galloping so, with his great wings outspread
he seemed the embodiment of all bitterness.

Across each high-hunched shoulder he had thrown
one haunch of a sinner, whom he held in place
with a great talon round each ankle bone.

"Blacktalons of our bridge," he began to roar,
"I bring you one of Santa Zita's Elders!
Scrub him down while I go back for more:

I planted a harvest of them in that city:
everyone there is a grafter except Bonturo.
There 'Yes' is 'No' and 'No' is 'Yes' for a fee."

Down the sinner plunged, and at once the Demon
spun from the cliff; no mastiff ever sprang
more eager from the leash to chase a felon.

Down plunged the sinner and sank to reappear
with his backside arched and his face and both his feet
glued to the pitch, almost as if in prayer.

But the Demons under the bridge, who guard that place
and the sinners who are thrown to them, bawled out:
"You're out of bounds here for the Sacred Face:

this is no dip in the Serchio: take your look
and then get down in the pitch. And stay below
unless you want a taste of a grappling hook."

Then they raked him with more than a hundred hooks
bellowing: "Here you dance below the covers.
Graft all you can there: no one checks your books."

They dipped him down into that pitch exactly
as a chef makes scullery boys dip meat in a boiler,
holding it with their hooks from floating free.

And the Master said: "*You* had best not be seen

by these Fiends till I am ready. Crouch down here.
One of these rocks will serve you as a screen.

And whatever violence you see done to me,
you have no cause to fear. I know these matters:
I have been through this once and come back safely."

With that, he walked on past the end of the bridge;
and it wanted all his courage to look calm
from the moment he arrived on the sixth ridge.

With that same storm and fury that arouses
all the house when the hounds leap at a tramp
who suddenly falls to pleading where he pauses—

so rushed those Fiends from below, and all the pack
pointed their gleaming pitchforks at my Guide.
But he stood fast and cried to them: "Stand back!

Before those hooks and grapples make too free,
send up one of your crew to hear me out,
then ask yourselves if you still care to rip me."

All cried as one: "Let Malacoda go."
So the pack stood and one of them came forward,
saying: "What good does he think *this* will do?"

"Do you think, Malacoda," my good Master said,
"you would see me here, having arrived this far
already, safe from you and every dread,

without Divine Will and propitious Fate?
Let me pass on, for it is willed in Heaven
that I must show another this dread state."

The Demon stood there on the flinty brim,
so taken aback he let his pitchfork drop;

then said to the others: "Take care not to harm him!"

"O you crouched like a cat," my Guide called to me,
"among the jagged rock piles of the bridge,
come down to me, for now you may come safely."

Hearing him, I hurried down the ledge;
and the Demons all pressed forward when I appeared,
so that I feared they might not keep their pledge.
So once I saw the Pisan infantry
march out under truce from the fortress at Caprona,
staring in fright at the ranks of the enemy.

I pressed the whole of my body against my Guide,
and not for an instant did I take my eyes
from those black fiends who scowled on every side.

They swung their forks saying to one another:
"Shall I give him a touch in the rump?" and answering:
"Sure; give him a taste to pay him for his bother."

But the Demon who was talking to my Guide
turned round and cried to him: "At ease there,
Snatcher!"
And then to us: "There's no road on this side:

the arch lies all in pieces in the pit.
If you *must* go on, follow along this ridge;
there's another cliff to cross by just beyond it.

In just five hours it will be, since the bridge fell,
a thousand two hundred sixty-six years and a day;
that was the time the big quake shook all Hell.

I'll send a squad of my boys along that way
to see if anyone's airing himself below:
you can go with them: there will be no foul play.

Front and center here, Grizzly and Hellken,"
he began to order them. "You too, Deaddog.
Curlybeard, take charge of a squad of ten.

Take Grafter and Dragontooth along with you.
Pigtusk, Catclaw, Cramper, and Crazyred.
Keep a sharp lookout on the boiling glue

as you move along, and see that these gentlemen
are not molested until they reach the crag
where they can find a way across the den."

"In the name of heaven, Master," I cried, "what sort
of guides are these? Let us go on alone
if you know the way. Who can trust such an escort!

If you are as wary as you used to be
you surely see them grind their teeth at us,
and knot their beetle brows so threateningly."

And he: "I do not like this fear in you.
Let them gnash and knot as they please; they menace only
the sticky wretches simmering in that stew."

They turned along the left bank in a line;
but before they started, all of them together
had stuck their pointed tongues out as a sign

to their Captain that they wished permission to pass,
and he had made a trumpet of his ass.

Canto XXII

The Poets set off with their escorts of demons. Dante sees the GRAFTERS lying in the pitch like frogs in water with only their muzzles out. They disappear as soon as they sight the demons and only a ripple on the surface betrays their presence.

One of the Grafters, AN UNIDENTIFIED NAVARRESE, ducks too late and is seized by the demons who are about to claw him, but CURLYBEARD holds them back while Virgil questions him. The wretch speaks of his fellow sinners, FRIAR GOMITA and MICHEL ZANCHE, while the uncontrollable demons rake him from time to time with their hooks.

The Navarrese offers to lure some of his fellow sufferers into the hands of the demons, and when his plan is accepted he plunges into the pitch and escapes. HELLKEN and GRIZZLY fly after him, but too late. They start a brawl in mid-air and fall into the pitch themselves. Curlybeard immediately organizes a rescue party and the Poets, fearing the bad temper of the frustrated demons, take advantage of the confusion to slip away.

I have seen horsemen breaking camp. I have seen
the beginning of the assault, the march and muster,
and at times the retreat and riot. I have been

where chargers trampled your land, O Aretines!
I have seen columns of foragers, shocks of tourney,
and running of tilts. I have seen the endless lines

march to bells, drums, trumpets, from far and near.
I have seen them march on signals from a castle.
I have seen them march with native and foreign gear.

But never yet have I seen horse or foot,
nor ship in range of land nor sight of star,
take its direction from so low a toot.

We went with the ten Fiends—ah, savage crew!—
but "In church with saints; with stewpots in the tavern,"
as the old proverb wisely bids us do.

All my attention was fixed upon the pitch:
to observe the people who were boiling in it,
and the customs and the punishments of that ditch.

As dolphins surface and begin to flip
their arched backs from the sea, warning the sailors
to fall-to and begin to secure ship—

So now and then, some soul, to ease his pain,
showed us a glimpse of his back above the pitch
and quick as lightning disappeared again.

And as, at the edge of a ditch, frogs squat about
hiding their feet and bodies in the water,
leaving only their muzzles sticking out—

so stood the sinners in that dismal ditch;
but as Curlybeard approached, only a ripple
showed where they had ducked back into the pitch.

I saw—the dread of it haunts me to this day—
one linger a bit too long, as it sometimes happens
one frog remains when another spurts away;

and Catclaw, who was nearest, ran a hook
through the sinner's pitchy hair and hauled him in.
He looked like an otter dripping from the brook.

I knew the names of all the Fiends by then;
I had made a note of them at the first muster,
and, marching, had listened and checked them over again.

"Hey, Crazyred," the crew of Demons cried

all together, "give him a taste of your claws.
Dig him open a little. Off with his hide."

And I then: "Master, can you find out, please,
the name and history of that luckless one
who has fallen into the hands of his enemies?"

My Guide approached that wraith from the hot tar
and asked him whence he came. The wretch replied:
"I was born and raised in the Kingdom of Navarre.

My mother placed me in service to a knight;
for she had borne me to a squanderer
who killed himself when he ran through his birthright.

Then I became a domestic in the service
of good King Thibault. There I began to graft,
and I account for it in this hot crevice."

And Pigtusk, who at the ends of his lower lip
shot forth two teeth more terrible than a boar's,
made the wretch feel how one of them could rip.

The mouse had come among bad cats, but here
Curlybeard locked arms around him crying:
"While I've got hold of him the rest stand clear!"

And turning his face to my Guide: "If you want to ask him
anything else," he added, "ask away
before the others tear him limb from limb."

And my Guide to the sinner: "I should like to know
if among the other souls beneath the pitch
are any Italians?" And the wretch: "Just now

I left a shade who came from parts near by.
Would I were still in the pitch with him, for then

these hooks would not be giving me cause to cry."

And suddenly Grafter bellowed in great heat:
"We've stood enough!" And he hooked the sinner's arm
and, raking it, ripped off a chunk of meat.
Then Dragontooth wanted to play, too, reaching down
for a catch at the sinner's legs; but Curlybeard
wheeled round and round with a terrifying frown,

and when the Fiends had somewhat given ground
and calmed a little, my Guide, without delay,
asked the wretch, who was staring at his wound:

"Who was the sinner from whom you say you made
your evil-starred departure to come ashore
among these Fiends?" And the wretch: "It was the
shade

of Friar Gomita of Gallura, the crooked stem
of every Fraud: when his master's enemies
were in his hands, he won high praise from them.

He took their money without case or docket,
and let them go. He was in all his dealings
no petty bursar, but a kingly pocket.

With him, his endless crony in the fosse,
is Don Michel Zanche of Logodoro;
they babble about Sardinia without pause.

But look! See that fiend grinning at your side!
There is much more that I should like to tell you,
but oh, I think he means to grate my hide!"

But their grim sergeant wheeled, sensing foul play,
and turning on Cramper, who seemed set to strike,
ordered: "Clear off, you buzzard. Clear off, I say!"

"If either of you would like to see and hear
Tuscans or Lombards," the pale sinner said,
"I can lure them out of hiding if you'll stand clear

and let me sit here at the edge of the ditch,
and get all these Blacktalons out of sight;
for while they're here, no one will leave the pitch.

In exchange for myself, I can fish you up as pretty
a mess of souls as you like. I have only to whistle
the way we do when one of us gets free."

Deaddog raised his snout as he listened to him;
then, shaking his head, said, "Listen to the grafter
spinning his tricks so he can jump from the brim!"

And the sticky wretch, who was all treachery:
"Oh I am more than tricky when there's a chance
to see my friends in greater misery."

Hellken, against the will of all the crew,
could hold no longer. "If you jump," he said
to the scheming wretch, "I won't come after you

at a gallop, but like a hawk after a mouse.
We'll clear the edge and hide behind the bank:
let's see if you're trickster enough for all of us."

Reader, here is new game! The Fiends withdrew
from the bank's edge, and Deaddog, who at first
was most against it, led the savage crew.

The Navarrese chose his moment carefully:
and planting both his feet against the ground,
he leaped, and in an instant he was free.

The Fiends were stung with shame, and of the lot
Hellken most, who had been the cause of it.
He leaped out madly bellowing: "You're caught!"

but little good it did him; terror pressed
harder than wings; the sinner dove from sight
and the Fiend in full flight had to raise his breast.

A duck, when the falcon dives, will disappear
exactly so, all in a flash, while he
returns defeated and weary up the air.
Grizzly, in a rage at the sinner's flight,
flew after Hellken, hoping the wraith would escape,
so he might find an excuse to start a fight.

And as soon as the grafter sank below the pitch,
Grizzly turned his talons against Hellken,
locked with him claw to claw above the ditch.

But Hellken was sparrowhawk enough for two
and clawed him well; and ripping one another,
they plunged together into the hot stew.

The heat broke up the brawl immediately,
but their wings were smeared with pitch and
they could not rise.
Curlybeard, upset as his company,

commanded four to fly to the other coast
at once with all their grapples. At top speed
the Fiends divided, each one to his post.

Some on the near edge, some along the far,
they stretched their hooks out to the clotted pair
who were already cooked deep through the scar

of their first burn. And turning to one side

we slipped off, leaving them thus occupied.

Canto XXIII

The Poets are pursued by the Fiends and escape them by sliding down the sloping bank of the next pit. They are now in the SIXTH BOLGIA. Here the HYPOCRITES, weighted down by great leaden robes, walk eternally round and round a narrow track. The robes are brilliantly gilded on the outside and are shaped like a monk's habit, for the hypocrite's outward appearance shines brightly and passes for holiness, but under that show lies the terrible weight of his deceit which the soul must bear through all eternity.

The Poets talk to TWO JOVIAL FRIARS and come upon CAIAPHAS, the chief sinner of that place. Caiaphas was the High Priest of the Jews who counseled the Pharisees to crucify Jesus in the name of public expedience. He is punished by being himself crucified to the floor of Hell by three great stakes, and in such a position that every passing sinner must walk upon him. Thus he must suffer upon his own body the weight of all the world's hypocrisy, as Christ suffered upon his body the pain of all the world's sins.

The Jovial Friars tell Virgil how he may climb from the pit, and Virgil discovers that Malacoda lied to him about the bridges over the Sixth Bolgia.

Silent, apart, and unattended we went
as Minor Friars go when they walk abroad,
one following the other. The incident

recalled the fable of the Mouse and the Frog
that Aesop tells. For compared attentively
point by point, "pig" is no closer to "hog"

than the one case to the other. And as one thought
springs from another, so the comparison
gave birth to a new concern, at which I caught

my breath in fear. This thought ran through my mind:
"These Fiends, through us, have been made ridiculous,
and have suffered insult and injury of a kind

to make them smart. Unless we take good care—
now rage is added to their natural spleen—
they will hunt us down as greyhounds hunt the hare."

Already I felt my scalp grow tight with fear.
I was staring back in terror as I said:
"Master, unless we find concealment here

and soon, I dread the rage of the Fiends: already
they are yelping on our trail: I imagine them
so vividly I can hear them now." And he:

"Were I a pane of leaded glass, I could not
summon your outward look more instantly
into myself, than I do your inner thought.

Your fears were mixed already with my own
with the same suggestion and the same dark look;
so that of both I form one resolution:

the right bank may be sloping: in that case
we may find some way down to the next pit
and so escape from the imagined chase."

He had not finished answering me thus
when, not far off, their giant wings outspread,
I saw the Fiends come charging after us.

Seizing me instantly in his arms, my Guide—
like a mother wakened by a midnight noise
to find a wall of flame at her bedside

(who takes her child and runs, and more concerned

for him than for herself, does not pause even
to throw a wrap about her) raised me, turned,

and down the rugged bank from the high summit
flung himself down supine onto the slope
which walls the upper side of the next pit.

Water that turns the great wheel of a land-mill
never ran faster through the end of a sluice
at the point nearest the paddles—as down that hill

my Guide and Master bore me on his breast,
as if I were not a companion, but a son.
And the soles of his feet had hardly come to rest

on the bed of the depth below, when on the height
we had just left, the Fiends beat their great wings.
But now they gave my Guide no cause for fright;

for the Providence that gave them the fifth pit
to govern as the ministers of Its will,
takes from their souls the power of leaving it.

About us now in the depth of the pit we found
a painted people, weary and defeated.
Slowly, in pain, they paced it round and round.

All wore great cloaks cut to as ample a size
as those worn by the Benedictines of Cluny.
The enormous hoods were drawn over their eyes.

The outside is all dazzle, golden and fair;
the inside, lead, so heavy that Frederick's capes,
compared to these, would seem as light as air.

O weary mantle for eternity!
We turned to the left again along their course,

listening to their moans of misery,
but they moved so slowly down that barren strip,
tired by their burden, that our company
was changed at every movement of the hip.

And walking thus, I said: "As we go on,
may it please you to look about among these people
for any whose name or history may be known."

And one who understood Tuscan cried to us there
as we hurried past: "I pray you check your speed,
you who run so fast through the sick air:

it may be I am one who will fit your case."
And at his words my Master turned and said:
"Wait now, then go with him at his own pace."

I waited there, and saw along that track
two souls who seemed in haste to be with me;
but the narrow way and their burden held them back.

When they had reached me down that narrow way
they stared at me in silence and amazement,
then turned to one another. I heard one say:

"This one seems, by the motion of his throat,
to be alive; and if they are dead, how is it
they are allowed to shed the leaden coat?"

And then to me "O Tuscan, come so far
to the college of the sorry hypocrites,
do not disdain to tell us who you are."

And I: "I was born and raised a Florentine
on the green and lovely banks of Arno's waters,
I go with the body that was always mine.

But who are *you*, who sighing as you go
distill in floods of tears that drown your cheeks?
What punishment is this that glitters so?"

"These burnished robes are of thick lead," said one,
"and are hung on us like counterweights, so heavy
that we, their weary fulcrums, creak and groan.

Jovial Friars and Bolognese were we.
We were chosen jointly by your Florentines
to keep the peace, an office usually

held by a single man; near the Gardingo
one still may see the sort of peace we kept.
I was called Catalano, he, Loderingo."

I began: "O Friars, your evil . . ."—and then I saw
a figure crucified upon the ground
by three great stakes, and I fell still in awe.

When he saw me there, he began to puff great sighs
into his beard, convulsing all his body;
and Friar Catalano, following my eyes,

said to me: "That one nailed across the road
counselled the Pharisees that it was fitting
one man be tortured for the public good.

Naked he lies fixed there, as you see,
in the path of all who pass; there he must feel
the weight of all through all eternity.

His father-in-law and the others of the Council
which was a seed of wrath to all the Jews,
are similarly staked for the same evil."

Then I saw Virgil marvel for a while

over that soul so ignominiously
stretched on the cross in Hell's eternal exile.

Then, turning, he asked the Friar: "If your law permit,
can you tell us if somewhere along the right
there is some gap in the stone wall of the pit

through which we two may climb to the next brink
without the need of summoning the Black Angels
and forcing them to raise us from this sink?"

He: "Nearer than you hope, there is a bridge
that runs from the great circle of the scarp
and crosses every ditch from ridge to ridge,

except that in this it is broken; but with care
you can mount the ruins which lie along the slope
and make a heap on the bottom." My Guide stood there

motionless for a while with a dark look.
At last he said: "He lied about this business,
who spears the sinners yonder with his hook."

And the Friar: "Once at Bologna I heard the wise
discussing the Devil's sins; among them I heard
that he is a liar and the father of lies."

When the sinner had finished speaking, I saw the face
of my sweet Master darken a bit with anger:
he set off at a great stride from that place,

and I turned from that weighted hypocrite
to follow in the prints of his dear feet.

Canto XXIV

CIRCLE EIGHT: BOLGIA SEVEN
The Thieves

The Poets climb the right bank laboriously, cross the bridge of the SEVENTH BOLGIA and descend the far bank to observe the THIEVES. They find the pit full of monstrous reptiles who curl themselves about the sinners like living coils of rope, binding each sinner's hands behind his back, and knotting themselves through the loins. Other reptiles dart about the place, and the Poets see one of them fly through the air and pierce the jugular vein of one sinner who immediately bursts into flames until only ashes remain. From the ashes the sinner re-forms painfully.

These are Dante's first observations of the Thieves and will be carried further in the next Canto, but the first allegorical retribution is immediately apparent. Thievery is reptilian in its secrecy; therefore it is punished by reptiles. The hands of the thieves are the agents of their crimes; therefore they are bound forever. And as the thief destroys his fellowmen by making their substance disappear, so is he painfully destroyed and made to disappear, not once but over and over again.

The sinner who has risen from his own ashes reluctantly identifies himself as VANNI FUCCI. He tells his story, and to revenge himself for having been forced to reveal his identity he utters a dark prophecy against Dante.

In the turning season of the youthful year,
when the sun is warming his rays beneath Aquarius
and the days and nights already begin to near

their perfect balance; the hoar-frost copies then
the image of his white sister on the ground,
but the first sun wipes away the work of his pen.

The peasants who lack fodder then arise
and look about and see the fields all white,
and hear their lambs bleat; then they smite their thighs, go back into the house,
walk here and there,

pacing, fretting, wondering what to do,
then come out doors again, and there, despair

falls from them when they see how the earth's face
has changed in so little time, and they take their staffs
and drive their lambs to feed—so in that place

when I saw my Guide and Master's eyebrows lower,
my spirits fell and I was sorely vexed;
and as quickly came the plaster to the sore:

for when he had reached the ruined bridge, he stood
and turned on me that sweet and open look
with which he had greeted me in the dark wood.

When he had paused and studied carefully
the heap of stones, he seemed to reach some plan,
for he turned and opened his arms and lifted me.

Like one who works and calculates ahead,
and is always ready for what happens next—
so, raising me above that dismal bed

to the top of one great slab of the fallen slate,
he chose another saying: "Climb here, but first
test it to see if it will hold your weight."

It was no climb for a lead-hung hypocrite:
for scarcely we—he light and I assisted—
could crawl handhold by handhold from the pit;

and were it not that the bank along this side
was lower than the one down which we had slid,
I at least—I will not speak for my Guide—

would have turned back. But as all of the vast rim
of Malebolge leans toward the lowest well,

so each succeeding valley and each brim
is lower than the last. We climbed the face
and arrived by great exertion to the point
where the last rock had fallen from its place.

My lungs were pumping as if they could not stop;
I thought I could not go on, and I sat exhausted
the instant I had clambered to the top.

"Up on your feet! This is no time to tire!"
my Master cried. "The man who lies asleep
will never waken fame, and his desire

and all his life drift past him like a dream,
and the traces of his memory fade from time
like smoke in air, or ripples on a stream.

Now, therefore, rise. Control your breath, and call
upon the strength of soul that wins all battles
unless it sink in the gross body's fall.

There is a longer ladder yet to climb:
this much is not enough. If you understand me,
show that you mean to profit from your time."

I rose and made my breath appear more steady
than it really was, and I replied: "Lead on
as it pleases you to go: I am strong and ready."

We picked our way up the cliff, a painful climb,
for it was narrower, steeper, and more jagged
than any we had crossed up to that time.

I moved along, talking to hide my faintness,
when a voice that seemed unable to form words
rose from the depths of the next chasm's darkness.

I do not know what it said, though by then the Sage
had led me to the top of the next arch;
but the speaker seemed in a tremendous rage.

I was bending over the brim, but living eyes
could not plumb to the bottom of that dark;
therefore I said, "Master, let me advise

that we cross over and climb down the wall:
for just as I hear the voice without understanding,
so I look down and make out nothing at all."

"I make no other answer than the act,"
the Master said: "the only fit reply
to a fit request is silence and the fact."

So we moved down the bridge to the stone pier
that shores the end of the arch on the eighth bank,
and there I saw the chasm's depths made clear;

and there great coils of serpents met my sight,
so hideous a mass that even now
the memory makes my blood run cold with fright.

Let Libya boast no longer, for though its sands
breed chelidrids, jaculi, and phareans,
cenchriads, and two-headed amphisbands,

it never bred such a variety
of vipers, no, not with all Ethiopia
and all the lands that lie by the Red Sea.

Amid that swarm, naked and without hope,
people ran terrified, not even dreaming
of a hole to hide in, or of heliotrope.

Their hands were bound behind by coils of serpents

which thrust their heads and tails between the loins
and bunched in front, a mass of knotted torments.

One of the damned came racing round a boulder,
and as he passed us, a great snake shot up
and bit him where the neck joins with the shoulder.
No mortal pen—however fast it flash
over the page—could write down *o* or *i*
as quickly as he flamed and fell in ash;

and when he was dissolved into a heap
upon the ground, the dust rose of itself
and immediately resumed its former shape.

Precisely so, philosophers declare,
the Phoenix dies and then is born again
when it approaches its five hundredth year.

It lives on tears of balsam and of incense;
in all its life it eats no herb or grain,
and nard and precious myrrh sweeten its cerements.

And as a person fallen in a fit,
possessed by a Demon or some other seizure
that fetters him without his knowing it,

struggles up to his feet and blinks his eyes
(still stupefied by the great agony
he has just passed), and, looking round him, sighs—

such was the sinner when at last he rose.
O Power of God! How dreadful is Thy will
which in its vengeance rains such fearful blows.

Then my Guide asked him who he was. And he
answered reluctantly: "Not long ago
I rained into this gullet from Tuscany.

I am Vanni Fucci, the beast. A mule among men,
I chose the bestial life above the human.
Savage Pistoia was my fitting den."

And I to my Guide: "Detain him a bit longer
and ask what crime it was that sent him here;
I knew him as a man of blood and anger."

The sinner, hearing me, seemed discomforted,
but he turned and fixed his eyes upon my face
with a look of dismal shame; at length he said:

"That you have found me out among the strife
and misery of this place, grieves my heart more
than did the day that cut me from my life.

But I am forced to answer truthfully:
I am put down so low because it was I
who stole the treasure from the Sacristy,

for which others once were blamed. But that you may
find less to gloat about if you escape here,
prick up your ears and listen to what I say:

First Pistoia is emptied of the Black,
then Florence changes her party and her laws.
From Valdimagra the God of War brings back

a fiery vapor wrapped in turbid air:
then in a storm of battle at Piceno
the vapor breaks apart the mist, and there

every White shall feel his wounds anew.
And I have told you this that it may grieve you."

Canto XXV

*Vanni's rage mounts to the point where he hurls an ultimate obscenity at God,
and the serpents immediately swarm over him, driving him off in great pain. The
Centaur, CACUS, his back covered with serpents and a fire-eating dragon, also
gives chase to punish the wretch.*

*Dante then meets FIVE NOBLE THIEVES OF FLORENCE and sees the
further retribution visited upon the sinners. Some of the thieves appear first in
human form, others as reptiles. All but one of them suffer a painful
transformation before Dante's eyes. AGNELLO appears in human form and is
merged with CIANFA, who appears as a six-legged lizard. BUOSO appears as a
man and changes form with FRANCESCO, who first appears as a tiny reptile.
Only PUCCIO SCIANCATO remains unchanged, though we are made to
understand that his turn will come.*

*For endless and painful transformation is the final state of the thieves. In life
they took the substance of others, transforming it into their own. So in Hell their
very bodies are constantly being taken from them, and they are left to steal back
a human form from some other sinner. Thus they waver constantly between man
and reptile, and no sinner knows what to call his own.*

When he had finished, the thief—to his disgrace—
raised his hands with both fists making figs,
and cried: "Here, God! I throw them in your face!"

Thereat the snakes became my friends, for one
coiled itself about the wretch's neck
as if it were saying: "You shall not go on!"

and another tied his arms behind him again,
knotting its head and tail between his loins
so tight he could not move a finger in pain.

Pistoia! Pistoia! why have you not decreed
to turn yourself to ashes and end your days,
rather than spread the evil of your seed!

In all of Hell's corrupt and sunken halls
I found no shade so arrogant toward God,
not even him who fell from the Theban walls!

Without another word, he fled; and there
I saw a furious Centaur race up, roaring:
"Where is the insolent blasphemer? Where?"

I do not think as many serpents swarm
in all the Maremma as he bore on his back
from the haunch to the first sign of our human form.

Upon his shoulders, just behind his head
a snorting dragon whose hot breath set fire
to all it touched, lay with its wings outspread.

My Guide said: "That is Cacus. Time and again
in the shadow of Mount Aventine he made
a lake of blood upon the Roman plain.

He does not go with his kin by the blood-red fosse
because of the cunning fraud with which he stole
the cattle of Hercules. And thus it was

his thieving stopped, for Hercules found his den
and gave him perhaps a hundred blows with his club,
and of them he did not feel the first ten."

Meanwhile, the Centaur passed along his way,
and three wraiths came. Neither my Guide nor I
knew they were there until we heard them say:

"You there—who are you?" There our talk fell still
and we turned to stare at them. I did not know them,
but by chance it happened, as it often will,
one named another. "Where is Cianfa?" he cried;
"Why has he fallen back?" I placed a finger
across my lips as a signal to my Guide.

Reader, should you doubt what next I tell,
it will be no wonder, for though I saw it happen,
I can scarce believe it possible, even in Hell.

For suddenly, as I watched, I saw a lizard
come darting forward on six great taloned feet
and fasten itself to a sinner from crotch to gizzard.

Its middle feet sank in the sweat and grime
of the wretch's paunch, its forefeet clamped his arms,
its teeth bit through both cheeks. At the same time

its hind feet fastened on the sinner's thighs:
its tail thrust through his legs and closed its coil
over his loins. I saw it with my own eyes!

No ivy ever grew about a tree
as tightly as that monster wove itself
limb by limb about the sinner's body;

they fused like hot wax, and their colors ran
together until neither wretch nor monster
appeared what he had been when he began:

just so, before the running edge of the heat
on a burning page, a brown discoloration
changes to black as the white dies from the sheet.

The other two cried out as they looked on:
"Alas! Alas! Agnello, how you change!

Already you are neither two nor one!"

The two heads had already blurred and blended;
now two new semblances appeared and faded,
one face where neither face began nor ended.
From the four upper limbs of man and beast
two arms were made, then members never seen
grew from the thighs and legs, belly and breast.

Their former likenesses mottled and sank
to something that was both of them and neither;
and so transformed, it slowly left our bank.

As lizards at high noon of a hot day
dart out from hedge to hedge, from shade to shade,
and flash like lightning when they cross the way,

so toward the bowels of the other two,
shot a small monster; livid, furious,
and black as a pepper corn. Its lunge bit through

that part of one of them from which man receives
his earliest nourishment; then it fell back
and lay sprawled out in front of the two thieves.

Its victim stared at it but did not speak:
indeed, he stood there like a post, and yawned
as if lack of sleep, or a fever, had left him weak.

The reptile stared at him, he at the reptile;
from the wound of one and from the other's mouth
two smokes poured out and mingled, dark and vile.

Now let Lucan be still with his history
of poor Sabellus and Nassidius,
and wait to hear what next appeared to me.

Of Cadmus and Arethusa be Ovid silent. I have no need to envy him those verses
where he makes one a fountain, and one a serpent:

for he never transformed two beings face to face
in such a way that both their natures yielded
their elements each to each, as in this case.
Responding sympathetically to each other,
the reptile cleft his tail into a fork,
and the wounded sinner drew his feet together.

The sinner's legs and thighs began to join:
they grew together so, that soon no trace
of juncture could be seen from toe to loin.

Point by point the reptile's cloven tail
grew to the form of what the sinner lost;
one skin began to soften, one to scale.

The armpits swallowed the arms, and the short shank
of the reptile's forefeet simultaneously
lengthened by as much as the man's arms shrank.

Its hind feet twisted round themselves and grew
the member man conceals; meanwhile the wretch
from his one member generated two.

The smoke swelled up about them all the while:
it tanned one skin and bleached the other; it stripped
the hair from the man and grew it on the reptile.

While one fell to his belly, the other rose
without once shifting the locked evil eyes
below which they changed snouts as they changed pose.

The face of the standing one drew up and in
toward the temples, and from the excess matter
that gathered there, ears grew from the smooth skin;

while of the matter left below the eyes
the excess became a nose, at the same time
forming the lips to an appropriate size.

Here the face of the prostrate felon slips,
sharpens into a snout, and withdraws its ears
as a snail pulls in its horns. Between its lips
the tongue, once formed for speech, thrusts out a fork;
the forked tongue of the other heals and draws
into his mouth. The smoke has done its work.

The soul that had become a beast went flitting
and hissing over the stones, and after it
the other walked along talking and spitting.

Then turning his new shoulders, said to the one
that still remained: "It is Buoso's turn to go
crawling along this road as I have done."

Thus did the ballast of the seventh hold
shift and reshift; and may the strangeness of it
excuse my pen if the tale is strangely told.

And though all this confused me, they did not flee
so cunningly but what I was aware
that it was Puccio Sciancato alone of the three

that first appeared, who kept his old form still.
The other was he for whom you weep, Gaville.

Canto XXVI

CIRCLE EIGHT: BOLGIA EIGHT
The Evil Counselors

Dante turns from the Thieves toward the Evil Counselors of the next Bolgia, and between the two he addresses a passionate lament to Florence prophesying the griefs that will befall her from these two sins. At the purported time of the Vision, it will be recalled, Dante was a Chief Magistrate of Florence and was forced into exile by men he had reason to consider both thieves and evil counselors. He seems prompted, in fact, to say much more on this score, but he restrains himself when he comes in sight of the sinners of the next Bolgia, for they are a moral symbolism, all men of gift who abused their genius, perverting it to wiles and stratagems. Seeing them in Hell he knows his must be another road: his way shall not be by deception.

So the Poets move on and Dante observes the EIGHTH BOLGIA in detail. Here the EVIL COUNSELORS move about endlessly, hidden from view inside great flames. Their sin was to abuse the gifts of the Almighty, to steal his virtues for low purposes. And as they stole from God in their lives and worked by hidden ways, so are they stolen from sight and hidden in the great flames which are their own guilty consciences. And as, in most instances at least, they sinned by glibness of tongue, so are the flames made into a fiery travesty of tongues.

Among the others, the Poets see a great doubleheaded flame, and discover that ULYSSES and DIOMEDE are punished together within it. Virgil addresses the flame, and through its wavering tongue Ulysses narrates an unforgettable tale of his last voyage and death.

Joy to you, Florence, that your banners swell,
beating their proud wings over land and sea,
and that your name expands through all of Hell!

Among the thieves I found five who had been
your citizens, to my shame; nor yet shall you
mount to great honor peopling such a den!

But if the truth is dreamed of toward the morning,
you soon shall feel what Prato and the others
wish for you. And were that day of mourning

already come it would not be too soon.
So may it come, since it must! for it will weigh
more heavily on me as I pass my noon.

We left that place. My Guide climbed stone by stone
the natural stair by which we had descended
and drew me after him. So we passed on,

and going our lonely way through that dead land
among the crags and crevices of the cliff,
the foot could make no way without the hand.

I mourned among those rocks, and I mourn again
when memory returns to what I saw:
and more than usually I curb the strain

of my genius, lest it stray from Virtue's course;
so if some star, or a better thing, grant me merit,
may I not find the gift cause for remorse.

As many fireflies as the peasant sees
when he rests on a hill and looks into the valley
(where he tills or gathers grapes or prunes his trees)

in that sweet season when the face of him
who lights the world rides north, and at the hour
when the fly yields to the gnat and the air grows dim—

such myriads of flames I saw shine through
the gloom of the eighth abyss when I arrived
at the rim from which its bed comes into view.

As he the bears avenged so fearfully

beheld Elijah's chariot depart—
the horses rise toward heaven—but could not see

more than the flame, a cloudlet in the sky,
once it had risen—so within the fosse
only those flames, forever passing by

were visible, ahead, to right, to left;
for though each steals a sinner's soul from view
not one among them leaves a trace of the theft.

I stood on the bridge, and leaned out from the edge;
so far, that but for a jut of rock I held to
I should have been sent hurtling from the ledge

without being pushed. And seeing me so intent,
my Guide said: "There are souls within those flames;
each sinner swathes himself in his own torment."

"Master," I said, "your words make me more sure,
but I had seen already that it was so
and meant to ask what spirit must endure

the pains of that great flame which splits away
in two great horns, as if it rose from the pyre
where Eteocles and Polynices lay?"

He answered me: "Forever round this path
Ulysses and Diomede move in such dress,
united in pain as once they were in wrath;

there they lament the ambush of the Horse
which was the door through which the noble seed
of the Romans issued from its holy source;

there they mourn that for Achilles slain
sweet Deidamia weeps even in death;

there they recall the Palladium in their pain."

"Master," I cried, "I pray you and repray
till my prayer becomes a thousand—if these souls
can still speak from the fire, oh let me stay

until the flame draws near! Do not deny me:
You see how fervently I long for it!"
And he to me: "Since what you ask is worthy,

it shall be. But be still and let me speak;
for I know your mind already, and they perhaps
might scorn your manner of speaking, since they were Greek."

And when the flame had come where time and place
seemed fitting to my Guide, I heard him say
these words to it: "O you two souls who pace

together in one flame!—if my days above
won favor in your eyes, if I have earned
however much or little of your love

in writing my High Verses, do not pass by,
but let one of you be pleased to tell where he,
having disappeared from the known world, went to die."

As if it fought the wind, the greater prong
of the ancient flame began to quiver and hum;
then moving its tip as if it were the tongue

that spoke, gave out a voice above the roar.
"When I left Circe," it said, "who more than a year
detained me near Gaëta long before

Aeneas came and gave the place that name,
not fondness for my son, nor reverence
for my aged father, nor Penelope's claim

to the joys of love, could drive out of my mind
the lust to experience the far-flung world
and the failings and felicities of mankind.

I put out on the high and open sea
with a single ship and only those few souls
who stayed true when the rest deserted me.
As far as Morocco and as far as Spain
I saw both shores; and I saw Sardinia
and the other islands of the open main.

I and my men were stiff and slow with age
when we sailed at last into the narrow pass
where, warning all men back from further voyage,

Hercules' Pillars rose upon our sight.
Already I had left Ceuta on the left;
Seville now sank behind me on the right.

'Shipmates,' I said, 'who through a hundred thousand
perils have reached the West, do not deny
to the brief remaining watch our senses stand

experience of the world beyond the sun.
Greeks! You were not born to live like brutes,
but to press on toward manhood and recognition!'

With this brief exhortation I made my crew
so eager for the voyage I could hardly
have held them back from it when I was through;

and turning our stern toward morning, our bow toward night,
we bore southwest out of the world of man;
we made wings of our oars for our fool's flight.

That night we raised the other pole ahead

with all its stars, and ours had so declined
it did not rise out of its ocean bed.

Five times since we had dipped our bending oars
beyond the world, the light beneath the moon
had waxed and waned, when dead upon our course

we sighted, dark in space, a peak so tall
I doubted any man had seen the like.
Our cheers were hardly sounded, when a squall
broke hard upon our bow from the new land:
three times it sucked the ship and the sea about
as it pleased Another to order and command.

At the fourth, the poop rose and the bow went down
till the sea closed over us and the light was gone."

Canto XXVII

CIRCLE EIGHT: BOLGIA EIGHT
The Evil Counselors

The double flame departs at a word from Virgil and behind it appears another
which contains the soul of COUNT GUIDO DA MONTEFELTRO, a Lord of
Romagna. He had overheard Virgil speaking Italian, and the entire flame in
which his soul is wrapped quivers with his eagerness to hear recent news of his
wartorn country. (As Farinata has already explained, the spirits of the damned
have prophetic powers, but lose all track of events as they approach.)
   Dante replies with a stately and tragic summary of how things stand in the
cities of Romagna. When he has finished, he asks Guido for his story, and Guido
recounts his life, and how Boniface VIII persuaded him to sin.

When it had finished speaking, the great flame
stood tall and shook no more. Now, as it left us
with the sweet Poet's license, another came

along that track and our attention turned
to the new flame: a strange and muffled roar
rose from the single tip to which it burned.

As the Sicilian bull—that brazen spit
which bellowed first (and properly enough)
with the lament of him whose file had tuned it—

was made to bellow by its victim's cries
in such a way, that though it was of brass,
it seemed itself to howl and agonize:

so lacking any way through or around
the fire that sealed them in, the mournful words
were changed into its language. When they found

their way up to the tip, imparting to it
the same vibration given them in their passage
over the tongue of the concealed sad spirit,

we heard it say: "O you at whom I aim
my voice, and who were speaking Lombard, saying:
'Go now, I ask no more,' just as I came—

though I may come a bit late to my turn,
may it not annoy you to pause and speak a while:
you see it does not annoy me—and I burn.

If you have fallen only recently
to this blind world from that sweet Italy
where I acquired my guilt, I pray you, tell me:

is there peace or war in Romagna? for on earth
I too was of those hills between Urbino
and the fold from which the Tiber springs to birth."

I was still staring at it from the dim
edge of the pit when my Guide nudged me, saying:
"This one is Italian; *you* speak to him."

My answer was framed already; without pause
I spoke these words to it: "O hidden soul,
your sad Romagna is not and never was

without war in her tyrants' raging blood;
but none flared openly when I left just now.
Ravenna's fortunes stand as they have stood

these many years: Polenta's eagles brood
over her walls, and their pinions cover Cervia.
The city that so valiantly withstood

the French, and raised a mountain of their dead,
feels the Green Claws again. Still in Verrucchio
the Aged Mastiff and his Pup, who shed
Montagna's blood, raven in their old ranges.
The cities of Lamone and Santerno
are led by the white den's Lion, he who changes
his politics with the compass. And as the city
the Savio washes lies between plain and mountain,
so it lives between freedom and tyranny.

Now, I beg you, let us know your name;
do not be harder than one has been to you;
so, too, you will preserve your earthly fame."

And when the flame had roared a while beneath
the ledge on which we stood, it swayed its tip
to and fro, and then gave forth this breath:

"If I believed that my reply were made
to one who could ever climb to the world again,
this flame would shake no more. But since no shade

ever returned—if what I am told is true—
from this blind world into the living light,
without fear of dishonor I answer you.

I was a man of arms: then took the rope
of the Franciscans, hoping to make amends:
and surely I should have won to all my hope

but for the Great Priest—may he rot in Hell!—
who brought me back to all my earlier sins;
and how and why it happened I wish to tell

in my own words: while I was still encased
in the pulp and bone my mother bore, my deeds
were not of the lion but of the fox: I raced

through tangled ways; all wiles were mine from birth,
and I won to such advantage with my arts
that rumor of me reached the ends of the earth.
But when I saw before me all the signs
of the time of life that cautions every man
to lower his sail and gather in his lines,

that which had pleased me once, troubled my spirit,
and penitent and confessed, I became a monk.
Alas! What joy I might have had of it!

It was then the Prince of the New Pharisees drew
his sword and marched upon the Lateran—
and not against the Saracen or the Jew,

for every man that stood against his hand
was a Christian soul: not one had warred on Acre,
nor been a trader in the Sultan's land.

It was he abused his sacred vows and mine:
his Office and the Cord I wore, which once
made those it girded leaner. As Constantine

sent for Silvestro to cure his leprosy,
seeking him out among Soracte's cells;
so this one from his great throne sent for me

to cure the fever of pride that burned his blood.
He demanded my advice, and I kept silent
for his words seemed drunken to me. So it stood

until he said: "Your soul need fear no wound;
I absolve your guilt beforehand; and now teach me
how to smash Penestrino to the ground.

The Gates of Heaven, as you know, are mine

to open and shut, for I hold the two Great Keys
so easily let go by Celestine."

His weighty arguments led me to fear
silence was worse than sin. Therefore, I said:
"Holy Father, since you clean me here

of the guilt into which I fall, let it be done:
long promise and short observance is the road
that leads to the sure triumph of your throne."

Later, when I was dead, St. Francis came
to claim my soul, but one of the Black Angels
said: 'Leave him. Do not wrong me. This one's name

went into my book the moment he resolved
to give false counsel. Since then he has been mine,
for who does not repent cannot be absolved;

nor can we admit the possibility
of repenting a thing at the same time it is willed,
for the two acts are contradictory.'

Miserable me! with what contrition
I shuddered when he lifted me, saying: 'Perhaps
you hadn't heard that I was a logician.'

He carried me to Minos: eight times round
his scabby back the monster coiled his tail,
then biting it in rage he pawed the ground

and cried: 'This one is for the thievish fire!'
And, as you see, I am lost accordingly,
grieving in heart as I go in this attire."

His story told, the flame began to toss
and writhe its horn. And so it left, and we

crossed over to the arch of the next fosse

where from the iron treasury of the Lord
the fee of wrath is paid the Sowers of Discord.

Canto XXVIII

The Poets come to the edge of the NINTH BOLGIA and look down at a parade of hideously mutilated souls. These are the SOWERS OF DISCORD, and just as their sin was to rend asunder what God had meant to be united, so are they hacked and torn through all eternity by a great demon with a bloody sword. After each mutilation the souls are compelled to drag their broken bodies around the pit and to return to the demon, for in the course of the circuit their wounds knit in time to be inflicted anew. Thus is the law of retribution observed, each sinner suffering according to his degree.

Among them Dante distinguishes three classes with varying degrees of guilt within each class. First come the SOWERS OF RELIGIOUS DISCORD. Mahomet is chief among them, and appears first, cleft from crotch to chin, with his internal organs dangling between his legs. His son-in-law, Ali, drags on ahead of him, cleft from topknot to chin. These reciprocal wounds symbolize Dante's judgment that, between them, these two sum up the total schism between Christianity and Mohammedanism. The revolting details of Mahomet's condition clearly imply Dante's opinion of that doctrine. Mahomet issues an ironic warning to another schismatic, FRA DOLCINO.

Next come the SOWERS OF POLITICAL DISCORD, among them PIER DA MEDICINA, the Tribune CURIO, and MOSCA DEI LAMBERTI, each mutilated according to the nature of his sin.

Last of all is BERTRAND DE BORN, SOWER OF DISCORD BETWEEN KINSMEN. He separated father from son, and for that offense carries his head separated from his body, holding it with one hand by the hair, and swinging it as if it were a lantern to light his dark and endless way. The image of Bertrand raising his head at arm's length in order that it might speak more clearly to the Poets on the ridge is one of the most memorable in the Inferno. For some reason that cannot be ascertained, Dante makes these sinners quite eager to be remembered in the world, despite the fact that many who lie above them in Hell were unwilling to be recognized.

Who could describe, even in words set free
of metric and rhyme and a thousand times retold,
the blood and wounds that now were shown to me!

At grief so deep the tongue must wag in vain;
the language of our sense and memory
lacks the vocabulary of such pain.

If one could gather all those who have stood
through all of time on Puglia's fateful soil
and wept for the red running of their blood

in the war of the Trojans; and in that long war
which left so vast a spoil of golden rings,
as we find written in Livy, who does not err;

along with those whose bodies felt the wet
and gaping wounds of Robert Guiscard's lances;
with all the rest whose bones are gathered yet

at Ceperano where every last Pugliese
turned traitor; and with those from Tagliacozzo
where Alardo won without weapons—if all these

were gathered, and one showed his limbs run through,
another his lopped off, that could not equal
the mutilations of the ninth pit's crew.

A wine tun when a stave or cant-bar starts
does not split open as wide as one I saw
split from his chin to the mouth with which man farts.

Between his legs all of his red guts hung
with the heart, the lungs, the liver, the gall bladder,
and the shriveled sac that passes shit to the bung.

I stood and stared at him from the stone shelf;
he noticed me and opening his own breast
with both hands cried: "See how I rip myself!

See how Mahomet's mangled and split open!
Ahead of me walks Ali in his tears,
his head cleft from the top-knot to the chin.

And all the other souls that bleed and mourn
along this ditch were sowers of scandal and schism:
as they tore others apart, so are they torn.

Behind us, warden of our mangled horde,
the devil who butchers us and sends us marching
waits to renew our wounds with his long sword

when we have made the circuit of the pit;
for by the time we stand again before him
all the wounds he gave us last have knit.

But who are you that gawk down from that sill—
probably to put off your own descent
to the pit you are sentenced to for your own evil?"

"Death has not come for him, guilt does not drive
his soul to torment," my sweet Guide replied.
"That he may experience all while yet alive

I, who am dead, must lead him through the drear
and darkened halls of Hell, from round to round:
and this is true as my own standing here."

More than a hundred wraiths who were marching under
the sill on which we stood, paused at his words
and stared at me, forgetting pain in wonder.

"And if you do indeed return to see

the sun again, and soon, tell Fra Dolcino
unless he longs to come and march with me

he would do well to check his groceries
before the winter drives him from the hills
and gives the victory to the Novarese."

Mahomet, one foot raised, had paused to say
these words to me. When he had finished speaking
he stretched it out and down, and moved away.

Another—he had his throat slit, and his nose
slashed off as far as the eyebrows, and a wound
where one of his ears had been—standing with those

who stared at me in wonder from the pit,
opened the grinning wound of his red gullet
as if it were a mouth, and said through it:

"O soul unforfeited to misery
and whom—unless I take you for another—
I have seen above in our sweet Italy;

if ever again you see the gentle plain
that slopes down from Vercelli to Marcabò,
remember Pier da Medicina in pain,

and announce this warning to the noblest two
of Fano, Messers Guido and Angiolello:
that unless our foresight sees what is not true

they shall be thrown from their ships into the sea
and drown in the raging tides near La Cattolica
to satisfy a tyrant's treachery.

Neptune never saw so gross a crime
in all the seas from Cyprus to Majorca,

not even in pirate raids, nor the Argive time.

The one-eyed traitor, lord of the demesne
whose hill and streams one who walks here beside me
will wish eternally he had never seen,

will call them to a parley, but behind
sweet invitations he will work it so
they need not pray against Focara's wind."

And I to him: "If you would have me bear
your name to time, show me the one who found
the sight of that land so harsh, and let me hear

his story and his name." He touched the cheek
of one nearby, forcing the jaws apart,
and said: "This is the one; he cannot speak.

This outcast settled Caesar's doubts that day
beside the Rubicon by telling him:
'A man prepared is a man hurt by delay.' "

Ah, how wretched Curio seemed to me
with a bloody stump in his throat in place of the tongue
which once had dared to speak so recklessly!

And one among them with both arms hacked through
cried out, raising his stumps on the foul air
while the blood bedaubed his face: "Remember, too,

Mosca dei Lamberti, alas, who said
'A thing done has an end!' and with those words
planted the fields of war with Tuscan dead."

"And brought about the death of all your clan!"
I said, and he, stung by new pain on pain,
ran off; and in his grief he seemed a madman.

I stayed to watch those broken instruments,
and I saw a thing so strange I should not dare
to mention it without more evidence

but that my own clear conscience strengthens me,
that good companion that upholds a man
within the armor of his purity.

I saw it there; I seem to see it still—
a body without a head, that moved along
like all the others in that spew and spill.
It held the severed head by its own hair,
swinging it like a lantern in its hand;
and the head looked at us and wept in its despair.

It made itself a lamp of its own head,
and they were two in one and one in two;
how this can be, He knows who so commanded.

And when it stood directly under us
it raised the head at arm's length toward our bridge
the better to be heard, and swaying thus

it cried: "O living soul in this abyss,
see what a sentence has been passed upon me,
and search all Hell for one to equal this!

When you return to the world, remember me:
I am Bertrand de Born, and it was I
who set the young king on to mutiny,

son against father, father against son
as Achitophel set Absalom and David;
and since I parted those who should be one

in duty and in love, I bear my brain

divided from its source within this trunk;
and walk here where my evil turns to pain,

an eye for an eye to all eternity:
thus is the law of Hell observed in me."

Canto XXIX

CIRCLE EIGHT: BOLGIA TEN
The Falsifiers (Class I, Alchemists)

Dante lingers on the edge of the Ninth Bolgia expecting to see one of his kinsmen, GERI DEL BELLO, among the Sowers of Discord. Virgil, however, hurries him on, since time is short, and as they cross the bridge over the TENTH BOLGIA, Virgil explains that he had a glimpse of Geri among the crowd near the bridge and that he had been making threatening gestures at Dante.

The Poets now look into the last bolgia *of the Eighth Circle and see THE FALSIFIERS. They are punished by afflictions of every sense: by darkness, stench, thirst, filth, loathsome diseases, and a shrieking din. Some of them, moreover, run ravening through the pit, tearing others to pieces. Just as in life they corrupted society by their falsifications, so in death these sinners are subjected to a sum of corruptions. In one sense they figure forth what society would be if all falsifiers succeeded—a place where the senses are an affliction (since falsification deceives the senses) rather than a guide, where even the body has no honesty, and where some lie prostrate while others run ravening to prey upon them.*

Not all of these details are made clear until the next Canto, for Dante distinguishes four classes of Falsifiers, and in the present Canto we meet only the first class, THE ALCHEMISTS, the Falsifiers of Things. Of this class are GRIFFOLINO D'AREZZO and CAPOCCHIO, with both of whom Dante speaks.

The sight of that parade of broken dead
had left my eyes so sotted with their tears
I longed to stay and weep, but Virgil said:

"What are you waiting for? Why do you stare
as if you could not tear your eyes away
from the mutilated shadows passing there?

You did not act so in the other pits.

Consider—if you mean perhaps to count them—
this valley and its train of dismal spirits

winds twenty-two miles round. The moon already
is under our feet; the time we have is short,
and there is much that you have yet to see."

"Had you known what I was seeking," I replied,
"you might perhaps have given me permission
to stay on longer." (As I spoke, my Guide

had started off already, and I in turn
had moved along behind him; thus, I answered
as we moved along the cliff.) "Within that cavern

upon whose brim I stood so long to stare,
I think a spirit of my own blood mourns
the guilt that sinners find so costly there."

And the Master then: "Hereafter let your mind
turn its attention to more worthy matters
and leave him to his fate among the blind;

for by the bridge and among that shapeless crew
I saw him point to you with threatening gestures,
and I heard him called Geri del Bello. You

were occupied at the time with that headless one
who in his life was master of Altaforte,
and did not look that way; so he moved on."

"O my sweet Guide," I answered, "his death came
by violence and is not yet avenged
by those who share his blood, and, thus, his shame.

For this he surely hates his kin, and, therefore,
as I suppose, he would not speak to me;

and in that he makes me pity him the more."

We spoke of this until we reached the edge
from which, had there been light, we could have seen
the floor of the next pit. Out from that ledge

Malebolge's final cloister lay outspread,
and all of its lay brethren might have been
in sight but for the murk; and from those dead

such shrieks and strangled agonies shrilled through me
like shafts, but barbed with pity, that my hands
flew to my ears. If all the misery

that crams the hospitals of pestilence
in Maremma, Valdichiano, and Sardinia
in the summer months when death sits like a presence

on the marsh air, were dumped into one trench—
that might suggest their pain. And through the screams,
putrid flesh spread up its sickening stench.

Still bearing left we passed from the long sill
to the last bridge of Malebolge. There
the reeking bottom was more visible.

There, High Justice, sacred ministress
of the First Father, reigns eternally
over the falsifiers in their distress.

I doubt it could have been such pain to bear
the sight of the Aeginian people dying
that time when such malignance rode the air

that every beast down to the smallest worm
shriveled and died (it was after that great plague
that the Ancient People, as the poets affirm,

were reborn from the ants)—as it was to see
the spirits lying heaped on one another
in the dank bottom of that fetid valley.
One lay gasping on another's shoulder,
one on another's belly; and some were crawling
on hands and knees among the broken boulders.

Silent, slow step by step, we moved ahead
looking at and listening to those souls
too weak to raise themselves from their stone bed.

I saw two there like two pans that are put
one against the other to hold their warmth.
They were covered with great scabs from head to foot.

No stable boy in a hurry to go home,
or for whom his master waits impatiently,
ever scrubbed harder with his currycomb

than those two spirits of the stinking ditch
scrubbed at themselves with their own bloody claws
to ease the furious burning of the itch.

And as they scrubbed and clawed themselves, their nails
drew down the scabs the way a knife scrapes bream
or some other fish with even larger scales.

"O you," my Guide called out to one, "you there
who rip your scabby mail as if your fingers
were claws and pincers; tell us if this lair

counts any Italians among those who lurk
in its dark depths; so may your busy nails
eternally suffice you for your work."

"We both are Italian whose unending loss

you see before you," he replied in tears.
"But who are you who come to question us?"

"I am a shade," my Guide and Master said,
"who leads this living man from pit to pit
to show him Hell as I have been commanded."
The sinners broke apart as he replied
and turned convulsively to look at me,
as others did who overheard my Guide.

My Master, then, ever concerned for me,
turned and said: "Ask them whatever you wish."
And I said to those two wraiths of misery:

"So may the memory of your names and actions
not die forever from the minds of men
in that first world, but live for many suns,

tell me who you are and of what city;
do not be shamed by your nauseous punishment
into concealing your identity."

"I was a man of Arezzo," one replied,
"and Albert of Siena had me burned;
but I am not here for the deed for which I died.

It is true that jokingly I said to him once:
'I know how to raise myself and fly through air';
and he—with all the eagerness of a dunce—

wanted to learn. Because I could not make
a Daedalus of him—for no other reason—
he had his father burn me at the stake.

But Minos, the infallible, had me hurled
here to the final bolgia of the ten
for the alchemy I practiced in the world."

And I to the Poet: "Was there ever a race
more vain than the Sienese? Even the French,
compared to them, seem full of modest grace."

And the other leper answered mockingly:
"Excepting Stricca, who by careful planning
managed to live and spend so moderately;

and Niccolò, who in his time above
was first of all the shoots in that rank garden
to discover the costly uses of the clove;

and excepting the brilliant company of talents
in which Caccia squandered his vineyards and his woods,
and Abbagliato displayed his intelligence.

But if you wish to know who joins your cry
against the Sienese, study my face
with care and let it make its own reply.

So you will see I am the suffering shadow
of Capocchio, who, by practicing alchemy,
falsified the metals, and you must know,

unless my mortal recollection strays
how good an ape I was of Nature's ways."

Canto XXX

CIRCLE EIGHT: BOLGIA TEN
The Falsifiers
(*The Remaining Three Classes:*
Evil Impersonators,
Counterfeiters,
False Witnesses)

Just as Capocchio finishes speaking, two ravenous spirits come racing through the pit; and one of them, sinking his tusks into Capocchio's neck, drags him away like prey. Capocchio's companion, Griffolino, identifies the two as GIANNI SCHICCHI and MYRRHA, who run ravening through the pit through all eternity, snatching at other souls and rending them. These are the EVIL IMPERSONATORS, Falsifiers of Persons. In life they seized upon the appearance of others, and in death they must run with never a pause, seizing upon the infernal apparition of these souls, while they in turn are preyed upon by their own furies.

Next the Poets encounter MASTER ADAM, a sinner of the third class, a Falsifier of Money, i.e., a COUNTERFEITER. Like the alchemists, he is punished by a loathsome disease and he cannot move from where he lies, but his disease is compounded by other afflictions, including an eternity of unbearable thirst. Master Adam identifies two spirits lying beside him as POTIPHAR'S WIFE and SINON THE GREEK, sinners of the fourth class, THE FALSE WITNESS, i.e., Falsifiers of Words.

Sinon, angered by Master Adam's identification of him, strikes him across the belly with the one arm he is able to move. Master Adam replies in kind, and Dante, fascinated by their continuing exchange of abuse, stands staring at them until Virgil turns on him in great anger, for "The wish to hear such baseness is degrading." Dante burns with shame, and Virgil immediately forgives him because of his great and genuine repentance.

At the time when Juno took her furious
revenge for Semele, striking in rage
again and again at the Theban royal house,

King Athamas, by her contrivance, grew
so mad, that seeing his wife out for an airing
with his two sons, he cried to his retinue:

"Out with the nets there! Nets across the pass!
for I will take this lioness and her cubs!"
And spread his talons, mad and merciless,

and seizing his son Learchus, whirled him round
and brained him on a rock; at which the mother
leaped into the sea with her other son and drowned.

And when the Wheel of Fortune spun about
to humble the all-daring Trojan's pride
so that both king and kingdom were wiped out;

Hecuba—mourning, wretched, and a slave—
having seen Polyxena sacrificed,
and Polydorus dead without a grave;

lost and alone, beside an alien sea,
began to bark and growl like a dog
in the mad seizure of her misery.

But never in Thebes nor Troy were Furies seen
to strike at man or beast in such mad rage
as two I saw, pale, naked, and unclean,

who suddenly came running toward us then,
snapping their teeth as they ran, like hungry swine
let out to feed after a night in the pen.

One of them sank his tusks so savagely
into Capocchio's neck, that when he dragged him,
the ditch's rocky bottom tore his belly.

And the Aretine, left trembling by me, said:

"That incubus, in life, was Gianni Schicchi;
here he runs rabid, mangling the other dead."

"So!" I answered, "and so may the other one
not sink its teeth in you, be pleased to tell us
what shade it is before it races on."

And he: "That ancient shade in time above
was Myrrha, vicious daughter of Cinyras
who loved her father with more than rightful love.

She falsified another's form and came
disguised to sin with him just as that other
who runs with her, in order that he might claim

the fabulous lead-mare, lay under disguise
on Buoso Donati's death bed and dictated
a spurious testament to the notaries."

And when the rabid pair had passed from sight,
I turned to observe the other misbegotten
spirits that lay about to left and right.

And there I saw another husk of sin,
who, had his legs been trimmed away at the groin,
would have looked for all the world like a mandolin.

The dropsy's heavy humors, which so bunch
and spread the limbs, had disproportioned him
till his face seemed much too small for his swollen paunch.

He strained his lips apart and thrust them forward
the way a sick man, feverish with thirst,
curls one lip toward the chin and the other upward.

"O you exempt from every punishment
of this grim world (I know not why)," he cried,

"look well upon the misery and debasement

of him who was Master Adam. In my first
life's time, I had enough to please me: here,
I lack a drop of water for my thirst.

The rivulets that run from the green flanks
of Casentino to the Arno's flood,
spreading their cool sweet moisture through their banks,

run constantly before me, and their plash
and ripple in imagination dries me
more than the disease that eats my flesh.

Inflexible Justice that has forked and spread
my soul like hay, to search it the more closely,
finds in the country where my guilt was bred

this increase of my grief; for there I learned,
there in Romena, to stamp the Baptist's image
on alloyed gold—till I was bound and burned.

But could I see the soul of Guido here,
or of Alessandro, or of their filthy brother,
I would not trade that sight for all the clear

cool flow of Branda's fountain. One of the three—
if those wild wraiths who run here are not lying—
is here already. But small good it does me

when my legs are useless! Were I light enough
to move as much as an inch in a hundred years,
long before this I would have started off

to cull him from the freaks that fill this fosse,
although it winds on for eleven miles
and is no less than half a mile across.

Because of them I lie here in this pig-pen;
it was they persuaded me to stamp the florins
with three carats of alloy." And I then:

"Who are those wretched two sprawled alongside
your right-hand borders, and who seem to smoke
as a washed hand smokes in winter?" He replied:

"They were here when I first rained into this gully,
and have not changed position since, nor may they,
as I believe, to all eternity.

One is the liar who charged young Joseph wrongly:
the other, Sinon, the false Greek from Troy.
A burning fever makes them reek so strongly."

And one of the false pair, perhaps offended
by the manner of Master Adam's presentation,
punched him in the rigid and distended

belly—it thundered like a drum—and he
retorted with an arm blow to the face
that seemed delivered no whit less politely,

saying to him: "Although I cannot stir
my swollen legs, I still have a free arm
to use at times when nothing else will answer."

And the other wretch said: "It was not so free
on your last walk to the stake, free as it was
when you were coining." And he of the dropsy:

"That's true enough, but there was less truth in you
when they questioned you at Troy." And Sinon then:
"For every word I uttered that was not true

you uttered enough false coins to fill a bushel:
I am put down here for a single crime,
but you for more than any Fiend in Hell."

"Think of the Horse," replied the swollen shade,
"and may it torture you, perjurer, to recall
that all the world knows the foul part you played."

"And to you the torture of the thirst that fries
and cracks your tongue," said the Greek, "and of the water
that swells your gut like a hedge before your eyes."

And the coiner: "So is your own mouth clogged
with the filth that stuffs and sickens it as always;
if I am parched while my paunch is waterlogged,

you have the fever and your cankered brain;
and were you asked to lap Narcissus' mirror
you would not wait to be invited again."

I was still standing, fixed upon those two
when the Master said to me: "Now keep on looking
a little longer and I quarrel with you."

When I heard my Master raise his voice to me,
I wheeled about with such a start of shame
that I grow pale yet at the memory.

As one trapped in a nightmare that has caught
his sleeping mind, wishes within the dream
that it were all a dream, as if it were not—

such I became: my voice could not win through
my shame to ask his pardon; while my shame
already won more pardon than I knew.

"Less shame," my Guide said, ever just and kind,

"would wash away a greater fault than yours.
Therefore, put back all sorrow from your mind;

and never forget that I am always by you
should it occur again, as we walk on,
that we find ourselves where others of this crew

fall to such petty wrangling and upbraiding.
The wish to hear such baseness is degrading."

Canto XXXI

Dante's spirits rise again as the Poets approach the Central Pit, a great well, at the bottom of which lies Cocytus, the Ninth and final circle of Hell. Through the darkness Dante sees what appears to be a city of great towers, but as he draws near he discovers that the great shapes he has seen are the Giants and Titans who stand perpetual guard inside the well-pit with the upper halves of their bodies rising above the rim.

Among the Giants, Virgil identifies NIMROD, builder of the Tower of Babel; EPHIALTES and BRIAREUS, who warred against the Gods; and TITYOS and TYPHON, who insulted Jupiter. Also here, but for no specific offense, is ANTAEUS, and his presence makes it clear that the Giants are placed here less for their particular sins than for their general natures.

These are the sons of earth, embodiments of elemental forces unbalanced by love, desire without restraint and without acknowledgment of moral and theological law. They are symbols of the earth-trace that every devout man must clear from his soul, the unchecked passions of the beast. Raised from the earth, they make the very gods tremble. Now they are returned to the darkness of their origins, guardians of earth's last depth.

At Virgil's persuasion, Antaeus takes the Poets in his huge palm and lowers them gently to the final floor of Hell.

One and the same tongue had first wounded me so that the blood came rushing to my cheeks, and then supplied the soothing remedy.

Just so, as I have heard, the magic steel of the lance that was Achilles' and his father's could wound at a touch, and, at another, heal.

We turned our backs on the valley and climbed from it to the top of the stony bank that walls it round, crossing in silence to the central pit.
Here it was less than night and less than day; my eyes could make out little through the gloom, but I heard the shrill note of a trumpet bray

louder than any thunder. As if by force, it drew my eyes; I stared into the gloom along the path of the sound back to its source.

After the bloody rout when Charlemagne had lost the band of Holy Knights, Roland blew no more terribly for all his pain.

And as I stared through that obscurity, I saw what seemed a cluster of great towers, whereat I cried: "Master, what is this city?"

And he: "You are still too far back in the dark to make out clearly what you think you see; it is natural that you should miss the mark:

You will see clearly when you reach that place how much your eyes mislead you at a distance; I urge you, therefore, to increase your pace."

Then taking my hand in his, my Master said: "The better to prepare you for strange truth, let me explain those shapes you see ahead:

they are not towers but giants. They stand in the well from the navel down; and stationed round its bank they mount guard on the final pit of Hell."

Just as a man in a fog that starts to clear begins little by little to piece together the shapes the vapor crowded from the air—

so, when those shapes grew clearer as I drew across the darkness to the central brink, error fled from me; and my terror grew.
For just as at Montereggione the great towers crown the encircling wall; so the grim giants whom Jove still threatens when the thunder roars

raised from the rim of stone about that well the upper halves of their bodies, which loomed up like turrets through the murky air of Hell.

I had drawn close enough to one already to make out the great arms along his sides, the face, the shoulders, the breast, and most of the belly.

Nature, when she destroyed the last exemplars on which she formed those beasts, surely did well to take such executioners from Mars.

And if she has not repented the creation of whales and elephants, the thinking man will see in that her justice and discretion:

for where the instrument of intelligence is added to brute power and evil will, mankind is powerless in its own defense.

His face, it seemed to me, was quite as high and wide as the bronze pine cone in St. Peter's with the rest of him proportioned accordingly:

so that the bank, which made an apron for him from the waist down, still left so much exposed that three Frieslanders standing on the rim,

one on another, could not have reached his hair; for to that point at which men's capes are buckled, thirty good hand-spans of brute bulk rose clear.

"Rafel mahee amek zabi almit," began a bellowed chant from the brute mouth for which no sweeter psalmody was fit.

And my Guide in his direction: "Babbling fool, stick to your horn and vent yourself with it when rage or passion stir your stupid soul.

Feel there around your neck, you muddle-head, and find the cord; and there's the horn itself, there on your overgrown chest." To me he said:

"His very babbling testifies the wrong he did on earth: he is Nimrod, through whose evil mankind no longer speaks a common tongue.

Waste no words on him: it would be foolish. To him all speech is meaningless; as his own, which no one understands, is simply gibberish."

We moved on, bearing left along the pit, and a crossbow-shot away we found the next one, an even huger and more savage spirit.

What master could have bound so gross a beast I cannot say, but he had his right arm pinned behind his back, and the left across his breast by an enormous chain that wound about him from the neck down, completing five great turns before it spiraled down below the rim.

"This piece of arrogance," said my Guide to me, "dared try his strength against the power of Jove; for which he is rewarded as you see.

He is Ephialtes, who made the great endeavour with the other giants who alarmed the Gods; the arms he raised then, now are bound forever."

"Were it possible, I should like to take with me," I said to him, "the memory of seeing the immeasurable Briareus." And he:

"Nearer to hand, you may observe Antaeus who is able to speak to us, and is not bound. It is he will set us down in Cocytus,

the bottom of all guilt. The other hulk stands far beyond our road. He too, is bound and looks like this one, but with a fiercer sulk."

No earthquake in the fury of its shock ever seized a tower more violently, than Ephialtes, hearing, began to rock.

Then I dreaded death as never before; and I think I could have died for very fear had I not seen what manacles he wore.

We left the monster, and not far from him we reached Antaeus, who to his shoulders alone soared up a good five ells above the rim.

"O soul who once in Zama's fateful vale—where Scipio became the heir of glory when Hannibal and all his troops turned tail—

took more than a thousand lions for your prey; and in whose memory many still believe the sons of earth would yet have won the day

had you joined with them against High Olympus—do not disdain to do us a small service, but set us down where the cold grips Cocytus.

Would you have us go to Tityos or Typhon?—this man can give you what is longed for here: therefore do not refuse him, but bend down.

For he can still make new your memory: he lives, and awaits long life, unless Grace call him before his time to his felicity."

Thus my Master to that Tower of Pride; and the giant without delay reached out the hands which Hercules had felt, and raised my Guide.

Virgil, when he felt himself so grasped, called to me: "Come, and I will hold you safe." And he took me in his arms and held me clasped.

The way the Carisenda seems to one who looks up from the leaning side when clouds are going over it from that direction,

making the whole tower seem to topple—so Antaeus seemed to me in the fraught moment when I stood clinging, watching from below

as he bent down; while I with heart and soul wished we had gone some other way, but gently he set us down inside the final hole

whose ice holds Judas and Lucifer in its grip. Then straightened like a mast above a ship.

Canto XXXII

CIRCLE NINE: COCYTUS
ROUND ONE: CAÏNA
ROUND TWO: ANTENORA

Compound Fraud
The Treacherous to Kin
The Treacherous to Country

At the bottom of the well Dante finds himself on a huge frozen lake. This is COCYTUS, the NINTH CIRCLE, the fourth and last great water of Hell, and here, fixed in the ice, each according to his guilt, are punished sinners guilty of TREACHERY AGAINST THOSE TO WHOM THEY WERE BOUND BY SPECIAL TIES. The ice is divided into four concentric rings marked only by the different positions of the damned within the ice.

This is Dante's symbolic equivalent of the final guilt. The treacheries of these souls were denials of love (which is God) and of all human warmth. Only the remorseless dead center of the ice will serve to express their natures. As they denied God's love, so are they furthest removed from the light and warmth of His Sun. As they denied all human ties, so are they bound only by the unyielding ice.

The first round is CAINA, named for Cain. Here lie those who were treacherous against blood ties. They have their necks and heads out of the ice and are permitted to bow their heads—a double boon since it allows them some protection from the freezing gale and, further, allows their tears to fall without freezing their eyes shut. Here Dante sees ALESSANDRO and NAPOLEONE DEGLI ALBERTI, and he speaks to CAMICION, who identifies other sinners of this round.

The second round is ANTENORA, named for Antenor, the Trojan who was believed to have betrayed his city to the Greeks. Here lie those guilty of TREACHERY TO COUNTRY. They, too, have their heads above the ice, but they cannot bend their necks, which are gripped by the ice. Here Dante accidentally

*kicks the head of BOCCA DEGLI ABBATI and then proceeds to treat him with a
savagery he has shown to no other soul in Hell. Bocca names some of his fellow
traitors, and the Poets pass on to discover two heads frozen together in one hole.
One of them is gnawing the nape of the other's neck.*

If I had rhymes as harsh and horrible
as the hard fact of that final dismal hole
which bears the weight of all the steeps of Hell,

I might more fully press the sap and substance from my conception; but since I
must do without them, I begin with some reluctance.

For it is no easy undertaking, I say,
to describe the bottom of the Universe;
nor is it for tongues that only babble child's play.

But may those Ladies of the Heavenly Spring
who helped Amphion wall Thebes, assist my verse,
that the word may be the mirror of the thing.

O most miscreant rabble, you who keep
the stations of that place whose name is pain,
better had you been born as goats or sheep!

We stood now in the dark pit of the well,
far down the slope below the Giant's feet,
and while I still stared up at the great wall,

I heard a voice cry: "Watch which way you turn:
take care you do not trample on the heads
of the forworn and miserable brethren."

Whereat I turned and saw beneath my feet
and stretching out ahead, a lake so frozen
it seemed to be made of glass. So thick a sheet

never yet hid the Danube's winter course,
nor, far away beneath the frigid sky,

locked the Don up in its frozen source:

for were Tanbernick and the enormous peak
of Pietrapana to crash down on it,
not even the edges would so much as creak.
The way frogs sit to croak, their muzzles leaning
out of the water, at the time and season
when the peasant woman dreams of her day's gleaning—

Just so the livid dead are sealed in place
up to the part at which they blushed for shame,
and they beat their teeth like storks. Each holds his face

bowed toward the ice, each of them testifies
to the cold with his chattering mouth, to his heart's grief
with tears that flood forever from his eyes.

When I had stared about me, I looked down
and at my feet I saw two clamped together
so tightly that the hair of their heads had grown

together. "Who are you," I said, "who lie
so tightly breast to breast?" They strained their necks,
and when they had raised their heads as if to reply,

the tears their eyes had managed to contain
up to that time gushed out, and the cold froze them
between the lids, sealing them shut again

tighter than any clamp grips wood to wood,
and mad with pain, they fell to butting heads
like billy-goats in a sudden savage mood.

And a wraith who lay to one side and below,
and who had lost both ears to frostbite, said,
his head still bowed: "Why do you watch us so?

If you wish to know who they are who share one doom,
they owned the Bisenzio's valley with their father,
whose name was Albert. They sprang from one womb,

and you may search through all Caïna's crew
without discovering in all this waste
a squab more fit for the aspic than these two;
not him whose breast and shadow a single blow
of the great lance of King Arthur pierced with light;
nor yet Focaccia; nor this one fastened so

into the ice that his head is all I see,
and whom, if you are Tuscan, you know well—
his name on the earth was Sassol Mascheroni.

And I—to tell you all and so be through—
was Camicion de' Pazzi. I wait for Carlin
beside whose guilt my sins will shine like virtue."

And leaving him, I saw a thousand faces
discolored so by cold, I shudder yet
and always will when I think of those frozen places.

As we approached the center of all weight,
where I went shivering in eternal shade,
whether it was my will, or chance, or fate,

I cannot say, but as I trailed my Guide
among those heads, my foot struck violently
against the face of one. Weeping, it cried:

"Why do you kick me? If you were not sent
to wreak a further vengeance for Montaperti,
why do you add this to my other torment?"

"Master," I said, "grant me a moment's pause
to rid myself of a doubt concerning this one;

then you may hurry me at your own pace."

The Master stopped at once, and through the volley
of foul abuse the wretch poured out, I said:
"Who are you who curse others so?" And he:

"And who are *you* who go through the dead larder
of Antenora kicking the cheeks of others
so hard, that were you alive, you could not kick harder?"
"I *am* alive," I said, "and if you seek fame,
it may be precious to you above all else
that my notes on this descent include your name."

"Exactly the opposite is my wish and hope,"
he answered. "Let me be; for it's little you know
of how to flatter on this icy slope."

I grabbed the hair of his dog's-ruff and I said:
"Either you tell me truly who you are,
or you won't have a hair left on your head."

And he: "Not though you snatch me bald. I swear
I will not tell my name nor show my face.
Not though you rip until my brain lies bare."

I had a good grip on his hair; already
I had yanked out more than one fistful of it,
while the wretch yelped, but kept his face turned from me;

when another said: "Bocca, what is it ails you?
What the Hell's wrong? Isn't it bad enough
to hear you bang your jaws? Must you bark too?"

"Now filthy traitor, say no more!" I cried,
"for to your shame, be sure I shall bear back
a true report of you." The wretch replied:

"Say anything you please but go away.
And if you *do* get back, don't overlook
that pretty one who had so much to say

just now. Here he laments the Frenchman's price.
'I saw Buoso da Duera,' you can report,
'where the bad salad is kept crisp on ice.'

And if you're asked who else was wintering here,
Beccheria, whose throat was slit by Florence,
is there beside you. Gianni de' Soldanier

is further down, I think, with Ganelon, and Tebaldello, who opened the gates of
Faenza and let Bologna steal in with the dawn."

Leaving him then, I saw two souls together
in a single hole, and so pinched in by the ice
that one head made a helmet for the other.

As a famished man chews crusts—so the one sinner
sank his teeth into the other's nape
at the base of the skull, gnawing his loathsome dinner.

Tydeus in his final raging hour
gnawed Menalippus' head with no more fury
than this one gnawed at skull and dripping gore.

"You there," I said, "who show so odiously
your hatred for that other, tell me why
on this condition: that if in what you tell me

you seem to have a reasonable complaint
against him you devour with such foul relish,
I, knowing who you are, and his soul's taint,

may speak your cause to living memory,
God willing the power of speech be left to me."

THE PURGATORIO
Canto I

ANTE-PURGATORY:
THE SHORE OF THE ISLAND
Cato of Utica

*The Poets emerge from Hell just before dawn of Easter Sunday (April 10, 1300),
and Dante revels in the sight of the rediscovered heavens. As he looks eagerly
about at the stars, he sees nearby an old man of impressive bearing. The ancient
is CATO OF UTICA, guardian of the shores of Purgatory. Cato challenges the
Poets as fugitives from Hell, but Virgil, after first instructing Dante to kneel in
reverence, explains Dante's mission and Beatrice's command. Cato then gives
them instructions for proceeding.*

*The Poets have emerged at a point a short way up the slope of Purgatory. It is
essential, therefore, that they descend to the lowest point and begin from there,
an allegory of Humility. Cato, accordingly, orders Virgil to lead Dante to the
shore, to wet his hands in the dew of the new morning, and to wash the stains of
Hell from Dante's face and the film of Hell's vapors from Dante's eyes. Virgil is
then to bind about Dante's waist one of the pliant reeds (symbolizing Humility)
that grow in the soft mud of the shore.*

*Having so commanded, Cato disappears. Dante arises in silence and stands
waiting, eager to begin. His look is all the communication that is necessary.
Virgil leads him to the shore and performs all that Cato has commanded.
Dante's first purification is marked by a miracle: when Virgil breaks off a reed,
the stalk immediately regenerates a new reed, restoring itself exactly as it had
been.*

For better waters now the little bark
of my indwelling powers raises her sails,
and leaves behind that sea so cruel and dark.

Now shall I sing that second kingdom given
the soul of man wherein to purge its guilt
and so grow worthy to ascend to Heaven.

Yours am I, sacred Muses! To you I pray. Here let dead poetry rise once more to
life, and here let sweet Calliope rise and play

some fair accompaniment in that high strain
whose power the wretched Pierides once felt
so terribly they dared not hope again.

Sweet azure of the sapphire of the east
was gathering on the serene horizon
its pure and perfect radiance—a feast

to my glad eyes, reborn to their delight,
as soon as I had passed from the dead air
which had oppressed my soul and dimmed my sight.

The planet whose sweet influence strengthens love
was making all the east laugh with her rays,
veiling the Fishes, which she swam above.

I turned then to my right and set my mind
on the other pole, and there I saw four stars
unseen by mortals since the first mankind.

The heavens seemed to revel in their light.
O widowed Northern Hemisphere, bereft
forever of the glory of that sight!

As I broke off my gazing, my eyes veered
a little to the left, to the other pole
from which, by then, the Wain had disappeared.

I saw, nearby, an ancient man, alone.
His bearing filled me with such reverence,
no father could ask more from his best son.

His beard was long and touched with strands of white,

as was his hair, of which two tresses fell
over his breast. Rays of the holy light

that fell from the four stars made his face glow
with such a radiance that he looked to me
as if he faced the sun. And standing so,

he moved his venerable plumes and said:
"Who are you two who climb by the dark stream
to escape the eternal prison of the dead?

Who led you? or what served you as a light
in your dark flight from the eternal valley,
which lies forever blind in darkest night?

Are the laws of the pit so broken? Or is new counsel
published in Heaven that the damned may wander
onto my rocks from the abyss of Hell?"

At that my Master laid his hands upon me,
instructing me by word and touch and gesture
to show my reverence in brow and knee,

then answered him: "I do not come this way
of my own will or powers. A Heavenly Lady
sent me to this man's aid in his dark day.

But since your will is to know more, my will
cannot deny you; I will tell you truly
why we have come and how. This man has still

to see his final hour, though in the burning
of his own madness he had drawn so near it
his time was perilously short for turning.

As I have told you, I was sent to show
the way his soul must take for its salvation;

and there is none but this by which I go.

I have shown him the guilty people. Now I mean
to lead him through the spirits in your keeping,
to show him those whose suffering makes them clean.
By what means I have led him to this strand
to see and hear you, takes too long to tell:
from Heaven is the power and the command.

Now may his coming please you, for he goes
to win his freedom; and how dear that is
the man who gives his life for it best knows.

You know it, who in that cause found death sweet
in Utica where you put off that flesh
which shall rise radiant at the Judgment Seat.

We do not break the Laws: this man lives yet,
and I am of that Round not ruled by Minos,
with your own Marcia, whose chaste eyes seem set

in endless prayers to you. O blessed breast
to hold her yet your own! for love of her
grant us permission to pursue our quest

across your seven kingdoms. When I go
back to her side I shall bear thanks of you,
if you will let me speak your name below."

"Marcia was so pleasing in my eyes
there on the other side," he answered then,
"that all she asked, I did. Now that she lies

beyond the evil river, no word or prayer
of hers may move me. Such was the Decree
pronounced upon us when I rose from there.

But if, as you have said, a Heavenly Dame
orders your way, there is no need to flatter:
you need but ask it of me in her name.

Go then, and lead this man, but first see to it
you bind a smooth green reed about his waist
and clean his face of all trace of the pit.

For it would not be right that one with eyes
still filmed by mist should go before the angel
who guards the gate: he is from Paradise.

All round the wave-wracked shore-line, there below,
reeds grow in the soft mud. Along that edge
no foliate nor woody plant could grow,

for what lives in that buffeting must bend.
Do not come back this way: the rising sun
will light an easier way you may ascend."

With that he disappeared; and silently
I rose and moved back till I faced my Guide,
my eyes upon him, waiting. He said to me:

"Follow my steps and let us turn again:
along this side there is a gentle slope
that leads to the low boundaries of the plain."

The dawn, in triumph, made the day-breeze flee
before its coming, so that from afar
I recognized the trembling of the sea.

We strode across that lonely plain like men
who seek the road they strayed from and who count
the time lost till they find it once again.

When we had reached a place along the way

where the cool morning breeze shielded the dew
against the first heat of the gathering day,

with gentle graces my Sweet Master bent
and laid both outspread palms upon the grass.
Then I, being well aware of his intent,

lifted my tear-stained cheeks to him, and there
he made me clean, revealing my true color
under the residues of Hell's black air.

We moved on then to the deserted strand
which never yet has seen upon its waters
a man who found his way back to dry land.

There, as it pleased another, he girded me.
Wonder of wonders! when he plucked a reed
another took its place there instantly,

arising from the humble stalk he tore
so that it grew exactly as before.

Canto II

ANTE-PURGATORY:
THE SHORE OF THE ISLAND
The Angel Boatman
Casella
Cato of Utica

It is dawn. Dante, washed, and girded by the reed, is standing by the shore when he sees a light approaching at enormous speed across the sea. The light grows and becomes visible as THE ANGEL BOATMAN who ferries the souls of the elect from their gathering place at THE MOUTH OF THE TIBER to the shore of Purgatory.

The newly arrived souls debark and, taking the Poets as familiars of the place, ask directions. Virgil explains that he and Dante are new arrivals but that they have come by the dark road through Hell. The newly arrived souls see by his breathing that Dante is alive and crowd about him. One of the new souls is CASELLA, a musician who seems to have been a dear friend of Dante's. Dante tries three times to clasp him to his bosom, but each time his arms pass through empty air. Casella explains the function of the Angel Boatman and then, at Dante's request, strikes up a song, one of Dante's own canzoni *that Casella had set to music. Instantly, CATO descends upon the group, berating them, and they break like startled pigeons up the slope toward the mountain.*

The sun already burned at the horizon,
while the high point of its meridian circle
covered Jerusalem, and in opposition

equal Night revolved above the Ganges
bearing the Scales that fall out of her hand
as she grows longer with the season's changes:

thus, where I was, Aurora in her passage
was losing the pale blushes from her cheeks

which turned to orange with increasing age.
We were still standing by the sea's new day
like travelers pondering the road ahead
who send their souls on while their bones delay;

when low above the ocean's western rim,
as Mars, at times, observed through the thick vapors
that form before the dawn, burns red and slim;

just so—so may I hope to see it again!—
a light appeared, moving above the sea
faster than any flight. A moment then

I turned my eyes to question my sweet Guide,
and when I looked back to that unknown body
I found its mass and brightness magnified.

Then from each side of it came into view
an unknown something-white; and from beneath it,
bit by bit, another whiteness grew.

We watched till the white objects at each side
took shape as wings, and Virgil spoke no word.
But when he saw what wings they were, he cried:

"Down on your knees! It is God's angel comes!
Down! Fold your hands! From now on you shall see
many such ministers in the high kingdoms.

See how he scorns man's tools: he needs no oars
nor any other sail than his own wings
to carry him between such distant shores.

See how his pinions tower upon the air,
pointing to Heaven: they are eternal plumes
and do not moult like feathers or human hair."

Then as that bird of heaven closed the distance
between us, he grew brighter and yet brighter
until I could no longer bear the radiance,

and bowed my head. He steered straight for the shore,
his ship so light and swift it drew no water;
it did not seem to sail so much as soar.

Astern stood the great pilot of the Lord,
so fair his blessedness seemed written on him;
and more than a hundred souls were seated forward,

singing as if they raised a single voice
in exitu Israel de Aegypto.
Verse after verse they made the air rejoice.

The angel made the sign of the cross, and they
cast themselves, at his signal, to the shore.
Then, swiftly as he had come, he went away.

The throng he left seemed not to understand
what place it was, but stood and stared about
like men who see the first of a new land.

The Sun, who with an arrow in each ray
had chased the Goat out of the height of Heaven,
on every hand was shooting forth the day,

when those new souls looked up to where my Guide
and I stood, saying to us, "If you know it,
show us the road that climbs the mountainside."

Virgil replied: "You think perhaps we two
have had some long experience of this place,
but we are also pilgrims, come before you

only by very little, though by a way

so steep, so broken, and so tortuous
the climb ahead of us will seem like play."

The throng of souls, observing by my breath
I was still in the body I was born to,
stared in amazement and grew pale as death.

As a crowd, eager for news, will all but smother
a messenger who bears the olive branch,
and not care how they trample one another—

so these, each one of them a soul elect,
pushed close to stare at me, well-nigh forgetting
the way to go to make their beauty perfect.

One came forward to embrace me, and his face
shone with such joyous love that, seeing it,
I moved to greet him with a like embrace.

O solid-seeming shadows! Three times there
I clasped my hands behind him, and three times
I drew them to my breast through empty air.

Amazed, I must have lost all color then,
for he smiled tenderly and drew away,
and I lunged forward as if to try again.

In a voice as gentle as a melody
he bade me pause; and by his voice I knew him,
and begged him stay a while and speak to me.

He answered: "As I loved you in the clay
of my mortal body, so do I love you freed:
therefore I pause. But what brings you this way?"

"Casella mine, I go the way I do
in the hope I may return here," I replied.

"But why has so much time been taken from you?"

And he: "I am not wronged if he whose usage
accepts the soul at his own time and pleasure
has many times refused to give me passage:

his will moves in the image and perfection
of a Just Will; indeed, for three months now
he has taken all who asked, without exception.

And so it was that in my turn I stood
upon that shore where Tiber's stream grows salt,
and there was gathered to my present good.

It is back to the Tiber's mouth he has just flown,
for there forever is the gathering place
of all who do not sink to Acheron."

"If no new law has stripped you of your skill
or of the memory of those songs of love
that once could calm all passion from my will,"

I said to him, "Oh sound a verse once more
to soothe my soul which, with its weight of flesh
and the long journey, sinks distressed and sore."

"Love that speaks its reasons in my heart,"
he sang then, and such grace flowed on the air
that even now I hear that music start.

My Guide and I and all those souls of bliss
stood tranced in song; when suddenly we heard
the Noble Elder cry: "What's this! What's this!

Negligence! Loitering! O laggard crew
run to the mountain and strip off the scurf
that lets not God be manifest in you!"

Exactly as a flock of pigeons gleaning
a field of stubble, pecking busily,
forgetting all their primping and their preening,

will rise as one and scatter through the air,
leaving their feast without another thought
when they are taken by a sudden scare—

so that new band, all thought of pleasure gone,
broke from the feast of music with a start
and scattered for the mountainside like one
who leaps and does not look where he will land.
Nor were my Guide and I inclined to stand.

Canto III

ANTE-PURGATORY:
THE BASE OF THE CLIFF
The Late-Repentant
Class One: The Contumacious
Manfred

The souls scatter for the mountain, and Dante draws close to Virgil as they both race ahead. The newly risen sun is at Dante's back. He runs, therefore, with his shadow stretched long and directly before him. Suddenly he becomes aware that there is only one shadow on the ground and he turns in panic, thinking Virgil is no longer at his side. Virgil reassures him, explaining that souls are so made as to cast no shadow. His remarks on the nature of souls give him occasion to define THE LIMITS OF REASON IN THE SCHEME OF CREATION.

The poets reach THE BASE OF THE CLIFF and are dismayed to find that it rises sheer, offering no way by which they may climb. While Virgil is pondering this new difficulty, Dante looks about and sees a band of souls approaching so slowly that they seem scarcely to move. These are the first of THE LATE-REPENTANT souls the Poets will encounter. In life they put off the desire for grace: now, as they were laggard in life, so must they wait before they may begin their purification. The souls in this band are all souls of THE CONTUMACIOUS: they died excommunicated, but surrendered their souls to God when they were at the point of death. Their punishment is that they must wait here at the Base of the Cliff for thirty times the period of their contumacy.

One soul among them identifies himself as MANFRED and begs Dante to bear a message to his daughter Constance in order that she may offer prayer for Manfred's soul and thereby shorten his period of waiting. Manfred explains that prayer can greatly assist the souls in Purgatory. He also explains how it is that though contumacy is punished, no act of priest or Pope may keep from salvation a soul that has truly given itself to God.

Those routed souls scattered across the scene,
their faces once again turned toward the mountain
where Reason spurs and Justice picks us clean;

but I drew ever closer to my Guide:
and how could I have run my course without him?
who would have led me up the mountainside?

He seemed gnawed by remorse for his offense:
O noble conscience without stain! how sharp
the sting of a small fault is to your sense!

When he had checked that haste that urges men
to mar the dignity of every act,
my mind, forced in upon itself till then,

broke free, and eager to see all before me,
I raised my eyes in wonder to that mountain
that soars highest to Heaven from the sea.

Low at my back, the sun was a red blaze;
its light fell on the ground before me broken
in the form in which my body blocked its rays.

I gave a start of fear and whirled around
seized by the thought that I had been abandoned,
for I saw one shadow only on the ground.

And my Comfort turned full to me then to say:
"Why are you still uncertain? Why do you doubt
that I am here and guide you on your way?

Vespers have rung already on the tomb
of the body in which I used to cast a shadow.
It was taken to Naples from Brindisium.

If now I cast no shadow, should that fact
amaze you more than the heavens which pass the light
undimmed from one to another? We react

within these bodies to pain and heat and cold

according to the workings of That Will
which does not will that all Its ways be told.

He is insane who dreams that he may learn
by mortal reasoning the boundless orbit
Three Persons in One Substance fill and turn.

Be satisfied with the *quia* of cause unknown,
O humankind! for could you have seen All,
Mary need not have suffered to bear a son.

You saw how some yearn endlessly in vain:
such as would, else, have surely had their wish,
but have, instead, its hunger as their pain.

I speak of Aristotle and Plato," he said.
"—Of them and many more." And here he paused,
and sorrowing and silent, bowed his head.

Meanwhile we reached the mountain's foot; and there
we found so sheer a cliff, the nimblest legs
would not have served, unless they walked on air.

The most forsaken and most broken goat-trace
in the mountains between Lerici and Turbia
compared to this would seem a gracious staircase.

My Guide exclaimed: "Now who is there to say
in which direction we may find some slope
up which one without wings may pick his way!"

While he was standing, head bowed to his shoulders,
and pondering which direction we might take,
I stood there looking up among the boulders,

and saw upon my left beside that cliff-face
a throng that moved its feet in our direction,

and yet seemed not to, so slow was its pace.

"Master," I said, "look up and you will find
some people coming who may solve the problem,
if you have not yet solved it in your mind."

He looked up then and, openly relieved,
said: "Let us go to them, since they lag so.
And you, dear son, believe as you have believed."

We were as far off yet from that slow flock
(I mean when we had gone a thousand paces)
as a strong slingsman could have thrown a rock,

when they drew in against the cliff and stood there
like men who fear what they see coming toward them
and, waiting for it, huddle close and stare.

"O well-concluded lives! O souls thus met
already among the chosen!" Virgil said,
"By that sweet crown of peace that shall be set

on each of you in time, tell us which way
leads to some slope by which we two may climb.
Who best knows time is most grieved by delay."

As sheep come through a gate—by ones, by twos,
by threes, and all the others trail behind,
timidly, nose to ground, and what the first does

the others do, and if the first one pauses,
the others huddle up against his back,
silly and mute, not knowing their own causes—

just so, I stood there watching with my Guide,
the first row of that happy flock come on,
their look meek and their movements dignified.

And when the souls that came first in that flock
saw the light broken on the ground to my right
so that my shadow fell upon the rock,

they halted and inched back as if to shy,
and all the others who came after them
did as the first did without knowing why.

"Let me confirm the thought you leave unspoken:
it is a living body you see before you
by which the sunlight on the ground is broken.

Do not be astonished: you may rest assured
he does not seek the way to climb this wall
without a power from Heaven."—Thus my Lord

addressed them, and those worthy spirits said,
waving the backs of their hands in our direction:
"First turn around, and then go straight ahead."

And one soul said to me: "Whoever you are,
as you move on, look back and ask yourself
if you have ever seen me over there."

I studied him with care, my head turned round:
gold-blond he was, and handsomely patrician,
although one brow was split by a sword wound.

When I, in all humility, confessed
I never before had seen him, he said, "Look"
—and showed me a great slash above his breast.

Then, smiling, added: "I am Manfred, grandson
of the blessed Empress Constance, and I beg you,
when you return there over the horizon,

go to my sweet daughter, noble mother
of the honor of Sicily and of Aragon
and speak the truth, if men speak any other.

My flesh had been twice hacked, and each wound mortal,
when, tearfully, I yielded up my soul
to Him whose pardon gladly waits for all.

Horrible were my sins, but infinite
is the abiding Goodness which holds out
Its open arms to all who turn to It.
If the pastor of Cosenza, by the rage
of Clement sent to hunt me down, had first
studied the book of God at this bright page,

my body's bones would still be in the ground
there by the bridgehead outside Benevento,
under the heavy guard of the stone mound.

Now, rattled by the wind, by the rain drenched,
they lie outside the kingdom, by the Verde,
where he transported them with tapers quenched.

No man may be so cursed by priest or pope
but what the Eternal Love may still return
while any thread of green lives on in hope.

Those who die contumacious, it is true,
though they repent their feud with Holy Church,
must wait outside here on the bank, as we do,

for thirty times as long as they refused
to be obedient, though by good prayers
in their behalf, that time may be reduced.

See, then, how great a service you may do me
when you return, by telling my good Constance

of my condition and of this decree

that still forbids our entrance to the kingdom.
For here, from those beyond, great good may come."

Canto IV

Listening to Manfred's discourse, Dante has lost track of time. Now, at midmorning, the Poets reach the opening in the cliff-face and begin the laborious climb. Dante soon tires and cries that he can go no farther, but Virgil urges him to pull himself a little higher yet—significantly—to the LEDGE OF THE INDOLENT, those souls whose sin was their delay in pulling themselves up the same hard path.

Seated on the ledge, Virgil explains that in the nature of the mountain, the beginning of the ascent (the First Turning from Sin to True Repentance) is always hardest. The higher one climbs from sin to repentance, the easier it becomes to climb still higher until, in the Perfection of Grace, the climb becomes effortless. But to that ultimate height, as Virgil knows, Human Reason cannot reach. It is Beatrice (Divine Love) who must guide him there.

As Virgil finishes speaking, an ironic reply comes from behind a boulder. The speaker is BELACQUA, an old friend of Dante's, and the laziest man in Florence. Because of his indolence, he put off good works and the active desire for grace until he lay dying. In life he made God wait. Now God makes him wait an equal period before he may pass through the Gate into Purgatory and begin his purification. Unless, as Belacqua adds, the prayers of the devout intercede for him.

But now Virgil points out that the sun is already at its noon-height and that Dante, unlike the Indolent, must not delay.

When any sense of ours records intense
pleasure or pain, then the whole soul is drawn
by such impressions into that one sense,

and seems to lose all other powers. And thus
do I refute the error that asserts

that one soul on another burns in us.

And, for this reason, when we see or hear
whatever seizes strongly on the soul,
time passes, and we lose it unaware.

For that which senses is one faculty;
and that which keeps the soul intact, another:
the first, as it were, bound; the second, free.

To this, my own experience bears witness,
for while I listened to that soul and marveled,
the sun had climbed—without my least awareness—

to fifty full degrees of its noon peak
when, at one point along the way, that band
cried out in chorus: "Here is what you seek."

Often when grapes hang full on slope and ledge
the peasant, with one forkful of his thorns,
seals up a wider opening in his hedge

than the gap we found there in that wall of stone;
up which—leaving that band of souls behind—
my Guide led and I followed: we two alone.

Go up to San Leo or go down to Noli;
go climb Bismantova—two legs suffice:
here nothing but swift wings will answer wholly.

The swift wings and the feathers, I mean to say,
of great desire led onward by that Guide
who was my hope and light along the way.

Squeezed in between two walls that almost meet
we labor upward through the riven rock:
a climb that calls for both our hands and feet.

Above the cliff's last rise we reached in time
an open slope. "Do we go right or left?"
I asked my Master, "or do we still climb?"

And he: "Take not one step to either side,
but follow yet, and make way up the mountain
till we meet someone who may serve as guide."

Higher than sight the peak soared to the sky:
much steeper than a line drawn from mid-quadrant
to the center, was the slope that met my eye.

The climb had sapped my last strength when I cried:
"Sweet Father, turn to me: unless you pause
I shall be left here on the mountainside!"

He pointed to a ledge a little ahead
that wound around the whole face of the slope.
"Pull yourself that much higher, my son," he said.

His words so spurred me that I forced myself
to push on after him on hands and knees
until at last my feet were on that shelf.

There we sat, facing eastward, to survey
the trail we had just climbed; for oftentimes
a backward look comforts one on the way.

I looked down first to the low-lying shore,
then upward to the sun—and stopped amazed,
for it was from the left its arrows bore.

Virgil was quick to note the start I gave
when I beheld the Chariot of the Sun
driven between me and the North Wind's cave.

"Were Castor and Pollux," he said, "in company
of that bright mirror which sends forth its rays
equally up and down, then you would see

the twelve-toothed cogwheel of the Zodiac
turned till it blazed still closer to the Bears
—unless it were to stray from its fixed track.

If you wish to understand why this is so,
imagine Zion and this Mount so placed
on earth, the one above, the other below,

that the two have one horizon though they lie
in different hemispheres. Therefore, the path
that Phaëthon could not follow in the sky

must necessarily, in passing here
on the one side, pass there upon the other,
as your own reasoning will have made clear."

And I then: "Master, I may truly vow
I never grasped so well the very point
on which my wits were most astray just now:

that the mid-circle of the highest Heaven,
called the Equator, always lies between
the sun and winter, and, for the reason given,

lies as far north of this place at all times
as the Hebrews, when they held Jerusalem,
were wont to see it toward the warmer climes.

But—if you please—I should be glad to know
how far we have yet to climb, for the peak soars
higher to Heaven than my eye can go."

And he: "Such is this Mount that when a soul

begins the lower slopes it most must labor;
then less and less the more it nears its goal.

Thus when we reach the point where the slopes seem
so smooth and gentle that the climb becomes
as easy as to float a skiff downstream,

then will this road be run, and not before
that journey's end will your repose be found.
I know this much for truth and say no more."

His words were hardly out when, from nearby,
we heard a voice say: "Maybe by that time
you'll find you need to sit before you fly!"

We turned together at the sound, and there,
close on our left, we saw a massive boulder
of which, till then, we had not been aware.

To it we dragged ourselves, and there we found
stretched in the shade, the way a slovenly man
lies down to rest, some people on the ground.

The weariest of them, judging by his pose,
sat hugging both knees while his head, abandoned,
dropped down between them halfway to his toes.

"Master," I said, "look at that sorry one
who seems so all-let-down. Were Sloth herself
his sister, he could not be so far gone!"

That heap took heed, and even turned his head
upon his thigh—enough to look at us.
"You climb it if you're such a flash," he said.

I knew him then, and all the agony
that still burned in my lungs and raced my pulse

did not prevent my going to him. He

raising his head—just barely—when I stood by,
drawled: "So you really know now why the sun
steers to the left of you across the sky?"

His short words and his shorter acts, combined,
made me half smile as I replied: "Belacqua,
your fate need never again trouble my mind.

Praise be for that. But why do you remain
crouched here? Are you waiting for a guide, perhaps?
Or are you up to your old tricks again?"

"Old friend," he said, "what good is it to climb?—
God's Bird above the Gate would never let me
pass through to start my trials before my time.

I must wait here until the heavens wheel past
as many times as they passed me in my life,
for I delayed the good sighs till the last.

Prayer could help me, if a heart God's love
has filled with Grace should offer it. All other
is worthless, for it is not heard above."

But now the Poet already led the way
to the slope above, saying to me: "Come now:
the sun has touched the very peak of day

above the sea, and night already stands
with one black foot upon Morocco's sands."

Canto V

ANTE-PURGATORY:
THE SECOND LEDGE
The Late-Repentant
Class Three: Those Who Died
by Violence Without Last Rites

The Poets continue up the mountain and Dante's shadow once more creates
excitement among the waiting souls. These are the souls of THOSE WHO DIED
BY VIOLENCE WITHOUT LAST RITES. Since their lives were cut off, they did
not have full opportunity to repent, and therefore they are placed a step higher
than the simply Indolent.

These souls crowd about Dante, eager to have him bear news of them back to
the world and so to win prayers that will shorten their delay. Virgil instructs
Dante to listen to these souls, but warns him not to interrupt his own climb to
Grace. The Poets, therefore, continue to press on while the souls cluster about
and follow them, each of them eager to tell his story and to beg that Dante speak
of them when he returns to the world.

I was following the footsteps of my Guide,
having already parted from those shades,
when someone at my back pointed and cried:

"Look there! see how the sun's shafts do not drive
through to the left of that one lower down,
and how he walks as if he were alive!"

I looked behind me to see who had spoken,
and I saw them gazing up at me alone,
at me, and at the light, that it was broken.

At which my Master said: "Why do you lag?
What has so turned your mind that you look back?

What is it to you that idle tongues will wag?

Follow my steps, though all such whisper of you:
be as a tower of stone, its lofty crown
unswayed by anything the winds may do.

For when a man lets his attention range
toward every wisp, he loses true direction,
sapping his mind's force with continual change."

What could I say except "I come"? I said it
flushed with that hue that sometimes asks forgiveness
for which it shows the asker to be fit.

Meanwhile across the slope a little before us
people approached chanting the *Miserere*
verse by verse in alternating chorus.

But when they noticed that I blocked the course
of the Sun's arrows when they struck my body,
their song changed to an "Oh! . . ." prolonged and
hoarse.

Out of that silenced choir two spirits ran
like messengers and, reaching us, they said:
"We beg to know—are you a living man?"

My Guide replied: "You may be on your way.
And bear back word to those who sent you here
he does indeed still walk in mortal clay.

If, as I think, it was his shadow drew them
to stand and stare, they know already. Tell them
to honor him: that may be precious to them."

I never saw hot vapors flashing through
the first sweet air of night, or through the clouds

of August sunsets, faster than those two

ran up to join their band, wheeled round again,
and, with the whole band following, came toward us,
like cavalry sent forward with a loose rein.

"There are hundreds in that troop that charges so,"
my Guide said, "and all come to beg a favor.
Hear them, but press on, listening as you go."

"Pure spirit," they came crying, "you who thus
while still inside the body you were born to
climb to your bliss—oh pause and speak to us.

Is there no one here you recognize? Not one
of whom you may bear tidings to the world?
Wait! Won't you pause? Oh please! Why do you run?

We all are souls who died by violence,
all sinners to our final hour, in which
the lamp of Heaven shed its radiance

into our hearts. Thus from the brink of death,
repenting all our sins, forgiving those
who sinned against us, with our final breath

we offered up our souls at peace with Him
who saddens us with longing to behold
His glory on the throne of Seraphim."

"Oh well-born souls," I said, "I can discover
no one among you that I recognize
however much I search your faces over;

but if you wish some service of me, speak,
and if the office is within my power
I will perform it, by that peace I seek

in following the footsteps of this Guide,
that peace that draws me on from world to world
to my own good." I paused, and one replied:

"No soul among us doubts you will fulfill
all you declare, without your need to swear it,
if lack of power does not defeat your will.

I, then, who am no more than first to plead,
beg that if ever you see that land that lies
between Romagna and Naples, you speak my need

most graciously in Fano, that they to Heaven
send holy prayers to intercede for me;
so may my great offenses be forgiven.

I was of Fano, but the wounds that spilled
my life's blood and my soul at once, were dealt me
among the Antenori. I was killed

where I believed I had the least to fear.
Azzo of Este, being incensed against me
beyond all reason, had me waylaid there.

Had I turned toward La Mira when they set
upon me first outside of Oriaco,
I should be drawing breath among men yet.

I ran into the swamp, and reeds and mud
tangled and trapped me. There I fell. And there
I watched my veins let out a pool of blood."

Another spoke: "So may the Love Divine
fulfill the wish that draws you up the mountain,
for sweet compassion, lend your aid to mine.

I am Bonconte, once of Montefeltro.
Because Giovanna and the rest forget me,
I go among these souls with head bowed low."

And I: "What force or chance led you to stray
so far from Campaldino that your grave
remains to be discovered to this day?"

And he: "There flows below the Casentino
a stream, the Archiana, which arises
above the hermitage in Appennino.

There where its name ends in the Arno's flood
I came, my throat pierced through, fleeing on foot
and staining all my course with my life's blood.

There my sight failed. There with a final moan
which was the name of Mary, speech went from me.
I fell, and there my body lay alone.

I speak the truth. Oh speak it in my name
to living men! God's angel took me up,
and Hell's cried out: 'Why do you steal my game?

If his immortal part is your catch, brother,
for one squeezed tear that makes me turn it loose,
I've got another treatment for the other!'

You are familiar with the way immense
watery vapors gather on the air,
then burst as rain, as soon as they condense.

To ill will that seeks only ill, his mind
added intelligence, and by the powers
his nature gives, he stirred the mist and wind.

From Pratomagno to the spine, he spread

a mist that filled the valley by day's end;
then turned the skies above it dark as lead.

The saturated air changed into rain
and down it crashed, flooding the rivulets
with what the sodden earth could not retain;

the rills merged into torrents, and a flood
swept irresistibly to the royal river.
The Archiana, raging froth and mud,

found my remains in their last frozen rest
just at its mouth, swept them into the Arno,
and broke the cross I had formed upon my breast
in my last agony of pain and guilt.
Along its banks and down its bed it rolled me,
and then it bound and buried me in silt."

A third spoke when that second soul had done:
"When you have found your way back to the world,
and found your rest from this long road you run,

oh speak my name again with living breath
to living memory. Pia am I.
Siena gave me birth; Maremma, death.

As he well knows who took me as his wife
with jeweled ring before he took my life."

Canto VI

ANTE-PURGATORY:
THE SECOND LEDGE
The Late-Repentant
Class Three: Those Who Died by Violence
Sordello

The Poets move along with the souls still crowding about them. Dante promises all of them that he will bear word of them back to the world, but he never pauses in his climb. Among that press of souls, Dante specifically mentions seeing BENINCASA DA LATERINA, GUCCIO DE' TARLATI, FEDERICO NOVELLO, COUNT ORSO, and PIERRE DE LA BROSSE.

Finally free of that crowd, Dante asks Virgil how it is that prayer may sway God's will. Virgil explains in part but once more finishes by declaring that the whole truth is beyond him and that Dante must refer the question to Beatrice when he meets her.

The sun passes behind the mountain as they climb (midafternoon of Easter Sunday). The poets press on, and there on the shady slope they encounter the majestic spirit of SORDELLO who, like Virgil, is a Mantuan. Dante watches Sordello and Virgil embrace in a transport of love for their common birthplace and is moved to denounce Italy for setting brothers to war on one another, to denounce the EMPEROR ALBERT for his failure to bring unity and peace to Italy, and finally to utter an invective against Florence as the type of the war-torn and corrupt state.

The loser, when a game of dice is done,
remains behind reviewing every roll
sadly, and sadly wiser, and alone.

The crowd leaves with the winner: one behind
tugs at him, one ahead, one at his side—
all calling their long loyalty to his mind.

Not stopping, he hands out a coin or two
and those he has rewarded let him be.

So he fights off the crowd and pushes through.

Such was I then, turning my face now here,
now there, among that rout, and promising
on every hand, till I at last fought clear.

There was the Aretine who came to woe
at the murderous hand of Tacco; and the other
who drowned while he was hunting down his foe.

There, hands outstretched to me as I pushed through,
was Federico Novello; and the Pisan
who made the good Marzucco shine so true.

I saw Count Orso; and the shade of one
torn from its flesh, it said, by hate and envy,
and not for any evil it had done—

Pierre de la Brosse, I mean: and of this word
may the Lady of Brabant take heed while here,
lest, there, she find herself in a worse herd.

When I had won my way free of that press
of shades whose one prayer was that others pray,
and so advance them toward their blessedness,

I said: "O my Soul's Light, it seems to me
one of your verses most expressly states
prayer may not alter Heaven's fixed decree:

yet all these souls pray only for a prayer.
Can all their hope be vain? Or have I missed
your true intent and read some other there?"

And he: "The sense of what I wrote is plain,
if you bring all your wits to bear upon it.
Nor is the hope of all these spirits vain.

The towering crag of Justice is not bent,
nor is the rigor of its edict softened
because the supplications of the fervent

and pure in heart cancel the debt of time
decreed on all these souls who linger here,
consumed with yearning to begin the climb.

The souls I wrote about were in that place
where sin is not atoned for, and their prayers—
they being pagan—were cut off from Grace.

But save all questions of such consequence
till you meet her who will become your lamp
between the truth and mere intelligence.

Do you understand me? I mean Beatrice.
She will appear above here, at the summit
of this same mountain, smiling in her bliss."

"My Lord," I said, "let us go faster now:
I find the climb less tiring than at first,
and see, the slope already throws a shadow."

"The day leads on," he said, "and we shall press
as far as we yet may while the light holds,
but the ascent is harder than you guess:

before it ends, the Sun must come around
from its present hiding place behind the mountain
and once more cast your shadow on the ground.

But see that spirit stationed all alone
and looking down at us: he will point out
the best road for us as we travel on."

We climbed on then. O Lombard, soul serene,
how nobly and deliberately you watched us!
how distant and majestic was your mien!

He did not speak to us as on we pressed
but held us fixed in his unblinking eyes
as if he were a lion at its rest.
Virgil, nonetheless, climbed to his side
and begged him to point out the best ascent.
The shade ignored the question and replied

by asking in what country we were born
and who we were. My gentle Guide began:
"Mantua . . ." And that shade, till then withdrawn,

leaped to his feet like one in sudden haste
crying: "O Mantuan, I am Sordello
of your own country!" And the two embraced.

Ah servile Italy, grief's hostelry,
ah ship unpiloted in the storm's rage,
no mother of provinces but of harlotry!

That noble spirit leaped up with a start
at the mere sound of his own city's name,
and took his fellow citizen to his heart:

while still, within you, brother wars on brother,
and though one wall and moat surrounds them all,
your living sons still gnaw at one another!

O wretched land, search all your coasts, your seas,
the bosom of your hills—where will you find
a single part that knows the joys of peace?

What does it matter that Justinian came
to trim the bit, if no one sits the saddle?

Without him you would have less cause for shame!

You priests who, if you heed what God decreed,
should most seek after holiness and leave
to Caesar Caesar's saddle and his steed—

see how the beast grows wild now none restrains
its temper, nor corrects it with the spur,
since you set meddling hands upon its reins!

O German Albert, you who turn away
while she grows vicious, being masterless;
you should have forked her long before today!

May a just judgment from the stars descend
upon your house, a blow so weirdly clear
that your line tremble at it to the end.

For you, sir, and your father, in your greed
for the cold conquests of your northern lands,
have let the Empire's Garden go to seed.

Come see the Montagues and Capulets,
the Monaldi and Filippeschi, reckless man!
those ruined already, these whom ruin besets.

Come, cruel Emperor, come and see your lords
hunted and holed; come tend their wounds and see
what fine security Santafior affords.

Come see your stricken Rome that weeps alone,
widowed and miserable, and day and night
laments: "O Caesar mine, why are you gone?"

Come see your people—everywhere the same—
united in love; and if no pity for us
can move you, come and blush for your good name.

O Supreme Jove, for mankind crucified,
if you permit the question, I must ask it:
are the eyes of your clear Justice turned aside?

Or is this the unfolding of a plan
shaped in your fathomless counsels toward some good
beyond all reckoning of mortal man?

For the land is a tyrant's roost, and any clod
who comes along playing the partisan
passes for a Marcellus with the crowd.

Florence, my Florence, may you not resent
the fact that my digression has not touched you—
thanks to your people's sober management.

Others have Justice at heart but a bow strung
by careful counsels and not quickly drawn:
yours shoot the word forever—from the tongue.

Others, offered public office, shun
the cares of service. Yours cry out unasked:
"I will! I'll take it on! I am the one!"

Rejoice, I say, that your great gifts endure:
your wealth, your peacefulness, and your good sense.
What truth I speak, the facts will not obscure.

Athens and Sparta when of old they drew
the codes of law that civilized the world,
gave only merest hints, compared to you,

of man's advance. But all time shall remember
the subtlety with which the thread you spin
in mid-October breaks before November.

How often within living recollection
have you changed coinage, custom, law, and office,
and hacked your own limbs off and sewed them on?

But if your wits and memory are not dead
you yet will see yourself as that sick woman
who cannot rest, though on a feather bed,

but flails as if she fenced with pain and grief.
Ah, Florence, may your cure or course be brief.

Canto VII

ANTE-PURGATORY:
THE SECOND LEDGE
THE FLOWERING VALLEY
The Late-Repentant
Class Four: The Negligent
Rulers

Sordello, discovering Virgil's identity, pays homage to him and offers to guide the Poets as far as Peter's Gate. It is nearly sunset, however, and Sordello explains that by THE LAW OF THE ASCENT no one may go upward after sundown. He suggests that they spend the night in the nearby FLOWERING VALLEY in which the souls of THE NEGLIGENT RULERS wait to begin their purification. The three together climb in the failing light to the edge of the valley. In it, they observe, among others: RUDOLPH OF HAPSBURG, OTTOCAR OF BOHEMIA, PHILIP THE BOLD OF FRANCE, HENRY OF NAVARRE, PEDRO III OF ARAGON, CHARLES I OF ANJOU, HENRY III OF ENGLAND, and WILLIAM VII, MARQUIS OF MONFERRATO.

All of the rulers, except Henry of England, were in one way or another connected with the Holy Roman Empire. Thus they were specially sanctified by the Divine Right of Kings and again sanctified for their place in the temporal hierarchy of Christ's Empire. Dante signalizes this elevation by the beauty of the valley in which he places them, a flower-strewn green hollow of unearthly beauty and fragrance. The valley is certainly a counterpart of the Citadel of the Virtuous Pagans in Limbo, but it outshines that lower splendor by as much as Divine Love outshines Human Reason.

Three or four times in brotherhood the two
embraced and re-embraced, and then Sordello
drew back and said: "Countryman, who are *you*?"

"Before those spirits worthy to be blessed
had yet been given leave to climb this mountain,

Octavian had laid my bones to rest.

I am Virgil, and I am lost to Heaven
for no sin, but because I lacked the faith."
In these words was my Master's answer given.

Just as a man who suddenly confronts
something too marvelous either to believe
or disbelieve, and so does both at once—

so did Sordello. Then his great head lowered,
and, turning, he once more embraced my Master,
but round the knees, as a menial does his lord.

"Eternal Glory of the Latin race,
through whom our tongue made all its greatness clear!
Of my own land the deathless pride and praise!

What grace or merit lets me see you plain?"
he said. "And oh, if I am worthy, tell me
if you come here from Hell, and from what pain."

"Through every valley of the painful kingdom
I passed," my Lord replied. "A power from Heaven
marked me this road, and in that power I come.

Not what I did but what I left undone,
who learned too late, denies my right to share
your hope of seeing the Eternal Sun.

There is a place below where sorrow lies
in untormented gloom. Its lamentations
are not the shrieks of pain, but hopeless sighs.

There do I dwell with souls of babes whom death
bit off in their first innocence, before
baptism washed them of their taint of earth.

There do I dwell with those who were not dressed
in the Three Sacred Virtues but, unstained,
recognized and practiced all the rest.

But if you know and are allowed to say,
show us how we may reach the true beginning
of Purgatory by the shortest way."

"We are not fixed in one place," he replied,
"but roam at will up and around this slope
far as the Gate, and I will be your guide.

But the day is fading fast, and in no case
may one ascend at night: we will do well
to give some thought to a good resting place.

Some souls are camped apart here on the right.
If you permit, I will conduct you to them:
I think you will find pleasure in the sight."

"What is it you say?" my Guide asked. "If one sought
to climb at night, would others block his way?
Or would he simply find that he could not?"

"Once the Sun sets," that noble soul replied,
"you would not cross this line"—and ran his finger
across the ground between him and my Guide.

"Nor is there anything to block the ascent
except the shades of night: they of themselves
suffice to sap the will of the most fervent.

One might, indeed, go down during the night
and wander the whole slope, were he inclined to,
while the horizon locks the day from sight."

I heard my Lord's voice, touched with wonder, say:
"Lead us to the place of which you spoke
where we may win some pleasure from delay."

We had not traveled very far from there
before I saw a hollow in the slope
such as one often finds in mountains here.

"There," said that spirit, "where the mountain makes
a lap among its folds: that is the place
where we may wait until the new day breaks."

The dell's rim sank away from left to right.
A winding path, half-level and half-steep,
led us to where the rim stood at mid-height.

Indigo, phosphorescent wood self-lit,
gold, fine silver, white-lead, cochineal,
fresh emerald the moment it is split—

all colors would seem lusterless as shade
if placed beside the flowers and grassy banks
that made a shining of that little glade.

Nor has glad Nature only colored there,
but of a thousand sweet scents made a single
earthless, nameless fragrance of the air.

Salve Regina!—from that green the hymn
was raised to Heaven by a choir of souls
hidden from outer view by the glade's rim.

"Sirs," said that Mantuan, "do not request
that I conduct you there while any light
remains before the Sun sinks to its nest.

You can observe them from this rise and follow

their actions better, singly and en masse,
than if you moved among them in the hollow.

He who sits highest with the look of one
ashamed to move his lips when others praise,
in life left undone what he should have done.

He was the Emperor Rudolph whose high state
could once have stayed the death of Italy.
Now, though another try, 't will be too late.

That one who comforts him ruled formerly
the land where rise the waters that flow down
the Moldau to the Elbe to the sea.

He was Ottocar, and more respected and feared
while still in diapers than his dissipated
son Wenceslaus is now with a full beard.

That Snubnose there who talks with head close-pressed
to the kindly looking one, died while in flight,
dishonoring the Lily on his crest.

Observe the way he beats his breast and cries.
And how the other one has made his palm
a bed to rest his cheek on while he sighs.

They are father and father-in-law of The Plague of France.
They know his dissolute and vicious ways,
and hence their grief among these holy chants.

The heavy-sinewed one beside that spirit
with the manly nose, singing in harmony,
bore in his life the seal of every merit.

And if that younger one who sits in place
behind him, had remained king after him,

true merit would have passed from vase to vase.

As it has not, alas, in their successors.
Frederick and James possess the kingdoms now.
Their father's better heritage none possesses.

Rare is the tree that lifts to every limb
the sap of merit—He who gives, so wills
that men may learn to beg their best from Him.

And what I say goes for that bignosed one
no less than for the other who sings with him.
On his account Provence and Puglia mourn.
By as much as Margaret and Beatrice
must yield when Constance speaks her husband's worth,
that much less than the tree the seedling is.

See Henry of England seated there alone,
the monarch of the simple life: his branches
came to good issue in a noble son.

The other lone one seated on the ground
below the rest and looking up to them
was the Marquis William Longsword, he who found

such grief in Allesandria, for whose pride
both Monferrato and Canavese cried."

Canto VIII

ANTE-PURGATORY:
THE FLOWERING VALLEY
The Negligent Rulers
Nightfall, Easter Sunday
The Guardian Angels
The Serpent

As the light fades, Dante, Virgil, and Sordello stand on the bank and watch the souls below gather and sing the COMPLINE HYMN, asking for protection in the night. In response to the hymn TWO GREEN ANGELS descend from Heaven and take their posts, one on each side of the valley. Full darkness now settles, and the Poets may make their DESCENT INTO THE VALLEY.

Dante immediately finds a soul he knows, JUDGE NINO DE' VISCONTI, and has a long conversation with him in which both bemoan the infidelity of widows who remarry.

When Judge Nino has finished speaking, Dante looks at the South Pole and sees that THREE STARS (the Three Theological Virtues) have replaced THE FOUR STARS (the Four Cardinal Virtues) he had seen at dawn.

As he is discussing them with Virgil THE SERPENT appears and is immediately routed by the Angels, who return to their posts. Dante then has a conversation with CONRAD MALASPINA, whom Judge Nino had summoned when he found out Dante was a living man. Dante owes a debt of gratitude to the Malaspina House for its hospitality to him in his exile, and he takes this opportunity to praise the house and to have Conrad prophesy that Dante shall live to know more about it.

It was the hour that turns the memories
of sailing men their first day out, to home,
and friends they sailed from on that morning's breeze;

that thrills the traveler newly on his way
with love and yearning when he hears afar
the bell that seems to mourn the dying day—

when I began, for lack of any sound,
to count my hearing vain: and watched a spirit
who signaled for attention all around.

Raising his hands, he joined his palms in prayer
and turned his rapt eyes east, as if to say:
"I have no thought except that Thou art there."

"Te lucis ante" swelled from him so sweetly,
with such devotion and so pure a tone,
my senses lost the sense of self completely.

Then all the others with a golden peal
joined in the hymn and sang it to the end,
their eyes devoutly raised to Heaven's wheel.

Reader, if you seek truth, sharpen your eyes,
for here the veil of allegory thins
and may be pierced by any man who tries.

I saw that host of kings, its supplication
sung to a close, stand still and pale and humble,
eyes raised to Heaven as if in expectation.

I saw two angels issue and descend
from Heaven's height, bearing two flaming swords
without a point, snapped off to a stub end.

Green as a leaf is at its first unfurling,
their robes; and green the wings that beat and blew
the flowing folds back, fluttering and whirling.

One landed just above me, and one flew
to the other bank. Thus, in the silent valley,
the people were contained between the two.

I could see clearly that their hair was gold,

but my eyes drew back bedazzled from their faces,
defeated by more light than they could hold.

"They are from Mary's bosom," Sordello said,
"and come to guard the valley from the Serpent
that in a moment now will show its head."

And I, not knowing where it would appear,
turned so I stood behind those trusted shoulders
and pressed against them icy-cold with fear.

Once more Sordello spoke: "Now let us go
to where the great souls are, and speak to them.
The sight of you will please them much, I know."

It was, I think, but three steps to the base
of the little bank; and there I saw a shade
who stared at me as if he knew my face.

The air was closing on its darkling hour,
yet not so fast but what it let me see,
at that close range, what it had veiled before.

I took a step toward him; he, one toward me—
Noble Judge Nin! how it rejoiced my soul
to see you safe for all eternity!

No welcome was left unsaid on either side.
Then he inquired: "How long since did you come
to the mountain's foot over that widest tide?"

"Oh," I replied, "I came by the pits of woe—
this morning. I am still in my first life,
though I gain the other on the road I go."

He and Sordello, when they heard me thus
answer the question, suddenly drew back

as if surprised by something marvelous.

One turned to Virgil, and one turned aside
to a shade who sat nearby. "Conrad! Get up!
See what the grace of God has willed!" he cried.

And then to me: "By all the thankful praise
you owe to Him who hides His primal cause
so deep that none may ever know His ways—

when you have once more crossed the enormous tide,
tell my Giovanna to cry out my name
there where the innocent are gratified.

I do not think her mother cares for me
since she put off the weeds and the white veil
that she will once more long for presently.

She shows all men how long love's fire will burn
within a woman's heart when sight and touch
do not rekindle it at every turn.

Nor will the Milanese viper she must bear
upon her tomb do her such honor in it
as would Gallura's cock emblazoned there."

So spoke he; and his features bore the seal
of that considered anger a good man
reaches in reason and may rightly feel.

I looked up at the Heavens next, and eyed
that center point at which the stars are slowest,
as a wheel is next the axle. And my Guide:

"My son, what is it that you stare at so?"
And I: "At those three stars there in whose light
the polar regions here are all aglow."

And he to me: "Below the rim of space
now ride the four bright stars you saw this morning,
and these three have arisen in their place."

Sordello started as my Guide said this;
and clutching him, he pointed arm and finger,
crying: "Our Adversary! There he is!"

Straight through the valley's unprotected side
a serpent came, perhaps the very one
that gave the bitter food for which Eve cried.

Through the sweet grass and flowers the long sneak drew,
turning its head around from time to time
to lick itself as preening beasts will do.

I did not see and cannot tell you here
how the celestial falcons took to flight;
but I did see that both were in the air.

Hearing their green wings beating through the night,
the serpent fled. The angels wheeled and climbed
back to their posts again in equal flight.

The shade the Judge had summoned with his cry
had not moved from his side; through all that fray
he stared at me without blinking an eye.

"So may the lamp that leads to what you seek
find oil enough," he said, "in your own will
to light your way to the enameled peak;

if you can say for certain how things stand
in Val di Magra or those parts, please do,
for I was once a great lord in that land.

Conrad Malaspina I was—the grandson
and not the Elder. Here I purify
the love I bore for those who were my own."

"Oh," I replied, "I never have been near
the lands you held; but is there in all Europe
a hamlet ignorant of the name you bear?

The glories of your noble house proclaim
its lords abroad, proclaim the lands that bear them;
and he who does not know them knows their fame.

I swear to you—so may my present course
lead me on high—your honored house has never
put by its strict sword and its easy purse.

Usage and nature have so formed your race
that, though the Guilty Head pervert all else,
it still shuns ill to walk the path of grace."

And he: "Go now, for the Sun shall not complete
its seventh rest in that great bed the Ram
bestrides and covers with its four spread feet,

before this testimony you have given
shall be nailed to the center of your head
with stouter nails, and more securely driven,

than ever hearsay was. And this shall be
certain as fate is in its fixed decree."

Canto IX

*Dawn is approaching. Dante has a dream of A GOLDEN EAGLE that descends
from the height of Heaven and carries him up to the Sphere of Fire. He wakes to
find he has been transported in his sleep, that it was LUCIA who bore him,
laying him down beside an enormous wall, through an opening in which he and
Virgil may approach THE GATE
OF PURGATORY.*

   *Having explained these matters, Virgil leads Dante to the Gate and its ANGEL
GUARDIAN. The Angel is seated on the topmost of THREE STEPS that
symbolize the three parts of a perfect ACT OF CONFESSION. Dante prostrates
himself at the feet of the Angel, who cuts SEVEN P's in Dante's forehead with
the point of a blazing sword. He then allows the Poets to enter. As the Gates
open with a sound of thunder, the mountain resounds with a great HYMN OF
PRAISE.*

Now pale upon the balcony of the East
ancient Tithonus' concubine appeared,
but lately from her lover's arms released.

Across her brow, their radiance like a veil,
a scroll of gems was set, worked in the shape
of the cold beast whose sting is in his tail.

And now already, where we were, the night
had taken two steps upward, while the third
thrust down its wings in the first stroke of flight;

when I, by Adam's weight of flesh defeated,
was overcome by sleep, and sank to rest
across the grass on which we five were seated.

At that new hour when the first dawn light grows

and the little swallow starts her mournful cry,
perhaps in memory of her former woes;

and when the mind, escaped from its submission
to flesh and to the chains of waking thought,
becomes almost prophetic in its vision;

in a dream I saw a soaring eagle hold
the shining height of heaven, poised to strike,
yet motionless on widespread wings of gold.

He seemed to hover where old history
records that Ganymede rose from his friends,
borne off to the supreme consistory.

I thought to myself: "Perhaps his habit is
to strike at this one spot; perhaps he scorns
to take his prey from any place but this."

Then from his easy wheel in Heaven's spire,
terrible as a lightning bolt, he struck
and snatched me up high as the Sphere of Fire.

It seemed that we were swept in a great blaze,
and the imaginary fire so scorched me
my sleep broke and I wakened in a daze.

Achilles must have roused exactly thus—
glancing about with unadjusted eyes,
now here, now there, not knowing where he was

when Thetis stole him sleeping, still a boy,
and fled with him from Chiron's care to Scyros,
whence the Greeks later lured him off to Troy.

I sat up with a start; and as sleep fled
out of my face, I turned the deathly white

of one whose blood is turned to ice by dread.

There at my side my comfort sat—alone.
The sun stood two hours high, and more. I sat
facing the sea. The flowering glen was gone.
"Don't be afraid," he said. "From here our course
leads us to joy, you may be sure. Now, therefore,
hold nothing back, but strive with all your force.

You are now at Purgatory. See the great
encircling rampart there ahead. And see
that opening—it contains the Golden Gate.

A while back, in the dawn before the day,
while still your soul was locked in sleep inside you,
across the flowers that made the valley gay,

a Lady came. 'I am Lucia,' she said.
'Let me take up this sleeping man and bear him
that he may wake to see his hope ahead.'

Sordello and the others stayed. She bent
and took you up. And as the light grew full,
she led, I followed, up the sweet ascent.

Here she put you down. Then with a sweep
of her sweet eyes she marked that open entrance.
Then she was gone; and with her went your sleep."

As one who finds his doubt dispelled, sheds fear
and feels it change into new confidence
as bit by bit he sees the truth shine clear—

so did I change; and seeing my face brim
with happiness, my Guide set off at once
to climb the slope, and I moved after him.

Reader, you know to what exalted height
I raised my theme. Small wonder if I now
summon still greater art to what I write.

As we drew near the height, we reached a place
from which—inside what I had first believed
to be an open breach in the rock face—

I saw a great gate fixed in place above
three steps, each its own color; and a guard
who did not say a word and did not move.

Slow bit by bit, raising my lids with care,
I made him out seated on the top step,
his face more radiant than my eyes could bear.

He held a drawn sword, and the eye of day
beat such a fire back from it, that each time
I tried to look, I had to look away.

I heard him call: "What is your business here?
Answer from where you stand. Where is your Guide?
Take care you do not find your coming dear."

"A little while ago," my Teacher said,
"A Heavenly Lady, well versed in these matters,
told us: 'Go there. That is the Gate ahead.' "

"And may she still assist you, once inside,
to your soul's good! Come forward to our three steps,"
the courteous keeper of the gate replied.

We came to the first step: white marble gleaming
so polished and so smooth that in its mirror
I saw my true reflection past all seeming.

The second was stained darker than blue-black

and of a rough-grained and a fire-flaked stone,
its length and breadth crisscrossed by many a crack.

The third and topmost was of porphyry,
or so it seemed, but of a red as flaming
as blood that spurts out of an artery.

The Angel of the Lord had both feet on
this final step and sat upon the sill
which seemed made of some adamantine stone.
With great good will my Master guided me
up the three steps and whispered in my ear:
"Now beg him humbly that he turn the key."

Devoutly prostrate at his holy feet,
I begged in mercy's name to be let in,
but first three times upon my breast I beat.

Seven *P*'s, the seven scars of sin,
his sword point cut into my brow. He said:
"Scrub off these wounds when you have passed within."

Color of ashes, of parched earth one sees
deep in an excavation, were his vestments,
and from beneath them he drew out two keys.

One was of gold, one silver. He applied
the white one to the gate first, then the yellow,
and did with them what left me satisfied.

"Whenever either of these keys is put
improperly in the lock and fails to turn it,"
the Angel said to us, "the door stays shut.

One is more precious. The other is so wrought
as to require the greater skill and genius,
for it is that one which unties the knot.

They are from Peter, and he bade me be
more eager to let in than to keep out
whoever cast himself prostrate before me."

Then opening the sacred portals wide:
"Enter. But first be warned: do not look back
or you will find yourself once more outside."

The Tarpeian rock-face, in that fatal hour
that robbed it of Metellus, and then the treasure,
did not give off so loud and harsh a roar
as did the pivots of the holy gate—
which were of resonant and hard-forged metal—
when they turned under their enormous weight.

At the first thunderous roll I turned half-round,
for it seemed to me I heard a chorus singing
Te deum laudamus mixed with that sweet sound.

I stood there and the strains that reached my ears
left on my soul exactly that impression
a man receives who goes to church and hears

the choir and organ ringing out their chords
and now does, now does not, make out the words.

Canto X

*The gate closes behind them and the Poets begin the ascent to The FIRST
CORNICE through a tortuous passage that Dante describes as a NEEDLE'S
EYE. They reach the Cornice about 9:00 or 10:00 of Monday morning.*

*At first the Cornice seems deserted. Dante's eye is caught by a series of three
marvelously wrought bas-reliefs in the marble of the inner cliff face. Three
panels depict three scenes that serve as THE WHIP OF PRIDE, exemplifying to
each sinner as he enters how far greater souls have put by far greater reasons
for pride in order to pursue the grace of humility.*

*As Dante stands in admiration before the carvings, Virgil calls his attention to
a band of souls approaching from the left, and Dante turns for his first sight of
the souls of THE PROUD, who crawl agonizingly round and round the Cornice
under the crushing weight of enormous slabs of rock. Their punishment is so
simple and so terrible that Dante can scarcely bear to describe it. He cries out in
anguish to the proud of this world to take heed of the nature of their sin and of
its unbearable punishment.*

When we had crossed the threshold of that gate
so seldom used because man's perverse love
so often makes the crooked path seem straight,

I knew by the sound that it had closed again;
and had I looked back, to what water ever
could I have gone to wash away that stain?

We climbed the rock along a narrow crack
through which a zigzag pathway pitched and slid
just as a wave swells full and then falls back.

"This calls for careful judgment," said my guide.
"Avoid the places where the rock swells up
and weave among the troughs from side to side."

Our steps became so difficult and few,
the waning moon had reached its western bed
and sunk to rest before we could work through

that needle's eye. But when we had won clear
to an open space above, at which the mountain
steps back to form a ledge, we halted there;

I tired, and both of us confused for lack
of any sign or guide. The ledge was level,
and lonelier even than a desert track.

From brink to cliff-face measured three men's height,
and the Cornice did not vary in its width
as far as I could see to left or right.

Our feet had not yet moved a step up there,
when I made out that all the inner cliff
which rose without a foothold anywhere

was white and flawless marble and adorned
with sculptured scenes beside which Polyclitus',
and even Nature's, best works would be scorned.

The Angel who came down from God to man
with the decree of peace the centuries wept for,
which opened Heaven, ending the long ban,

stood carved before us with such force and love,
with such a living grace in his whole pose,
the image seemed about to speak and move.

One could have sworn an *Ave!* sounded clear,
for she who turned the key that opened to us
the Perfect Love, was also figured there;
and all her flowing gesture seemed to say—
impressed there as distinctly as a seal
impresses wax—*Ecce ancilla Dei.*

"Do not give all your thoughts to this one part,"
my gentle Master said. (I was then standing
on that side of him where man has his heart.)

I turned my eyes a little to the right
(the side on which he stood who had thus urged
me) and there, at Mary's back, carved in that white

and flawless wall, I saw another scene,
and I crossed in front of Virgil and drew near it
the better to make out what it might mean.

Emerging from the marble were portrayed
the cart, the oxen, and the Ark from which
the sacrilegious learned to be afraid.

Seven choirs moved there before it, bringing
confusion to my senses; with my hearing
I thought "No," with my sight, "Yes, they are singing."

In the same way, the smokes the censers poured
were shown so faithfully that eyes and nose
disputed yes and no in happy discord.

And there before the Holy Vessel, dancing
with girt-up robes, the humble Psalmist moved,
less than a king, and more, in his wild prancing.

Facing him, portrayed with a vexed frown
of mingled sadness and contempt, Michal

stood at a palace window looking down.

I moved a little further to the right,
the better to observe another panel
that shone at Michal's back, dazzling and white.

Here was portrayed from glorious history
that Roman Prince whose passion to do justice
moved Gregory to his great victory.

I speak of Trajan, blessed Emperor.
And at his bridle was portrayed a widow
in tears wept from the long grief of the poor.

Filling the space on both sides and behind
were mounted knights on whose great golden banners
the eagles seemed to flutter in the wind.

The widow knelt and by consummate art
appeared to say: "My Lord, avenge my son
for he is slain and I am sick at heart."

And he to answer: "Justice shall be done;
wait only my return." And she: "My Lord"—
speaking from the great grief that urged her on—

"If you do not?" And he: "Who wears my crown
will right your wrong." And she: "Can the good deed
another does grace him who shuns his own?"

And he, then: "Be assured. For it is clear
this duty is to do before I go.
Justice halts me, pity binds me here."

The Maker who can never see or know
anything new, produced that "visible speaking":
new to us, because not found below.

As I stood relishing the art and thought
of those high images—dear in themselves,
and dearer yet as works His hand had wrought—

the Poet said: "Look there: they seem to crawl
but those are people coming on our left:
they can tell us where to climb the wall."
My eyes, always intent to look ahead
to some new thing, finding delight in learning,
lost little time in doing as he said.

Reader, I would not have you be afraid,
nor turn from your intention to repent
through hearing how God wills the debt be paid.

Do not think of the torments: think, I say,
of what comes after them: think that at worst
they cannot last beyond the Judgment Day.

"Master," I said, "those do not seem to me
people approaching us; nor do I know—
they so confuse my sight—what they may be."

And he to me: "Their painful circumstance
doubles them to the very earth: my own eyes
debated what they saw there at first glance.

Look hard and you will see the people pressed
under the moving boulders there. Already
you can make out how each one beats his breast."

O you proud Christians, wretched souls and small,
who by the dim lights of your twisted minds
believe you prosper even as you fall—

can you not see that we are worms, each one

born to become the Angelic butterfly
that flies defenseless to the Judgment Throne?

What have your souls to boast of and be proud?
You are no more than insects, incomplete
as any grub until it burst the shroud.

Sometimes at roof or ceiling-beam one sees
a human figure set there as a corbel,
carved with its chest crushed in by its own knees,
so cramped that what one sees imagined there
makes his bones ache in fact—just such a sense
grew on me as I watched those souls with care.

True, those who crawled along that painful track
were more or less distorted, each one bent
according to the burden on his back;

yet even the most patient, wracked and sore,
seemed to be groaning: "I can bear no more!"

Canto XI

As the souls of the Proud creep near, the Poets hear them recite a long and humble prayer based on the Paternoster. When the prayer is ended, Virgil asks one of the souls, hidden from view under its enormous burden, the way to the ascent. The sinner, who identifies himself as OMBERTO ALDOBRANDESCO, instructs the Poets to follow along in the direction the souls are crawling. He recites his history in brief, and it becomes clear that Dante means him to exemplify PRIDE OF BIRTH. The conversation between Dante and Omberto is overheard by ODERISI D'AGOBBIO, who turns in pain and speaks to Dante, explaining his sin of PRIDE OF TALENT, the avidity of the artist for pre-eminence. Oderisi also points out the soul that struggles along just ahead of him as PROVENZANO SALVANI, once war lord of Siena, who is being punished for PRIDE OF TEMPORAL POWER, though he has been advanced toward his purification in recognition of a single ACT OF GREAT HUMILITY performed in order to save the life of a friend.

Oderisi concludes with a DARK PROPHECY OF DANTE'S EXILE from Florence.

Our Father in Heaven, not by Heaven bounded
but there indwelling for the greater love
Thou bear'st Thy first works in the realm first-
founded,

hallowed be Thy name, hallowed Thy Power
by every creature as its nature grants it
to praise Thy quickening breath in its brief hour.

Let come to us the sweet peace of Thy reign,
for if it come not we cannot ourselves
attain to it however much we strain.

And as Thine Angels kneeling at the throne
offer their wills to Thee, singing Hosannah,
so teach all men to offer up their own.

Give us this day Thy manna, Lord we pray,
for if he have it not, though man most strive
through these harsh wastes, his speed is his delay.

As we forgive our trespassers the ill
we have endured, do Thou forgive, not weighing
our merits, but the mercy of Thy will.

Our strength is as a reed bent to the ground:
do not Thou test us with the Adversary,
but deliver us from him who sets us round.

This last petition, Lord, with grateful mind,
we pray not for ourselves who have no need,
but for the souls of those we left behind.

—So praying godspeed for themselves and us,
those souls were crawling by under such burdens
as we at times may dream of. Laden thus,

unequally tormented, weary, bent,
they circled the First Cornice round and round,
purging away the world's foul sediment.

If they forever speak our good above,
what can be done for their good here below
by those whose will is rooted in God's love?

Surely, we should help those souls grow clear
of time's deep stain, that each at last may issue
spotless and weightless to his starry sphere.

"Ah, so may Justice and pity soon remove
the load you bear, that you may spread your wings
and rise rejoicing to the Perfect Love—

help us to reach the stairs the shortest way,
and should there be more than one passage, show us
the one least difficult to climb, I pray;

for my companion, who is burdened still
with Adam's flesh, grows weak in the ascent,
though to climb ever higher is all his will."

I heard some words in answer to my Lord's,
but could not tell which of those souls had spoken,
nor from beneath which stone. These were the words:

"Your way is to the right, along with ours.
If you will come with us, you will discover
a pass within a living person's powers.

And were I not prevented by the stone
that masters my stiff neck and makes me keep
my head bowed to the dust as I move on,

I would look up, hoping to recognize
this living and still nameless man with you,
and pray to find compassion in his eyes.

I was Italian. A Tuscan of great fame—
Guglielmo Aldobrandesco—was my father.
I do not know if you have heard the name.

My ancient lineage and the hardihood
my forebears showed in war, went to my head.
With no thought that we all share the one blood

of Mother Eve, I scorned all others so

I died for it; as all Siena knows,
and every child in Campagnatico.

I am Omberto, and my haughty ways
were not my ruin alone, but brought my house
and all my followers to evil days.

Here until God be pleased to raise my head
I bear this weight. Because I did not do so
among the living, I must among the dead."

I had bowed low, better to know his state,
when one among them—not he who was speaking—
twisted around beneath his crushing weight,

saw me, knew me, and cried out. And so
he kept his eyes upon me with great effort
as I moved with those souls, my head bowed low.

"Aren't you Od'risi?" I said. "He who was known
as the honor of Agobbio, and of that art
Parisians call *illumination*?"

"Brother," he said, "what pages truly shine
are Franco Bolognese's. The real honor
is all his now, and only partly mine.

While I was living, I know very well,
I never would have granted him first place,
so great was my heart's yearning to excel.

Here pride is paid for. Nor would I have been
among these souls, had I not turned to God
while I still had in me the power to sin.

O gifted men, vainglorious for first place,
how short a time the laurel crown stays green

unless the age that follows lacks all grace!

Once Cimabue thought to hold the field
in painting, and now Giotto has the cry
so that the other's fame, grown dim, must yield.

So from one Guido has another shorn
poetic glory, and perhaps the man
who will un-nest both is already born.

A breath of wind is all there is to fame
here upon earth: it blows this way and that,
and when it changes quarter it changes name.

Though loosed from flesh in old age, will you have
in, say, a thousand years, more reputation
than if you went from child's play to the grave?

What, to eternity, is a thousand years?
Not so much as the blinking of an eye
to the turning of the slowest of the spheres.

All Tuscany once sounded with the fame
of this one who goes hobbling on before me;
now, one hears scarce a whisper of his name,

even in Siena, where he was in power
when he destroyed the rage of Florence (then,
as much a shrew as she is, now, a whore).

The fame of man is like the green of grass:
it comes, it goes; and He by whom it springs
bright from earth's plenty makes it fade and pass."

And I to him: "These truths bend my soul low
from swollen pride to sweet humility.
But who is he of whom you spoke just now?"

"That's Provenzan Salvani, and the stone
is on him," he replied, "for his presumption
in making all Siena his alone.

So he goes on and has gone since his death,
without a pause. Such coin must one pay here
for being too presumptuous on earth."

And I: "But if the souls that do not mend
their sinful ways until the brink of life,
must wait below before they can ascend

(unless the prayers of those whom God holds dear
come to their aid) the period of their lives—
how was he given license to be here?"

"At the peak of his life's glory," said the ghost,
"in the Campo of Siena, willingly,
and putting by all pride, he took his post;

and there, to free his dear friend from the pains
he suffered in the dungeons of King Charles,
stood firm, although he trembled in his veins.

I say no more; and though you well may feel
I speak in riddles, it will not be long
before your neighbors' actions will reveal

all you need know to fathom what I say.
—It was this good work spared him his delay."

Canto XII

THE FIRST CORNICE
The Proud

The Rein of Pride The Angel of Humility

VIRGIL instructs Dante to arise from where he has been walking bent beside Oderisi and to move on. Dante follows obediently, and soon Virgil points out to him THE REIN OF PRIDE carved in thirteen scenes into the stone beneath their feet. The scenes portray dreadful examples of the destruction that follows upon great pride.

The Poets pass on and find THE ANGEL OF HUMILITY approaching to welcome them. The Angel strikes Dante's forehead with his wings and, though Dante does not discover it till later, THE FIRST P instantly disappears without a trace, symbolizing the purification from the sin of Pride. The Poets pass on, up a narrow ASCENT TO THE SECOND CORNICE, but though the way is narrow, Dante finds it much easier than the first, since steps have been cut into it, and since he is lighter by the weight of the first P. As they climb they hear the first beatitude, Beati pauperes spiritu, *ring out behind them, sung by the Angel of Humility.*

As oxen go in yoke—step matched, head bowed—
I moved along beside that laden soul
as long as the sweet pedagogue allowed.

But when he said: "Leave him his weary trail:
here each must speed his boat as best he can
urging it onward with both oars and sail"—

I drew myself again to the position
required for walking: thus my body rose,
but my thoughts were still bent double in contrition.

I was following my Guide, and we had put
those laden souls behind us far enough
to make it clear that we were light of foot,

when he said, without turning back his head:
"Look down. You will find solace on the way
in studying what pavement your feet tread."

In order that some memory survive
of those who die, their slabs are often carved
to show us how they looked while yet alive.

And often at the sight a thought will stir
the passer-by to weep for what has been—
though only the compassionate feel that spur.

Just so, but with a far more lifelike grace—
they being divinely wrought—stone figures covered
the track that jutted from the mountain's face.

Mark there, on one side, him who had been given
a nobler form than any other creature.
He plunged like lightning from the peak of Heaven.

Mark, on the other, lying on the earth,
stricken by the celestial thunderbolt,
Briareus, heavy with the chill of death.

Mark there, still armed, ranged at their father's side,
Thymbraeus, Mars, and Pallas looking down
at the Giants' severed limbs strewn far and wide.

Mark Nimrod at the foot of his great tower,
bemused, confounded, staring at his people
who shared at Shinar his mad dream of power.

Ah, Niobe! with what eyes wrung with pain
I saw your likeness sculptured on that road
between your seven and seven children slain!

Ah, Saul! how still you seemed to me, run through
with your own sword, dead upon Mount Gilboa,
which never after that felt rain nor dew.

Ah mad Arachne! so I saw you there—
already half turned spider—on the shreds
of what you wove to be your own despair.

Ah Rehoboam! your image in that place
no longer menaces; a chariot bears it
in panic flight, though no one gives it chase.

Now see Alcmaeon, there on the hard pavement,
standing above her mother when she learned
the full cost of the fatal ornament.

Now see there how his own sons fell upon
Sennacherib at prayer within the temple,
and how they left him dead when they were done.

Now see Tomyris bloody with her kill
after the ruin she wrought, saying to Cyrus:
"Your thirst was all for blood. Now drink your fill."

Now see how the Assyrians broke and ran
from Israel after Holofernes' murder;
and showed the slaughtered remnants of the man.

Mark Troy there in its ashes overthrown.
Ah, Ilion! how lowly and how lost!
Now see your hollow shell upon that stone!

What brush could paint, or etching-stylus draw
such lineaments and shadings? At such skill
the subtlest genius would have stared in awe.

The dead seemed dead, the living alive. A witness

to the event itself saw it no better
than I did, looking down there at its likeness.

Now swell with pride and cut your reckless swath
with head held high, you sons of Eve, and never
bow down to see the evil in your path!

We had, I found, gone round more of the mount,
and the sun had run more of its daily course,
than my bound soul had taken into account;

when Virgil, ever watchful, ever leading,
commanded: "Lift your head. This is no time
to be shut up in your own thoughts, unheeding.

Look there and see an Angel on his way
to welcome us; and see—the sixth handmaiden
returns now from her service to the day.

That he may gladly send us up the mountain,
let reverence grace your gestures and your look.
Remember, this day will not dawn again."

I was well used to his warnings to abjure
all that delayed me from my good: on that point
nothing he said to me could be obscure.

Toward us, dressed in white, and with a face
serenely tremulous as the Morning Star,
the glorious being came, radiant with Grace.

First his arms and then his wings spread wide.
"Come," he said, "the stars are near, and now
the way is easy up the mountainside.

Few, all too few, come answering to this call.
O sons of man, born to ascend on high,

how can so slight a wind-puff make you fall?"

Straight to where the rock was cut he led.
There he struck my forehead with his wings,
then promised us safe journeying ahead.

When a man has climbed the first slope toward the crown
on which is built the church that overhangs
at the Rubaconte, the well-managed town,

the abrupt ascent is softened on his right
by steps cut in the rock in other days,
before the stave and ledger had grown light—

just so the bank here, plunging like a slide
from the Round above, has been made easier,
though towering cliffs squeeze us from either side.

We set out on the climb, and on the way
Beati pauperes spiritu rang out,
more sweetly sung than any words could say.

Ah, what a difference between these trails
and those of Hell: here every entrance fills
with joyous song, and there with savage wails!

We were going up the holy steps, and though
the climb was steep, I seemed to feel much lighter
than I had felt on level ground below.

"Master," I said, "tell me what heaviness
has been removed from me that I can climb
yet seem to feel almost no weariness."

He answered: "When the *P*'s that still remain,
though fading, on your brow, are wiped away
as the first was, without a trace of stain—

then will your feet be filled with good desire:
not only will they feel no more fatigue
but all their joy will be in mounting higher."

A man with some strange thing lodged on his hat
will stroll, not knowing, till the stares of others
set him to wonder what they're staring at:

whereat his hand seeks out and verifies
what he suspected, thus performing for him
the office he could not serve with his eyes—

just so, I put my right hand to my brow,
fingers outspread, and found six letters only
of those that had been carved there down below

by the Angel with the keys to every grace;
at which a smile shone on my Master's face.

Canto XIII

THE SECOND CORNICE
The Envious

The Whip of Envy

*The Poets reach THE SECOND CORNICE and find the blue-black rock
unadorned by carvings. There are no souls in sight to guide them and Virgil,
therefore, turns toward the Sun as his Guide, BEARING RIGHT around the
Cornice.*

*As they walk on, Dante hears voices crying out examples of great love of
others (CARITAS), the virtue opposed to Envy. These voices are THE WHIP OF
ENVY.*

*A short way beyond, Dante comes upon the souls of THE ENVIOUS and
describes THEIR PUNISHMENT. The Cornice on which they sit is the color of a
bruise, for every other man's good fortune bruised the souls of the Envious. They
offended with their eyes, envying all the good they saw of others, and therefore
their eyes are wired shut. So blinded, they sit supporting one another, as they
never did in life, and all of them lean for support against the blue-black cliff
(God's Decree). They are dressed in haircloth, the further to subdue their souls,
and they intone endlessly THE LITANY OF THE SAINTS.*

*Among them Dante encounters SAPÌA OF SIENA and has her relate her story.
When she questions him in turn, Dante confesses his fear of HIS OWN
BESETTING SIN, which is Pride.*

We climbed the stairs and stood, now, on the track
where, for a second time, the mount that heals
all who ascend it, had been terraced back.

The terrace circles the entire ascent
in much the same way as the one below,
save that the arc it cuts is sooner bent.

There were no spirits and no carvings there.

Bare was the cliff-face, bare the level path.
The rock of both was livid, dark and bare.

"Were we to wait till someone came this way
who might direct us," Virgil said to me,
"I fear that would involve a long delay."

Then he looked up and stared straight at the sun;
and then, using his right side as a pivot,
he swung his left around; then he moved on.

"O Blessed Lamp, we face the road ahead
placing our faith in you: lead us the way
that we should go in this new place," he said.

"You are the warmth of the world, you are its light;
if other cause do not urge otherwise,
your rays alone should serve to lead us right."

We moved on with a will, and in a while
we had already gone so far up there
as would be reckoned, here on earth, a mile;

when we began to hear in the air above
invisible spirits who flew toward us speaking
sweet invitations to the feast of love.

The first voice that flew past rang to the sky
"Vinum non habent." And from far behind us
we heard it fade repeating the same cry.

Even before we heard it cry its last
far round the slope, another voice rang out:
"I am Orestes!"—and it, too, sped past.

"Sweet Father," I began, "what are these cries?"—
and even as I asked, I heard a third

bodiless voice say: "Love your enemies."

And my good Master then: "This circle purges
the guilt of Envious spirits, and for these
who failed in Love, Love is the lash that scourges.

The Rein must cry the opposite of Love:
you will hear it, I expect, before you reach
the pass of absolution that leads above.

But now look carefully across the air
ahead of us, and you will see some people
seated against the inner cliff up there."

I opened my eyes wider: further on
I saw a group of spirits dressed in cloaks
exactly the same color as the stone.

As we drew nearer I heard prayers and plaints.
"O Mary, pray for us," I heard them cry;
and to Michael, and to Peter, and all Saints.

I cannot think there walks the earth today
a man so hard that he would not be moved
by what I saw next on that ashen way.

For when I drew near and could see the whole
penance imposed upon those praying people,
my eyes milked a great anguish from my soul.

Their cloaks were made of haircloth, coarse and stiff.
Each soul supported another with his shoulder,
and all leaned for support against the cliff.

The impoverished blind who sit all in a row
during Indulgences to beg their bread
lean with their heads together exactly so,

the better to win the pity they beseech,
not only with their cries, but with their look
of fainting grief, which pleads as loud as speech.

Just as the sun does not reach to their sight,
so to those shades of which I spoke just now
God's rays refuse to offer their delight;

for each soul has its eyelids pierced and sewn
with iron wires, as men sew new-caught falcons,
sealing their eyes to make them settle down.

Somehow it seemed to me a shameful act
to stare at others and remain unseen.
I turned to Virgil. He, with perfect tact,

knew what the mute was laboring to say
and did not wait my question. "Speak," he said,
"but count your words and see they do not stray."

Virgil was walking by me down the ledge
on the side from which—because no parapet
circled the cliff—one might plunge off the edge.

On the other side those spirits kept their places
absorbed in prayer, while through the ghastly stitches
tears forced their way and flowed down from their faces.

I turned to them and said: "O souls afire
with hope of seeing Heaven's Light, and thus
already certain of your heart's desire—

so may High Grace soon wash away the scum
that clogs your consciousness, that memory's stream
may flow without a stain in joys to come—

tell me if there is any Latin soul
among you here: I dearly wish to know,
and telling me may help him to his goal."

—"We are all citizens of one sublime
and final city, brother; you mean to ask
who lived in Italy in his pilgrim-time."

These are the words I heard a spirit say
from somewhere further on. I moved up, therefore,
in order to direct my voice that way.

I saw one shade who seemed to have in mind
what I had said.—How could I tell? She sat
chin raised, the waiting gesture of the blind.

"O soul self-humbled for the climb to Grace,"
I said, "if it was you who spoke, I beg you,
make yourself known either by name or place."

"I was Sienese," she answered. "On this shelf
I weep away my world-guilt with these others
in prayers to Him that he vouchsafe Himself.

Sapìa was I, though sapient I was not;
I found more joy in the bad luck of others
than in the good that fell to my own lot.

If this confession rings false to your ears,
hear my tale out; then see if I was mad.
—In the descending arc of my own years,

the blood of my own land was being spilled
in battle outside Colle's walls, and I
prayed God to do what He already willed.

So were they turned—their forces overthrown—

to the bitter paths of flight; and as I watched
I felt such joy as I had never known;

such that I raised my face, flushed with false power,
and screamed to God: 'Now I no longer fear you'—
like a blackbird when the sun comes out an hour.

Not till my final hour had all but set
did I turn back to God, longing for peace.
Penance would not yet have reduced my debt

had not Pier Pettinaio in saintly love
grieved for my soul and offered holy prayers
that interceded for me there above.

But who are you that you come here to seek
such news of us; and have your eyes unsewn,
as I believe; and breathe yet when you speak?"

"My eyes," I said, "will yet be taken from me
upon this ledge, but not for very long:
little they sinned through being turned in envy.

My soul is gripped by a far greater fear
of the torment here below, for even now
I seem to feel the burden those souls bear."

And she: "Then who has led you to this Round,
if you think to go below again?" And I:
"He who is with me and who makes no sound.

And I still live: if you would have me move
my mortal feet down there in your behalf,
ask what you will, O soul blessed by God's love."

"Oh," she replied, "this is a thing so rare
it surely means that God has loved you greatly;

from time to time, then, help me with a prayer.

I beg by all you most desire to win
that if you walk again on Tuscan soil
you will restore my name among my kin.

You will find them in that foolish mob whose dream
is Talamone now, and who will lose there
more than they did once in their silly scheme

to find the lost Diana. Though on that coast
it is the admirals who will lose the most."

Canto XIV

Dante's conversation with Sapìa of Siena is overheard by two spirits who sit side by side against the inner cliff-face. They are GUIDO DEL DUCA and RINIERI DA CALBOLI.

Dante enters into conversation with them, and Guido denounces the inhabitants of the cities of the Valley of the Arno. He then prophesies the slaughter that Rinieri's grandson, FULCIERI, shall visit upon Florence. And he prophesies also that Fulcieri's actions will have a bearing on Dante's approaching exile from Florence. Guido concludes with a lament for the past glories of Romagna as compared to its present degeneracy.

Leaving the two spirits in tears, Dante and Virgil move on, and they have hardly left when Dante is struck with terror by two bodiless voices that break upon them like thunder. The voices are THE REIN OF ENVY. The first is THE VOICE OF CAIN lamenting that he is forever cut off from mankind. The second is THE VOICE OF AGLAUROS, who was changed to stone as a consequence of her envy of her sister.

Virgil concludes the Canto with a denunciation of mankind's stubborn refusal to heed the glory of the Heavens and to prepare for eternal Grace.

"Who do you think that is? He roams our hill
before death gives him wings, and he's left free
to shut his eyes or open them at will."

"I don't know, but I know he's not alone. Ask him—you're nearer—but put in a way that won't offend him. Take a careful tone."

Thus, on my right, and leaning head to head,
two of those spirits were discussing me.
Then they turned up their faces, and one said:

"O soul that though locked fast within the flesh
still makes its way toward Heaven's blessedness,
in charity, give comfort to our wish:

tell us your name and city, for your climb
fills us with awe at such a gift of grace
as never has been seen up to this time."

And I: "In Falterona lies the source
of a brook that grows and winds through Tuscany
till a hundred miles will not contain its course.

From its banks I bring this flesh. As for my name—
to tell you who I am would serve no purpose:
I have as yet won very little fame."

And the first spirit: "If I rightly weigh
your words upon the balance of my mind,
it is the Arno you intend to say."

And the other to him: "Why is he so careful
to avoid the river's name? He speaks as men do
when they refer to things too foul or fearful."

To which the shade he had addressed replied:
"That I don't know; but it would be a mercy
if even the name of such a valley died.

From its source high in the great range that outsoars
almost all others (from whose chain Pelorus
was cut away), to the point where it restores

in endless soft surrender what the sun
draws from the deep to fall again as rain,
that every rill and river may flow on,

men run from virtue as if from a foe

or poisonous snake. Either the land is cursed,
or long-corrupted custom drives them so.

And curse or custom so transform all men
who live there in that miserable valley,
one would believe they fed in Circe's pen.

It sets its first weak course among sour swine,
indecent beasts more fit to grub and grunt
for acorns than to sit to bread and wine.

It finds next, as it flows down and fills out,
a pack of curs, their snarl worse than their bite;
and in contempt it turns aside its snout.

Down, down it flows, and as the dogs grow fewer
the wolves grow thicker on the widening banks
of that accursed and God-forsaken sewer.

It drops through darkened gorges, then, to find
the foxes in their lairs, so full of fraud
they fear no trap set by a mortal mind.

Nor will I, though this man hear what I say,
hold back the prophecy revealed to me;
for well may he recall it on his way.

I see your grandson riding to the chase.
He hunts the wolves that prowl by the fierce river.
He has become the terror of that place.

He sells their living flesh, then—shame on shame—
the old beast slaughters them himself, for sport.
Many will die, and with them, his good name.

He comes from that sad wood covered with gore,
and leaves it in such ruin, a thousand years

will not serve to restock its groves once more."

Just as a man to whom bad chance announces
a dreadful ill, distorts his face in grief,
no matter from what quarter the hurt pounces—

just so that shade, who had half turned his head
better to listen, showed his shock and pain
when he had registered what the other said.

So moved by one's words and the other's face,
I longed to know their names. I asked them, therefore,
phrasing my plea with prayers to win their grace;

at which the spokesman of the two replied:
"You beg me of my good grace that I grant you
what I have asked of you and been denied;

but God has willed His favor to shine forth
so greatly in you, I cannot be meager:
Guido del Duca was my name on earth.

The fires of envy raged so in my blood
that I turned livid if I chanced to see
another man rejoice in his own good.

This seed I sowed; this sad straw I reap here.
O humankind, why do you set your hearts
on what it is forbidden you to share?

This is Rinier, the honor and the pride
of the house of the Calboli, of which no one
inherited his merit when he died.

Nor in that war-torn land whose boundary-lines
the sea and the Reno draw to the east and west;
and, north and south, the Po and the Apennines,

is his the only house that seems to be
bred bare of those accomplishments and merits
which are the good and truth of chivalry.

For the land has lost the good of hoe and plow,
and poisonous thorns so choke it that long years
of cultivation would scarce clear it now.

Where is Mainardi? Have you lost the seed
of Lizio? Traversaro? di Carpigna?
O Romagnoles changed to a bastard breed!

When will a Fabbro evermore take root
in all Bologna? or in Faenza, a Fosco?—
who was his little plant's most noble shoot.

O Tuscan, can I speak without a tear
of Ugolino d'Azzo and Guido da Prata,
who shared our time on earth? and with them there

Federico di Tignoso and his train?
the house of the Traversari and the Anastagi,
both heirless now? or, dry-eyed, think again

of knights and ladies, of the court and field
that bonded us in love and courtesy
where now all hearts are savagely self-sealed?

O Brettinoro, why do you delay?
Your lords and many more have fled your guilt;
and why, like them, will you not melt away?

Bagnacaval does well to have no heirs;
and Castrocaro badly, and Conio worse
in bothering to breed such Counts as theirs.

The Pagani will do well enough, all told,
when once their fiend is gone, but not so well
their name will ever again shine as pure gold.

O Ugolin de' Fantolini, your name
remains secure, since you have none to bear it
and, in degeneracy, bring it to shame.

But leave me, Tuscan, I am more inclined
to spell my grief in tears now than in words;
for speaking thus has wrung my heart and mind."

We knew those dear souls heard us go away.
Their silence, therefore, served as our assurance
that, leaving them, we had not gone astray.

We had scarce left those spirits to their prayer,
when suddenly a voice that ripped like lightning
struck at us with a cry that split the air:

"All men are my destroyers!" It rolled past
as thunder rolls away into the sky
if the cloud bursts to rain in the first blast.

Our ears were scarcely settled from that burst
when lo, the second broke, with such a crash
it seemed the following thunder of the first:

"I am Aglauros who was turned to stone!"
Whereat, to cower in Virgil's arms, I took
a step to my right instead of going on.

The air had fallen still on every hand
when Virgil said: "That was the iron bit
that ought to hold men hard to God's command.

But still you gulp the Hellbait hook and all

and the Old Adversary reels you in.
Small good to you is either curb or call.

The Heavens cry to you, and all around
your stubborn souls, wheel their eternal glory,
and yet you keep your eyes fixed on the ground.

And for each turning from the joys of Love
the All-Discerning flails you from above."

Dante's riddle-like answer to a simple question, though it appears to be mere

Canto XV

THE SECOND CORNICE
THE ASCENT
THE THIRD CORNICE
The Envious
The Angel of Caritas
The Wrathful

The Whip of Wrath

*It is 3:00 P.M. and the Poets are walking straight into the sun when an even
greater radiance blinds Dante and he finds himself in the presence of THE
ANGEL OF CARITAS who passes the Poets on to the ledge above. As they
ascend, they hear the Angel sing THE FIFTH BEATITUDE.*

*As soon as the Poets enter THE THIRD CORNICE, Dante is entranced by
THREE VISIONS which constitute THE WHIP OF WRATH, extolling the virtue
of MEEKNESS toward kin, toward friends, and toward enemies.*

*These events consume three hours. It is, therefore, 6:00 P.M. of THE SECOND
DAY IN PURGATORY when the Poets, moving forward, observe an enormous
CLOUD OF SMOKE ahead of them.*

Of that bright Sphere that, like a child at play,
skips endlessly, as much as lies between
the third hour's end and the first light of day

remained yet of the Sun's course toward the night.
Thus, it was Vespers there upon the mountain
and midnight here in Italy, where I write.

The Sun's late rays struck us full in the face,
for in our circling course around the mountain
we now were heading toward his resting place.

Suddenly, then, I felt my brow weighed down
by a much greater splendor than the first.
I was left dazzled by some cause unknown

and raised my hands and joined them in the air
above my brows, making a sunshade of them
which, so to speak, blunted the piercing glare.

When a ray strikes glass or water, its reflection
leaps upward from the surface once again
at the same angle but opposite direction

from which it strikes, and in an equal space
spreads equally from a plumb-line to mid-point,
as trial and theory show to be the case.

Just so, it seemed to me, reflected light
struck me from up ahead, so dazzlingly
I had to shut my eyes to spare my sight.

"Dear Father, what is that great blaze ahead
from which I cannot shade my eyes enough,
and which is still approaching us?" I said.

"Do not be astonished," answered my sweet Friend
"if those of the Heavenly Family still blind you.
He has been sent to bid us to ascend.

Soon now, such sights will not aggrieve your sense
but fill you with a joy as great as any
Nature has fitted you to experience."

We stand before the Blessed Angel now.
With joyous voice he cries: "Enter. The stair
is far less steep than were the two below."

We had gone past him and were climbing on
when *Blessed are the merciful* hymned out
behind us, and *Rejoice you who have won.*

My Guide and I were going up the stair—

we two alone—and I, thinking to profit
from his wise words as we were climbing there,

questioned him thus: "What deep intent lay hidden
in what the spirit from Romagna said?
He spoke of 'sharing' and said it was 'forbidden.' "

And he: "He knows the sad cost of his own
besetting sin: small wonder he reviles it
in hope that you may have less to atone.

It is because you focus on the prize
of worldly goods, which every sharing lessens
that Envy pumps the bellows for your sighs.

But if, in true love for the Highest Sphere,
your longing were turned upward, then your hearts
would never be consumed by such a fear;

for the more there are there who say 'ours'—not 'mine'—
by that much is each richer, and the brighter
within that cloister burns the Love Divine."

"I am left hungrier being thus fed,
and my mind is more in doubt being thus answered,
than if I had not asked at all," I said.

"How can each one of many who divide
a single good have more of it, so shared,
than if a few had kept it?" He replied:

"Because within the habit of mankind
you set your whole intent on earthly things,
the true light falls as darkness on your mind.

The infinite and inexpressible Grace
which is in Heaven, gives itself to Love

as a sunbeam gives itself to a bright surface.

As much light as it finds there, it bestows;
thus, as the blaze of Love is spread more widely,
the greater the Eternal Glory grows.

As mirror reflects mirror, so, above,
the more there are who join their souls, the more
Love learns perfection, and the more they love.

And if this answer does not yet appease
your hunger, you will soon see Beatrice,
and this, and every wish, shall find surcease.

Only strive hard that soon no trace may show
of the five scars which true contrition heals—
as the first two have faded from your brow."

I was about to say, "I am satisfied,"
when suddenly we came to the next Round,
and my eyes' avidity left me tongue-tied.

Here suddenly, in an ecstatic trance,
I find myself caught up into a vision.
I see a crowded temple, and in the entrance

a lady by herself, her eyes aglow
with the sweet grace of a mother, saying gently:
"My son, my son, why do you treat us so?

Your father and I were seeking you in tears."
So saying, she falls silent, and as quickly
as it first came, the vision disappears.

Another lady now appears, her cheeks
bathed in those waters that are born of grief
when grief is born of anger. Now she speaks:

"O Pisistratus, if you are true Lord
of the city for whose name the Gods debated,
and whence all learning shone forth afterward,

avenge yourself on the presumptuous one
who dared embrace our daughter." And her
master, sweetly forbearing, in a placid tone,

and smiling gently at her, answers thus:
"What shall we do to those that wish us harm
if we take vengeance upon those that love us?"

Then there appears a wild and murderous spill
of people hate-incensed, stoning a boy,
and roaring to each other's wrath: "Kill! Kill!"

I see the boy sink to the ground, his death
already heavy on him, but his eyes,
like gates of Heaven, open through such wrath;

and even in his last extremity
he prays God to forgive his murderers,
turning to Him the look that unlocks pity.

When finally my soul could see and feel
things which were true outside it, I understood
my not-false errors had been dreams, though real.

My Guide, who watched me as I moved along
like one just wakened and still sleep-stunned, said:
"You barely seem to keep your feet—what's wrong?

You've stumbled on now for a good half-league
with eyes half-shut and legs too-wide, like one
groggy with wine or dropping with fatigue."

"O my sweet Father, if you wish to know,
listen, and I shall tell you what I saw,"
I answered, "when my legs were stricken so."

"Were you to wear a hundred masks," he said,
"to hide your face, it would lie open to me
so that your slightest thought might yet be read.

These visions warn your soul on no account
still to refuse the water of that peace
which flows to man from the Eternal Fount.

I did not ask 'what's wrong' as a man might
who sees with eyes alone, and when the body
is lying senseless has no other sight;

but rather to put strength into your stride:
for so must laggards be spurred on to use
their reawakening senses as a guide."

Through the last vesper-hour we traveled on,
looking ahead as far as eye could see
against the level rays of the late sun.

And there ahead of us against the light
we saw come billowing in our direction
by slow degrees, a smoke as black as night.

Nor was there refuge from it anywhere.
It took our sight from us, and the pure air.

NOTES

1-6. *that bright Sphere that . . . skips endlessly:* Despite the fact that Dante
says "Sphere" rather than "great circle" or "zone," the reference here is best
taken to be to the zodiac, which dips above and below the horizon and may,

48. *you:* You living men. Mankind in general.
51. *that Envy pumps the bellows for your sighs:* A Dantean figure. Envy seems

Canto XVI

THE THIRD CORNICE
The Wrathful
Marco Lombardo

The Poets enter the acrid and blinding smoke in which THE WRATHFUL suffer their purification. As Wrath is a corrosive state of the spirit, so the smoke stings and smarts. As Wrath obscures the true light of God, so the smoke plunges all into darkness. Within it, Dante hears souls singing THE LITANY OF THE LAMB OF GOD. The Lamb, of course, is the symbol of the MEEKNESS of Divine Love. As such, it is the opposite of Wrath. A further purification is implicit in the fact that the souls all sing as if with one voice, for Wrath is the sin that soonest breeds division among men, and only Spiritual Concord can reunite them.

MARCO LOMBARDO hears Dante speak and calls to him. Invited by Dante, Marco accompanies the Poets to the edge of the smoke, discoursing on the causes of the modern world's corruption, which he locates in the usurpation of temporal power and wealth by the Church. As Marco concludes, a light begins to appear through the smoke. Marco explains that it is the radiance of the Angel who waits ahead. He then turns back, for he is not yet fit to show himself to the Angel of the Lord.

No gloom of Hell, nor of a night allowed
no planet under its impoverished sky,
the deepest dark that may be drawn by cloud;

ever drew such a veil across my face,
nor one whose texture rasped my senses so,
as did the smoke that wrapped us in that place.

The sting was more than open eyes could stand.
My wise and faithful Guide drew near me, therefore,
and let me grasp his shoulder with my hand.

Just as a blindman—lest he lose his road
or tumble headlong and be hurt or killed—

walks at his guide's back when he goes abroad;

so moved I through that foul and acrid air,
led by my sweet Friend's voice, which kept repeating:
"Take care. Do not let go of me. Take care."

And I heard other voices. They seemed to pray
for peace and pardon to the Lamb of God
which, of Its mercy, takes our sins away.

They offered up three prayers, and every one
began with *Agnus Dei*, and each word
and measure rose in perfect unison.

"Master, do I hear spirits on this path?"
I said. And he to me: "You do indeed,
and they are loosening the knot of Wrath."

"And who are you, then, that you cleave our smoke,
yet speak of us as if you still kept time
by kalends?"—without warning, someone spoke

these words to me; at which my Lord and Guide
said: "Answer. And inquire respectfully
if one may find a way-up on this side."

And I: "O spirit growing pure and free
to go once more in beauty to your Maker—
you will hear wonders if you follow me."

"As far as is permitted me," he said,
"I will. And if the smoke divide our eyes,
our ears shall serve to join us in their stead."

So I began: "I make my way above
still in these swathings death dissolves. I came here
through the Infernal grief. Now, since God's love

incloses me in Grace so bounteous
that he permits me to behold His court
by means wholly unknown to modern use—

pray tell me who you were before you died,
and if I go the right way to the pass
that leads above. Your words shall be our guide."

"I was a Lombard. Marco was my name.
I knew the ways of the world, and loved that good
at which the bows of men no longer aim.

You are headed the right way to reach the stair
that leads above," he added. And: "I pray you
to pray for me when you have mounted there."

And I: "On my faith I vow it. But a doubt
has formed within me and has swelled so large
I shall explode unless I speak it out.

It was a simple doubt at first, but now
it doubles and grows sure as I compare
your words with what was said to me below.

The world, as you have said, is truly bare
of every trace of good; swollen with evil;
by evil overshadowed everywhere.

But wherein lies the fault? I beg to know
that I may see the truth and so teach others.
Some see it in the stars; some, here below."

A deep sigh wrung by grief, almost a moan
escaped as a long "Ah!" Then he said: "Brother,
the world is blind and you are its true son.

Mankind sees in the heavens alone the source
of all things, good and evil; as if by Law
they shaped all mortal actions in their course.

If that were truly so, then all Free Will
would be destroyed, and there would be no justice
in giving bliss for virtue, pain for evil.

The spheres *do* start your impulses along.
I do not say *all*, but suppose I did—
the light of reason still tells right from wrong;

and Free Will also, which, though it be strained
in the first battles with the heavens, still
can conquer all if it is well sustained.

You are free subjects of a more immense
nature and power which grants you intellect
to free you from the heavens' influence.

If, therefore, men today turn from God's laws,
the fault is in yourselves to seek and find;
and I shall truly explicate the cause:

From the hand of God, whose love shines like a ray
upon it, even before birth, comes forth
the simple soul which, like a child at play,

cries, laughs, and ignorant of every measure
but the glad impulse of its joyous Maker,
turns eagerly to all that gives it pleasure.

It tastes small pleasures first. To these it clings,
deceived, and seeks no others, unless someone
curb it, or guide its love to higher things.

Men, therefore, need restraint by law, and need

a monarch over them who sees at least
the towers of The True City. Laws, indeed,

there are, but who puts nations to their proof?
No one. The shepherd who now leads mankind
can chew the cud, but lacks the cloven hoof.

The people, then, seeing their guide devour
those worldly things to which their hunger turns
graze where he grazes, and ask nothing more.

The bad state of the modern world is due—
as you may see, then—to bad leadership;
and not to natural corruption in you.

Rome used to shine in two suns when her rod
made the world good, and each showed her its way:
one to the ordered world, and one to God.

Now one declining sun puts out the other.
The sword and crook are one, and only evil
can follow from them when they are together;

for neither fears the other, being one.
Look closely at the ear, if still you doubt me,
for by the seed it bears is the plant known.

Honor and Courtesy once made their home
in the land the Po and the Adige water—
till Frederick came to loggerheads with Rome.

Now any man who has good cause to fear
the sound of truth or honest company
may cross it safely—he will find none there.

True, three old men are left in whom the past
reproves the present. How time drags for them

till God remove them to their joy at last—

Conrad da Palazzo, the good Gherard',
and Guido da Castel, who is better named,
in the fashion of the French, 'The Honest Lombard.'

Say, then, that since the Church has sought to be
two governments at once, she sinks in muck,
befouling both her power and ministry."

"O Marco mine," I said, "you reason well!
And now I know why Levi's sons alone
could not inherit wealth in Israel.

But who is this Gherard' in whom you say
the past survives untarnished to reprove
the savage breed of this degenerate day?"

"Your question seeks to test me," said Lombardo,
"or else to trick me. How can you speak Tuscan
and still seem to know nothing of Gherardo?

Just what his surname is, I do not know—
unless he might be known as Gaia's father.
Godspeed: this is as far as I may go.

See there across the smoke, like dawn's first rays,
the light swell like a glory and a guide.
The Angel of this place gives forth that blaze,

and it is not fit he see me." Thus he spoke,
and said no more, but turned back through the smoke.

Canto XVII

THE FOURTH CORNICE
The Wrathful

The Rein of Wrath

THE ASCENT
The Angel of Meekness

The Poets emerge from the smoke and Dante is immediately enrapt by the visions that make up THE REIN OF WRATH. In succession he beholds THE DESTRUCTION CAUSED BY WRATH to PROCNE, to HAMAN, and to QUEEN AMATA. Dante emerges from his trance to hear THE ANGEL OF MEEKNESS calling to him to show him the ascent, and the Poets mount at once as the Beatitude, Blessed are the Peacemakers, *is sounded behind them.*

They reach the top of the Ascent just as night falls, and though they might normally continue along the level way Dante feels his body so weighed down that he has to pause and rest.

As the Poets rest, Virgil gives Dante a DISCOURSE ON LOVE, demonstrating to him that all actions spring from either NATURAL or SPIRITUAL LOVE, and that it is the various PERVERSIONS OF LOVE that lead to the sins that are punished in Purgatory.

Reader, if you have ever been closed in
by mountain mist that left you with no eyes
to see with, save as moles do, through the skin;

think how those dense damp vapors thinned away
slow bit by bit till through them the sun's ball
was once more dimly visible—thus you may,

and without strain, imagine from your own
recalled experience how I came again
to see the Sun, which now was almost down.

Thus, matching steps with my true Guide once more,
I passed beyond the cloud into those rays

which lay already dead on the low shore.

O Fantasy, which can entrance us so
that we at times stand and are not aware
though in our ears a thousand trumpets blow!—

what moves you since our senses lie dead then?
—A light that forms in Heaven of itself,
or of His will who sends its rays to men.

A vision grew within me of the wrong
she did who for her cruelty was changed
into that bird which most delights in song;

and my imagination was so shut
into itself that what I saw revealed
could never have come to me from without.

Next, down like rain, a figure crucified
fell into my high fantasy, his face
fierce and contemptuous even as he died.

Nearby him great Ahasuerus stood,
Esther his wife, and the just Mordecai
whose word and deed were always one in good.

And as soap bubbles rise in air and seem
full-bodied things, then rupture of themselves
when the film about them breaks, just so that dream

vanished, and through my vision rose an image
in which a maid cried: "O Queen! Queen no more!
Your very being canceled by your rage!

All not to lose Lavinia? Ah, mother,
now have you truly lost her. I am she,
and mourn your death before I mourn another."

When strong light beats against a man's closed eyes
his sleep is broken in him; yet, though broken,
gives a last twitch before it wholly dies:

my vision fell from me exactly so
the instant a new light beat on my face,
a light outshining any that men know.

I was looking all about, as if to find
where I might be, when a new voice that cried,
"Here is the ascent" drove all else from my mind;

and kindled in my spirit such a fire
to see who spoke, as cannot ever rest
till it stand face to face with its desire.

But, as in looking at the sun, whose rays
keep his form hidden from our stricken eyes—
so I lacked power to look into that blaze.

"A spirit of Heaven guides us toward the height:
he shows us the ascent before we ask,
and hides himself in his own holy light.

He does for us what men in the world's uses
do only for themselves; for who sees need
and waits a plea, already half refuses.

To such sweet bidding let our feet reply
by striving as they may before night fall;
for then they may not, till day light the sky."

So spoke my Guide, and he and I as one
moved toward the ascent; and soon as I had mounted
the first step cut into that ramp of stone,

I felt what seemed to be a great wing fan
my face and heard: "Blessèd are the peacemakers,
who feel no evil wrath toward any man."

The last rays, after which night rules the air,
were now so far above us that already
the stars began to shine through, here and there.

"O strength, why do you melt away?" I said
several times over to myself, for now
it seemed my legs were turning into lead.

We had come to where the stair ascends no more
and we were stuck fast on the topmost step
like a vessel half drawn up upon the shore.

I waited with my head cocked to one side
for any sound that might reveal the nature
of the new ledge. Then, turning to my Guide,

I said: "Dear Father, what impurity
is washed in pain here? Though our feet must stay,
I beg you not to stay your speech." And he:

"That love of good which in the life before
lay idle in the soul is paid for now.
Here Sloth strains at the once-neglected oar.

But that you may more clearly know The Way,
give your entire attention to my words;
thus shall you gather good fruit from delay.

Neither Creator nor his creatures move,
as you well know," he said, "but in the action
of animal or of mind-directed love.

Natural love may never fall to error.

The other may, by striving to bad ends,
or by too little, or by too much fervor.

While it desires the Eternal Good and measures
its wish for secondary goods in reason,
this love cannot give rise to sinful pleasures.

But when it turns to evil, or shows more
or less zeal than it ought for what is good,
then the creature turns on its Creator.

Thus you may understand that love alone
is the true seed of every merit in you,
and of all acts for which you must atone.

Now inasmuch as love cannot abate
its good wish for the self that loves, all things
are guarded by their nature from self-hate.

And since no being may exist alone
and apart from the First Being, by their nature,
all beings lack the power to hate That One.

Therefore, if I have parsed the truth of things,
the evil that man loves must be his neighbor's.
In mortal clay such bad love has three springs:

some think they see their own hope to advance
tied to their neighbor's fall, and thus they long
to see him cast down from his eminence;

some fear their power, preferment, honor, fame
will suffer by another's rise, and thus,
irked by his good, desire his ruin and shame;

and some at the least injury catch fire
and are consumed by thoughts of vengeance; thus,

their neighbor's harm becomes their chief desire.

Such threefold love those just below us here
purge from their souls. The other, which seeks good,
but without measure, I shall now make clear.—

All men, though in a vague way, apprehend
a good their souls may rest in, and desire it;
each, therefore, strives to reach his chosen end.

If you are moved to see good or pursue it,
but with a lax love, it is on this ledge—
after a proper penance—you will rue it.

There is another good which bears bad fruit:
it is not happiness, nor the true essence
of the Eternal Good, its flower and root.

The love that yields too much to this false good
is mourned on the three Cornices above us;
but in what way it may be understood

as a tripartite thing, I shall not say.
That, you may learn yourself upon our way."

Canto XVIII

THE FOURTH CORNICE
The Sloth ful

The Whip of Sloth
The Rein of Sloth

Virgil continues his DISCOURSE ON LOVE, explaining THE RELATION OF LOVE AND FREE WILL, but warns Dante that Reason is limited. Dante must seek the final answer from Beatrice, for the question involves one of the mysteries of faith.

It is near midnight when Virgil concludes, and Dante is starting to drowse, when he is suddenly brought awake by a long train of souls who come running and shouting from around the mountain. They are THE SLOTHFUL, the souls of those who recognized The Good but were not diligent in pursuit of it. As once they delayed, so now they are all hurry and zeal, and will not even pause to speak to the Poets.

Two souls run before the rest shouting aloud THE WHIP OF SLOTH, one citing Mary as an example of holy zeal, the other citing Caesar as an example of temporal zeal.

Virgil hails the racing souls to ask the nearer way to the ascent, but not even the news that Dante is still alive slows them. One soul, a former ABBOT OF SAN ZENO, shouts back an answer while still running.

Behind the train come two more souls shouting THE REIN OF SLOTH, citing as examples of the downfall of the laggard, the Israelites in the desert, and those followers of Aeneas who remained in Sicily.

The souls pass from sight and hearing. Dante, his head full of confused thoughts, sinks into sleep. Instantly, his thoughts are transformed into A DREAM.

His explanation at an end, My Guide,
that lofty scholar, scrutinized my face
as if to see if I seemed satisfied.

And I, my thirst already sprung anew,
said nothing, thinking "He may well be tired
of all this questioning I put him through."

But that true Father, sensing both my thirst
and that I was too timid to reveal it,
encouraged me to speak by speaking first.

I, therefore: "Master, in the light you shed
my sight grows so acute that I see clearly
all that your argument implied or said.

But, dear and gentle Father, please discourse
more fully on that love in which you say
all good and evil actions have their source."

And he: "Focus the keen eyes of your mind
on what I say, and you will see made clear
the error of the blind who lead the blind.

The soul, being created prone to Love,
is drawn at once to all that pleases it,
as soon as pleasure summons it to move.

From that which really is, your apprehension
extracts a form which it unfolds within you;
that form thereby attracts the mind's attention,

then if the mind, so drawn, is drawn to it,
that summoning force is Love; and thus within you,
through pleasure, a new natural bond is knit.

Then, just as fire yearns upward through the air,
being so formed that it aspires by nature
to be in its own element up there;

so love, which is a spiritual motion,

fills the trapped soul, and it can never rest
short of the thing that fills it with devotion.

By now you will, of course, have understood
how little of the truth they see who claim
that every love is, in itself, a good;

for though love's substance always will appear
to be a good, not every impress made,
even in finest wax, is good and clear."

"Your words and my own eager mind reveal
exactly what Love is," I said, "but now
there is an even greater doubt I feel:

if love springs from outside the soul's own will,
it being made to love, what merit is there
in loving good, or blame in loving ill?"

And he to me: "As far as reason sees,
I can reply. The rest you must ask Beatrice.
The answer lies within faith's mysteries.

Every substantial form distinct from matter
and yet united with it in some way,
has a specific power in it. This latter

is not perceivable save as it gives
evidence of its workings and effects—
as the green foliage tells us a plant lives.

Therefore, no man can know whence springs the light
of his first cognizance, nor of the bent
of such innate primordial appetite

as springs within you, as within the bee
the instinct to make honey; and such instincts

are, in themselves, not blamable nor worthy.

Now, that all later wills and this first bent
may thrive, the innate counsel of your Reason
must surely guard the threshold of consent.

This is the principle from which accrue
your just desserts, according as it reaps
and winnows good or evil love in you.

Those masters who best reasoned nature's plan
discerned this innate liberty, and therefore
they left their moral science to guide Man.

Or put it this way: all love, let us say,
that burns in you, springs from necessity;
but you still have the power to check its sway.

These noble powers Beatrice will comprehend
as 'The Free Will.' Keep that term well in mind
if she should speak of it when you ascend."

It was near midnight. The late-risen moon,
like a brass bucket polished bright as fire,
thinned out the lesser stars, which seemed to drown.

It traveled retrograde across that sign
the sun burns when the Romans look between
the Sards and Corsicans to its decline.

And he who made Piètola shine above
all other Mantuan towns, had discharged fully
the burden I had laid on him for love;

because of which I, being pleased to find
such clear and open answers to my questions,
was rambling drowsily within my mind.

I wakened in an instant to a pack
of people running toward us, a great mob
that broke around the mountain at my back:

as once, of old, wild hordes ran through the night
along Ismenus' and Asopus' banks
when Thebes invoked no more than Bacchus' might;

in such a frenzy, far as I could see,
those who were spurred by good will and high love
ran bent like scythes along that Cornice toward me.

They were upon us soon, for all that rout
was running furiously, and out in front
two spirits streaming tears were calling out:

"Mary *ran* to the hills"—so one refrain;
and the other: "Caesar, to subdue Ilerda
struck at Marseilles, and then *swooped* down on Spain."

"Faster! Faster! To be slow in love
is to lose time," cried those who came behind;
"Strive on that grace may bloom again above."

"O souls in whom the great zeal you now show
no doubt redeems the negligence and delay
that marred your will to do good, there below;

this man lives—truly—and the instant day
appears again, he means to climb. Please show him
how he may reach the pass the nearer way."

So spoke my Master, and one running soul
without so much as breaking step replied:
"Come after us, and you will find the hole.

The will to move on with all speed so fills us
we cannot stop; we humbly beg your pardon
if duty makes us seem discourteous.

I was abbot of San Zeno in the reign
of the good emperor Frederick Barbarossa,
of whom the Milanese still speak with pain.

And another with one foot now in the grave
will shed tears for that monastery soon,
and rue the evil orders he once gave.

For he has set his son up as the head—
a man deformed in body, worse in mind,
and bastard born—in its true Pastor's stead."

He had by then left us so far behind
that if he said more, it was lost to me:
but I was pleased to keep this much in mind.

My aid on all occasion, the prompt Master,
said: "Look, for here come two who cry aloud
the Scourge of Sloth, that souls may flee it faster."

At the tail end one runner cried: "They died
before the Jordan saw its heirs, those people
for whom the Red Sea's waters stood aside."

The other: "Those who found it too laborious
to go the whole way with Anchises' son
cut from their own lives all that was most glorious."

Then when those shades had drawn so far ahead
that I could not make out a trace of them,
a new thought seized upon me, and it bred

so many more, so various, and so scrambled,

that turning round and round inside itself
so many ways at once, my reason rambled;

I closed my eyes and all that tangled theme
was instantly transformed into a dream.

Canto XIX

THE FOURTH CORNICE
The Slothful

Dante's Dream of Sirena

THE ASCENT
THE FIFTH CORNICE
The Angel of Zeal
The Hoarders and Wasters (The Avaricious)

Just before morning (when the truth is dreamed) Dante dreams of THE SIREN that lures the souls of men to incontinent worldliness. Hideous in her true form, the Siren grows irresistible in men's eyes as they look upon her. A HEAVENLY LADY races in upon the dream and calls to Virgil who, thus summoned, strips the Siren, exposing her filthy body. Such a stench rises from her, so exposed, that Dante wakens shuddering, to find Virgil calling him to resume the journey.

THE ANGEL OF ZEAL shows them the passage, and when his wings have fanned the Poets, Dante casts off his depression and lethargy, and rushes up the remaining length of the passage.

Arrived at THE FIFTH CORNICE, Virgil inquires the way of one of the souls of THE HOARDERS AND WASTERS, who lie motionless and outstretched, bound hand and foot, with their faces in the dust.

The soul of POPE ADRIAN V replies that, if they have incurred no guilt by Hoarding or Wasting, they may pass on to the right. Dante kneels in reverence to Adrian and is scolded for doing so. Adrian then dismisses Dante in order to resume his purification. Adrian's last request is that his niece, ALAGIA, be asked to pray for his soul.

At the hour when the heat of the day is overcome
by Earth, or at times by Saturn, and can no longer
temper the cold of the moon; when on the dome

of the eastern sky the geomancers sight
Fortuna Major rising on a course
on which, and soon, it will be drowned in light;

there came to me in a dream a stuttering crone,
squint-eyed, clubfooted, both her hands deformed,
and her complexion like a whitewashed stone.

I stared at her; and just as the new sun
breathes life to night-chilled limbs, just so my look
began to free her tongue, and one by one

drew straight all her deformities, and warmed
her dead face, till it bloomed as love would wish it
for its delight. When she was thus transformed,

her tongue thus loosened, she began to sing
in such a voice that only with great pain
could I have turned from her soliciting.

"I am," she sang, "Sirena. I am she
whose voice is honeyed with such sweet enticements
it trances sailing men far out to sea.

I turned Ulysses from his wanderer's way
with my charmed song, and few indeed who taste
how well I satisfy would think to stray."

Her mouth had not yet shut when at my side
appeared a saintly lady, poised and eager
to heap confusion on the Siren's pride.

"O Virgil, Virgil! Who," she cried, "is this?"
Roused by her indignation, Virgil came:
his eyes did not once leave that soul of bliss.

He seized the witch, and with one rip laid bare
all of her front, her loins and her foul belly:
I woke sick with the stench that rose from there.

I turned then, and my Virgil said to me:

"I have called at least three times now. Rise and come
and let us find your entrance." Willingly

I rose to my feet. Already the high day
lit all the circles of the holy mountain.
The sun was at our backs as we took our way.

I followed in his steps, my brow as drawn
as is a man's so bowed with thought he bends
like half an arch of a bridge. And moving on,

I heard the words: "Come. This is where you climb,"
pronounced in such a soft and loving voice
as is not heard here in our mortal time.

With swanlike wings outspread, he who had spoken
summoned us up between the walls of rock.
He fanned us with his shining pinions then,

affirming over us as we went by
"blessed are they that mourn"—for they shall have
their consolation given them on high.

"What ails you?" said my Guide. "What heavy mood
makes you stare at the ground?" (We were by then
above the point at which the Angel stood.)

And I: "An apparition clouds my spirit,
a vision from a dream so strange and dreadful
I cannot seem to leave off thinking of it."

"Did you see that ageless witch," he said, "for whom
—and for no other—those above us weep?
And did you see how men escape her doom?

Let it teach your heels to scorn the earth, your eyes
to turn to the high lure the Eternal King

spins with his mighty spheres across the skies."

As falcons stare at their feet until they hear
the wished-for call, then leap with wings outspread
in eagerness for the meat that waits them there;

so did I move: filled with desire, I ran
up the remaining length of the rock passage
to the point at which the next great Round began.

When I stood on the fifth ledge and looked around,
I saw a weeping people everywhere
lying outstretched and face-down on the ground.

"My soul cleaves to the dust," I heard them cry
over and over as we stood among them;
and every word was swallowed by a sigh.

"O Chosen of God, spirits whose mournful rites
both Hope and Justice make less hard to bear,
show us the passage to the further heights."

"If you have not been sentenced to lie prone
in the bitter dust, and seek the nearest way,
keep the rim to your right as you go on."

So spoke the Poet, and so a voice replied
from the ground in front of us. I took good note
of what its way of speaking did not hide.

I turned my eyes to Virgil then, and he
gave me a happy sign of his permission
to do what my eyes asked. Being thus free

to act according to my own intention,
I moved ahead and stood above that soul
whose speaking had attracted my attention,

saying: "O Soul in whom these tears prepare
that without which no soul can turn to God,
put off a while, I beg, your greater care,

to tell me who you were, why you lie prone,
and if there is some way that I may serve you
in the world I left while still in flesh and bone."

"Why Heaven makes us turn our backs shall be
made known to you," the spirit said, "but first
scias quod ego fui successor Petri.

Between Sestri and Chiaveri, flowing on
through a fair land, there is a pleasant river
from which the title of my line is drawn.

A single month, a month and some few days
I came to know on my own weary body
how heavily the Papal Mantle weighs

upon the wearer who would take good care
to keep it from the mire; compared to that
all other burdens are as light as air.

My conversion, alas, came late; for only when
I had been chosen Pastor of Holy Rome
did I see the falseness in the lives of men.

I saw no heart's rest there, nor ease from strife,
nor any height the flesh-bound soul might climb,
and so I came to love this other life.

My soul was lost to God until that moment,
and wholly given over to avarice;
such was my sin, such is my punishment.

The nature of avarice is here made plain
in the nature of its penalty; there is not
a harsher forfeit paid on the whole mountain.

We would not raise our eyes to the shining spheres
but kept them turned to mundane things: so Justice
bends them to earth here in this place of tears.

As Avarice, there, quenched all our souls' delight
in the good without which all our works are lost,
so, here, the hand of Justice clamps us tight.

Taken and bound here hand and foot, we lie
outstretched and motionless; and here we stay
at the just pleasure of the Father on High."
I had knelt to him. Now I spoke once more.
That spirit sensed at once my voice was nearer
and guessed my reverence. "Why do you lower

your knees into the dust?" he said to me.
And I: "My conscience troubled me for standing
in the presence of your rank and dignity."

"Straighten your legs, my brother! Rise from error!"
he said. "I am, like you and all the others,
a fellow servant of one Emperor.

It is written in holy scripture *Neque nubent*;
if ever you understood that sacred text,
my reason for speaking will be evident.

Now go your way. I wish to be alone.
Your presence here distracts me from the tears
that make me ready. And to your last question:

I have a niece, Alagia, still on earth.
If she can but avoid the bad example

those of our line have set, her native worth

will lead her yet the way the blessed go.
And she alone remains to me below."

Canto XX

THE FIFTH CORNICE
The Hoarders and Wasters
(*The Avaricious*)

The Whip of Avarice
The Rein of Avarice

Dante walks on after Adrian has dismissed him, wishing he might have continued the conversation, but bowing to Adrian's wish to resume his purification.

The Poets find the ledge so crowded with the souls of the Avaricious that only one narrow passage is left open to them. Dante hears a soul cry out THE WHIP OF AVARICE, a litany in praise of MARY, FABRICIUS, and ST. NICHOLAS. The sinner identifies himself as HUGH CAPET and proceeds to a DENUNCIATION OF THE CAPETIAN KINGS, the dynasty he himself founded, but which has degenerated into a succession of kings distinguished only for their bloodthirsty avarice.

Hugh Capet then explains THE REIN OF AVARICE, citing seven examples of the downfall of the Avaricious.

Dante has hardly left Capet when he feels the mountain shake as if stricken by AN EARTHQUAKE, and he hears A SHOUT OF TRIUMPH. Dante is frightened but Virgil reassures him. The Poets move on at top speed, but Dante remains deep in thought, his mind pondering these new phenomena.

What's willed must bow to what is stronger willed: against my pleasure, to please him, I drew my sponge back from the water still unfilled.

I turned: my Guide set off along the space left clear next to the rock; for they who drain, slow tear by tear, the sin that eats the race left little room along the outer edge.

Thus, as one hugs the battlements in walking atop a wall, we moved along the ledge.

Hell take you, She-Wolf, who in the sick feast of your ungluttable appetite have taken more prey on earth than any other beast!

You Heavens, in whose turnings, as some say, things here below are changed—
when will he come whose power shall drive her from the light of day?

We moved along with measured step and slow, and all my thoughts were
centered on those shades, their tears and lamentations moved me so.

And walking thus, I heard rise from the earth before us: "Blessed Mary!"—with
a wail such as is wrung from women giving birth.

"How poor you were," the stricken voice went on, "is testified to all men by the
stable in which you laid your sacred burden down."

And then: "O good Fabricius, you twice refused great wealth that would have
stained your honor, and chose to live in poverty, free of vice."

These words had pleased me so that I drew near the place from which they
seemed to have been spoken, eager to know what soul was lying there.

The voice was speaking now of the largesse St. Nicholas bestowed on the three
virgins to guide their youth to virtuous steadiness.

"O soul," I said, "whose words recite such good, let me know who you were,
and why no other joins in your praises of such rectitude.

If I return to finish the short race remaining of that life that ends so soon, your
words will not lack some reward of grace."

"Not for such comfort as the world may give do I reply," he said, "but that such
light of grace should shine on you while yet you live.

I was the root of that malignant tree which casts its shadow on all Christendom
so that the soil bears good fruit only rarely.

But if Douay and Lille and Bruges and Ghent were strong again, their vengeance
would be swift; and that it may, I pray the King of Judgment.

I was Hugh Capet in my mortal state. From me stem all the Philips and the Louis' who have occupied the throne of France of late.

I was born in Paris as a butcher's son. When the old line of kings had petered out to one last heir, who wore a monk's gray gown,

I found that I held tight in my own hand the reins of state, and that my new wealth gave me such power, and such allies at my command,

that my son's head, with pomp and sacrament rose to the widowed crown of France. From him those consecrated bones took their descent.

Till the great dowry of Provence increased my race so that it lost its sense of shame, It came to little, but did no harm at least.

That was the birth of its rapacity, its power, its lies. Later—to make amends—it took Normandy, Ponthieu, and Gascony.

Charles came to Italy, and—to make amends—he victimized Conradin. Then he sent Saint Thomas back to Heaven—to make amends.

I see a time, not far off, that brings forth another Charles from France. It shall make clear to many what both he and his are worth.

He comes alone, unarmed but for the lance of Judas, which he drives so hard he bursts the guts of Florence with the blow he plants.

He wins no land there; only sin and shame. And what is worse for him is that he holds such crimes too lightly to repent his blame.

The third, once hauled from his own ship, I see selling his daughter, haggling like a pirate over a girl sold into slavery.

O Avarice, what more harm can you do? You have taken such a hold on my descendants they sell off their own flesh and blood for you!

But dwarfing all crimes, past or yet to be, I see Alagna entered, and, in His

Vicar, Christ Himself dragged in captivity.

I see Him mocked again and crucified, the gall and vinegar once more sent up. He dies again—with *live* thieves at His side.

I see another Pilate, so full of spite not even that suffices: his swollen sails enter the very Temple without right.

O God, my Lord, when shall my soul rejoice to see Thy retribution, which, lying hidden, sweetens Thine anger in Thy secret choice?

What you first heard me cry in adoration of that one only Bride of the Holy Ghost, which made you turn and ask an explanation, is the litany we add to every prayer as long as it is day. When the sun sets we raise the counter-cry on the night air.

We cry then how Pygmalion of old was made a traitor, thief, and parricide by his insatiable sick lust for gold;

how Midas suffered when his miser's prayer was answered, and became forever after the legend of a ludicrous despair;

and then we tell how Achan, covetous, stole from the booty, for which Joshua's rage still falls upon him—so it seems to us.

We cry Sapphira's and her husband's blame; we praise the hooves that battered Heliodorus; then round the ledge runs Polymnestor's name,

foul to all time with Polydorus' blood. Then we conclude the litany crying: 'Crassus, you supped on gold—tell us, did it taste good?'

We wail or mutter in our long remorse according to the inner spur that drives us, at times with more, at others with less force:

thus I was not the only one who praised the good we tell by day; but, as it happened, the only one nearby whose voice was raised."

We had already left him to his prayers and were expending every ounce of strength on the remaining distance to the stairs,

when suddenly I felt the mountain shake as if it tottered. Such a numb dread seized me as a man feels when marching to the stake.

Not even Delos, in that long ago before Latona went there to give birth to Heaven's eyes, was ever shaken so.

Then there went up a cry on every side, so loud that the sweet Master, bending close said: "Do not fear, for I am still your Guide."

"Glory to God in the Highest!" rang a shout from every throat—as I could understand from those nearby, whose words I could make out.

We stood there motionless, our souls suspended—as had the shepherds who first heard that hymn—until the ground grew still and the hymn ended.

Then we pushed on our holy way once more, studying those prostrate souls who had already resumed their lamentation, as before.

I never felt my soul assaulted so—unless my memory err—as in that war between my ignorance and desire to know

the explanation of that shock and shout; nor dared I ask, considering our haste; nor could I of myself, looking about,

find anywhere the key to what I sought. So I moved on, timid and sunk in thought.

Canto XXI

Burning with desire to know the cause of the "shock and shout," Dante hurries after Virgil along the narrow way. Suddenly they are overtaken by a figure that salutes them. Virgil answers, and the new soul, taking the Poets to be souls who may not enter Heaven, expresses astonishment at finding them in this place.

Virgil explains his and Dante's state and asks the explanation of the earthquake and of the great cry. The new soul explains that these phenomena occur only when a soul arises from its final purification and begins its final ascent to Heaven. The newcomer then reveals that he is STATIUS and recites his earthly history, ending with a glowing statement of his love for the works of Virgil. To have lived in Virgil's time, says Statius, he would have endured another year of the pains he has just ended.

Virgil warns Dante, with a glance, to be silent, but Dante cannot suppress a half smile, which Statius notices, and asks Dante to explain. He thus learns that he is, in fact, standing in the presence of Virgil. Immediately he kneels to embrace Virgil's knees, but Virgil tells him to arise at once, for such earthly vanities are out of place between shades.

The natural thirst that nothing satisfies
except that water the Samaritan woman
begged of Our Lord, as St. John testifies,

burned me; haste drove me on the encumbered way
behind my Guide, and I was full of grief
at the just price of pain those spirits pay;

when suddenly—just as Luke lets us know
that Christ, new risen from the tomb, appeared
to the two travelers on the road—just so

as we moved there with bowed heads lest we tread
upon some soul, a shade appeared behind us;
nor did we guess its presence till it said:

"Brothers, God give you peace." My Guide and I
turned quickly toward his voice, and with a sign
my Master gave the words their due reply.

Then he began: "May the True Court's behest,
which relegates me to eternal exile,
establish you in peace among the blest."

"But how, If you are souls denied God's bliss,"
he said—and we forged onward as he spoke—
"have you climbed up the stairs as far as this?"

My Teacher then: "You cannot fail to see,
if you observe the Angel's mark upon him,
that he will reign among the just. But she

whose wheel turns day and night has not yet spun
the full length of the thread that Clotho winds
into a hank for him and everyone.

Therefore, his soul, sister to yours and mine,
since it cannot see as we do, could not
climb by itself. And, therefore, Will Divine

has drawn me out of the great Throat of Woe
to guide him on his way, and I shall lead him
far as my knowledge gives me power to go.

But tell me, if you can, what was the shock
we felt just now? And why did all the mountain
cry with one voice down to its last moist rock?"

He struck the needle's eye of my desire
so surely with his question, that my thirst,
by hope alone, lost something of its fire.

The shade began: "The holy rules that ring
the mountain round do not permit upon it
any disordered or unusual thing,

nor any change. Only what Heaven draws
out of itself into itself again—
that and nothing else—can be a cause.

Therefore, there never can be rain nor snow,
nor hail, nor dew, nor hoarfrost higher up
than the little three-step stairway there below.

Neither dense clouds nor films of mist appear,
nor lightning's flash, nor Thaumas' glowing daughter,
who shifts about from place to place back there;

nor can dry vapors raise their shattering heat
above the top of these three steps I mentioned
upon which Peter's vicar plants his feet.

Shocks may occur below, severe or slight,
but tremors caused by winds locked in the earth
—I know not how—do not reach to this height.

It trembles here whenever a soul feels
so healed and purified that it gets up
or moves to climb; and then the great hymn peals.

The soul, surprised, becomes entirely free
to change its cloister, moved by its own will,
which is its only proof of purity.

Before purgation it does wish to climb,

but the will High Justice sets against that wish
moves it to will pain as it once willed crime.

And I, who in my torments have lain here
five hundred years and more, have only now
felt my will free to seek a better sphere.

It was for that you felt the mountain move
and heard the pious spirits praise the Lord—
ah may He call them soon to go above!"

These were the spirit's words to us, and mine
cannot express how they refreshed my soul,
but as the thirst is greater, the sweeter the wine.

And my wise Leader: "Now I see what snare
holds you, how you slip free, why the mount trembles,
and why your joint rejoicing fills the air.

Now it would please me greatly, if you please,
to know your name and hear in your own words
why you have lain so many centuries."

"In the days when the good Titus, with the aid
of the Almighty King, avenged the wounds
that poured the blood Iscariot betrayed,

I lived renowned back there," replied that soul,
"in the most honored and enduring name,
but still without the faith that makes us whole.

My verses swelled with such melodious breath
that, from Toulouse, Rome called me to herself,
and there I merited a laurel wreath.

Statius my name, and it still lives back there.
I sang of Thebes, then of the great Achilles,

but found the second weight too great to bear.

The sparks that were my seeds of passion came
from that celestial fire which has enkindled
more than a thousand poets; I mean the flame

of the *Aeneid*, the mother that brought forth,
the nurse that gave suck to my song. Without it
I could not have weighed half a penny's worth.

And to have lived back there in Virgil's time
I would agree to pass another year
in the same banishment from which I climb."

Virgil, at these last words, shot me a glance
that said in silence, "Silence!" But man's will
is not supreme in every circumstance:

for tears and laughter come so close behind
the passions they arise from, that they least
obey the will of the most honest mind.

I did no more than half smile, but that shade
fell still and looked me in the eye—for there
the secrets of the soul are most betrayed.

"So may the road you travel lead to grace,"
he said, "what was the meaning of the smile
that I saw flash, just now, across your face?"

Now am I really trapped on either side:
one tells me to be still, one begs me speak.
So torn I heave a sigh, and my sweet Guide

understands all its meaning. "Never fear,"
he says to me, "speak up, and let him know
what he has asked so movingly to hear."

At which I said: "Perhaps my smiling thus
has made you marvel, Ancient Soul; but now
listen to something truly marvelous:

this one who guides my eyes aloft is he,
Virgil, from whom you drew the strength to sing
the deeds of men and gods in poetry.

The only motive for my smiling lay
in your own words. If you conceived another,
as you love truth, pray put the thought away."

He was bending to embrace my Teacher's knee,
but Virgil said: "No, brother. Shade you are,
and shade am I. You must not kneel to me."

And Statius, rising, said: "So may you find
the measure of the love that warms me to you
when for it I lose all else from my mind,

forgetting we are empty semblances
and taking shadows to be substances."

Canto XXII

THE ASCENT TO THE SIXTH CORNICE
THE SIXTH CORNICE
The Gluttons
                    The Tree
                The Whip of Gluttony

The Poets have passed the Angel who guards the ascent, and Dante has had one
more P removed from his forehead. So lightened, he walks easily behind Virgil
and Statius despite their rapid ascent, listening eagerly to their conversation.

Virgil declares his great regard for Statius, and Statius explains that he was on
the Fifth Cornice for Wasting rather than for Hoarding. He adds that he would
certainly have been damned, had Virgil's poetry not led him to see his error. For
Virgil, he acknowledges, not only inspired his song, but showed him the road to
faith, whereby he was baptized, though secretly, for fear of the persecutions—a
lukewarmness for which he spent four hundred years on the Fourth Cornice.

Statius then names his favorite poets of antiquity and asks where they are.
Virgil replies that they are with him in Limbo. He then cites many who have not
been mentioned before as being among his eternal companions.

At this point the Poets arrive at THE SIXTH CORNICE and, moving to the
right, come upon AN ENORMOUS TREE laden with fruits. From its foliage a
voice cries out the examples of abstinence that constitute THE WHIP OF
GLUTTONY.

We had, by now, already left behind
the Angel who directs to the Sixth Round.
He had erased a stigma from my brow,

and said that they who thirst for rectitude
are blessèd, but he did not say "who hunger"
when he recited that Beatitude.

I, lighter than on any earlier stairs,
followed those rapid spirits, and I found it
no strain at all to match my pace to theirs.

Virgil began: "When virtue lights in us
a fire of love, that love ignites another
within the soul that sees its burning. Thus,

ever since Juvenal came down to be
one of our court in the Infernal Limbo,
and told me of your great regard for me,

my good will toward you has been of a sort
I had not felt for any unseen person;
such as will make the climb ahead seem short.

But tell me—and if I presume too much
in slackening the rein this way, forgive me
as a friend would and answer me as such:

how, amid all the wisdom you possessed—
and which you won to by such diligence—
could Avarice find a place within your breast?"

At these words Statius let a brief smile play
across his lips, and fade. Then he replied:
"I hear love's voice in every word you say.

Often, indeed, appearances give rise
to groundless doubts in us, and false conclusions,
the true cause being hidden from our eyes.

Seeing me on the ledge from which I rose,
you have inferred my sin was Avarice;
an inference your question clearly shows.

Know then that my particular offense
was all too far from Avarice: I wept
thousands of months for riotous expense.

Had I not turned from prodigality
in pondering those lines in which you cry,
as if you raged against humanity:

'To what do you not drive man's appetite
O cursèd gold-lust!'—I should now be straining
in the grim jousts of the Infernal night.

I understood then that our hands could spread
their wings too wide in spending, and repented
of that, and all my sins, in grief and dread.

How many shall rise bald to Judgment Day
because they did not know this sin to grieve it
in life, or as their last breaths slipped away!

For when the opposite of a sin, as here,
is as blameworthy as the sin itself,
both lose their growth together and turn sere.

If, then, I lay so long in my distress
among the Avaricious where they weep,
it was to purge the opposite excess."

"But when you sang of the fierce warfare bred
between the twin afflictions of Jocasta,"
the singer of the sweet *Bucolics* said,

"from what you said when Clio tuned your strain,
it would not seem that you had found the faith
without the grace of which good works are vain.

If that be so, what Sun or beacon shone
into your mist that you set sail to follow
the Fisherman?" And that long-waiting one:

"You were the lamp that led me from that night.

You led me forth to drink Parnassian waters;
then on the road to God you shed your light.

When you declared, 'A new birth has been given.
Justice returns, and the first age of man.
And a new progeny descends from Heaven'—

you were as one who leads through a dark track
holding the light behind—useless to you,
precious to those who followed at your back.

Through you I flowered to song and to belief.
That you may know all, let me stretch my hand
to paint in full what I have sketched in brief.

The world, by then, was swollen with the birth
of True Belief sown by those messengers
the Everlasting Kingdom had sent forth.

Those words of yours I quoted, so agreed
with the new preachers', that I took to going
to where they gathered to expound the Creed.

In time, they grew so holy in my eyes
that in the persecutions of Domitian
the tears burst from me when I heard their cries.

And long as I remained upon the vexed
shores of that life, I helped them, and they taught me,
by their strict ways, to scorn all other sects.

Before my poem sang how the Greeks drew near
the Theban rivers, I had been baptized,
but kept my faith a secret, out of fear,

pretending to be pagan as before;
for which lukewarmness I was made to circle

the Ledge of Sloth four hundred years and more.

Now may you please to tell me—you who rent
the veil that hid me from this good I praise—
while we have time to spare in the ascent,

where is our ancient Terence now? and where
Caecilius, Varro, Plautus?—are they damned?
and if they are, what torments must they bear?"

—"All these are there with Persius and the rest,
myself among them, who surround that Greek
who outsucked all men at the Muses' breast.

All walk the first ledge of the dark of Hell;
and we speak often of the glorious mountain
on which the Nine who suckled us still dwell.

Euripides is with us, Antiphon,
Athenian Agathon, Simonides,
and many more who wore the laurel crown.

And there, of your own people, one may see
Ismene, mournful as she was before,
Deiphyle, Argia, Antigone,

Hypsipyle, who led to Langia's water,
Thetis, Deidamia with her sisters,
and there, too, one may see Tiresias' daughter."

We stepped from the walled stairs to level ground,
and both the Poets now had fallen still,
attentive once again to look around.

Of the day's handmaids, four had fallen back,
and now the fifth stood at the chariot's pole,
pointing the bright tip on its upward track,

when Virgil said: "I think we ought to go
with our right shoulders to the outer edge,
circling the slope as we have done below."

So custom served to guide us, and we went
as Virgil said, with all the more assurance
since Statius' silence gave us his consent.

They walked ahead and I came on behind
treasuring their talk, which was of poetry,
and every word of which enriched my mind.

But soon, in mid-road, there appeared a tree
laden with fragrant and delicious fruit,
and at that sight the talk stopped instantly.

As fir trees taper up from limb to limb,
so this tree tapered down; so shaped, I think,
that it should be impossible to climb.

From that side where the cliff closed-off our way
a clear cascade fell from the towering rock
and broke upon the upper leaves as spray.

The poets drew nearer, reverent and mute,
and from the center of the towering tree
a voice cried: "You shall not eat of the fruit!"

Then said: "Mary thought more of what was due
the joy and honor of the wedding feast
than of her mouth, which still speaks prayers for you.

Of old, the mothers of Rome's noble blood
found joy in water. And great wisdom came
to holy Daniel in despising food.

Bright as pure gold was mankind's state at first:
then, hunger seasoned acorns with delight,
and every rill ran sweet to honest thirst.

No wine nor meat were in the wilderness.
Honey and locusts—that and nothing more
nourished the Baptist in his holiness;

and to that fact is his great glory due,
as the Gospel clearly testifies to you."

Canto XXIII

THE SIXTH CORNICE
The Gluttons

Dante stares up into the tree to see who has spoken but he is called away by Virgil who leads on, talking to Statius, while Dante walks behind, drinking in their conversation. Suddenly, from behind him, Dante hears a psalm, and turning, he sees a band of GLUTTONS overtaking them, souls so emaciated that one can read in their sunken eyes and in the lines of the cheeks and nose the word "OMO."

After some difficulty Dante recognizes one of the hideously wasted souls as his old friend FORESE who had died only five years before, but who had been advanced into Purgatory and directly to this Cornice by the prayers of his widow, Nella.

In praising Nella for her devotion, Forese takes occasion to deliver a rather salty INVECTIVE AGAINST THE WOMEN OF FLORENCE for their immodest dress and behavior.

In answer to Forese's plea (for the souls have all seen Dante's shadow), Dante explains how he has mounted into Purgatory and with whom he is traveling.

In hope of seeing who had cried those words
I drew near and peered up at the green boughs
like one who wastes his lifetime stalking birds.

At that, my more-than-father said: "My son,
come now, for we must portion out more wisely
the time allotted us." And he moved on.

I looked down and turned round to join those sages
in the same instant. And their talk was such
that every step I took paid double wages.

Then suddenly at my back I heard the strain

of *Labia mea, Domine,* so sung
that it was both a hymn and cry of pain.

"Father," I said, "what is this sound?" And he:
"Spirits who, circling so, loosen perhaps
the knot of debt they owe Eternity."

As pilgrims wrapped in holy meditation,
when they encounter strangers on the way,
look, but do not pause for conversation;

so from behind us, turning half about
to stare as they went by, a band of souls
came up and passed us, silent and devout.

The sockets of their eyes were caves agape;
their faces death-pale, and their skin so wasted
that nothing but the gnarled bones gave it shape.

I doubt that even Erysichthon's skin,
even when he most feared that he would starve,
had drawn so tight to bone, or worn so thin.

"Behold," I thought, although I did not speak,
"the face of those who lost Jerusalem
when Miriam ripped her son with her own beak."

Their eye pits looked like gem-rims minus gem.
Those who read OMO in the face of man
would easily have recognized the *M.*

Who could imagine, without knowing how,
craving could waste souls so at the mere smell
of water and of fruit upon the bough?

I was still wondering how they could have grown
so thin and scabby (since what famished them

had not yet been made clear to me), when one

turning his eyes from deep inside his skull,
stared at me fixedly, then cried aloud:
"How have I earned a grace so bountiful?"

I never would have recognized his face,
but in his voice I found that which his features
had eaten from themselves without a trace.

That spark relit my memory and, in awe,
I understood beneath those altered features
it was Forese's very self I saw.

"Ah, do not stare," he pleaded, "at my hide,
bleached like a leper's by these flaming scabs,
nor at the fleshless bones I bear inside;

but tell me all about yourself, and who
these two souls are that bear you company;
and tell me with all haste, I beg of you."

"I wept to see your face once when it lay
in death," I said, "and I weep no less now
to see what pain has wasted it away;

in God's name tell me how. Do not demand
I speak while still bemused, for he speaks badly
whose mind is too full to be at command."

And he: "From the Eternal Counsel flow
the powers whereby the water and the tree
we have just passed, emaciate us so.

All those who sing while weeping in their pain
once loved their stomach-sacs beyond all measure.
Here, thirst and hunger wring them clean again.

Hunger and thirst that nothing can assuage
grow in us from the fragrance of the fruit
and of the spray upon the foliage.

And not once only as we round this place
do we endure renewal of our pain.
—Did I say 'pain'? I should say 'gift of grace.'

For the same will that drives us to the Tree
drove Christ on gladly to cry 'Eli! Eli!'
when he paid with his blood to set us free."

And I to him: "Forese, from the day
in which you changed worlds for the better life,
less than five years, as yet, have passed away.

If your ability to sin had fled
before the hour of that sublime sweet sorrow
that weds us back to God, among his blessèd,

how have you reached so high in the great climb?
I thought to find you still below, with those
who sit and wait, repaying time for time."

"My Nella's flood of tears," he answered me,
"Have borne me up so soon to let me drink
the blessed wormwood of my agony.

Her sighs and prayers were heard where Love abounds:
they raised me from the slope where I lay waiting
and set me free of all the other Rounds.

The dearer and more pleasing in God's sight
is the poor widow of my love, as she
is most alone in doing what is right.

For the Barbagia of Sardinia breeds
chaste women as compared to that Barbagia
in which I left her to her widow's weeds.

O my dear brother, what is there to say?
In vision I already see a time—
and it is not far distant from this day—

in which the pulpit shall denounce by writ
the shameless jades that Florentines call ladies,
who go about with breasts bare to the tit.

What Moslem woman ever has required
a priestly discipline, or any other,
before she would go decently attired?

But if the chippies only could foresee
swift Heaven's punishment, they'd have their mouths
already open to howl misery.

For if what we foresee here does not lie,
they shall be sad before those sons grow beards
who can be soothed now with a lullaby.

Now, brother, answer in your turn. You see
your shadow there, and how these other souls
are staring at the spot along with me."

I then: "If you call back to mind from here
my past life in your company, yours in mine,
memory will seem too great a load to bear.

I was recalled from such ways by that one
who leads me here, and just the other day
when that one's sister (pointing to the Sun)

was at the full. Through the profoundest night

of final death he led me in this flesh
which follows him to find the final Right.

From there with many a sweet encouragement
he led me upward and around the mountain
which straightens in you what the world has bent.

And he has pledged himself to go with me
until I stand by Beatrice, above.
Then I must do without his company.

The one who pledges this (and as I spoke
I pointed to him standing there) is Virgil.
The other is the shade of him who woke
to blessedness just now when every rim,
the mountain round, shook in releasing him."

Canto XXIV

THE SIXTH CORNICE
The Gluttons

The Tree of Knowledge
The Rein of Gluttony

The Poets move on as Dante continues his talk with Forese, who identifies many of the souls of the Gluttons, among them BONAGIUNTA OF LUCCA. Bonagiunta mutters a prophecy concerning Dante's future meeting with GENTUCCA. He then questions Dante about THE SWEET NEW STYLE and ends by concluding that had he and the others of his school of poetry grasped the principle of natural expression, they would have written as well as do the poets of Dante's school.

All the other souls speed ahead, but Forese remains to prophesy the death of his brother, CORSO DONATI, leader of the Black Guelphs. Then he speeds away and soon disappears.

The Poets move on and come to THE TREE OF KNOWLEDGE from which a voice cries THE REIN OF GLUTTONY, citing EVE, THE CENTAURS, and THE ARMY OF GIDEON. Having skirted the tree carefully, warned away by the voice, the Poets move ahead and meet THE ANGEL OF ABSTINENCE, who shows them to the ascent.

Talk did not slow our steps, nor they in turn
our talk, but still conversing we moved on
like ships at sea with a brisk wind astern.

And all those shades, looking like things twice dead,
were drinking in through their sepulchral eyes
the awe of seeing me as I had been bred.

And I, continuing as I had begun,
said: "His ascent, I think, is somewhat slower
than it would be but for that other one.

—But where now is Piccarda? Do you know?

And is there anyone of special note
among these people who stare at me so?"

"My sister, who was good as she was fair,
and fair as good, sits crowned on High Olympus,
rejoicing in eternal triumph there."

Thus he began. Then: "To identify
anyone here is certainly permitted,
for abstinence has milked our features dry.

This" (and he pointed to him) "dearest brother,
was Bonagiunta of Lucca. That behind him,
his face more sunken in than any other,

once fathered Holy Church. Of Tours his line;
and here in the long fast he expiates
Bolsena's eels and the Vernaccia wine."

Then he named many others, one by one,
at which I saw not one black look among them,
but all seemed pleased at being thus made known.

Ubaldino della Pila hungered there,
and Boniface, shepherd to all those bellies—
they were so starved they used their teeth on air.

I saw my Lord Marchese. Before he died
he drank with somewhat less thirst at Forlì,
yet no man ever saw him satisfied.

As one who notes one face especially
among a crowd, I noted him of Lucca
who seemed most to desire a word with me.

He muttered something, and I seemed to hear
the word "Gentucca" issue from the wound

where most he felt High Justice pluck him bare.

"Spirit," I said, "since you seem so intent
on talking to me, do so audibly,
and speaking so, make both of us content."

"Though men may mock my city," he replied,
"she who will teach you how to treasure it
is born there, though she is not yet a bride.

This presage you shall take with you from here,
and if you misconstrued what I first muttered
the facts themselves, in time, will make it clear.

But is this really the creator of
those new *canzoni*, one of which begins
'Ladies who have the intellect of Love'?"

And I: "When Love inspires me with delight,
or pain, or longing, I take careful note,
and as he dictates in my soul, I write."

And he: "Ah, brother, now I see the thong
that held Guittone, and the Judge, and me
short of that sweet new style of purest song.

I see well how your pens attained such powers
by following exactly Love's dictation,
which certainly could not be said of ours.

And if one scan the two styles side by side,
that is the only difference he will find."
With that he fell still, as if satisfied.

Just as the cranes that winter by the Nile
form close-bunched flights at times, then, gathering speed,
streak off across the air in single file;

so all the people there faced straight ahead,
and being lightened by both will and wasting,
quickened their paces, and away they sped.

And as a runner who must take a rest
lets his companions pull ahead, and walks
till he has eased the panting in his chest;

just so Forese let that blessed train
outdistance him, and held his pace to mine,
and said to me: "When shall we meet again?"

"I do not know how long my life will be,"
I said, "but I cannot return so soon
but what my wish will reach the shore before me;

for from that city where I came to life
goodness is disappearing day by day;
a place foredoomed to ruin by bloody strife."

"Take heart," he said, "for I see him whose crime
exceeds all others' dragged at a beast's tail
to where sin lasts beyond the end of time.

At every stride the beast goes faster, faster,
until its flashing hooves lash out, and leave
the foul ruin of what was once its master.

Those Spheres (and he looked toward the Heavens here)
will not turn far before what I have said,
and may not add to now, shall be made clear.

Now I must leave you far behind: your pace
has cost me a considerable delay;
and time is precious to us in this place."

At times during a horse charge, one brave knight
will spur ahead, burning to claim the honor
of having struck the first blow in the fight;

just so his lengthened stride left us behind,
and I trailed on, accompanied by those two
who were such mighty marshals of mankind.

And when, in such haste, he had pulled ahead
so far that I could only make him out
as I could understand what he had said;

we turned a corner and there came in sight,
not far ahead, a second tree, its boughs
laden with fruit, its foliage bursting bright.

Sometimes when greedy children beg and screech
for what they may not have, the one they cry to
holds it in plain sight but beyond their reach

to whet their appetites: so, round that tree,
with arms raised to the boughs, a pack of souls
begged and was given nothing. Finally

they gave up and moved on unsatisfied,
and we drew close in our turn to that plant
at which such tears and pleadings were denied.

"Pass on. Do not draw near. The tree whose fruit
Eve took and ate grows further up the slope,
and this plant sprouted from that evil root."

—Thus, from the boughs, an unknown voice called down.
And thus warned, Virgil, Statius, and myself
drew close, and hugged the cliff, and hurried on.

"Recall," the voice went on, "those cursed beasts

born of a cloud. When they had swilled the wine,
Theseus had to slash their double breasts.

Recall those Jews who once showed Gideon
how to abandon all to thirst, whereat
he would not lead them down the hills to Midian."

So we strode on along the inner way
while the voice cried the sins of Gluttony
which earn, as we had seen, such fearful pay.

Then the road cleared, and with more room for walking
we spread out, and had gone a thousand paces
in meditation, with no thought of talking;

when suddenly a voice cried, startling me
as if I were a panic-stricken colt:
"What are you thinking of alone, you three?"

I looked up to see who had spoken so:
no man has ever seen in any furnace,
metal or glass raised to so red a glow.

"If your wish is to ascend," I heard one say,
"this is the place where you must turn aside.
All you who search for Peace—this is the way."

His glory blinded me. I groped and found
my Teacher's back and followed in his steps
as blind men do who guide themselves by sound.

Soft on my brow I felt a zephyr pass,
soft as those airs of May that herald dawn
with breathing fragrances of flowers and grass;

and unmistakably I felt the brush
of the soft wing releasing to my senses

ambrosial fragrances in a soft rush.

And soft I heard the Angel voice recite:
"Blessed are they whom Grace so lights within
that love of food in them does not excite

excessive appetite, but who take pleasure
in keeping every hunger within measure."

19. (*and he pointed to him*): Dante seems to have discovered this device at the

Canto XXV

DEPARTURE FROM THE SIXTH CORNICE
The Ascent
                    The Discourse of Statius
THE SEVENTH CORNICE
                    The Whip of Lust
The Lustful

It is 2:00 P.M. as the Three Poets leave the Cornice of the Gluttonous and begin their hurried ASCENT TO THE SEVENTH CORNICE.

Dante, burning with eagerness to ask how the Gluttons could give the appearance of advanced starvation despite the fact that they are airy bodies and do not need food, fears to speak but is finally encouraged to do so by Virgil. Dante immediately offers his question, and Virgil, as an act of courtesy, invites Statius to answer it. The rest of the rapid ascent is then occupied by THE DISCOURSE OF STATIUS ON

THE NATURE OF THE GENERATIVE PRINCIPLE, THE BIRTH OF THE HUMAN SOUL, and THE NATURE OF AERIAL BODIES.

By the time Statius is finished, the Poets have reached the Seventh Cornice. There, enwrapped in sheets of flame, the souls of THE LUSTFUL sing over and over the hymn Summae Deus Clementiae. *At each conclusion of the hymn, they cry out in praise of an example of High Chastity. These examples form THE WHIP OF LUST. It is in this way, singing and praising as they move through the flames, that the Lustful perform their purification.*

It was an hour to climb without delay.
Taurus succeeded to the Sun's meridian,
and Scorpio to Night's—a world away;

thus, as a man spurred on by urgent cause will push ahead, no matter what appears along the way inviting him to pause—

just so we filed, one of us at a time,

into the gap, and started up those stairs
whose narrowness divides all those who climb.

And as a little stork, eager to fly
but afraid to leave the nest, will raise a wing
then let it fall again—just such was I,

the will within me now strong and now weak,
eager to ask, but going only so far
as to make me clear my throat, and then not speak.

The pace was swift; nor did my Sweet Lord slow
his stride, but said: "I see the bow of speech
drawn back to the very iron. Let It go."

My doubts resolved, I did not hesitate
to use my mouth. "How can they grow so thin,"
I said, "who need no food in their new state?"

"Recall Meleager wasting as the brand
wasted in fire," he said, "and you will find
the matter not so hard to understand.

Or think how your least move before a glass
is answered by your image, and what seemed hard
is bound to grow much clearer than it was.

But this wish burns you, I know, and to put out
all of its flames, I shall beg Statius now
to be the one to heal the wounds of doubt."

"If, in your presence," Statius first replied,
"I explain eternal things, let my excuse
be only that your wish be not denied."

And then to me: "Son, let it be your task
to hear and heed my words, and they will be

a light upon the 'how' of what you ask.

Perfect blood—that pure blood that remains
as one might say, like food upon the table,
and never goes to slake the thirsty veins—
acquires, within the heart, formative power
over all human organs; as that which flows
into the veins forms *them*. It is once more

changed in the heart, then flows down to that place
the better left unmentioned. Thence, it drips
over another blood in its natural vase.

There, the two commingle; and one blood shows
a passive bent, while the other blood is active,
due to the perfect place from which it flows.

So joined, the active force within the latter
first clots, then quickens what it has made firm
of the former blood to serve as working matter.

The active force has now become a soul
like that of a plant, but with the difference
that this begins where that achieves its goal.

Soon, like some sea-thing, half-beast and half-weed,
it moves and feels. It then begins to form
those powers of sense of which it is the seed.

Now, my son, the formative power expands
and elongates within, till every member
takes form and place as nature's plan commands.

But how this animal-thing grows human powers
you do not yet see; and this very point
has led astray a wiser head than yours.

By him, the *possible intellect* was thought
(since it occupied no organ) to be disjoined
from the *vegetative soul*—and so he taught.

Open your heart to the truth I shall explain,
and know that at the instant articulation
has been perfected in the foetal brain,

that instant the First Mover turns to it.
And there, rejoicing at such art in nature,
breathes into it a new and powerful spirit.

All that is active there, this spirit draws
into itself, forming a single soul
that lives, and feels, and measures its own cause.

(Consider, if you find these words of mine
too strange to understand, how the Sun's heat
joined to the sap of the vine turns into wine.)

Then when Lachesis' flax is drawn, it frees
itself from flesh, but takes with it the essence
of its divine and human faculties—

its lower powers grown passive now and mute;
but memory, intelligence, and will
more active than they were, and more acute.

Miraculously then, by its own will,
it falls at once to one or the other shore.
There it first learns its way, for good or ill.

And once inclosed in that new atmosphere,
the *formative power* rays out, as it did first
in shaping the bodily parts it left back there.

Then, as the air after a rain will glow

inside itself, reflecting an outer ray,
and clothe itself in many colors—so

wherever the soul may stop in its new hour,
the air about it takes on that soul's image.
Such is the virtue of the *formative power*.

Thereafter, in the same way one may see
flame follow fire wherever it may shift,
the new form follows the soul eternally.

From air it draws its visibility. Hence,
it is called a *shade*. And out of air it forms
the organs of sight, speech, and every sense.

Thus are we able to speak and laugh. And thus
are we able to weep such tears and breathe such sighs
as you have seen and heard, passing among us.

As desire, or other feelings move us, so
our shades change their appearances. And that
is that cause of what amazed you just below."

—We had come, by then, to the last turn of the stairs
from which we bore to the right along the cornice,
and our minds were drawn already to other cares.

Here, from the inner wall, flames blast the ledge,
while from the floor an air-blast bends them back,
leaving one narrow path along the edge.

This path we were forced to take as best we might,
in single file. And there I was—the flames
to the left of me, and the abyss to the right.

My Leader said: "In this place, it is clear,
we all must keep a tight rein on our eyes.

To take a false step would be easy here."

"*Summae Deus clementiae*," sang a choir
inside that furnace, and despite my road
I could not help but look into the fire.

Then I saw spirits moving through the flames,
and my eyes turned now to them, now to my feet,
as if divided between equal claims.

When they had sung the hymn, those souls in pain
cried out in full voice: "*Virum non cognosco.*"
Then, softly, they began the hymn again.

That done, they cried: "Diana kept to the wood,
and drove Helicé from her when that nymph
had felt Venus's poison in her blood."

Then, once again, the hymn swelled from their choir;
and after it they praised husbands and wives
who were chaste as virtue and marriage vows require.

And in this way, I think, they sing their prayer
and cry their praise for as long as they must stay
within the holy fire that burns them there.

Such physic and such diet has been thought fit
before the last wound of them all may knit.

Canto XXVI

THE SEVENTH CORNICE
The Lustful

The Rein of Lust

Dante's shadow falls on the wall of flame and it is noticed by the souls of the Lustful who approach (without leaving the flames) to question him. Dante's answer, however, is interrupted by the approach of a second band of souls from the opposite direction. These are THE SODOMITES. The two bands of souls exchange brief embraces and then cry out THE REIN OF LUST as they move on, drawing rapidly apart.

The first group again approaches Dante and the soul of GUIDO GUINIZELLI speaks to him. Dante pays high homage to Guinizelli and discusses with him the growth of the Sweet New Style.

With a final request for a prayer for his soul, Guido withdraws and Dante then addresses ARNAUT DANIEL, who answers in the langue d'oc, *and also begs that Dante say a prayer for him. His petition made, Daniel disappears into the purifying flame.*

So, one before the other, we moved there
along the edge, and my Sweet Guide kept saying:
"Walk only where you see me walk. Take care."

The Sun, already changing from blue to white
the face of the western sky, struck at my shoulder,
its rays now almost level on my right;

and my shadow made the flames a darker red.
Even so slight an evidence, I noticed,
made many shades that walked there turn their head.

And when they saw my shadow, these began
to speak of me, saying to one another:
"He seems to be no shade, but a living man!"

And some of them drew near me then—as near
as they could come, for they were ever careful
to stay within the fire that burned them there.

"O you who trail the others—with no desire
to lag, I think, but out of deference—
speak to me who am burned by thirst and fire.

Not I alone need what your lips can tell:
all these thirst for it more than Ethiopes
or Indians for a drink from a cold well:

how is it that you cast a shadow yet,
making yourself a barrier to the Sun,
as if death had not caught you in its net?"

—So one addressed me. And I should have been
explaining myself already, but for a new
surprising sight that caught my eye just then;

for down the center of that fiery way
came new souls from the opposite direction,
and I forgot what I had meant to say.

I saw them hurrying from either side,
and each shade kissed another, without pausing,
each by the briefest greeting satisfied.

(Ants, in their dark ranks, meet exactly so,
rubbing each other's noses, to ask perhaps
what luck they've had, or which way they should go.)

As soon as they break off their friendly greeting,
before they take the first step to pass on,
each shade outshouts the other at that meeting.

"Sodom and Gomorrah," the new souls cry.

And the others: "Pasiphaë enters the cow
to call the young bull to her lechery."

As if cranes split into two flocks, and one
flew to the Rhipheans, one to the sands,
these to escape the ice, and those the Sun—

so, then, those shades went their opposing ways;
and all returned in tears to their first song,
and each to crying an appropriate praise.

Then those who came my way drew close once more—
the same shades that had first entreated me.
They seemed as eager to hear me as before.

I, having had their wish presented twice,
replied without delay: "O souls assured—
whenever it may be—of Paradise,

I did not leave my limbs beyond the flood,
not green nor ripe, but bear them with me here
in their own jointure and in their own blood.

I go to be no longer blind. Above
there is a lady wins us grace, and I,
still mortal, cross your world led by her love.

But now I pray—so may it soon befall
you have your greater wish to be called home
into that heaven of love that circles all—

tell me, that I may write down what you say
for all to read, who are you? and those others
who move away behind you—who are they?"

Just as our mountaineers, their first time down,
half-wild and shaggy, gape about the streets

and stare in dumb amazement at the town—

just such a look I saw upon those shades;
but when they had recovered from their stupor
(which from a lofty heart the sooner fades),

the first shade spoke again: "Blessèd are you
who for a better life, store in your soul
experience of these realms you travel through!

Those souls you saw going the other way
grew stained in that for which triumphant Caesar
heard his own legions call him "Queen" one day.

Therefore their band, at parting from us, cries
'Sodom!'—as you have heard—that by their shame
they aid the fire that makes them fit to rise.

We were hermaphroditic in our offenses,
but since we did not honor human laws,
yielding like animals to our lusting senses,

we, when we leave the other band, repent
by crying to our shame the name of her
who crouched in the mock-beast with beast's intent.

And now you know our actions and our crime.
But if you wish our names, we are so many
I do not know them all, nor is there time.

Your wish to know mine shall be satisfied:
I am Guido Guinizelli, here so soon
because I repented fully before I died."

In King Lycurgus' darkest hour, two sons
discovered their lost mother: I was moved
as they had been (but could not match their actions)

when I heard his name, for he had fathered me
and all the rest, my betters, who have sung
sweet lilting rhymes of love and courtesy.

Enraptured, I can neither speak nor hear
but only stare at him as we move on,
although the flames prevent my drawing near.

When at last my eyes had fed, I spoke anew;
and in such terms as win belief, I offered
to serve him in whatever I could do.

And he to me then: "What you say has made
such a profound impression on my mind
as Lethe cannot wash away, nor fade.

But if the words you swore just now are true,
let me know why you show by word and look
such love as I believe I see in you?"

And I to him: "Your songs so sweet and clear
which, for as long as modern usage lives,
shall make the very ink that writes them dear."

"Brother," he said, "that one who moves along
ahead there," (and he pointed) "was in life
a greater craftsman of the mother tongue.

He, in his love songs and his tales in prose,
was without peer—and if fools claim Limoges
produced a better, there are always those

who measure worth by popular acclaim,
ignoring principles of art and reason
to base their judgments on the author's name.

So, once, our fathers sent Guittone's praise,
and his alone, bounding from cry to cry,
though truth prevails with most men nowadays.

And now, if you enjoy such privilege
that you are free to go up to that cloister
within which Christ is abbot of the college,

say an Our Father for me in that host,
as far as it may serve us in this world
in which the very power to sin is lost."

With that, perhaps to yield his place with me
to someone else he vanished through the fire
as a fish does to the dark depths of the sea.

I drew ahead till I was by that shade
he had pointed to, and said that in my heart
a grateful place to feast his name was laid.

And he replied at once and willingly:
"Such pleasaunce have I of thy gentilesse,
that I ne can, ne will I hide from thee.

Arnaut am I, and weepe and sing my faring.
In grievousnesse I see my follies past;
in joie, the blisiful daie of my preparing.

And by that eke virtue, I thee implour,
that redeth thee, that thou amount the staire,
be mindful in thy time of my dolour."

Then he, too, hid himself within the fire
that makes those spirits ready to go higher.

Canto XXVII

THE SEVENTH CORNICE
The Angel of Chastity

The Wall of Fire

THE EARTHLY PARADISE
The Angel Guardian

A little before sunset of the third day on the Mountain the Poets come to the further limit of the Seventh Cornice and are greeted by THE ANGEL OF CHASTITY, who tells them they must pass through the wall of fire. Dante recoils in terror, but Virgil persuades him to enter in Beatrice's name.

They are guided through the fire by a chant they hear coming from the other side. Emerging, they find it is sung by THE ANGEL GUARDIAN of the Earthly Paradise, who stands in a light so brilliant that Dante cannot see him. (It is probably here that THE LAST P is stricken from Dante's brow. Or perhaps it was consumed by the fire.)

The Angel hurries them toward the ascent, but night overtakes them, and the Poets lie down to sleep, each on the step on which he finds himself. (For Statius it will be the last sleep, since there is no night in Heaven.) There, just before dawn, Dante has a prophetic DREAM OF LEAH AND RACHEL, which foreshadows the appearance, above, of Matilda and Beatrice.

Day arrives; the Poets rise and race up the rest of the ascent until they come in sight of THE EARTHLY PARADISE. Here VIRGIL SPEAKS HIS LAST WORDS, for the Poets have now come to the limit of Reason, and Dante is now free to follow his every impulse, since all motion of sin in him has been purged away.

As the day stands when the Sun begins to glow
over the land where his Maker's blood was shed,
and the scales of Libra ride above the Ebro,

while Ganges' waters steam in the noonday glare—
so it stood, the light being nearly faded,
when we met God's glad Angel standing there

on the rocky ledge beyond the reach of the fire,

and caroling *"Beati mundo corde"*
in a voice to which no mortal could aspire.

Then: "Blessèd ones, till by flame purified
no soul may pass this point. Enter the fire
and heed the singing from the other side."

These were his words to us when we had come
near as we could, and hearing them, I froze
as motionless as one laid in his tomb.

I lean forward over my clasped hands and stare
into the fire, thinking of human bodies
I once saw burned, and once more see them there.

My kindly escorts heard me catch my breath
and turned, and Virgil said: "Within that flame
there may be torment, but there is no death.

Think well, my son, what dark ways we have trod . . .
I guided you unharmed on Geryon:
shall I do less now we are nearer God?

Believe this past all doubt: were you to stay
within that womb of flame a thousand years,
it would not burn a single hair away.

And if you still doubt my sincerity,
but reach the hem of your robe into the flame:
your hands and eyes will be your guarantee.

My son, my son, turn here with whole assurance.
Put by your fears and enter to your peace."
And I stood fixed, at war with my own conscience.

And seeing me still stubborn, rooted fast,
he said, a little troubled: "Think, my son,

you shall see Beatrice when this wall is past."

As Pyramus, but one breath from the dead,
opened his eyes when he heard Thisbe's name,
and looked at her, when the mulberry turned red—

just so my hard paralysis melted from me,
and I turned to my Leader at that name
which wells forever in my memory;

at which he wagged his head, as at a child
won over by an apple. Then he said:
"Well, then, what are we waiting for?" and smiled.

He turned then and went first into the fire,
requesting Statius, who for some time now
had walked between us, to bring up the rear.

Once in the flame, I gladly would have cast
my body into boiling glass to cool it
against the measureless fury of the blast.

My gentle father, ever kind and wise,
strengthened me in my dread with talk of Beatrice,
saying: "I seem already to see her eyes."

From the other side, to guide us, rose a paean,
and moving toward it, mindless of all else,
we emerged at last where the ascent began.

There I beheld a light that burned so brightly
I had to look away; and from it rang:
"*Venite benedicti patris mei.*"

"Night falls," it added, "the sun sinks to rest;
do not delay but hurry toward the height
while the last brightness lingers in the west."

Straight up through the great rock-wall lay the way
on such a line that, as I followed it,
my body blocked the sun's last level ray.

We had only climbed the first few stairs as yet
when I and my two sages saw my shadow
fade from me; and we knew the sun had set.

Before the vast sweep of the limned horizon
could fade into one hue and night win all
the immeasurable air to its dominion,

each made the step on which he stood his bed,
for the nature of the Mount not only stopped us
but killed our wish to climb, once day had fled.

As goats on a rocky hill will dance and leap,
nimble and gay, till they find grass, and then,
while they are grazing, grow as tame as sheep

at ease in the green shade when the sun is high
and the shepherd stands by, leaning on his staff,
and at his ease covers them with his eye—

and as the herdsman beds down on the ground,
keeping his quiet night watch by his flock
lest it be scattered by a wolf or hound;

just so we lay there, each on his stone block,
I as the goat, they as my guardians,
shut in on either side by walls of rock.

I could see little ahead—rock blocked the way—
but through that little I saw the stars grow larger,
brighter than mankind sees them. And as I lay,

staring and lost in thought, a sleep came on me—
the sleep that oftentimes presents the fact
before the event, a sleep of prophecy.

At the hour, I think, when Venus, first returning
out of the east, shone down upon the mountain—
she who with fires of love comes ever-burning—

I dreamed I saw a maiden innocent
and beautiful, who walked a sunny field
gathering flowers, and caroling as she went:

"Say I am Leah if any ask my name,
and my white hands weave garlands wreath on wreath
to please me when I stand before the frame

of my bright glass. For this my fingers play
among these blooms. But my sweet sister Rachel
sits at her mirror motionless all day.

To stare into her own eyes endlessly
is all her joy, as mine is in my weaving.
She looks, I do. Thus live we joyously."

Now eastward the new day rayed Heaven's dome
(the sweeter to the returning wanderer
who wakes from each night's lodging nearer home),

and the shadows fled on every side as I
stirred from my sleep and leaped upon my feet,
seeing my Lords already standing by.

"This is the day your hungry soul shall be
fed on the golden apples men have sought
on many different boughs so ardently."

These were the very words which, at the start,

my Virgil spoke to me, and there have never
been gifts as dear as these were to my heart.

Such waves of yearning to achieve the height
swept through my soul, that at each step I took
I felt my feathers growing for the flight.

When we had climbed the stairway to the rise
of the topmost step, there with a father's love
Virgil turned and fixed me with his eyes.

"My son," he said, "you now have seen the torment
of the temporal and the eternal fires;
here, now, is the limit of my discernment.

I have led you here by grace of mind and art;
now let your own good pleasure be your guide;
you are past the steep ways, past the narrow part.

See there the sun that shines upon your brow,
the sweet new grass, the flowers, the fruited vines
which spring up without need of seed or plow.

Until those eyes come gladdened which in pain
moved me to come to you and lead your way,
sit there at ease or wander through the plain.

Expect no more of me in word or deed:
here your will is upright, free, and whole,
and you would be in error not to heed

whatever your own impulse prompts you to:
lord of yourself I crown and mitre you."

Canto XXVIII

*It is the morning of the Wednesday after Easter, Dante's fourth day on the
Mountain, and having been crowned Lord of Himself by Virgil, Dante now takes
the lead for the first time, wandering at his leisure into THE SACRED WOOD of
the Earthly Paradise until his way is blocked by the waters of LETHE.*

*His feet stopped, Dante sends his eyes on to wander that Wood and there
suddenly appears to him a solitary lady singing and gathering flowers. She is
MATILDA, who symbolizes THE ACTIVE LIFE OF THE SOUL.*

*In reply to Dante's entreaty, Matilda approaches to the other bank of the river.
So standing, three paces across from him, she offers to answer all that Dante
wishes to ask. Dante replies that he is in some confusion about the sources of the
wind and the water of the Earthly Paradise. Matilda promises to dispel the mists
from his understanding and proceeds to explain in great detail THE NATURAL
PHENOMENA OF THE EARTHLY PARADISE, which is to say, the source of
the wind, the vegetation, and the water. She further explains the special powers
of the waters of LETHE and of EUNOË and concludes with some remarks on the
errors of the ancient poets in the location of the Earthly Paradise. At her last
words, Dante turns to his two ancient poets to see how they are taking her
remarks. Finding them smiling, he turns back once more to Matilda.*

Eager now to explore in and about
the luxuriant holy forest evergreen
that softened the new light, I started out,

without delaying longer, from the stair
and took my lingering way into the plain
on ground that breathed a fragrance to the air.

With no least variation in itself
and with no greater force than a mild wind,
the sweet air stroked my face on that sweet shelf,

and at its touch the trembling branches swayed,
all bending toward that quarter into which
the holy mountain cast its morning shade;

yet not so far back that in any part
of that sweet wood the small birds in the tops
had reason to stop practicing their art;

but bursting with delight those singing throngs
within their green tents welcomed the new breeze
that murmured a sweet burden to their songs

like that one hears gathering from bough to bough
of the pine wood there on Chiassi's shore
when Aeolus lets the Sirocco blow.

I had already come, slow bit by bit,
so far into that ancient holy wood
I could not see where I had entered it;

when I came upon a stream that blocked my way.
To my left it flowed, its wavelets bending back
the grasses on its banks as if in play.

The purest waters known to man would seem
to have some taint of sediment within them
compared to those, for though that holy stream

flows darkly there, its surface never lit
in its perpetual shade by any shaft
of sun or moon, nothing could hide in it.

My feet stopped, but my eyes pursued their way
across that stream, to wander in delight
the variousness of everblooming May.

And suddenly—as rare sights sometimes do,

the wonder of them driving from the mind
all other thoughts—I saw come into view

a lady, all alone, who wandered there
singing, and picking flowers from the profusion
with which her path was painted everywhere.

"Fair lady who—if outward looks and ways
bear, as they ought, true witness to the heart—
have surely sunned yourself in Love's own rays,

be pleased," I said to her, "to draw as near
the bank of this sweet river as need be
for me to understand the song I hear.

You make me see in my imagining
Persephone as she appeared that day
her mother lost a daughter; she, the Spring."

As a dancer, keeping both feet on the ground
and close together, hardly putting one
before the other, spins herself around—

so did she turn to me upon the red
and yellow flowerlets, virgin modesty
making her lower her eyes and bow her head.

And she did all I asked, for she came forward
till I not only heard the melody
of what she sang, but made out every word.

And when she stood where the bright grasses are
bathed and bent by the waves of the clear river,
she raised her eyes—and gave my soul a star.

I cannot think so glorious a ray
shot out of Venus' eyes that time her son

wounded her inadvertently in play.

There, on the other bank, smiling she stood
and gathered to her arms more of the flowers
that sprang up without seeds in that high wood.

The stream between us was three paces wide,
but the Hellespont where Persian Xerxes crossed
to leave a dire example to all pride,

in its raging between Sestos and Abydos,
caused less hate in Leander than this in me,
for not dividing so that I might cross.

"You are newcomers, and perhaps you find
because I smile," she said, "here in this place
chosen to be the nest of humankind,

some doubt that makes you wonder at the sight.
To pierce such mists as gather on your thoughts
the psalm, *Delectasti me,* will give you light.

And you in front who first entreated me,
speak if you would know more. I came prepared
to answer you as fully as need be."

"The way the wood hums and the waters flow,"
I said then, "are at odds with the conclusions
I drew from what I heard a while ago."

"I shall explain from what cause," she replied,
"these things that have confused your mind proceed,
and thus brush its obscuring mist aside.

That Highest Good which only Itself can please
made man good, and for goodness, and It gave him
this place as earnest of eternal peace.

But man defaulted. All too brief his stay.
Defaulted, and exchanged for tears and toil
his innocent first laughter and sweet play.

When vapors of the earth and water meet
a storm is born, below there. Now these vapors
reach up, as far as possible, toward heat.

To guard man from such warring elements
this mountain soared so high that no earth vapor
could rise above the gate of penitence.

Now since the air revolves in one conjoint
and perfect circuit with The Primal Motion,
unless its wheel is broken at some point;

here at this altitude, where it goes round
in its pure state, it strikes the foliage
which, being dense, is made to give off sound.

The stricken plant impregnates the pure air
with its particular powers, which are then borne
on the great wheel and scattered everywhere;

and the other earth, according to the powers
of soil and climate in its various zones,
conceives and bears its various fruits and flowers.

When this is understood there, no man need
believe it strange when plants take root and spring
out of the earth without apparent seed.

Know, too, the sacred soil on which you stand
is bursting-full of species of all sorts,
and bears fruits never picked by human hand.

The water you see here is from no source
that needs replenishment from cloudy vapors,
like streams that rise and fall: with constant force

it leaves a fountain that receives again,
from God's Will, every drop that it pours forth
to the two streams it sends across this plain.

On this side, it removes as it flows down
all memory of sin; on that, it strengthens
the memory of every good deed done.

It is called Lethe here: Eunoë there.
And one must drink first this and then the other
to feel its powers. No sweetness can compare

with the savor of these waters. And although
you may at once, and with no more instruction,
drink your soul's fill from the eternal flow,

let me bestow one thing more for good measure.
Though I exceed my promise, I cannot think
what I add now will meet with your displeasure.

Those ancients who made songs to celebrate
man's Age of Gold, placed probably on Parnassus
this perfect garden of his first pure state.

Here mankind lived its innocent first days.
Here is the Eternal Spring and every fruit.
This is the nectar that the poets praise."

She paused. I turned around to face my lords,
the poets whose strains had honored ancient song,
and saw they had received her final words

with smiles that lingered yet upon their faces;

then turned back to that lady of glad graces.

45. *sunned yourself in Love's own rays:* In the light of God.
50. *Persephone:* Daughter of Demeter (whose name signifies "Mother Earth"), the goddess of vegetation. One day, as Persephone was gathering flowers in a

Canto XXIX

The Heavenly Pageant

Chanting a blessing on those whose sins are forgiven, Matilda moves upstream along one bank of Lethe, and Dante keeps pace with her on the other side. A glorious light and a sweet melody grow on the air, filling Dante with such rapture that he cries out against Eve's daring, through which such joys were lost to mankind.

Soon thereafter he sees the approach of THE HEAVENLY PAGEANT. It is led by SEVEN GOLDEN CANDELABRA that paint A SEVEN-STRIPED RAINBOW on the sky. Behind them come TWENTY-FOUR ELDERS (the Books of the Old Testament), and behind them FOUR BEASTS (the Four Gospels), who guard A TRIUMPHAL CHARIOT (the Church), drawn by a GRIFFON (Christ). At the right wheel of the Chariot dance THE THREE THEOLOGICAL VIRTUES; at its left wheel, THE FOUR CARDINAL VIRTUES. This group is followed, in order, by TWO ELDERS representing Luke as the author of Acts and Paul as the author of the fourteen epistles; by FOUR ELDERS representing James, Peter, John, and Jude as authors of the four Catholic epistles; and finally by A SINGLE ELDER representing John as the author of Revelation.

When the Chariot reaches a point directly across from Dante, a thunderclap resounds, and the entire pageant halts upon that signal.

Her words done, she began her song again—
Beati quorum tecta sunt peccata—
as if in love when love is free of pain.

As nymphs of old went wandering alone
through the deep-shaded woodlands, some pursuing,
and others seeking to evade, the Sun;

so, then, she started up the riverside
and, on my own bank, I kept pace with her,
matching her little steps with shortened stride.

Some fifty paces each we moved this way,
when both banks curved as one; and now I found
my face turned to the cradle of the day.

Nor had we gone as far again, all told,
beyond the curve, when she turned to me, saying:
"Dear brother, look and listen." And behold!—

through all that everlasting forest burst
an instantaneous flood of radiance.
I took it for a lightning-flash at first.

But lightning comes and goes. The light I saw
not only stayed on but grew more resplendent.
"What can this be?" I asked myself in awe.

And a sweet melody filled the bright air—
so sweet that I reproached in righteous zeal
Eve's fatal recklessness. How could she dare?—

one woman alone, made but a moment since—
all heaven and earth obedient—to refuse
the one veil willed by High Omnipotence;

beneath which, had she stayed God's acolyte,
I should have known before then, and for longer
those raptures of ineffable delight.

My soul hung tranced in joy beyond all measure
and yearning for yet more, as I moved on
through those first fruits of the eternal pleasure;

when, under the green boughs that spread before us
the air became a blaze, and the sweet sound
we had been hearing grew into a chorus.

O holy, holy Virgins, if for you
I ever suffered vigils, cold, or fasts,
occasion spurs me now to claim my due.

Empty all Helicon! Now is the time!
Urania, help me here with your full choir,
to bring things scarce conceivable to rhyme!

I saw next, far ahead, what I believed
were seven golden trees (at such a distance
and in such light the eye can be deceived);

but in a while, when I had drawn so near
that chance resemblances confused by distance
no longer made false images appear,

that power that reaps for reason's mill could see
that they were candelabra; and in the chant
it heard the word *Hosanna!* ringing free.

Above the gold array flamed seven times seven
candles more lucent than the mid-month moon
at midnight in the calm of clearest heaven.

I turned about, amazed at what I saw,
to my good Virgil, and he answered me
in silence, with a look of equal awe.

I turned back then to those sublimities
that were approaching at so slow a pace
that new brides might outdistance them with ease.

The lady cried: "Why have you set your mind
so fixedly upon those living lights
that you do not observe what comes behind?"

Then I saw people walking like attendants

behind their lords, and clothed in robes so white
earth has no snow of such a pure resplendence.

Upon my left the polished river shone
bright as a mirror, and when I looked in
I saw my left side there, perfectly drawn.

And when I had moved close enough to be
kept at a distance by no more than water,
I halted my slow steps, better to see.

I saw the flames advance, leaving the air
painted behind, as if by massive strokes,
or by bright pennons they were trailing there;

thus, all the trailing heavens were aglow
with seven bands of light of the same color
as Delia's girdle or Apollo's bow.

Those bands stretched back further than I could see,
and the distance separating side from side
came to ten paces, as it seemed to me.

And there, advancing two by two beneath
that seven-striped sky came four-and-twenty elders,
each crowned in glory with a lily-wreath.

And all sang with one voice, triumphantly:
"Blessèd art thou among the daughters of Adam!
Blessèd thy beauty to eternity!"

And when those souls elect, as in a dream,
had left behind the flowers and the new grass
that shone before me, there across the stream,

as star follows on star in the serene
of heaven's height, there came on at their backs

four beasts, and these wore wreaths of living green.

Each had three pairs of wings, and every pair
was full of eyes. Were Argus living yet,
his eyes would be most like what I saw there.

I cannot spend my rhymes as liberally
as I should like to in describing them,
for, reader, other needs are pressing me:

but read Ezekiel where he sets forth
how they appeared to him in a great storm
of wind and cloud and fire out of the North;

and such as he recounts, such did I see;
except that in the number of their wings
John differs with him, and agrees with me.

Within the space they guarded there came on
a burnished two-wheeled chariot in triumph,
and harnessed to the neck of a great Griffon

whose wings, upraised into the bands of light,
inclosed the middle one so perfectly
they cut no part of those to left or right.

Higher than sight its wing-tips soared away.
Its bird-like parts were gold; and white the rest
with blood-red markings. Will it serve to say

Rome never saw such a caparison,
no, not for Africanus, nor yet Augustus?
The Sun's own would seem shabby by comparison;

yes, even the Sun's own chariot, which strayed
and was destroyed in fire by Jove's dark justice
that day the frightened Earth devoutly prayed.

Beside the right wheel, dancing in a gyre,
three maidens came. The first one was so red
she would be barely visible in fire.

The second looked as if both flesh and bone
were made of flawless emerald. The third
seemed a new snow no slightest wind has blown.

And now the white one led the dance, and now
the red: and from the song the red one sang
the others took their measure, fast or slow.

Beside the left wheel, dancing in a flame
of purple robes, and led by one who had
three eyes within her head, four glad nymphs came.

Behind these seven came on, side by side,
two elders, different in dress, but both
by the same massive bearing dignified.

One showed he was a follower of the art
of great Hippocrates, whom Nature made
to heal the creatures dearest to her heart.

The other, his counterpart, carried a blade
so sharp and bright that at the sight of it,
even across the stream, I was afraid.

Next I saw four who walked with humble mien.
And last of all, one who moved in a trance,
as if asleep, but his face was firm and keen.

These seven were robed like the first twenty-four
in flowing robes of white, but, for their crowns,
it was not wreaths of lilies that they wore,

but roses and whatever blooms most red.
One would have sworn, seeing them at a distance,
that they were wearing flames about the head.

And when the chariot had reached the place
across from me, I heard a thunderclap
that seemed a signal to those souls in grace,

for there, in unison with the exalted
first flaming standards, all that pageant halted.

Canto XXX

Beatrice

Virgil Vanishes

The procession halts and the Prophets turn to the chariot and sing "Come, my bride, from Lebanon." They are summoning BEATRICE, who appears on the left side of the chariot, half-hidden from view by showers of blossoms poured from above by A HUNDRED ANGELS. Dante, stirred by the sight, turns to Virgil to express his overflowing emotions, and discovers that VIRGIL HAS VANISHED.

Because he bursts into tears at losing Virgil DANTE IS REPRIMANDED BY BEATRICE. The Angel Choir overhead immediately breaks into a Psalm of Compassion, but Beatrice, still severe, answers by detailing Dante's offenses in not making proper use of his great gifts. It would violate the ordering of the Divine Decree, she argues, to let Dante drink the waters of Lethe, thereby washing all memory of sin from his soul, before he had shed the tears of a real repentance.

When the Septentrion of the First Heaven,
which does not rise nor set, and which has never
been veiled from sight by any mist but sin,

and which made every soul in that high court
know its true course (just as the lower Seven
direct the helmsman to his earthly port),
had stopped; the holy prophets, who till then
had walked between the Griffon and those lights,
turned to the car like souls who cry "Amen."

And one among them who seemed sent from Heaven
clarioned: *"Veni, sponsa, de Libano,"*
three times, with all the others joining in.

As, at the last trump every saint shall rise
out of the grave, ready with voice new-fleshed

to carol *Alleluliah* to the skies;

just so, above the chariot, at the voice
of such an elder, rose a hundred Powers
and Principals of the Eternal Joys,

all saying together: *"Benedictus qui venis";*
then, scattering flowers about on every side:
"Manibus o date lilia plenis."

Time and again at daybreak I have seen
the eastern sky glow with a wash of rose
while all the rest hung limpid and serene,

and the Sun's face rise tempered from its rest
so veiled by vapors that the naked eye
could look at it for minutes undistressed.

Exactly so, within a cloud of flowers
that rose like fountains from the angels' hands
and fell about the chariot in showers,

a lady came in view: an olive crown
wreathed her immaculate veil, her cloak was green,
the colors of live flame played on her gown.

My soul—such years had passed since last it saw
that lady and stood trembling in her presence,
stupefied by the power of holy awe—

now, by some power that shone from her above
the reach and witness of my mortal eyes,
felt the full mastery of enduring love.

The instant I was smitten by the force,
which had already once transfixed my soul
before my boyhood years had run their course,

I turned left with the same assured belief
that makes a child run to its mother's arms
when it is frightened or has come to grief,

to say to Virgil: "There is not within me
one drop of blood unstirred. I recognize
the tokens of the ancient flame." But he,

he had taken his light from us. He had gone.
Virgil had gone. Virgil, the gentle Father
to whom I gave my soul for its salvation!

Not all that sight of Eden lost to view
by our First Mother could hold back the tears
that stained my cheeks so lately washed with dew.

"Dante, do not weep yet, though Virgil goes.
Do not weep yet, for soon another wound
shall make you weep far hotter tears than those!"

As an admiral takes his place at stern or bow
to observe the handling of his other ships
and spur all hands to do their best—so now,

on the chariot's left side, I saw appear
when I turned at the sound of my own name
(which, necessarily, is recorded here),

that lady who had been half-veiled from view
by the flowers of the angel-revels. Now her eyes
fixed me across the stream, piercing me through.

And though the veil she still wore, held in place
by the wreathed flowers of wise Minerva's leaves,
let me see only glimpses of her face,

her stern and regal bearing made me dread
her next words, for she spoke as one who saves
the heaviest charge till all the rest are read.

"Look at me well. I am she. I am Beatrice.
How dared you make your way to this high mountain?
Did you not know that here man lives in bliss?"
I lowered my head and looked down at the stream.
But when I saw myself reflected there,
I fixed my eyes upon the grass for shame.

I shrank as a wayward child in his distress
shrinks from his mother's sternness, for the taste
of love grown wrathful is a bitterness.

She paused. At once the angel chorus sang
the blessed psalm: *"In te, Domine, speravi."*
As far as *"pedes meos"* their voices rang.

As on the spine of Italy the snow
lies frozen hard among the living rafters
in winter when the northeast tempests blow;

then, melting if so much as a breath stir
from the land of shadowless noon, flows through itself
like hot wax trickling down a lighted taper—

just so I froze, too cold for sighs or tears
until I heard that choir whose notes are tuned
to the eternal music of the spheres.

But when I heard the voice of their compassion
plead for me more than if they had cried out:
"Lady, why do you treat him in this fashion?";

the ice, which hard about my heart had pressed,
turned into breath and water, and flowed out

through eyes and throat in anguish from my breast.

Still standing at the chariot's left side,
she turned to those compassionate essences
whose song had sought to move her, and replied:

"You keep your vigil in the Eternal Day
where neither night nor sleep obscures from you
a single step the world takes on its way;

but I must speak with greater care that he
who weeps on that far bank may understand
and feel a grief to match his guilt. Not only

by the workings of the spheres that bring each seed
to its fit end according to the stars
that ride above it, but by gifts decreed

in the largesse of overflowing Grace,
whose rain has such high vapors for its source
our eyes cannot mount to their dwelling place;

this man, potentially, was so endowed
from early youth that marvelous increase
should have come forth from every good he sowed.

But richest soil the soonest will grow wild
with bad seed and neglect. For a while I stayed him
with glimpses of my face. Turning my mild

and youthful eyes into his very soul,
I let him see their shining, and I led him
by the straight way, his face to the right goal.

The instant I had come upon the sill
of my second age, and crossed and changed my life,
he left me and let others shape his will.

When I rose from the flesh into the spirit,
to greater beauty and to greater virtue,
he found less pleasure in me and less merit.

He turned his steps aside from the True Way,
pursuing the false images of good
that promise what they never wholly pay.

Not all the inspiration I won by prayer
and brought to him in dreams and meditations
could call him back, so little did he care.
He fell so far from every hope of bliss
that every means of saving him had failed
except to let him see the damned. For this

I visited the portals of the dead
and poured my tears and prayers before that spirit
by whom his steps have, up to now, been led.

The seal Almighty God's decree has placed
on the rounds of His creation would be broken
were he to come past Lethe and to taste

the water that wipes out the guilty years
without some scot of penitential tears!"

Canto XXXI

Beatrice continues her reprimand, forcing Dante to confess his faults until he swoons with grief and pain at the thought of his sin. He wakes to find himself in Lethe, held in the arms of Matilda, who leads him to the other side of the stream and there immerses him that he may drink the waters that wipe out all memory of sin.

Matilda then leads him to THE FOUR CARDINAL VIRTUES, who dance about him and lead him before THE GRIFFON where he may look into THE EYES OF BEATRICE. In them Dante sees, in a FIRST BEATIFIC VISION, the radiant reflection of the Griffon, who appears now in his human and now in his godly nature.

THE THREE THEOLOGICAL VIRTUES now approach and beg that Dante may behold THE SMILE OF BEATRICE. Beatrice removes her veil, and in a SECOND BEATIFIC VISION, Dante beholds the splendor of the unveiled shining of Divine Love.

"You, there, who stand upon the other side—"
(turning to me now, who had thought the edge
of her discourse was sharp, the point) she cried

without pause in her flow of eloquence,
"Speak up! Speak up! Is it true? To such a charge
your own confession must give evidence."

I stood as if my spirit had turned numb:
the organ of my speech moved, but my voice
died in my throat before a word could come.

Briefly she paused, then cried impatiently:
"What are you thinking? Speak up, for the waters

have yet to purge sin from your memory."

Confusion joined to terror forced a broken
"yes" from my throat, so weak that only one
who read my lips would know that I had spoken.

As an arbalest will snap when string and bow
are drawn too tight by the bowman, and the bolt
will strike the target a diminished blow—

so did I shatter, strengthless and unstrung,
under her charge, pouring out floods of tears,
while my voice died in me on the way to my tongue.

And she: "Filled as you were with the desire
I taught you for That Good beyond which nothing
exists on earth to which man may aspire,

what yawning moats or what stretched chain-lengths lay
across your path to force you to abandon
all hope of pressing further on your way?

What increase or allurement seemed to show
in the brows of others that you walked before them
as a lover walks below his lady's window?"

My breath dragged from me in a bitter sigh;
I barely found a voice to answer with;
my lips had trouble forming a reply.

In tears I said: "The things of the world's day,
false pleasures and enticements, turned my steps
as soon as you had ceased to light my way."

And she: "Had you been silent, or denied
what you confess, your guilt would still be known
to Him from Whom no guilt may hope to hide.

But here, before our court, when souls upbraid
themselves for their own guilt in true remorse,
the grindstone is turned back against the blade.

In any case that you may know your crime
truly and with true shame and so be stronger
against the Siren's song another time,

control your tears and listen with your soul
to learn how my departure from the flesh
ought to have spurred you to the higher goal.

Nothing in Art or Nature could call forth
such joy from you, as sight of that fair body
which clothed me once and now sifts back to earth.

And if my dying turned that highest pleasure
to very dust, what joy could still remain
in mortal things for you to seek and treasure?

At the first blow you took from such vain things
your every thought should have been raised to follow
my flight above decay. Nor should your wings

have been weighed down by any joy below—
love of a maid, or any other fleeting
and useless thing—to wait a second blow.

The fledgling waits a second shaft, a third;
but nets are spread and the arrow sped in vain
in sight or hearing of the full-grown bird."

As a scolded child, tongue-tied for shame, will stand
and recognize his fault, and weep for it,
bowing his head to a just reprimand,

so did I stand. And she said: "If to hear me
grieves you, now raise your beard and let your eyes
show you a greater cause for misery."

The blast that blows from Libya's hot sand,
or the Alpine gale, overcomes less resistance
uprooting oaks than I, at her command,

overcame then in lifting up my face;
for when she had referred to it as my "beard"
I sensed too well the venom of her phrase.

When I had raised my eyes with so much pain,
I saw those Primal Beings, now at rest,
who had strewn blossoms round her thick as rain;

and with my tear-blurred and uncertain vision
I saw Her turned to face that beast which is
one person in two natures without division.

Even veiled and across the river from me
her face outshone its first-self by as much
as she outshone all mortals formerly.

And the thorns of my repentance pricked me so
that all the use and substance of the world
I most had loved, now most appeared my foe.

Such guilty recognition gnawed my heart
I swooned for pain; and what I then became
she best knows who most gave me cause to smart.

When I returned to consciousness at last
I found the lady who had walked alone
bent over me. "Hold fast!" she said, "Hold fast!"

She had drawn me into the stream up to my throat,

and pulling me behind her, she sped on
over the water, light as any boat.

Nearing the sacred bank, I heard her say
in tones so sweet I cannot call them back,
much less describe them here: *"Asperges me."*

Then the sweet lady took my head between
her open arms, and embracing me, she dipped me
and made me drink the waters that make clean.

Then raising me in my new purity
she led me to the dance of the Four Maidens;
each raised an arm and so joined hands above me.

"Here we are nymphs; stars are we in the skies.
Ere Beatrice went to earth we were ordained
her handmaids. We will lead you to her eyes;

but that your own may see what joyous light
shines in them, yonder Three, who see more deeply,
will sharpen and instruct your mortal sight."

Thus they sang, then led me to the Griffon.
Behind him, Beatrice waited. And when I stood
at the Griffon's breast, they said in unison:

"Look deep, look well, however your eyes may smart.
We have led you now before those emeralds
from which Love shot his arrows through your heart."

A thousand burning passions, every one
hotter than any flame, held my eyes fixed
to the lucent eyes she held fixed on the Griffon.

Like sunlight in a glass the twofold creature
shone from the deep reflection of her eyes,

now in the one, now in the other nature.

Judge, reader, if I found it passing strange
to see the thing unaltered in itself
yet in its image working change on change.

And while my soul in wonder and delight
was savoring that food which in itself
both satisfies and quickens appetite,

the other Three, whose bearing made it clear
they were of higher rank, came toward me dancing
to the measure of their own angelic air.

"Turn, Beatrice, oh turn the eyes of grace,"
was their refrain, "upon your faithful one
who comes so far to look upon your face.

Grant us this favor of your grace: reveal
your mouth to him, and let his eyes behold
the Second Beauty, which your veils conceal."

O splendor of the eternal living light!
who that has drunk deep of Parnassus' waters,
or grown pale in the shadow of its height,

would not, still, feel his burdened genius fail
attempting to describe in any tongue
how you appeared when you put by your veil

in that free air open to heaven and earth
whose harmony is your shining shadowed forth!

THE PARADISO
Canto I

THE EARTHLY PARADISE
ASCENT TO HEAVEN
The Invocation
The Sphere of Fire
The Music of the Spheres

DANTE STATES his supreme theme as Paradise itself and invokes the aid not only of the Muses but of Apollo.

Dante and Beatrice are in THE EARTHLY PARADISE, the Sun is at the Vernal Equinox, it is noon at Purgatory and midnight at Jerusalem when Dante sees Beatrice turn her eyes to stare straight into the Sun and reflexively imitates her gesture. At once it is as if a second Sun had been created, its light dazzling his senses, and Dante feels the ineffable change of his mortal soul into Godliness.

These phenomena are more than his senses can grasp, and Beatrice must explain to him what he himself has not realized: that he and Beatrice are soaring toward the height of Heaven at an incalculable speed.

Thus Dante climaxes the master metaphor in which purification is equated to weightlessness. Having purged all dross from his soul he mounts effortlessly, without even being aware of it at first, to his natural goal in the Godhead. So they pass through THE SPHERE OF FIRE, and so Dante first hears THE MUSIC OF THE SPHERES.

The glory of Him who moves all things rays forth
through all the universe, and is reflected
from each thing in proportion to its worth.

I have been in that Heaven of His most light,
and what I saw, those who descend from there
lack both the knowledge and the power to write.

For as our intellect draws near its goal

it opens to such depths of understanding
as memory cannot plumb within the soul.

Nevertheless, whatever portion time
still leaves me of the treasure of that kingdom
shall now become the subject of my rhyme.

O good Apollo, for this last task, I pray
you make me such a vessel of your powers
as you deem worthy to be crowned with bay.

One peak of cleft Parnassus heretofore
has served my need, now must I summon both
on entering the arena one time more.

Enter my breast, I pray you, and there breathe
as high a strain as conquered Marsyas
that time you drew his body from its sheath.

O power divine, but lend to my high strain
so much as will make clear even the shadow
of that High Kingdom stamped upon my brain,

and you shall see me come to your dear grove
to crown myself with those green leaves which you
and my high theme shall make me worthy of.

So seldom are they gathered, Holy Sire,
to crown an emperor's or a poet's triumph
(oh fault and shame of mortal man's desire!)

that the glad Delphic god must surely find
increase of joy in the Peneian frond
when any man thirsts for it in his mind.

Great flames are kindled where the small sparks fly.
So after me, perhaps, a better voice

shall raise such prayers that Cyrrha will reply.

The lamp of the world rises to mortal view
from various stations, but that point which joins
four circles with three crosses, it soars through

to a happier course in happier conjunction
wherein it warms and seals the wax of the world
closer to its own nature and high function.

That glad conjunction had made it evening here
and morning there; the south was all alight,
while darkness rode the northern hemisphere;

when I saw Beatrice had turned left to raise
her eyes up to the Sun; no eagle ever
stared at its shining with so fixed a gaze.

And as a ray descending from the sky
gives rise to another, which climbs back again,
as a pilgrim yearns for home; so through my eye

her action, like a ray into my mind,
gave rise to mine: I stared into the Sun
so hard that here it would have left me blind;

but much is granted to our senses there,
in that garden made to be man's proper place,
that is not granted us when we are here.

I had to look away soon, and yet not
so soon but what I saw him spark and blaze
like new-tapped iron when it pours white-hot.

And suddenly, as it appeared to me,
day was added to day, as if He who can
had added a new Sun to Heaven's glory.

Beatrice stared at the eternal spheres
entranced, unmoving; and I looked away
from the Sun's height to fix my eyes on hers.

And as I looked, I felt begin within me
what Glaucus felt eating the herb that made him
a god among the others in the sea.

How speak trans-human change to human sense?
Let the example speak until God's grace
grants the pure spirit the experience.

Whether I rose in only the last created
part of my being, O Love that rulest Heaven
Thou knowest, by whose lamp I was translated.

When the Great Wheel that spins eternally,
in longing for Thee, captured my attention
by that harmony attuned and heard by Thee,

I saw ablaze with Sun from side to side
a reach of Heaven: not all the rains and rivers
of all of time could make a sea so wide.

That radiance and that new-heard melody
fired me with such a yearning for their Cause
as I had never felt before. And she

who saw my every thought as well as I,
saw my perplexity: before I asked
my question she had started her reply.

Thus she began: "You dull your own perceptions
with false imaginings and do not grasp
what would be clear but for your preconceptions.

You think you are still on earth: the lightning's spear
never fled downward from its natural place
as rapidly as you are rising there."

I grasped her brief and smiling words and shed
my first perplexity, but found myself
entangled in another, and I said:

"My mind, already recovered from the surprise
of the great marvel you have just explained,
is now amazed anew: how can I rise

in my gross body through such aery substance?"
She sighed in pity and turned as might a mother
to a delirious child. "The elements

of all things," she began, "whatever their mode,
observe an inner order. It is this form
that makes the universe resemble God.

In this the higher creatures see the hand
of the Eternal Worth, which is the goal
to which these norms conduce, being so planned.

All Being within this order, by the laws
of its own nature is impelled to find
its proper station round its Primal Cause.

Thus every nature moves across the tide
of the great sea of being to its own port,
each with its given instinct as its guide.

This instinct draws the fire about the Moon.
It is the mover in the mortal heart.
It draws the earth together and makes it one.

Not only the brute creatures, but all those

possessed of intellect and love, this instinct
drives to their mark as a bow shoots forth its arrows.

The Providence that makes all things hunger here
satisfies forever with its light
the heaven within which whirls the fastest sphere.

And to it now, as to a place foretold,
are we two soaring, driven by that bow
whose every arrow finds a mark of gold.

It is true that oftentimes the form of a thing
does not respond to the intent of the art,
the matter being deaf to summoning—

just so, the creature sometimes travels wide
of this true course, for even when so driven
it still retains the power to turn aside

(exactly as we may see the heaven's fire
plunge from a cloud) and its first impulse may
be twisted earthward by a false desire.

You should not, as I see it, marvel more
at your ascent than at a river's fall
from a high mountain to the valley floor.

If you, free as you are of every dross,
had settled and had come to rest below,
that would indeed have been as marvelous

as a still flame there in the mortal plain."
So saying, she turned her eyes to Heaven again.

Canto II

ASCENT TO THE MOON
THE FIRST SPHERE: THE MOON
Warning to the Reader
Beatrice Explains the
Markings on the Moon

*DANTE AND BEATRICE are soaring to THE SPHERE OF THE MOON at a
speed approaching that of light. Dante warns back the shallow reader: only
those who have eaten of the knowledge of God may hope to follow him into the
last reaches of his infinite voyage, for it will reveal such wonders as only faith
can grasp.*

*His warning concluded, he and Beatrice enter the Sphere of the Moon and
pass into the substances of the Moon as light into water, as God incarnated
himself into man, or as the saved soul reenters God, without disruption of the
substance thus entered.*

*Still unenlightened by the ultimate revelation, Dante does not understand how
there can appear on the diamond-smooth surface on the Moon (as he conceived
it) those markings we know as THE MAN IN THE MOON, and which the
Italians knew as CAIN WITH HIS BUSH OF THORNS.*

*Beatrice asks for his explanation, refutes it, and proceeds to explain the truth
of the Moon's markings.*

O you who in your wish to hear these things
have followed thus far in your little skiffs
the wake of my great ship that sails and sings,

turn back and make your way to your own coast.
Do not commit yourself to the main deep,
for, losing me, all may perhaps be lost.

My course is set for an uncharted sea.
Minerva fills my sail. Apollo steers.
And nine new Muses point the Pole for me.

You other few who have set yourselves to eat

the bread of angels, by which we live on earth,
but of which no man ever grew replete;

you may well trust your keel to the salt track
and follow in the furrow of my wake
ahead of the parted waters that close back.

Those heroes who sailed to Colchis, there to see
their glorious Jason turned into a plowman,
were not as filled with wonder as you will be.

The connate and perpetual thirst we feel
for the Godlike realm, bore us almost as swiftly
as the sight soars to see the heavens wheel.

Beatrice was looking upward and I at her
when—in the time it takes a bolt to strike,
fly, and be resting in the bowstring's blur—

I found myself in a place where a wondrous thing
drew my entire attention; whereat she
from whom I could not hide my mind's
least yearning

turned and said, as much in joy as beauty:
"To God, who has raised us now to the first star
direct your thoughts in glad and grateful duty."

It seemed to me a cloud as luminous
and dense and smoothly polished as a diamond
struck by a ray of sun, enveloped us.

We were received into the elements
of the eternal pearl as water takes
light to itself, with no change in its substance.

If I was a body (nor need we in this case

conceive how one dimension can bear another,
which must be if two bodies fill one space)

the more should my desire burn like the Sun
to see that Essence in which one may see
how human nature and God blend into one.
There we shall witness what we hold in faith,
not told by reason but self-evident;
as men perceive an axiom here on earth.

"My lady," I replied, "in every way
my being can, I offer up my thanks
to Him who raised me from the world of clay.

But tell me what dark traces in the grain
of this bright body show themselves below
and cause men to tell fables about Cain?"

She smiled a moment and then answered me:
"If the reckoning of mortals fails to turn
the lock to which your senses hold no key,

the arrows of wonder should not run you through:
even when led by the evidence of the senses
the wings of reason often do not fly true.

But what do *you* believe the cause to be?"
And I: "That these variations we observe
are caused by bodies of varying density."

And she: "You will certainly come to know your view
is steeped in falsehood. If you listen well
to the counter-arguments I shall offer you.

The eighth sphere shines with many lamps, and these
may be observed to shine with various aspects,
both in their qualities and quantities.

If rare or dense alone could have produced
all this, one power would have to be in all,
whether equally or variously diffused.

Diversity of powers can only spring
from formal principles, and all but one
would be excluded by your reasoning.

Now if rarity produced the marks you mention,
then the matter of this planet must be transparent
at certain points, due to its rarefaction;

or it must be arranged like fat and lean
within a body, as, so to speak, a book
alternates pages. But it may be seen

in an eclipse that the first cannot be true,
for then the sun's light, as it does in striking
rare matter of any sort, would pass right through.

Since it does not, we may then pass along
to the second case, and if I prove it false,
I shall have shown that your whole thought is wrong.

If this rare matter is not spread throughout
the planet's mass, then there must be a limit
at which the denser matter will turn about

the sun's rays, which, not being allowed to pass,
will be reflected as light and color are
from the leaded back of a clear looking glass.

Now you may argue, in Avicenna's track,
that the ray seems darker in one place than in others
since it is being reflected from further back.

From such an *instance* (if you will do your part)
you may escape by experiment (that being
the spring that feeds the rivers of man's art).

Take three clear mirrors. Let two be set out
at an equal distance from you, and a third
between them, but further back. Now turn about

to face them, and let someone set a light
behind your back so that it strikes all three
and is reflected from them to your sight.

Although the image from the greater distance
is smaller than the others, you must note
that all three shine back with an equal brilliance.

Now, as the power of the Sun's rays will strip
the wintry ground on which the snow has lain
of the cold and color that held it in their grip,

so you, with mind stripped clean, shall I delight
with such a radiance of the living truth
that it will leap and tremble in your sight.

Within the heaven of peace beyond the sky
there whirls a body from whose power arises
the being of all things that within it lie.

The next sphere, that which is so richly lit,
distributes this power to many essences
distinct from itself, yet all contained within it.

The other spheres, in various degrees,
dispose the special powers they have within
to their own causes and effects. All these

great universal organs, as you now know,

proceed from grade to grade. Each in its order
takes power from above and does its work below.

Now then, note carefully how I move on
through this pass to the truth you seek, for thus
you shall learn how to hold the ford alone.

The motion and the power of the sacred gyres—
as the hammer's art is from the smith—must flow
from the Blessed Movers. It is their power inspires.

And thus that Heaven made loveliest in its wheel
by many lamps, from the deep mind that turns it
takes the image and makes itself the seal.
And as the soul within your mortal clay
is spread through different organs, each of which
is shaped to its own end; in the same way

the high angelic Intelligence spreads its goodness
diversified through all the many stars
while yet revolving ever in its Oneness.

This varying power is variously infused
throughout the precious body that it quickens,
in which, like life in you, it is diffused.

Because of the glad nature from which it flows,
this many-faceted power shines through that body
as through the living eye the glad soul glows.

From this source only, not from rare and dense,
comes that by which one light and another differs—
the formal principle whose excellence,

conforming to its own purposes, makes appear
those markings you observe as dark and clear.

Canto III

AS DANTE IS ABOUT TO SPEAK to Beatrice he sees the dim traceries of human faces and taking them to be reflections, he turns to see what souls are being so reflected. Beatrice, as ever, explains that these pallid images are the souls themselves. They are THE INCONSTANT, the souls of those who registered holy vows in Heaven, but who broke or scanted them.

Among them PICCARDA DONATI identifies herself, and then identifies THE EMPRESS CONSTANCE. Both, according to Dante's beliefs, had taken vows as nuns but were forced to break them in order to contract a political marriage. Not all the souls about them need have failed in the same vows, however. Any failure to fulfill a holy vow (of holy orders, to go on a pilgrimage, to offer special services to God) might place the soul in this lowest class of the blessed.

Piccarda explains that every soul in Heaven rejoices in the entire will of God and cannot wish for a higher place, for to do so would be to come into conflict with the will of God. In the perfect harmony of bliss, everywhere in Heaven is Paradise.

That Sun that breathed love's fire into my youth
had thus resolved for me, feature by feature—
proving, disproving—the sweet face of truth.
I, raising my eyes to her eyes to announce
myself resolved of error, and well assured,
was about to speak; but before I could pronounce

my first word, there appeared to me a vision.
It seized and held me so that I forgot
to offer her my thanks and my confession.

As in clear glass when it is polished bright,
or in a still and limpid pool whose waters
are not so deep that the bottom is lost from sight,

a footnote of our lineaments will show,
so pallid that our pupils could as soon
make out a pearl upon a milk-white brow—
so I saw many faces eager to speak,
and fell to the error opposite the one
that kindled love for a pool in the smitten Greek.

And thinking the pale traces I saw there
were reflected images, I turned around
to face the source—but my eyes met empty air.

I turned around again like one beguiled,
and took my line of sight from my sweet guide
whose sacred eyes grew radiant as she smiled.

"Are you surprised that I smile at this childish act
of reasoning?" she said, "since even now
you dare not trust your sense of the true fact,

but turn, as usual, back to vacancy?
These are true substances you see before you.
They are assigned here for inconstancy
to holy vows. Greet them. Heed what they say,
and so believe; for the True Light that fills them
permits no soul to wander from its ray."

So urged, I spoke to those pale spirits, turning
to one who seemed most eager, and began
like one whose mind goes almost blank with yearning.

"O well-created soul, who in the sun
of the eternal life drinks in the sweetness
which, until tasted, is beyond conception;

great would be my joy would you confide
to my eager mind your earthly name and fate."
That soul with smiling eyes, at once replied:

"The love that fills us will no more permit
hindrance to a just wish than does that Love
that wills all of Its court to be like It.

I was a virgin sister there below,
and if you search your memory with care,
despite my greater beauty, you will know

I am Piccarda, and I am placed here
among these other souls of blessedness
to find my blessedness in the slowest sphere.

Our wishes, which can have no wish to be
but in the pleasure of the Holy Ghost,
rejoice in being formed to His decree.

And this low-seeming post which we are given
is ours because we broke, or, in some part,
slighted the vows we offered up to Heaven."

And I then: "Something inexpressibly
divine shines in your face, subliming you
beyond your image in my memory:

therefore I found you difficult to place;
but now, with the assistance of your words,
I find the memory easier to retrace.

But tell me, please: do you who are happy here
have any wish to rise to higher station,
to see more, or to make yourselves more dear?"

She smiled, as did the spirits at her side;
then, turning to me with such joy she seemed
to burn with the first fire of love, replied:

"Brother, the power of love, which is our bliss,
calms all our will. What we desire, we have.
There is in us no other thirst than this.

Were we to wish for any higher sphere,
then our desires would not be in accord
with the high will of Him who wills us here;

and if love is our whole being, and if you weigh
love's nature well, then you will see that discord
can have no place among these circles. Nay,

the essence of this blessed state of being
Is to hold all our will within His will,
whereby our wills are one and all-agreeing.

And so the posts we stand from sill to sill
throughout this realm, please all the realm as much
as they please Him who wills us to His will.

In His will is our peace. It is that sea
to which all moves, all that Itself creates
and Nature bears through all Eternity."

Then was it clear to me that everywhere
in Heaven is Paradise, though the Perfect Grace
does not rain down alike on all souls there.

But as at times when we have had our fill
of one food and still hunger for another,
we put this by with gratitude, while still

asking for that—just so I begged to know,
by word and sign, through what warp she had not
entirely passed the shuttle of her vow.

"The perfection of her life and her great worth

enshrine a lady hereabove," she said,
"in whose rule some go cloaked and veiled on earth,

that till their death they may live day and night
with that sweet Bridegroom who accepts of love
all vows it makes that add to His delight.

As a girl, I fled the world to walk the way
she walked, and closed myself into her habit,
pledged to her sisterhood till my last day.

Then men came, men more used to hate than love.
They tore me away by force from the sweet cloister.
What my life then became is known above.

This other splendor who lets herself appear
here to my right to please you, shining full
of every blessedness that lights this sphere,

understands in herself all that I say.
She, too, was a nun. From her head as from mine
the shadow of the veil was ripped away.

Against her will and all propriety
she was forced back to the world. Yet even there
her heart was ever veiled in sanctity.

She is the radiance of the Empress Constance,
who by the second blast of Swabia
conceived and bore its third and final puissance."

She finished, and at once began to sing
Ave Maria, and singing, sank from view
like a weight into deep water, plummeting

out of my sight, which followed while it could,
and then, having lost her, turned about once more

to the target of its greater wish and good,

and wholly gave itself to the delight
of the sweet vision of Beatrice. But she
flashed so radiantly upon my sight

that I, at first, was blinded, and thus was slow
to ask of her what I most wished to know.

Canto IV

THE FIRST SPHERE: THE MOON
Beatrice Discourses:
The True Seat of the Blessed
Plato's Error
Free Will
Recompense for Broken Vows

PICCARDA HAS TOLD DANTE that she inhabits the sphere of the inconstant Moon because she broke her vows against her will. Dante is torn by doubts that could lead to heresy. Was Plato right in saying souls come from their various stars preformed, and then return to them? If so, what of FREE WILL? And if Heaven is Justice, how have these souls sinned in being forced against their wills? And if Heaven is truth, what of the contradiction between Piccarda's statements and Beatrice's?

Beatrice resolves all of Dante's doubts. When she has finished Dante asks if men may offer OTHER RECOMPENSE FOR BROKEN VOWS.

A man given free choice would starve to death
between two equal equidistant foods,
unable to get either to his teeth.

So would a lamb, in counterbalanced fear,
tremble between two she-wolves and stand frozen.
So would a hound stand still between two deer.

If I stood mute, then, tugged to either side,
I neither blame myself, nor take my doubt—
it being necessary—as cause for pride.

I did not speak, but on my face, at once,
were written all my questions and my yearnings,
far more distinctly than I could pronounce.

And Beatrice did as Daniel once had done
when he raised Nebuchadnezzar from the wrath
that made him act unjustly in Babylon.

"I see full well how equal wish and doubt
tear you two ways," she said, "so that your zeal
tangles upon itself and cannot breathe out.

You reason: 'If the will that vowed stays true,
how can another's violence take away
from the full measure of bliss that is my due?'

And I see a second doubt perplex that thought
because the souls you see seem to return
to the stars from which they came, as Plato taught.

These are the questions that bear down your will
with equal force. Therefore, I shall treat first
the one whose venom has more power to kill.

Choose the most God-like of the Seraphim—
take Moses, or Samuel, or take either John,
or even Mary—not one is nearer Him,

nor holds his seat atop the blessed spheres
in any heaven apart from those you saw;
nor has his being more or fewer years.

All add their beauty to the Highest Wheel,
share the sweet life, and vary in it only
by how much of the Eternal Breath they feel.

They showed themselves here not because this post
has been assigned them, but to symbolize
that they stand lowest in the Heavenly host.

So must one speak to mortal imperfection,

which only from the *sensible* apprehends
whatever it then makes fit for intellection.

Scripture in like manner condescends,
describing God as having hands and feet
as signs to men of what more it portends.

So Holy Church shows you in mortal guise
the images of Gabriel and of Michael,
and of the other who gave back Tobit's eyes.

For if Timaeus—as seems rather clear—
spoke literally, what he says about souls
is nothing like the truth shown to us here.

He says the soul finds its own star again,
from which, as he imagines, nature chose it
to give form to the flesh and live with men.

But it may be the words he uses hide
a second meaning, which, if understood,
reveals a principle no man may deride.

If he means that the blame or honor due
the influence of each sphere returns to it,
his arrow does hit something partly true.

This principle, misunderstood, once drove
almost the whole world to attach to planets
such names as Mars and Mercury and Jove.

The other doubt that agitates your mind
is not as venomous, for not all its malice
could drive you from my side to wander blind.

For mortal men to argue that they see
injustice in our justice is in itself

a proof of faith, not poisonous heresy.

But since the truth of this lies well within
the reach of your own powers, I shall explain it,
just as you wish.—If violence, to begin,

occurs when those who suffer its abuse
contribute nothing to what forces them,
then these souls have no claim to that excuse.

For the will, if it will not, cannot be spent,
but does as nature does within a flame
a thousand or ten thousand winds have bent.

If it yields of itself, even in the least,
then it assists the violence—as did these
who could have gone back to their holy feast.

If their whole will had joined in their desire—
as whole will upheld Lawrence on the grill,
and Mucius with his hand thrust in the fire,

just so, it would have forced them to return
to their true way the instant they were free.
But such pure will is too rare, we must learn!

If you have gleaned them diligently, then
these words forever destroy the argument
that would have plagued your mind time and again.

But now another pass opens before you,
so strait and tortuous that without my help
you would tire along the way and not win through.

I made you understand beyond all doubt
that these souls cannot lie, for they exist
in the First Truth and cannot wander out.

Later you heard Piccarda say that she
who stood beside her kept her love of the veil;
and it seems that what she said contradicts me.

Time and again, my brother, men have run
from danger by a path they would not choose,
and on it done what ought not to be done.

So, bending to his father's prayer, did he
who took his mother's life. Alcmaeon I mean,
who sought his piety in impiety.

Now weigh within your own intelligence
how will and violence interact, so joining
that no excuse can wipe out the offense.

Absolute will does not will its own harm,
but fearing worse may come if it resists,
consents the more, the greater its alarm.

Thus when Piccarda spoke as she did to you,
she meant the absolute will; and I, the other.
So both of us spoke only what was true."

—Such was the flowing of that stream so blest
it flows down from the Fountain of All Truth.
Such was the power that laid my doubts to rest.

"Beloved of the First Love! O holy soul!"
I said then, "You whose words flow over me,
and with their warmth quicken and make me whole,

there is not depth enough within my love
to offer you due thanks, but may the One
who sees and can, answer for me above.

Man's mind, I know, cannot win through the mist
unless it is illumined by that Truth
beyond which truth has nowhere to exist.

In That, once it has reached it, it can rest
like a beast within its den. And reach it can;
else were all longing vain, and vain the test.

Like a new tendril yearning from man's will
doubt sprouts to the foot of truth. It is that in us
that drives us to the summit from hill to hill.

By this am I encouraged, by this bidden,
my lady, in all reverence, to ask
your guidance to a truth that still lies hidden:

can such as these who put away their veils
so compensate by other good works done
that they be not found wanting on your scales?"

Beatrice looked at me, and her glad eyes,
afire with their divinity, shot forth
such sparks of love that my poor faculties

gave up the reins. And with my eyes cast down
I stood entranced, my senses all but flown.

Canto V

ASCENT TO THE SECOND SPHERE
THE SECOND SPHERE: MERCURY
Beatrice Discourses
The Seekers of Honor
The Emperor Justinian

BEATRICE EXPLAINS the SANCTITY OF THE VOW, its RELATION TO FREE WILL, THE LIMITED RANGE WITHIN WHICH VOWS MAY BE ALTERED, and the DANGERS OF EVIL VOWS.

When she has finished, she and Dante soar to the SECOND SPHERE. There a host of radiant souls gathers to dance homage around Beatrice and Dante. These are the SEEKERS OF HONOR, souls who were active in their pursuit of the good, but who were motivated in their pursuit by a desire for personal honor, a good enough motive, but the least of all good motives.

One soul among them addresses Dante with particular joy. In Canto VI this soul identifies itself as the radiance that in mortal life was the EMPEROR JUSTINIAN.

"If, in the warmth of love, I manifest
more of my radiance than the world can see,
rendering your eyes unequal to the test,

do not be amazed. These are the radiancies
of the perfected vision that sees the good
and step by step moves nearer what it sees.
Well do I see how the Eternal Ray,
which, once seen, kindles love forevermore,
already shines on you. If on your way

some other thing seduce your love, my brother,
it can only be a trace, misunderstood,
of this, which you see shining through the other.

You ask if there is any compensation

the soul may offer for its unkept vows
that will secure it against litigation."

So Beatrice, alight from Heaven's Source,
began this canto; and without a pause,
continued thus her heavenly discourse:

"Of all creation's bounty realized,
God's greatest gift, the gift in which mankind
is most like Him, the gift by Him most prized,

is the freedom He bestowed upon the will.
All His intelligent creatures, and they alone,
were so endowed, and so endowed are still.

From this your reasoning should make evident
the value of the vow, if it is so joined
that God gives His consent when you consent.

When, therefore, God and man have sealed the pact,
the man divests himself of that great treasure
of which I speak—and by his own free act.

What can you offer, then, to make amends?
How can you make good use of what is His?
Would you employ extortion to good ends?

This much will make the main point clear to you.
But since the church grants dispensations in this,
whereby what I have said may seem untrue;

you must yet sit at table, for the food
you have just taken is crusty; without help
you will not soon digest it to your good.

Open your mind to what I shall explain,
then close around it, for it is no learning

to understand what one does not retain.

The essence of this sacrificial act
lies, first, in *what* one does, and, second, in *how*—
the *matter* and the *manner* of the pact.

This second part cannot be set aside
except by full performance; on this point
what I said earlier stands unqualified.

Thus it was mandatory to sacrifice
among the Jews, though the offering itself
might vary, or a substitute might suffice.

The other—what I have called the *matter*—may
be of the sort for which a substitution
will serve without offending in any way.

But let no man by his own judgment or whim
take on himself that burden unless the keys
of gold and silver have been turned for him.

And let him think no change a worthy one
unless what he takes up contains in it,
at least as six does four, what he puts down.

There are, however, things whose weight and worth
tip every scale, and for these there can be
no recompense by anything on earth.

Let no man make his vow a sporting thing.
Be true and do not make a squint-eyed choice
as Jephthah did in his first offering.

He had better have cried, 'I had no right to speak!'
than, keeping his vow, do worse. And in like case
will you find that chief war leader, the great Greek

whose Iphigenia wept her loveliness,
and made both fools and wise men share her tears
hearing of such dark rites and her distress.

Be slower to move, Christians, be grave, serene.
Do not be like a feather in the wind,
nor think that every water washes clean.

You have the Testaments, both old and new,
and the shepherd of the church to be your guide;
and this is all you need to lead you true.

If cunning greed comes promising remission,
be men, not mad sheep, lest the Jew among you
find cause to point his finger in derision.

Do not be like the lamb that strays away
from its mother's milk and, simple and capricious,
fights battles with itself in silly play!"

—Thus Beatrice to me, just as I write.
Then she turned, full of yearning, to that part
where the world is quickened most by the True Light.

Her silence, her transfigured face ablaze
made me fall still although my eager mind
was teeming with new questions I wished to raise.

And like an arrow driven with such might
it strikes its mark before the string is still,
we soared to the second kingdom of the light.

My lady glowed with such a joyous essence
giving herself to the light of that new sky
that the planet shone more brightly with her presence.

And if the star changed then and laughed with bliss,
what did I do, who in my very nature
was made to be transformed through all that is?

As in a fish pond that is calm and clear
fish swim to what falls in from the outside,
believing it to be their food, so, here,

I saw at least a thousand splendors move
toward us, and from each one I heard the cry:
"Here is what will give increase to our love!"

And as those glories came to where we were
each shade made visible, in the radiance
that each gave off, the joy that filled it there.

Imagine, reader, that I had started so
and not gone on—think what an anguished famine
would then oppress your hungry will to know.

So may you, of yourself, be able to see
how much I longed to know their names and nature
the instant they had shown themselves to me.

—"O well born soul, permitted by God's grace
to see the thrones of the Eternal Triumph
while still embattled in the mortal trace,

the lamp that shines through all the vaults of Heaven
is lit in us; if, therefore, you seek light
on any point, ask and it shall be given."

—So spoke one of those pious entities.
And my lady said: "Speak. Speak with full assurance.
And credit them as you would deities!"

"I do indeed see that you make your nest

in your own light, and beam it through your eyes
that dazzle when you smile, o spirit blest.

But I know not who you are, nor why you are
assigned here, to this sphere that hides itself
from men's eyes in the rays of another star."

These were my words, my face turned to the light
that had just spoken; at which it made itself
far more resplendent yet upon my sight.

Just as the sun, when its rays have broken through
a screen of heavy vapors, will itself
conceal itself in too much light—just so,

in its excess of joy that sacred soul
hid itself from my sight in its own ray,
and so concealed within its aureole,

it answered me, unfolding many things,
the manner of which the following canto sings.

Canto VI

THE SECOND SPHERE: MERCURY
Seekers of Honor: Justinian
The Roman Eagle

THE SPIRIT IDENTIFIES ITSELF *as the soul of* THE EMPEROR JUSTINIAN *and proceeds to recount its life on earth, its conversion by* AGAPETUS, *and its subsequent dedication to* THE CODIFICATION OF THE LAW.

It proceeds next to a DISCOURSE ON THE HISTORY OF THE ROMAN EAGLE. *It concludes by identifying the spirit of* ROMEO DA VILLANOVA *as one among the souls of the Second Heaven.*

"Once Constantine had turned the eagle's wing
against the course of Heaven, which it had followed
behind the new son of the Latian king,

two hundred years and more, as mankind knows,
God's bird stayed on at Europe's furthest edge,
close to the mountains out of which it rose.

And there, his wings spread over land and sea,
he ruled the world, passing from hand to hand;
and so, through many changes, came to me.

Caesar I was, Justinian I am.
By the will of the First Love, which I now feel,
I pruned the law of waste, excess, and sham.

Before my work absorbed my whole intent
I knew Christ in one nature only, not two;
and so believing, I was well content.

But Agapetus, blessed of the Lord,
he, the supreme shepherd pure in faith,
showed me the true way by his holy word.

Him I believed, and in my present view
I see the truth as clearly as you see
how a contradiction is both false and true.

As soon as I came to walk in the True Faith's way
God's grace moved all my heart to my great work;
and to it I gave myself without delay.

To my Belisarius I left my spear
and God's right hand so moved his that the omen
for me to rest from war was more than clear.

Of the two things you asked about before
this puts a period to my first reply.
But this much said impels me to say more

that you may see with how much right men go
against the sacred standard when they plot
its subornation or its overthrow.

You know what heroes bled to consecrate
its holy destiny from that first hour
when Pallas died to give it its first state.

You know that for two centuries then its home
was Alba, till the time came when the three
fought with the three and carried it to Rome.

What it did then from the Sabine's day of woe
to good Lucretia's, under the seven kings
who plundered the neighboring lands, you also know,

and how it led the Chosen Romans forward
against the powers of Brennus, and of Pyrrhus,
and of many a rival state and warring lord.

Thence the fame of Torquatus, curly Quintius,
and the Decii and Fabii. How gladly
I bring it myrrh to keep it glorious.
It dashed to earth the hot Arabian pride
that followed Hannibal through the rocky Alps,
from which, you, Po, sweet river, rise and glide.

Under it triumphed at an early age
Scipio and Pompey. Against the mountain
that looked down on your birth it screamed its rage.

Then as that age dawned in which Heaven planned
the whole world to its harmony, Caesar came,
and by the will of Rome, took it in hand.

What it did then from the Var to the Rhine is known
to Isère, Arar, Seine, and every valley
from which the waters of the Rhone flow down.

And what it did when it had taken flight
from Ravenna and across the Rubicon
no tongue may hope to speak nor pen to write.

It turned and led the cohorts into Spain;
then to Dyrrachium; and then struck Pharsalus
so hard that even the hot Nile felt the pain.

Antandros and the Simoïs, where it first saw light,
it saw again, and Hector's grave, and then—
woe to Ptolemy—sprang again to flight.

Like a thunderbolt it struck at Juba next;
then turned once more and swooped down on your West
and heard again the Pompeian trumpet vexed.

For what it did above its next great chief
Brutus and Cassius wail in Cocytus;

and Modena and Perugia came to grief.

For that, the tears still choke the wretched wraith
of Cleopatra, who running to escape it,
took from the asp her black and sudden death.

With him it traveled far as the Red Sea;
and with him brought the world such peace that Janus
was sealed up in his temple with lock and key.

But what this sign that moves my present theme
had done before, all it was meant to do
through the mortal realm it conquered—all must seem

dim shadows of poor things, if it be scanned
with a clear eye and pure and honest heart,
as it appears in the third Caesar's hand;

for the Living Justice whose breath I here breathe in
gave it the glory, while in that same hand,
of avenging His just wrath at Adam's sin.

Now ponder the double marvel I unfold:
later, under Titus, it *avenged*
the vengeance taken for that crime of old!

And when the sharp tooth of the Lombard bit
the Holy Church, victorious Charlemagne,
under those same wings, came and rescued it.

Now are you truly able to judge those
whom I accused above, and their wrongdoing,
which is the cause of all your present woes.

One speeds the golden lilies on to force
the public standard; and one seizes it
for private gain—and who knows which is worse?

Let them scheme, the Ghibellines, let them plot and weave
under some other standard, for all who use
this bird iniquitously find cause to grieve!

Nor let the new Charles think his Guelphs will be
its overthrow, but let him fear the talons
that have ripped the mane from fiercer lions than he.

Many a father's sinfulness has sealed
his children's doom: let him not think his lilies
will take the place of God's bird on His shield.

—This little star embellishes its crown
with the light of those good spirits who were zealous
in order to win honor and renown;

and when desire leans to such things, being bent
from the true good, the rays of the true Love
thrust upward with less force for the ascent;

but in the balance of our reward and due
is part of our delight, because we see
no shade of difference between the two.

By this means the True Judge sweetens our will,
so moving us that in all eternity
nothing can twist our beings to any ill.

Unequal voices make sweet tones down there.
Just so, in our life, these unequal stations
make a sweet harmony from sphere to sphere.

Within this pearl shines, too, the radiance
of Romeo, whose good and beautiful works
were answered by ingratitude and bad chance.

But the Provençals who worked his overthrow
have no last laugh: he walks an evil road
who finds his loss in the good that others do.

Four daughters had Count Raymond, each the wife
of a Christian king, thanks to this Romeo,
a humble man, a pilgrim in his life.

Envy and calumny so moved Raymond then
that he demanded accounting of this just soul
whose management had returned him twelve for ten.

For this he wandered, aged, poor, and bent,
into the world again; and could the world
know what was in his heart that road he went

begging his life by crusts from door to door,
much as it praises him now, it would praise him more.

Canto VII

*JUSTINIAN AND HIS COMPANIONS break into a HYMN TO THE GOD OF
BATTLES and, dancing, disappear into the distance. Dante, torn by doubt, longs
to ask how a just vengeance may justly be avenged, but dares not speak.
Beatrice, sensing his confusion, answers his question before he can ask it.*

*She explains the DOUBLE NATURE OF THE CRUCIFIXION, and why the
Jews, though blameless in the crucifixion of the man, were still guilty of
sacrilege against the God. She then explains why God chose this means of
redemption, and why that choice was THE GREATEST ACT OF ALL
ETERNITY.*

*She then explains the difference between DIRECT AND INDIRECT
CREATION and concludes by proving WHY THE RESURRECTION OF THE
FLESH IS CERTAIN.*

*"Osanna sanctus Deus Sabaoth
superillustrans claritate tua
felices ignes horum malachoth!"*

—So, giving itself to its own harmony,
the substance of that being, over which
two lights were joined as one, appeared to me.

And all those souls joined in a holy dance,
and then, like shooting sparks, gone instantly,
they disappeared behind the veil of distance.

I stood, torn by my doubts. "Speak up. Speak up,"
I said inside myself. "Ask the sweet lady

who slakes your every thirst from the sweet cup."

But the awe that holds my being in its sway
even at the sound of BEA or of TRICE
kept my head bent as if I dozed away.

But she soon soothed my warring doubt and dread,
for with a smile whose ray could have rejoiced
the soul of a man tied to the stake, she said:

"I know by my infallible insight
you do not understand how a just vengeance
can justly be avenged. To set you right

I shall resolve your mind's ambivalence.
Listen and learn, for what I shall now say
will be a gift of lofty consequence.

Because he would not, for his own good, take
God's bit and rein, the man who was not born,
damning himself, damned mankind for his sake.

Therefore, for many centuries, men lay
in their sick error, till the Word of God
chose to descend into the mortal clay.

There, moved by His Eternal Love alone,
he joined in His own person that other nature
that had wandered from its Maker and been cast down.

Now heed my reasoning: so joined again
to its First Cause, this nature (as it had been
at its creation) was good and without stain.

But by its own action, when it turned its face
from the road of truth that was its road of life,
it was driven from the garden of God's grace.

If the agony on the cross, considering this,
was a punishment of the nature thus assumed,
no verdict ever bit with greater justice;

Just so, no crime to match this can be cited
when we consider the Person who endured it
in whom that other nature was united.

Thus, various sequels flow from one event:
God and the Jews concurred in the same death;
for it the earth shook and the heavens were rent.

You should no longer find it hard to see
what is meant in saying that just vengeance taken
was afterwards avenged by just decree.

I see now that your mind, thought upon thought,
is all entangled, and that it awaits
most eagerly the untying of the knot.

You think: 'I grasp the truth of what I hear.
But why God chose this means for our redemption—
this and no other—I cannot make clear.'

No one may grasp the hidden meaning of
this edict, brother, till his inborn senses
have been made whole in the sweet fire of love.

Truly, therefore, since so many sight,
and so few hit, this target, I shall now
explain exactly why this means was right.

That Good, which from Itself spurns every trace
of envy, in Itself sends out such sparks
as manifest the everlasting grace.

Whatever is uttered by Its direct expression
thereafter is eternal; His seal once stamped,
nothing can ever wipe out the impression.

Whatever is poured directly from Its spring
is wholly free; so made, it is not subject
to the power of any secondary thing.

The Sacred Fire that rays through all creation
burns with most joy in what is most like It;
the more alike, the greater Its elation.

All of these attributes endow the nature
of humankind; and if it fail in one,
it cannot help but lose its noble stature.

Sin is the one power that can take away
its freedom and its likeness to True Good,
whereby it shines less brightly in Its ray.

Its innate worth, so lost, it can regain
only by pouring back what guilt has spilled,
repaying evil pleasure with just pain.

Your nature, when it took sin to its seed,
sinned totally. It lost this innate worth,
and it lost Paradise by the same deed.

Nor could they be regained (if you heed my words
with scrupulous attention) by any road
that does not lead to one of these two fords:

either that God, by courtesy alone,
forgive his sin; or that the man himself,
by his own penitence and pain, atone.

Now fix your eye, unmoving, on the abyss

of the Eternal Wisdom, and your mind
on every word I say concerning this!

Limited man, by subsequent obedience,
could never make amends; he could not go
as low in his humility as once,

rebellious, he had sought to rise in pride.
Thus was he shut from every means himself
to meet God's claim that He be satisfied.

Thus it was up to God, to Him alone
in His own ways—by one or both, I say—
to give man back his whole life and perfection.

But since a deed done is more prized the more
it manifests within itself the mark
of the loving heart and goodness of the doer,

the Everlasting Love, whose seal is plain
on all the wax of the world was pleased to move
in all His ways to raise you up again.

There was not, nor will be, from the first day
to the last night, an act so glorious
and so magnificent, on either way.

For God, in giving Himself that man might be
able to raise himself, gave even more
than if he had forgiven him in mercy.

All other means would have been short, I say,
of perfect justice, but that God's own Son
humbled Himself to take on mortal clay.

And now, that every wish be granted you,
I turn back to explain a certain passage,

that you may understand it as I do.

You say: 'I see the water, I see the fire,
the air, the earth; and all their combinations
last but a little while and then expire.

Yet all these were creations! Ought not they—
if what you said of them before is true—
to be forever proof against decay?'

Of angels and this pure kingdom of the soul
in which you are, it may be said they sprang
full-formed from their creation, their beings whole.

But the elements, and all things generated
by their various compoundings, take their form
from powers that had themselves to be created.

Created was the matter they contain.
Created, too, was the informing power
of the stars that circle them in Heaven's main.

From the given potencies of these elements
the rays and motions of the sacred lamps
draw forth the souls of all brutes and all plants.

But the Supreme Beneficence inspires
your life directly, filling it with love
of what has made it, so that it desires

that love forever.—And from this you may
infer the sure proof of your resurrection,
if you once more consider in what way

man's flesh was given being like no other
when He made our first father and first mother."

Canto VIII

THE THIRD SPHERE: VENUS
The Amorous: Charles Martel

DANTE AND BEATRICE reach the Sphere of Venus, the Third Heaven. Instantly, a band of souls that had been dancing in the Empyrean descends to the travelers. These are the souls of the AMOROUS. As we learn in Canto IX, many of them, perhaps all, were so full of the influence of Venus that they were in danger of being lost to carnality. Through the love of God, however, their passion was converted from physical love to true caritas, and thus do they rejoice in Heaven.

Their spokesman is CHARLES MARTEL OF ANJOU. He identifies himself and prophesies dark days for the Kingdom of Naples because of the meanness of King Robert, his brother. Dante asks how it is that mean sons can be born of great fathers, and Charles answers with a DISCOURSE ON THE DIVERSITY OF NATURAL TALENTS, a diversity he assigns to the influence of the stars, as God provided them for man's own good as a social being, for only by diversity of gifts can society function. God had planned all these variations to a harmonious end. It is mankind, by forcing men into situations not in harmony with their talents, that strays from God's plan.

The world, to its own jeopardy, once thought
that Venus, rolling in the third epicycle,
rayed down love-madness, leaving men distraught.

Therefore the ancients, in their ignorance,
did honor not to her alone, but offered
the smokes of sacrifice and votive chants

to Dione and to Cupid, her mother and son,
and claimed that he had sat on Dido's lap
when she was smitten by love's blinding passion.

From her with whom my song began just now
they took the name of the star that woos the Sun,

now shining at its nape, now at its brow.

I reached it unaware of my ascent,
but my lady made me certain I was there
because I saw her grow more radiant.

And as a spark is visible in the fire,
and as two voices may be told apart
if one stays firm and one goes lower and higher;

so I saw lights circling within that light
at various speeds, each, I suppose, proportioned
to its eternal vision of delight.

No blast from cold clouds ever shot below,
whether visible or not, so rapidly
but what it would have seemed delayed and slow

to one who had seen those holy lights draw nigh
to where we were, leaving the dance begun
among the Seraphim in Heaven on high.

And from the first who came, in purest strain
"Hosannah" rang; so pure that, ever since,
my soul has yearned to hear that sound again.

Then one of them came forward and spoke thus:
"We are ready, all of us, and await your pleasure
that you may take from us what makes you joyous.

In one thirst and one spiraling and one sphere
we turn with those High Principalities
to whom you once cried from the world down there:

'O you whose intellects turn the third great wheel!'
So full of love are we that, for your pleasure,
it will be no less bliss to pause a while."

I raised my eyes to the holy radiance
that was my lady, and only after she
had given them her comfort and assurance,

did I turn to the radiance that had made
such promises. "Who are you?" were my words,
my voice filled with the love it left unsaid.

Ah, how it swelled and grew even more bright,
taking increase of bliss from my few words,
and adding new delight to its delight.

So changed, it said: "My life there among men
was soon concluded; had it lasted longer
great evils yet to be would not have been.

The ecstasy that is my heavenly boon
conceals me: I am wrapped within its aura
as a silkworm is enclosed in a cocoon.

You loved me much, and you had reason to,
for had I stayed below, you would have seen
more than the green leaves of my love for you.

The left bank of the land washed by the Rhone
after its waters mingle with the Sorgue's
waited, in due course, to become my own;

as did that horn of Italy that lies
south of the Tronto and Verde, within which
Bari, Gaeta, and Catona rise.

Already on my brow there shone the crown
of the land the Danube bathes when it has left
its German banks. And though not yet my own,

beautiful Sicily, the darkened coast
between the Capes of Faro and Passero,
there on the gulf that Eurus lashes most,

(not dimmed by Typhoeus, as mythology
would have men think, but by its rising sulfur)
would yet have looked to have its kings, through me,

from Charles and Rudolph, but that the bitter breath
of a populace subjected to misrule
cried out through all Palermo's streets 'Death! Death!'

And could Robert have foreseen how tyranny
will drive men mad, he would have fled in fear
from Catalonia's greedy poverty.

For some provision surely must be made,
by him or by another, lest on his ship,
already heavy laden, more be laid.

His nature, born to avarice from the loins
of a liberal sire, would have required lieutenants
who cared for more than filling chests with coins."

—"Sire, I hold dearer this felicity
that fills me when you speak, believing it
as visible to you as it is to me,

there where every good begins and ends.
And this, too, I hold dear—that you discern it
in looking on Him from whom all love descends.

You have given me joy. Now it is in your power
to give me light. For your words leave me in doubt:
how, if the seed is sweet, may the fruit be sour?"

Thus I. And he: "Could I make you recognize

one truth of what you ask, then what is now
behind your back, would be before your eyes.

The Good by which this kingdom you now climb
is turned and gladdened, makes its foresight shine
as powers of these great bodies to all time.

Not only does that Perfect Mind provide
for the diversities of every nature
but for their good and harmony beside.

And thus whatever arrow takes its arc
from this bow flies to a determined end,
it being aimed unerringly to its mark.

Else would these heavens you now move across
give rise to their effect in such a way
that there would be not harmony, but chaos.

This cannot be unless the intellects
that move these stars are flawed, and flawed the first,
which, having made them, gave them such defects.

—Should I expound this further?" he said to me.
And I: "There is no need, for now I know
nature cannot fall short of what must be."

And he: "Would man be worse off than he is,
there on earth, without a social order?"
"Yes!" I replied. "Nor need I proof of this."

"And can that be, unless men there below
lived variously to serve their various functions?
Your master, if he knows, answers you 'no.' "

So point by point that radiant soul disputes.
Now he concludes: "Your various aptitudes,

it follows, therefore, must have various roots,

So one man is born Xerxes, another Solon;
one Melchizedek, and another he
who, flying through the air, lost his own son.

That ever-revolving nature whose seal is pressed
into our mortal wax does its work well,
but takes no heed of where it comes to rest.

So Esau parted from Jacob in the seed;
and Romulus was born of such humble stock
that Mars became his father, as men agreed.

Begotten and begetter, but for the force
of overruling providence, the son's nature
would always follow in the father's course.

—And now what was behind shines out before.
But to make you understand how much you please me,
I would wrap you in one corollary more:

what Nature gives a man Fortune must nourish
concordantly, or nature, like any seed
out of its proper climate, cannot flourish.

If the world below would learn to heed the plan
of nature's firm foundation, and build on that,
it then would have the best from every man.

But into holy orders you deflect
the man born to strap on a sword and shield;
and make a king of one whose intellect

is given to writing sermons. And in this way
your footprints leave the road and go astray."

Canto IX

THE THIRD SPHERE: VENUS
The Amorous:
Cunizza, Folquet, Rahab

CUNIZZA DA ROMANO next appears, lamenting the woes that have befallen her native Venetia and prophesying great grief to her country-men for pursuing false fame on earth. Cunizza had begun her remarks by pointing out a soul who rejoices beside her in Heaven as one who pursued good ends. When she finishes speaking that soul identifies itself as FOLQUET, once BISHOP OF MARSEILLES. Folquet narrates his life and indicates that, like Cunizza, his amorous nature first led him to carnality but later filled him with passion for the True Love of God. Folquet then answers Dante's questions about the NATURE OF THE THIRD HEAVEN, identifies RAHAB, the Whore of Jericho, as the first soul to ascend to that sphere, and concludes with a DENUNCIATION OF BONIFACE VIII for neglecting the Holy Land and all things spiritual, and a further DENUNCIATION OF FLORENCE as a corrupt state and as the source of Papal corruption. A just vengeance, he prophesies, will not be long delayed.

Fair Clemence, when your Charles, in speaking thus
had shone his light into my mind, he told me
of the schemes and frauds that would attack his house.

But he said to me: "Say nothing. Let the years turn as they must." And so I can
say only that they who wrong you shall find cause for tears.

Now to the Sun, the all-sufficing good,
the eternal being of that sacred lamp
had turned itself again to be renewed.

O souls deceived! ill-born impieties
who turn your hearts away from the True Love
and fix your eyes on empty vanities!

—And lo! another of those splendors now

draws near me, and his wish to give me pleasure
shows in the brightening of his outward glow.
The eyes of Beatrice, which, as before
were fixed on me, saw all my wish and gave it
the assurance of their dear consent once more.

"O blessed spirit, be pleased to let me find
my joy at once," I said. "Make clear to me
that you are a true mirror of my mind!"

Thereat the unknown spirit of that light,
who had been singing in its depths, now spoke,
like one whose whole delight is to delight.

"In that part of the sinful land men know
as the Italy which lies between Rialto
and the springs from which the Brenta and Piave flow,

there stands a hill of no imposing height;
down from it years ago there came a firebrand
who laid waste all that region like a blight.

One root gave birth to both of us. My name
was Cunizza, of Romano, and I shine here
because this star conquered me with its flame.

Yet gladly I embrace the fate that so
arranged my lot, and I rejoice in it,
although it may seem hard to the crowd below.

This bright and precious jewel of our sky,
whose ray shines here beside me, left great fame
behind him on the earth; nor will it die

before this centenary is five times told.
Now ask yourself if man should seek that good
that lives in name after the flesh is cold.

The rabble that today spills through the land
bound by the Tagliamento and the Adige
think little of that, nor, though war's bloody hand

rips them, do they repent. But Paduan blood,
having shunned its duty, shall soon stain the water
that bathes Vicenza and drains into mud.

And there rules one who yet holds high his head,
there where the Sile and the Cagnano join,
for whom the net already has been spread.

And Feltro shall yet weep the treachery
of its foul priest; no man yet entered Malta
for a crime as infamous as his shall be.

Great would that ewer be that could hold at once
the blood Ferrara will spill, and tired the man
who set himself to weigh it ounce by ounce;

—all this the generous priest will freely give
to prove his party loyalty; but then
such gifts conform to how those people live.

On high are mirrors (you say 'Thrones') and these
reflect God's judgment to us; so enlightened,
we have thought it well to speak these prophecies."

Here she fell still and, turning, made it clear
she was drawn to other things, joining once more
the wheel of souls that dance through that third sphere.

That other Bliss, he I had heard her say
was precious to her, now showed himself to me
like a fine ruby struck by the sun's ray.

Up there, joy makes those souls add light to light,
as here it makes us laugh, while down below
souls darken as they grieve through Hell's long night.

"God sees all, and your insight, blessed being,
makes itself one with His," I said, "and thus
no thought or wish may hide beyond your seeing.

Why does your voice, then, which forever sings
Heaven's delight as one with those Blest Flames
who wrap themselves about with their six wings,

not grant my wish? Had I the intuition
with which to read your wish as you read mine,
I should not be still waiting for your question!"

"The greatest basin to which earth's waters flow
—aside from the sea that girdles all the land—"
his voice began when I had spoken so,

"extends so far against the course of the sun,
between opposing shores, that at its zenith
the sun must cross what first was its horizon.

I first saw light on that basin's shore between
the Ebro and that river whose short course
parts Tuscan from Genoese—the Magra, I mean.

Sunrise and sunset are about the same
for Bougiah and my city, whose blood flowed
to warm its harbor's waters when Caesar came.

My name—to such as knew it on the earth
was Folquet; here eternally my ray
marks all this sphere, as its ray marked my birth.

Dido did not burn hotter with love's rage,

when she offended both Sichaeus and Creusa,
than I, before my locks grew thin with age.

Nor she of Rhodopè who felt the smart
of Demophoön's deception, nor Hercules
when he had sealed Iole in his heart.

But none repents here; joy is all our being:
not at the sin—that never comes to mind—
but in the All-Ordering and All-Foreseeing.

Here all our thoughts are fixed upon the Love
that beautifies creation, and here we learn
how world below is moved by world above.

But that you may take with you from this sphere
full knowledge of all it makes you wish to know,
I must speak on a little further here.

You wish to know who is within this blaze
you see in all its splendor here beside me,
like purest water lit by the sun's rays.

Know, then, that in it Rahab finds her good;
and that, one with our choir, she seals upon it
the highest order of beatitude.

Of all Christ's harvest, her soul was the one
first summoned by this Heaven, on which the shadow
the earth casts rests the point of its long cone.

It was fitting in every way that she should thus
adorn one of these heavens as a palm
of the high victory two palms won for us,

for she it was who helped win the first glory
of Joshua's victory in the Holy Land

(which seems to have slipped from the Pope's memory).

Your Florence—which was planted by the One
who first turned on his Maker, and whose envy
has given men such cause for lamentation—

brings forth and spreads the accursed flower of gold
that changes the shepherd into a ravening wolf
by whom the sheep are scattered from the fold.

And so the Gospels and Great Doctors lie
neglected, and the Decretals alone
are studied, as their margins testify.

So Pope and Cardinal heed no other things.
Their thoughts do not go out to Nazareth
where the blessed Gabriel opened wide his wings.

But the Vatican, and the other chosen parts
of Holy Rome that have been, from the first,
the cemetery of those faithful hearts

that followed Peter and were his soldiery,
shall soon be free of this adultery."

Canto X

ASCENT TO THE SUN
THE FOURTH SPHERE: THE SUN
Doctors of the Church
The First Garland of Souls:
Aquinas

DANTE REVELS in the joy of God's creation and especially in the art shown by the placement of THE EQUINOCTIAL POINT. So rejoicing, he enters the SPHERE OF THE SUN, unaware of his approach until he has arrived.

A GARLAND OF TWELVE SOULS immediately surrounds him and Beatrice, the glory of each soul shining so brilliantly that it is visible even against the background of the Sun itself. These are TWELVE DOCTORS OF THE CHURCH, philosophers and theologians whose writings have guided the Church in creed and canon law. Their spokesman, appropriately, is THOMAS AQUINAS. He identifies the souls in order around the ring.

When Aquinas has finished, the souls dance around Dante and Beatrice, raising their voices in harmonies unknown except to Heaven itself.

Contemplating His Son with that Third Essence
of Love breathed forth forever by Them both,
the omnipotent and ineffable First Presence

created all that moves in mind and space
with such perfection that to look upon it
is to be seized by love of the Maker's grace.

Therefore, reader, raise your eyes across
the starry sphere. Turn with me to that point
at which one motion and another cross,

and there begin to savor your delight
in the Creator's art, which he so loves
that it is fixed forever in His sight.

Note how the wheel on which the planets ride
branches from there obliquely: only thus
may the earth that calls to them be satisfied.

For if these two great motions never crossed,
the influence of the heavens would be weakened
and most of its power upon the earth be lost.

For if its deviation were to be
increased or lessened, much would then be wanting,
both north and south, from the earth's harmony.

Stay on at table, reader, and meditate
upon this foretaste if you wish to dine
on joy itself before it is too late.

I set out food, but you yourself must feed!
For the great matters I record demand
all my attention and I must proceed.

Nature's majestic minister, the Sun,
who writes the will of Heaven on the earth
and with his light measures the hours that run,

now in conjunction (as I have implied)
with Aries, rode those spirals whose course brings him
ever earlier from the eastern side.

And I was with the Sun; but no more aware
of my ascent than a man is of a thought
that comes to mind, until he finds it there.

It is Beatrice, she it is who leads our climb
from good to better, so instantaneously
that her action does not spread itself through time.

How radiant in its essence that must be

which in the Sun (where I now was) shows forth
not by its color but its radiancy.

Though genius, art, and usage stored my mind,
I still could not make visible what I saw;
but yet may you believe and seek to find!

And if our powers fall short of such a height,
why should that be surprising, since the Sun
is as much as any eye has known of light?

Such, there, was the fourth family of splendors
of the High Father who fills their souls with bliss,
showing them how He breathes forth and engenders.

"Give thanks!" my lady said. "With all devotion
give thanks to the Sun of Angels, by whose grace
you have been lifted to this physical one!"

The heart of mortal never could so move
to its devotion, nor so willingly
offer itself to God in thankful love,

as mine did when these words had passed her lips.
So wholly did I give my love to Him
that she sank to oblivion in eclipse.

Nothing displeased, she laughed so that the blaze
of her glad eyes pierced my mind's singleness
and once again divided it several ways.

Splendors of living and transcendent light
circle us now and make a glowing crown,
sweeter in voice than radiant in sight.

Latona's daughter sometimes seems to us
so banded when the vaporous air weaves round her

the thread that makes her girdle luminous.

In Heaven's courts, from which height I have come,
are many gems so precious and so lovely
that they cannot be taken from the kingdom.

Of such those splendors sang. Who does not grow
wings that will fly him there, must learn these things
from the tidings of the tongueless here below.

When, so singing, those Sun-surpassing souls
had three times turned their blazing circuit round us,
like stars that circle close to the fixed poles,

they stood like dancers still caught in the pleasure
of the last round, who pause in place and listen
till they have caught the beat of the new measure.

And from within its blaze I heard one start:
"Since the ray of grace from which true love is kindled—
and then by loving, in the loving heart

grows and multiplies—among all men
so shines on you to lead you up these stairs
that none descend except to climb again;

whoever refused your soul, it being thirsty,
wine from his flask, would be no freer to act
than water blocked from flowing to the sea.

You wish to know what flowering plants are woven
into this garland that looks lovingly
on the lovely lady who strengthens you for Heaven.

I was a lamb among the holy flock
Dominic leads to where all plenty is,
unless the lamb itself stray to bare rock.

This spirit on my right, once of Cologne,
was my teacher and brother. Albert was his name,
and Thomas, of Aquinas, was my own.

If you wish, similarly, to know the rest
let your eyes follow where my words shall lead
circling through all this garland of the blest.

The next flame springs from the glad smile of Gratian
who so assisted one court and the other
that in him Heaven found good cause for elation.

The next to adorn our chorus of the glad
was the good Peter who, like the poor widow,
offered to Holy Church all that he had.

The fifth light, and the loveliest here, shines forth
from so magnificent a love that men
hunger for any news of it on earth;

within it is that mind to which were shone
such depths of wisdom that, if truth be true,
no mortal ever rose to equal this one.

See next the taper whose flame, when formerly
it burned in mortal flesh, saw most profoundly
the nature of angels and their ministry.

Within the lesser lamp next on my right
shines the defender of the Christian Age
whose treatise led Augustine toward the light.

Now if your mind has followed on my praise
from light to light, you are already eager
to know what spirit shines in the eighth blaze.

In it, for having seen the sum of good,
there sings a soul that showed the world's deceit
to any who would heed. The bones and blood

from which it was cruelly driven have their tomb
down there in Cieldauro: to this peace
it came from exile and from martyrdom.

See next the flames breathed forth by Isidore,
by Bede, and by that Richard whose 'Contemplations'
saw all that a mere man can see, and more.

The next, from whom your eyes return to me,
is the glory of a soul in whose grave thoughts
death seemed to be arriving all too slowly:

it is the flame, eternally elated,
of Siger, who along the Street of Straws
syllogized truths for which he would be hated."

Then as a clock tower calls us from above
when the Bride of God rises to sing her matins
to the Sweet Spouse, that she may earn his love,

with one part pulling and another thrusting,
tin-tin, so glad a chime the faithful soul
swells with the joy of love almost to bursting—

just so, I saw that wheel of glories start
and chime from voice to voice in harmonies
so sweetly joined, so true from part to part

that none can know the like till he go free
where joy begets itself eternally.

Canto XI

Doctors of the Church
The First Garland of Souls:
Aquinas
Praise of St. Francis
Degeneracy of Dominicans

THE SPIRITS complete their song and their joyous dance and once more gather around Dante and Beatrice.

Aquinas reads Dante's mind and speaks to make clear several points about which Dante was in doubt. He explains that Providence sent two equal princes to guide the Church, St. Dominic, the wise law-giver, being one, and St. Francis, the ardent soul, being the other. Aquinas was himself a Dominican. To demonstrate the harmony of Heaven's gift and the unity of the Dominicans and Franciscans, Aquinas proceeds to pronounce a PRAISE OF THE LIFE OF ST. FRANCIS. His account finished, he returns to the theme of the unity of the Dominicans and Franciscans, and proceeds to illustrate it further by himself lamenting the DEGENERACY OF THE DOMINICAN ORDER.

O senseless strivings of the mortal round!
how worthless is that exercise of reason
that makes you beat your wings into the ground!

One man was giving himself to law, and one
to aphorisms; one sought sinecures,
and one to rule by force or sly persuasion;

one planned his business, one his robberies;
one, tangled in the pleasure of the flesh,
wore himself out, and one lounged at his ease;

while I, of all such vanities relieved
and high in Heaven with my Beatrice,
arose to glory, gloriously received.

—When each had danced his circuit and come back
to the same point of the circle, all stood still,
like votive candles glowing in a rack.

And I saw the splendor of the blazing ray
that had already spoken to me, smile,
and smiling, quicken; and I heard it say:

"Just as I take my shining from on high,
so, as I look into the Primal Source,
I see which way your thoughts have turned, and why.

You are uncertain, and would have me find
open and level words in which to speak
what I expressed too steeply for your mind

when I said 'leads to where all plenty is,'
and 'no mortal ever rose to equal this one.'
And it is well to be exact in this.

The Providence that governs all mankind
with wisdom so profound that any creature
who seeks to plumb it might as well be blind,

in order that the Bride seek her glad good
in the Sweet Groom who, crying from on high,
took her in marriage with His blessed blood,

sent her two Princes, one on either side
that she might be secure within herself,
and thereby be more faithfully His Bride.

One, in his love, shone like the seraphim.
The other, in his wisdom, walked the earth
bathed in the splendor of the cherubim.

I shall speak of only one, though to extol
one or the other is to speak of both
in that their works led to a single goal.

Between the Tupino and the little race
sprung from the hill blessèd Ubaldo chose,
a fertile slope spreads up the mountain's face.

Perugia breathes its heat and cold from there
through Porta Sole, and Nocera and Gualdo
behind it mourn the heavy yoke they bear.

From it, at that point where the mountainside
grows least abrupt, a sun rose to the world
as this one does at times from Ganges' tide.

Therefore, let no man speaking of that place
call it *Ascesi*—'I have risen'—but rather,
Oriente—so to speak with proper grace.

Nor was he yet far distant from his birth
when the first comfort of his glorious powers
began to make its warmth felt on the earth:

a boy yet, for that lady who, like death
knocks on no door that opens to her gladly,
he had to battle his own father's wrath.

With all his soul he married her before
the diocesan court *et coram patre*;
and day by day he grew to love her more.

Bereft of her First Groom, she had had to stand
more than eleven centuries, scorned, obscure;
and, till he came, no man had asked her hand:

none, at the news that she had stood beside

the bed of Amyclas and heard, unruffled,
the voice by which the world was terrified;

and none, at word of her fierce constancy,
so great, that even when Mary stayed below,
she climbed the Cross to share Christ's agony.

But lest I seem obscure, speaking this way,
take Francis and Poverty to be those lovers.
That, in plain words, is what I meant to say.

Their harmony and tender exultation
gave rise in love, and awe, and tender glances
to holy thoughts in blissful meditation.

The venerable Bernard, seeing them so,
kicked off his shoes, and toward so great a peace
ran, and running, seemed to go too slow.

O wealth unknown! O plenitude untried!
Egidius went unshod. Unshod, Sylvester
followed the groom. For so it pleased the bride!

Thenceforth this father and this happy lord
moved with his wife and with his family,
already bound round by the humble cord.

He did not grieve because he had been born
the son of Bernardone; he did not care
that he went in rags, a figure of passing scorn.

He went with regal dignity to reveal
his stern intentions to Pope Innocent,
from whom his order first received the seal.

Then as more souls began to follow him
in poverty—whose wonder-working life

were better sung among the seraphim—

Honorius, moved by the Eternal Breath,
placed on the holy will of this chief shepherd
a second crown and everflowering wreath.

Then, with a martyr's passion, he went forth
and in the presence of the haughty Sultan
he preached Christ and his brotherhood on earth;

but when he found none there would take Christ's pardon,
rather than waste his labors, he turned back
to pick the fruit of the Italian garden.

On the crag between Tiber and Arno then, in tears
of love and joy, he took Christ's final seal,
the holy wounds of which he wore two years.

When God, whose loving will had sent him forward
to work such good, was pleased to call him back
to where the humble soul has its reward,

he, to his brothers, as to rightful heirs
commended his dearest Lady, and he bade them
to love her faithfully for all their years.

Then from her bosom, that dear soul of grace
willed its return to its own blessed kingdom;
and wished its flesh no other resting place.

Think now what manner of man was fit to be
his fellow helmsman, holding Peter's ship
straight to its course across the dangerous sea.

Such was our patriarch. Hence, all who rise
and follow his command will fill the hold,
as you can see, with fruits of paradise.

But his flock has grown so greedy for the taste
of new food that it cannot help but be
far scattered as it wanders through the waste.

The more his vagabond and distant sheep
wander from him, the less milk they bring back
when they return to the fold. A few do keep

close to the shepherd, knowing what wolf howls
in the dark around them, but they are so few
it would take little cloth to make their cowls.

Now, if my words have not seemed choked and blind,
if you have listened to me and taken heed,
and if you will recall them to your mind,

your wish will have been satisfied in part,
for you will see how the good plant is broken,
and what rebuke my words meant to impart

when I referred, a while back in our talk,
to 'where all plenty is' and to 'bare rock.' "

Canto XII

THE FOURTH SPHERE: THE SUN
Doctors of the Church
The Second Garland of Souls:
Bonaventure
Praise of St. Dominic
Degeneracy of Franciscans

*AS SOON AS Aquinas has finished speaking the wheel of souls begins to turn,
and before it has completed its first revolution it is surrounded by a SECOND
GARLAND OF TWELVE SOULS.*

*The spokesman of this second company is ST. BONAVENTURE. In the
harmonious balances of Heaven the Dominican Aquinas had spoken the praise
of the life of St. Francis. In the same outgoing motion of love the Franciscan
Bonaventure now speaks the PRAISE OF THE LIFE OF ST. DOMINIC. And as
Aquinas had concluded by lamenting the degeneracy of the Dominican Order, so
Bonaventure concludes his account with a LAMENT FOR THE DEGENERACY
OF THE FRANCISCAN ORDER. He then identifies the other souls in his
Garland.*

So spoke the blessed flame and said no more;
and at its final word the holy millstone
began revolving round us as before.

And had not finished its first revolution
before a second wheel had formed around it,
matching it tone for tone, motion for motion.

As a reflection is to the source of light,
such is the best our sirens and muses sing
to the chanting of those sheaths of pure delight.

As through thin clouds or mists twin rainbows bend

parallel arcs and equal coloring
when Juno calls her handmaid to attend—

the outer band born of the inner one,
like the voice of that wandering nymph of love consumed,
as vapors are consumed by the summer sun—

whereby all men may know what God made plain
in the pledge he gave to Noah that the waters
of the great deluge would not come again—

just so, those sempiternal roses wove
their turning garland round us, and the outer
answered the inner with the voice of love.

And when the exalted festival and dance
of love and rapture, sweet song to sweet song,
and radiance to flashing radiance,

had in a single instant fallen still
with one accord—as our two eyes make one,
being moved to open and close by a single will—

from one of those new splendors a voice came;
and as the North Star draws a needle's point,
so was my soul drawn to that glorious flame.

Thus he began: "The love that makes me shine
moves me to speak now of that other leader
through whom so much good has been said of mine

When one is mentioned the other ought to be;
for they were militant in the same cause
and so should shine in one light and one glory.

The troops of Christ, rearmed at such great cost,
were struggling on behind the Holy Standard,

fearful, and few, and laggard, and half lost,

when the Emperor who reigns eternally—
of His own grace and not for their own merit—
took thought of his imperiled soldiery;

and, as you have heard said, He sent His bride
two champions by whose teachings and example
the scattered companies were reunified.

In the land to which the West wind, soft and glad,
returns each Spring to open the new leaves
with which, soon, all of Europe will be clad,

at no great distance from the beat and bite
of those same waves behind which, in its course,
the sun, at times, hides from all mortal sight,

a fortunate village lies in the protection
of the great shield on which two lions are,
one subjugating and one in subjection.

Within its walls was born the ardent one,
true lover and true knight of the Christian faith;
bread to his followers, to his foes a stone.

His mind, from the instant it began to be,
swelled with such powers that in his mother's womb
he made her capable of prophecy.

And when he and his Lady Faith before
the holy font had married and endowed
each other with new gifts of holy power,

the lady who had spoken for him there
saw, in a dream, the wonder-working fruit
that he and his inheritors would bear.

To speak him as he was, a power from Heaven
was moved to give him the possessive form
of His name unto Whom he was wholly given.

Dominicus he was called. Let him be known
as the good husbandman chosen by Christ
to help Him in the garden He had sown.

A fitting squire and messenger of Christ
he was, for his first love was poverty,
and such was the first counsel given by Christ.

Often his nurse found him in meditation at night on the bare floor, awake and
silent, as if he were saying, 'This is my vocation.'

O Felix his father in true 'felicity!'
O mother truly Joan, 'whom God has graced!'
—if the names can be translated literally!

Not as men toil today for wealth and fame,
in the manner of the Ostian and Taddeo,
but for love of the true manna, he soon became

a mighty doctor, and began to go
his rounds of that great vineyard where the vine,
if left untended, pales and cannot grow.

Before that Seat where once the poor were fed
and tended (now, through no fault of its own,
but by its degenerate occupant, corrupted)

he did not ask the right to keep as pay
three out of every six, nor a benifice,
nor *decimas quae sunt pauperum Dei*;

but license in the sick world there below

to battle for that seed from which are sprung
the four and twenty plants that ring you now.

Then, will and doctrine joined, and in the light
of apostolic office, he burst forth,
like a torrent from a mountain vein, to smite

the stumps and undergrowths of heresy.
And where the thickets were least passable,
there his assault bore down most heavily.

And from him many rivulets sprang to birth
by which the Catholic orchard is so watered
that its little trees spring greener from the earth.

If such was the one wheel of the great car
in which the Church rode to defend herself
and win in open field her civil war,

you cannot fail to see with a clear mind
the excellence of that other, about whom,
before I joined you, Thomas was so kind.

But the track its great circumference cut of old
is so abandoned that the casks are empty,
and where there once was crust, now there is mold.

His family, that formerly used to go
in his very footsteps, is so turned around
that it prints toe on heel, and heel on toe.

Soon shall we see the harvest of these years
of lazy cultivation, and hear the darnel,
the storehouse shut against it, shed its tears.

Search our book leaf by leaf and you will see,
I have no doubt, written upon some page:

'I am today all that I used to be.'

But not at Casal' nor Acquasparta—there
they come to keep our rule, and in the keeping
one loosens it, one tightens it like a snare.

I am the life of Bonaventure, on earth
of Bagnoregio, who in great offices
always put back the things of lesser worth.

Illuminato and Augustine are here,
two of the first-come of the barefoot poor.
For the cord they wore God holds them ever dear.

The prior Hugo is here, and the deathless glow
of Peter Mangiadore, and Peter of Spain
whose light still shines in twelve small books below.

And the prophet Nathan, and the eternal part
of Chrysostom, and Anselm, and that Donatus
who gladly turned his hand to the first art.

Rabanus is also here; and here beside me
shines the Calabrian abbot Joachim
whose soul was given the power of prophecy.

The ardent courtesy of my holy brother
and his apt praise of one great paladin
moved me to say this much about the other

in emulous and loving eulogy;
and so moved all these of my company."

Canto XIII

THE FOURTH SPHERE: THE SUN
The Intellect of the Faith:
Theologians and Doctors
of the Church: Aquinas

THE TWENTY-FOUR blessed spirits, moved by the concluding words of Bonaventure, manifest themselves as a mystical constellation while ringing forth a hymn of praise that fills all Heaven.

When the hymn has been sung Aquinas speaks again. He has read Dante's mind and addresses its perplexity, explaining WHY NONE EVER ROSE TO EQUAL SOLOMON'S WISDOM. He concludes with a WARNING AGAINST HASTY JUDGMENT.

If you would understand what I now write
of what I saw next in that Heaven, imagine
(and hold the image rock-fast in your sight)

the fifteen brightest stars the heavens wear
in their living crown, stars of so clear a ray
it pierces even the mist-thickened air;

imagine that Wain that on our heaven's breast
lies night and day, because the tiller's turning
causes no part of it to sink to rest;

imagine the bright mouth of the horn one sees
flower from the axle star, around which spins
the first wheel—and imagine all of these

forming two constellations, each a wreath
(like that the daughter of King Minos made
when through her limbs she felt the chill of death)

and imagine, last, that one wreath has its rays

inside the other, and that both are turning
around one center but in opposite ways.

So might you dimly guess (if mankind could)
what actual stars, joined in their double dance,
circled around the point on which I stood;

though such experiences outrun our knowing
as the motion of the first and fastest heaven
outruns the low Chiana's sluggish flowing.

There they sang no Bacchic chant nor Paean,
but Three Persons in One Divine Nature
and It and human nature in One Person.

The song and circling dance ran through their measure,
and now those holy lights waited on us,
turning rejoiced from pleasure to new pleasure.

The silence of these numina was broken
by the same lamp from which the glorious life
of God's beloved pauper had been spoken.

It said: "Since one sheaf has been thrashed, my brother,
and the good grain of it has been put by,
sweet love invites me now to thrash the other.

Into that breast, you think, from which was carved
the rib that went to form the lovely cheek
for whose bad palate all mankind was starved,

and into that the lance pierced when it made
such restitution for the past and future
that every guilt of mankind was outweighed,

as much of wisdom's light, to the last ray,
as human nature can contain, He breathed

by whose power they were clad in mortal clay.

And, therefore, you were puzzled when I came
to the fifth light and said no mortal ever
had matched the wisdom sheathed within its flame.

Now open your eyes to what I shall say here
and see your thought and my words form one truth,
like the center and circumference of a sphere.

All things that die and all that cannot die
are the reflected splendor of the Form
our Father's love brings forth beyond the sky.

For the Living Light that streams forth from the Source
in such a way that it is never parted
from Him, nor from the Love whose mystic force

joins them in Trinity, lets its grace ray down,
as if reflected, through nine subsistant natures
that sempiternally remain as one.

From thing to thing to the last least potencies
the ray comes down, until it is so scattered
it brings forth only brief contingencies;

and these contingencies, I would have you see,
are those *generated things* the moving heavens
bring forth from seeds or not, as the case may be.

The wax of these things, and the powers that press
and shape it, vary; thus the Ideal Seal
shines through them sometimes more and sometimes less.

So trees of the same species may bring forth
fruit that is better or worse; so men are born
different in native talent and native worth.

Were the wax most ready and free of every dross,
and were the heavens in their supreme conjunction,
the light of the seal would shine through without loss:

but nature scants that light in all it makes,
working in much the manner of a painter
who knows the true art, but whose brush hand shakes.

But if the Fervent Love move the Pure Ray
of the First Power to wield the seal directly,
the thing so stamped is perfect in every way.

So once a quickening of the dust of earth
issued the form of the animal perfection;
so once the Virgin Womb quickened toward birth.

Therefore I say that I am one with you
in the opinion that mankind was never,
nor will be, what it once was in those two.

Having said this much, I must yet go on
or you would ask: 'How then can it be said,
no mortal ever rose to equal this one?'

But to make clear what yet seems not to be,
think who he was, and what it was that moved him
to answer when God said, 'What shall I give thee?'

I speak these words that you may understand
he was a king, and asked the Lord for wisdom
in governing his people and his land,

and not to know the number and degree
of our motor-angels, nor if a premised 'may'
can ever conclude, in logic, 'this must be,'

nor if there is prime motion, nor if in the space
of a semicircle a non-right triangle
may be drawn with the diameter as its base.

Hence you may see that when I spoke before
of unmatched wisdom, it was on royal prudence
that the drawn arrow of my intention bore.

Note well that I said 'rose' when I spoke of it.
Thus you will see I spoke only of kings,
of whom there are many, though so few are fit.

Such were my words, and taken in this light
they are consistent with all that you believe
of our first father and of our Best Delight.

And lead weights to your feet may my words be,
that you move slowly, like a weary man,
to the 'yes' and 'no' of what you do not see.

For he is a fool, and low among his kind,
who answers yea or nay without reflection,
nor does it matter on which road he runs blind.

Opinions too soon formed often deflect
man's thinking from the truth into gross error,
in which his pride then binds his intellect.

It is worse than vain for men to leave the shore
and fish for truth unless they know the art;
for they return worse off than they were before.

Of this, Parmenides and Melissus bear
their witness to all men, along with Bryson,
and others who set out without knowing where;

so Arius, Sabellius, and their schools

who were to Scripture like a mirroring sword,
distorting the straight faces to mislead fools.

Men should not be too smug in their own reason;
only a foolish man will walk his field
and count his ears too early in the season;

for I have seen a briar through winter's snows
rattle its tough and menacing bare stems,
and then, in season, open its pale rose;

and I have seen a ship cross all the main,
true to its course and swift, and then go down
just as it entered its home port again.

Let Tom and Jane not think, because they see
one man is picking pockets and another
is offering all his goods to charity,

that they can judge their neighbors with God's eyes:
for the pious man may fall, and the thief may rise."

Canto XIV

THE FOURTH SPHERE: THE SUN
The Two Circles of Souls
Philosophers and Theologians
Solomon
The Third Circle of Souls
Warriors of God
The Vision of Christ on the Cross
ASCENT TO MARS
THE FIFTH SPHERE: MARS

THOMAS AQUINAS has finished speaking. Now, anticipating the wish Dante has not yet realized is his own, Beatrice begs the double circle of Philosophers and Theologians to explain to Dante the state in which the blessed will find themselves after the RESURRECTION OF THE FLESH. The radiant spirit of SOLOMON answers.

As Solomon finishes his discourse and the souls about him cry "Amen!" Dante becomes aware of a THIRD CIRCLE OF SOULS, higher and more radiant even than the first two. Its radiance dawns slowly and indistinctly at first, and then suddenly bursts upon him. Only then does he realize that he and Beatrice have been ascending and that he has entered the FIFTH SPHERE, MARS. The souls he had seen in the third great circle are those of the WARRIORS OF GOD. There Dante beholds, shining through the Sphere of Mars (in about the way the rays of a star sapphire shine within the stone), the VISION OF CHRIST ON THE CROSS.

"The water in a round vessel moves about from center to rim if it is struck from within, from rim to center if it is struck from without."

—Such was the thought that suddenly occurred to my rapt mind when the immortal ray of Thomas had pronounced its final word, occasioned by the likeness to the flow of his speech and my lady's, she being moved to speak when he had done, beginning so:

"There is another need this man must find the holy root of, though he does not speak it, nor know, as yet, he has the thought in mind.

Explain to him if the radiance he sees flower about your beings will remain forever exactly as it shines forth in this hour; and if it will remain so, then explain how your restored eyes can endure such brilliance when your beings have grown visible again."

As dancers in a country reel flush brighter as they spin faster, moved by joy of joy, their voices higher, and all their gestures lighter—so at my lady's prompt and humble plea the sacred circles showed yet greater joy in their dance and in their heavenly harmony.

Those who mourn, here, that we must die to gain the life up there, have never visualized that soul-refreshing and eternal rain.

That One and Two and Three that is eternal, eternally reigning in Three and Two and One, uncircumscribed, and circumscribing all, was praised in three great paeans by each spirit of those two rings, and in such melody as would do fitting honor to any merit.

And I heard, then, from the most glorious ray of the inner circle, a voice as sweetly low as the angel's must have sounded to Mary, say:

"Long as the feast of Paradise shall be, so long shall our love's bliss shine forth from us and clothe us in these radiant robes you see.

Each robe reflects love's ardor shining forth; the ardor, the vision; the vision shines down to us as each is granted grace beyond his worth.

When our flesh, made glorious at the Judgment Seat, dresses us once again, then shall our persons become more pleasing in being more complete.

Thereby shall we have increase of the light Supreme Love grants, unearned, to make us fit to hold His glory ever in our sight.

Thereby, it follows, the vision shall increase; increase the ardor that the vision kindles; increase the ray its inner fires release.

But as a coal, in giving off its fire, outshines it by its living incandescence, its form remaining visible and entire;

so shall this radiance that wraps us round be outshone in appearance by the flesh that lies this long day through beneath the ground; nor will it be overborne by so much light; for the organs of the body shall be strengthened in all that shall give increase of delight."

And "Amen!" cried the souls of either chain with such prompt zeal as to make evident how much they yearned to wear their flesh again; perhaps less for themselves than for the love of mothers, fathers, and those each soul held dear before it became an eternal flame above.

And lo! all round me, equal in all its parts, a splendor dawned above the splendor there like a horizon when the new day starts.

And as, at the first coming on of night, new presences appear across the sky, seeming to be, and not to be, in sight;

so did I start to see Existences I had not seen before, forming a ring around the other two circumferences.

Oh sparkling essence of the Holy Ghost! How instantly it blazed before my eyes, defeating them with glory, their function lost!

But Beatrice let herself appear to me so glad in beauty, that the vision must lie with those whose glory outdoes memory.

From her I drew again the power of sight, and looked up, and I saw myself translated, with her alone, to the next estate of light.

I was made aware that I had risen higher by the enkindled ardor of the red star that glowed, I thought, with more than usual fire.

With all my heart, and in the tongue which is one in all men, I offered God my soul as a burnt offering for this new bliss.

Nor had the flame of sacrifice in my breast burned out, when a good omen let me know my prayer had been received by the Most Blest;

for with such splendor, in such a ruby glow, within two rays, there shone so great a glory I cried, "O Helios that arrays them so!"

As, pole to pole, the arch of the Milky Way so glows, pricked out by greater and lesser stars, that sages stare, not knowing what to say— so constellated, deep within that Sphere, the two rays formed into the holy sign a circle's quadrant lines describe. And here

memory outruns my powers. How shall I write that from that cross there glowed a vision of Christ? What metaphor is worthy of that sight?

But whoso takes his cross and follows Christ will pardon me what I leave here unsaid when *he* sees that great dawn that rays forth Christ.

From arm to arm, from root to crown of that tree, bright lamps were moving, crossing and rejoining. And when they met they glowed more brilliantly.

So, here on earth, across a slant of light that parts the air within the sheltering shade man's arts and crafts contrive, our mortal sight

observes bright particles of matter ranging up, down, aslant; darting or eddying; longer and shorter; but forever changing.

And as a viol and a harp in a harmony of many strings, make only a sweet tinkle to one who has not studied melody;

so from that choir of glories I heard swell so sweet a melody that I stood tranced, though what hymn they were singing, I could not tell.

That it was raised in lofty praise was clear, for I heard "Arise" and "Conquer"— but as one may hear, not understanding, and still hear.

My soul was so enraptured by those strains of purest song, that nothing until then had bound my being to it in such sweet chains.

My saying so may seem too bold at best, since I had not yet turned to those dear eyes in which my every yearning found its rest.

But think how the living seals of every beauty grow stronger toward their heights, and though I had not turned to those others yet in love and duty,

reason may yet dismiss the charge I bring against myself in order to dismiss it; and see the holy truth of what I sing;

for my sacred pleasure in those sacred eyes can only become purer as we rise.

Canto XV

THE FIFTH SPHERE: MARS
The Warriors of God
Cacciaguida

*THE SOULS OF THE GREAT CROSS stop their singing in order to encourage
Dante to speak, and one among them descends to the foot of the cross like a
shooting star, glowing with joy at the sight of Dante. It is, as Dante will
discover, CACCIAGUIDA, Dante's own great-great-grandfather.*

*Cacciaguida addresses Dante as "Blood of mine," and though he already
knows Dante's thoughts, he begs his descendant to speak them for the joy of
hearing his voice.*

*Dante does as he is bid, and Cacciaguida, in answer to Dante's request,
identifies himself, gives an ACCOUNT OF ANCIENT FLORENCE, and explains
how he followed CONRAD in the Crusades, BECAME A KNIGHT, and died in
battle passing from MARTYRDOM TO BLISS.*

Good will, in which there cannot fail to be the outgoing love of right (just as we
find self-seeking love in all iniquity),

stopped the sweet trembling harp, and let fall still the blessed viol, upon whose
many strings the Hand of Heaven plays Its sacred will.

How shall those beings not heed a righteous prayer when, to encourage me to
speak my wish, they stopped with one accord, and waited there?
Justly they mourn in their eternal wasting who, in their love for what does not
endure, stripped off the hope of this love everlasting.

As through the pure sky of a peaceful night there streaks from time to time a
sudden fire, and eyes that had been still move at the sight, as if they saw a star
changing its post (except that none is gone from where it started, and blazed its
little while, and soon was lost)—

so, in a trail of fire across the air, from the right arm to the foot of the great
cross, a star streaked from the constellation there.

Nor did that gemstone leave its diadem. Like fire behind an alabaster screen, it crossed those radiant ranks, still one with them.

Just so did the shade of ancient Ilium (if we may trust our greatest muse) go forth to greet Aeneas in Elysium.

"O sanguis meus, o superinfusa gratia Dei, sicut tibi, cui bis unquam coeli ianua reclusa?"

So spoke that radiance as I stared wide-eyed. Then I turned my eyes back to my blessed lady, and between those two souls I stood stupefied,

for such a fire of love burned in her eyes that mine, I thought, had touched the final depth both of my Grace and of my Paradise.

Then, radiating bliss in sight and sound, the spirit added to his opening words others I could not grasp: they were too profound.

Nor did the spirit's words elude my mind by his own choice. Rather, his thoughts took place above the highest target of mankind.

And when the bow recovered from the effect of its own ardor, and its words arced down nearer the target of our intellect,

the first on which my straining powers could feed were: "Praised be Thou, O Triune Unity which showeth me such favor in my seed!"

Continuing: "The sight of you assuages a long dear hunger that grew within this lamp from which I speak, as I perused the pages

of the Great Book where neither black nor white can ever change. I give thanks to this spirit whose love gave you the wings for this high flight.

You believe that what you think rays forth to me from the Primal Intellect, as five and six, if understood, ray forth from unity.

And for that reason you do not inquire who I may be, nor why I am more joyous than the other spirits of this joyous choir.

And you are right: for here in Paradise greatest and least alike gaze in that Mirror where thoughts outsoar themselves before they rise.

But, that the Sacred Love in which I wake to the eternal vision, and which fills me with a sweet thirst, you may the sooner slake, let your own voice, assured, frank, and elated, sound forth your will, sound forth your soul's desire, to which my answer is already fated!"

I turned to Beatrice and while I still sought words, she heard, and smiled such glad assent the joy of it gave wings to my glad will.

Thus I began: "When the First Equipoise shone forth to you, love and the power to speak love became in each of you an equal voice;

because the Sun that warmed and lighted you contains its heat and light so equally that though we seek analogies, none will do.

But mortal utterance and mortal feelings—for reasons that are evident to you— have no such equal feathers to their wings.

I, then, being mortal, in the perturbation of my unequal powers, with heart alone give thanks for your paternal salutation.

I do indeed beseech you, holy flame, and living topaz of this diadem, that you assuage my hunger to know your name."

"O leaf of mine, which even to foresee has filled me with delight, I was your root." —So he began in answer to my plea.

And then: "The first to take your present surname (whose soul has crawled the first round of the mountain a century and more), he who became

father of your grandfather, was my son. You would do well, by offering up good works, to shorten his long striving at his stone.

Florence, within her ancient walls secure—from them she still hears *tierce* and *nones* ring down—lived in sweet peace, her sons sober and pure.

No golden chains nor crowns weighed down her spirit, nor women in tooled sandals and studded belts more to be admired than the wearer's merit.

A father, in those days, was not terrified by the birth of a daughter, for marriage and marriage portion had not escaped all bounds on either side.

No mansions then stood uninhabited. No Sardanapalus had yet arrived to show what may be done in hall and bed.

Montemario had not yet been outshone by your Uccellatoio, which having passed it in the race up, shall pass it going down.

Bellincion Berti, with whom I was acquainted, went belted in leather and bone; and his good wife came from the mirror with her face unpainted.

I have seen the lords of Vecchio and of Nerli content to wear plain leather, and their wives working the spindle and distaff late and early.

Fortunate they! And blest their circumstance! Each sure of her own burial place; none yet deserted in her bed because of France.

One watched the cradle, babbling soft and low to soothe her child in the sweet idiom that is the first delight new parents know.

Another, spinning in her simple home, would tell old tales to children gathered round her, of Troy, and of Fiesole, and of Rome.

A Cornelia or Cincinnatus would amaze a modern Florentine as a Cianghella or a Lapo would have startled men in those days.

To so serene, so fair a townsman's life, to a citizenry so wedded in good faith, to such sweet dwelling, free of vice and strife,

Mary gave me—called in the pain of birth—and in your ancient Baptistry I became a Christian—and Cacciaguida, there on earth.

Moronto and Eliseo my brothers were. My wife came from the valley of the Po. The surname you now bear derives from her.

I served with Conrad in the Holy Land, and my valor so advanced me in his favor that I was knighted in his noble band.

With him I raised my sword against the might of the evil creed whose followers take from you—because your shepherds sin—what is yours by right.

There, by that shameless and iniquitous horde, I was divested of the flesh and weight of the deceitful world, too much adored

by many souls whose best hope it destroys; and came from martyrdom to my present joys."

Canto XVI

DANTE THRILLS WITH PLEASURE on learning that his ancestor had been elevated to knighthood, and feeling the power of pride of ancestry even in Heaven, in which there is no temptation to evil, he has a new insight into the family pride in which mortals glory. Moved by pride, Dante addresses Cacciaguida with the formal "voi," an affectation at which Beatrice, half amused, admonishes him with a smile.

Dante then asks Cacciaguida for details of his birth and ancestry and of THE HISTORY OF EARLY FLORENCE. Cacciaguida, as if to warn Dante away from pride of ancestry, dismisses the question of his birth and of his forebears as a matter best passed over in silence, and proceeds to a detailed account of the lords and people of Florence in the days when her bloodlines and traditions had not been diluted by the arrival of new families. It is to this "mongrelization" of the Florentines that Cacciaguida attributes all the subsequent degeneracy of Florence.

O trivial pride of ours in noble blood! that in possessing you men are possessed, down here, where souls grow sick and lose their good,

will never again amaze me, for there, too, where appetite is never drawn to evil
—in Heaven, I say—my own soul gloried in you!

You are a mantle that soon shrinks and tears. Unless new cloth is added day by day, time will go round you, snipping with its shears!

I spoke again, addressing him with that *"voi"* whose usage first began among the Romans—and which their own descendants least employ—

at which my Lady, who stood apart, though near, and smiling, seemed to me like her who coughed at the first recorded fault of Guinevere.

"You are my father," I started in reply. "You give me confidence to speak out boldly. You so uplift me, I am more than I.

So many streams of happiness flow down into my mind that it grows self-delighting at being able to bear it and not drown.

Tell me, then, dear source of my own blood, who were your own forefathers? when were you born? and what transpired in Florence in your boyhood?

Tell me of St. John's sheepfold in those days. How many souls were then within the flock, and which of them was worthy of high place?"

As glowing coals fanned by a breath of air burst into flames, so did I see that light increase its radiance when it heard my prayer.

And as its light gave off a livelier ray, so, in a sweeter and a softer voice— though not in the idiom we use today—

it said: "From the day when *Ave* sounded forth to that in which my mother, now a saint, being heavy laden with me, gave me birth,

this flame had come back to its Leo again to kindle itself anew beneath his paws five hundred times plus fifty plus twenty plus ten.

My ancestors and I were born in the place where the last quarter of the course begins for those who take part in your annual race.

Of my fathers, be content with what you have heard. Of who they were and whence they came to Florence silence is far more fitting than any word.

Of men who could bear arms there were counted then, between Mars and the Baptist, the fifth part of what may be mustered there from living men.

But the citizenry, now mongrelized by the blood of Campi, of Certaldo, and of Figghine, was pure then, down to the humblest planer of wood.

Oh how much better to have been neighbors of these of whom I speak, and to have Trespiano and Galuzzo still fixed as your boundaries,

than to have swallowed them and to bear the stink of the yokel of Aguglione, and of Signa's boor who still has eyes to swindle and hoodwink.

Had the world's most despicable crew not shown a hard stepmother's face and greed to Caesar but been a loving mother, one who is known

as a Florentine, and who trades in goods and debt, would be back in Simifonti, where his grandsire once gypsied in the streets for what he could get.

Montemurlo would still be owned by its own counts, the Cerchi would be in the parish of Acone, and in Valdigreve, still, the Bondelmounts.

It has always been a fact that confusion of blood has been a source of evil to city-states, just as our bodies are harmed by too much food;

and that a bull gone blind will fall before a blind lamb does. And that one sword may cut better than five has been proved in many a war.

If you will think of Luni and Urbisaglia, how they have passed away, and how, behind them, are dying now Chiusi and Sinigaglia,

it should not be too hard to comprehend, or strange to hear, that families dwindle out, when even cities come at last to an end.

All mankind's institutions, of every sort, have their own death, though in what long endures it is hidden from you, your own lives being short.

And as the circling of the lunar sphere covers and bares the shore with never a pause, so Fortune alters Florence year by year.

It should not, therefore, seem too wondrous strange to hear me speak of the good Florentines whose fame is veiled behind time's endless change.

I knew the Ughi, the Catellini, the line of the Greci, Filippi, Ormanni, and

Alberichi—illustrious citizens, even in decline.

I knew those of Sannella, and those of the Bow, and the Soldanieri, Ardinghi, and Bostichi; as grand as they were ancient, there below.

Not far from the portal that now bears the weight of such a cargo of new iniquity as soon, now, will destroy the ship of state,

once lived the Ravignani, from whom came Count Guido Guerra, and whoever else has since borne Bellincione's noble name.

The della Pressa were already furnished with knowledge of how to rule, and Galigaio had his gold hilt and pommel already burnished.
Great already were the lands of the vair, Sacchetti, Giuochi, Fifanti, Barucci, and Galli, and of those who blush now for the stave affair.

The trunk that bore the many-branched Calfucci had grown already great; already called to the curule were Sizii and Arrigucci.

How great I have seen them who are now undone by their own pride! And even the balls of gold—in all great deeds of Florence, how they shone!

So shone the fathers of that gang we see in the bishop's palace when your See falls vacant, fattening themselves as a consistory.

That overweening and presumptuous tribe—a dragon to all who run from it, a lamb to any who stand and show a tooth or bribe—

were coming up, though still so parvenu Donato was hardly pleased when his father-in-law made him a relative of such a crew.

The Caponsacchi had come down by then from Fiesole to market; the Infangati and Giudi were established as good townsmen.

And here's an astonishing fact, though little known: in ancient times a gate of the inner wall was named for those of the Pera, now all gone.

All those whose various quarterings display the staves of the great baron whose name and worth are kept alive every St. Thomas' Day

owe him the rank and privilege they enjoy, though one who binds those arms with a gold fringe makes common cause today with the hoi polloi.

Gualterotti and Importuni were then well known. And Borgo would still be a peaceful place had it not acquired new neighbors from Montebuon'.

The line from which was born your grief and strife because of the righteous anger that ruined you, and put an end to all your happier life,

was honored in itself and its allies. O Buondelmonti, what ill you did in fleeing its nuptials to find comfort in other ties!

Many would still be happy whom we now pity, had God seen fit to let the Ema drown you on the first day you started for the city.

But it was fitting that to the broken stone that guards the bridge, Florence should offer a victim to mark the last day's peace she has ever known.

With such as these, and others, my first life's years saw Florence live and prosper in such peace that she had, then, no reason to shed tears.

With such as these I saw there in my past so valiant and so just a populace that none had ever seized the ensign's mast

and hung the lily on it upside down. Nor was the red dye of division known."

Canto XVII

THE FIFTH SPHERE: MARS
The Warriors of God: Cacciaguida

BEATRICE AND CACCIAGUIDA already know what question is burning in Dante's mind, but Beatrice nevertheless urges him to speak it, that by practicing Heavenly discourse he be better able to speak to men when he returns to Earth. So urged, Dante asks Cacciaguida to make clear the recurring DARK PROPHECIES OF DANTE'S FUTURE.

Cacciaguida details DANTE'S COMING BANISHMENT FROM FLORENCE, identifies the patrons Dante will find, and assures Dante of his future fame. He warns Dante not to become bitter in adversity, assuring him that the Divine Comedy, once it becomes known, will outlive the proudest of the Florentines and bring shame to their evil memories for ages to come.

Like him who went to Clymene to learn if what he had heard was true, and who makes fathers unwilling to yield to their sons at every turn—

such was I, and such was I taken to be by Beatrice and by the holy lamp that, earlier, had changed its place for me.

Therefore my lady: "Speak. And let the fire of your consuming wish come forth," she said, "well marked by the inner stamp of your desire;

not that we learn more by what you say, but that you better learn to speak your thirst, that men may sooner quench it on your way."

"Dear root of my existence, you who soar so high that, as men grasp how a triangle may contain one obtuse angle and no more,

you grasp contingent things before they find essential being, for you can see that focus where all time is time-present in God's mind.

While I was yet with Virgil, there below, climbing the mountain where the soul is healed, and sinking through the dead world of its woe,

dark words of some dark future circumstance were said to me; whereby my soul is set four-square against the hammering of chance:

and, therefore, my desire will be content with knowing what misfortune is approaching; for the arrow we see coming is half spent."

—Such were the words of my reply, addressed to the light that had spoken earlier; and with them as Beatrice wished, my own wish was confessed.

Not in dark oracles like those that glued the foolish like limed birds, before the Lamb that takes our sins away suffered the rood;

but in clear words and the punctilious style of ordered thought, that father-love replied, concealed in and revealed by his own smile:

"*Contingency*, whose action is confined to the few pages of the world of matter, is fully drawn in the Eternal Mind;

but it no more derives *necessity* from being so drawn, than a ship dropping down river derives its motion from a watcher's eye.

As a sweet organ-harmony strikes the ear, so, from the Primal Mind, my eyes receive a vision of your future drawing near.

As Hippolytus left Athens, forced to roam by his two-faced and merciless stepmother, just so shall you leave Florence, friends, and home.

So is it willed, so does it already unfold, so will it soon be done by him who plots it there where Christ is daily bought and sold.

The public cry, as usual, will blame you of the offended party, but the vengeance truth will demand will yet show what is true.

All that you held most dear you will put by and leave behind you; and this is the arrow the longbow of your exile first lets fly.

You will come to learn how bitter as salt and stone is the bread of others, how hard the way that goes up and down stairs that never are your own.

And what will press down on your shoulders most will be the foul and foolish company you will fall into on that barren coast.

Ingrate and godless, mad in heart and head will they become against you, but soon thereafter it will be they, not you, whose cheeks turn red.

Their bestiality will be made known by what they do; while your fame shines the brighter for having become a party of your own.

Your first inn and first refuge you shall owe to the great Lombard whose escutcheon bears the sacred bird above, the ladder below.

In such regard and honor shall he hold you, that in the act of granting and requesting, what others do late, shall be first between you two.

With him you will see another, born of this star and so stamped by the iron of its virtues that he shall be renowned for deeds of war.

The world has not yet noticed him: these spheres in their eternal course above his youth have turned about him now only nine years.

Before the Gascon sets his low intrigue to snare high Henry, men will start to speak of his disregard of money and fatigue.

The knowledge of his magnanimities will spread so far that men will hear of it out of the mouths of his very enemies.

Look you to him and his great works. The fate of many shall be altered by his deeds, the rich and poor exchanging their estate.

And write this in your mind but remain silent concerning it . . ."—and he said things about him to astonish even those who shall be present.

Then added: "Son, these are the annotations to what was told you. These are the snares that hide behind a few turns of the constellations.

But do not hate your neighbors: your future stretches far beyond the reach of what they do and far beyond the punishment of wretches."

—When, by his silence, that blessed soul made clear that he had finished passing his dark shuttle across the threads I had combed for him there,

I then, as one who has not understood longs for the guidance of a soul that sees, and straightway wills, and wholly loves the good:

"Father, I do indeed see time's attacks hard spurred against me to strike such a blow as shall fall most on him who is most lax.

And it is well I arm myself with foresight. Thus, if the dearest place is taken from me, I shall not lose all place by what I write.

Down through that world of endless bitter sighs, and on the mountain from whose flowering crown I was uplifted by my lady's eyes,

and then through Heaven from ray to living ray, I have learned much that would, were it retold, offend the taste of many alive today.

Yet if, half friend to truth, I mute my rhymes, I am afraid I shall not live for those who will think of these days as 'the ancient times.' "

The light in which my heaven-found treasure shone smiled brighter in its rapture, coruscating like a gold mirror in a ray of sun;

then answered me: "A conscience overcast by its own shame, or another's, may indeed be moved to think your words a bitter blast.

Nevertheless, abjure all lies, but match your verses to the vision in fullest truth; and if their hides are scabby, let them scratch!

For if your voice is bitter when first tested upon the palate, it shall yet become a living nutriment when it is digested.

This cry you raise shall strike as does the wind hardest at highest peaks—and this shall argue no little for your honor, as you will find.

Therefore you have been shown—here in these spheres, there on the mount, and in the valley of woe—those souls whose names most ring in mortal ears;

for the feelings of a listener do not mark examples of things unknown, nor place their trust in instances whose roots hide in the dark;

nor will men be persuaded to give ear to arguments whose force is not made clear."

Canto XVIII

THE FIFTH SPHERE: MARS
The Courageous:
Cacciaguida
Great Warriors of God
ASCENT TO JUPITER
THE SIXTH SPHERE: JUPITER
The Just and Temperate Rulers
The Vision of the Flashing Lights
and of the Eagle

BEATRICE COMFORTS DANTE, who is pondering the bitter and the sweet of
Cacciaguida's prophecy, then instructs him to turn back to Cacciaguida, who
proceeds to name among the souls who form the Cross of Mars THE GREAT
WARRIORS OF GOD. They flash like shooting stars along the arms of the cross.
Finished, Cacciaguida reascends to his original place in the right arm and the
whole choir resumes its hymn.

Dante turns back to Beatrice, sees her grow yet more beautiful, and knows
they have made the ASCENT TO THE SIXTH SPHERE. He sees the pale glow of
Jupiter replace the red glow of Mars and in that silvery sheen he sees THE
VISION OF EARTHLY JUSTICE, a spectacular arrangement of lights that spell
out a message, letter by letter, and then form as an EAGLE (The Empire)
ornamented by glowing lilies (France).

Moved by this vision of Justice, Dante prays that these souls of Heavenly
Justice will visit their wrath upon the corrupt Pope, who, like a money-changer
in the temple, denies the sacraments of God's people by excommunication and
interdiction, in order to sell back to them what is rightfully theirs. So, for the
love of money does the successor of Peter and Paul betray holy office.

Now that holy mirror rejoiced alone, rapt in its own reflections; and I tasted the
bitterness and sweetness of my own.

My guide to God said: "Turn your thoughts along a happier course. Remember I
dwell near the One who lifts the weight of every wrong."

I turned to the loving sound of my soul's aid, and the love my eyes beheld in her sacred eyes I leave unsaid—not only am I afraid

my powers of speech fail, but my memory cannot return so far above itself unless Another's grace be moved to guide me.

This much of what I felt I can report—that as I looked at her my will was freed of every other wish of any sort,

for the Eternal Bliss that rayed down whole into my Beatrice, shone back from her face and its reflection there gladdened my soul.

And with a smile so radiant that my eyes were overcome, she said then: "Turn and listen: not in my eyes alone is Paradise."

As, here on earth, the face sometimes reveals the wish within, if it is wished so strongly that all the soul is gripped by what it feels—

so, in the flaming of the holy ray to which I turned, I read the inner will, and knew that it had something more to say.

It spoke thus: "In this fifth limb of the tree whose life is from its crown, and bears forever, and never sheds a leaf, I would have you see

elected spirits who, in the world's use, before they came to Heaven, were so renowned their great worth would make greater every Muse.

Look at the arms of the cross. As the swift flame within a flame does, so, within that choir, shall flash the splendor of each soul I name."

I saw along the cross a streak of light as he pronounced the name of Joshua: nor did the saying reach me before the sight.

And at the name of the great Maccabee I saw another, spinning; and the string that whirled that top was its own ecstasy.

And just as hunters follow their falcons' flights, so, at the names of Charlemagne and Roland, my rapt attention followed two more lights.

Then William of Orange, and then Rinoard drew my eyes after them along that cross. And then the good duke Godfrey, and Robert Guiscard.

Then, moving once more through those lights, the light that had come down to greet me, let me hear its art among the choir of Heaven's height.

I turned to my right to learn from Beatrice, whether by word or sign, what I should do, and I beheld her eyes shine with such bliss,

with such serenity, that she surpassed the vision of every other accustomed beauty in which she had shone, including even the last.

And as a man, perceiving day by day an increase of delight in doing good, begins to sense his soul is gaining way—

so, seeing that Miracle surpass the mark of former beauty, I sensed that I was turning, together with Heaven, through a greater arc.

And such a change as fair-skinned ladies show in a short space of time, when from their faces they lift the weight of shame that made them glow—

such change grew on my eyes when I perceived the pure white radiance of the temperate star—the sixth sphere—into which I was received.

Within that jovial face of Paradise I saw the sparkling of the love that dwelt there forming our means of speech before my eyes.

As birds arisen from a marshy plain almost as if rejoicing in their forage form, now a cluster, now a long-drawn skein—

so, there, within their sheaths of living light, blest beings soared and sang and joined their rays, and *D*, then *I*, then *L* formed on my sight.

First they sang and moved to their own song; then having formed themselves into a letter, they stopped their song and flight, though not for long.

O holy Pegasean who consecrates the power of genius, giving it long life, as it, through you, gives life to cities and states—

so fill me with your light, that as it shines I may show forth their image as I conceive it: let your own power appear in these few lines!

In five times seven vowels and consonants they showed themselves, and I grasped every part as if those lights had given it utterance.

The first words of that message as it passed before me were *DILIGITE IUSTITIAM. QUI IUDICATIS TERRAM* were the last.

Then, in the fifth word, at the final *M* they stayed aligned, and silvery Jupiter seemed to be washed in a gold glow around them.

More lights descended then and took their place on top of the *M*, and sang, as I believe, a hymn to the Good that draws them to Its grace.

Then—just as burning logs, when poked, let fly a fountain of innumerable sparks (from which fools used to think to prophesy)—

more than a thousand of those lights arose, some to a greater height, some to a lesser, each to the place the Sun that lit it chose.

And as each took its place in that still choir I saw the head and shoulders of an eagle appear in the fixed pattern of that fire.

The One who paints there needs no guide's behest. He is Himself the guide. From Him derives the skill and essential form that builds a nest.

The other sparks, at first content to twine in the form of golden lilies round the *M* now moved a bit, completing the design.

O lovely star, how rich a diadem shown forth to let me understand our justice flows to us from the heaven you begem.

Therefore I pray the mind that initiated your power and motion, to observe the source of the smoke by which your ray is vitiated;

that it be moved to anger once again against the buyers and sellers in the temple whose walls were built of blood and martyr's pain.

O soldiery of Heaven to whose array my mind returns, pray for all those on earth who follow bad example and go astray.

In earlier eras wars were carried on by swords; now, by denying this man or that the bread the Heavenly Father denies to none.

But you who scribble only to scratch out, remember that Peter and Paul, who died for the vineyard you trample, still defend the good you flout.

Well may you say: "My heart's wish is so set on the image of the saint who lived alone and who was forced to give his head in forfeit,

as if it were a favor at a ball—what do I care for the Fisherman or old Paul!"

Canto XIX

THE SIXTH SPHERE: JUPITER
The Just and Temperate
Rulers
The Eagle

THE EAGLE *made up of the many souls of the Just and Temperate Rulers moves*
its beak and speaks as if it were a single entity, announcing that it is the chosen
symbol of DIVINE JUSTICE. Dante is afire to understand the nature of the
Divine Justice and begs the Eagle to explain it, but he is told that the infinity of
God's excellence must forever exceed his creation, and that none may fathom
His will, whereby it is presumptuous of any creature to question the Divine
Justice. Man must be content with the guidance of Scripture and with the sure
knowledge that God is perfect, good, and just.

Dante had once pondered the justice of denying salvation to virtuous pagans.
The Eagle tells him it is not for him to sit in judgment on God's intent. It affirms
that except as he believes in Christ no soul may ascend to Heaven, yet it adds
that the virtuous pagan shall sit nearer Christ than many another who takes
Christ's name in vain.

The Eagle concludes with a DENUNCIATION OF THE BESTIALIZED KINGS
OF CHRISTENDOM in 1300.

Before me, its great wings outspread, now shone the image of the eagle those
bright souls had given form to in glad unison.

Each seemed a little ruby in the sky, and the sun's ray struck each in such a way
the light reflected straight into my eye.

What I must now call back from memory no voice has ever spoken, nor ink
written. Nor has its like been known to fantasy.

For I saw and heard the beak move and declare in its own voice the pronouns "I"
and "mine" when "we" and "our" were what conceived it there.

"For being just and pious in my time," it said, "I am exalted here in glory to which, by wish alone, no one may climb;

and leave behind me, there upon the earth, a memory honored even by evildoers, though they shun the good example it sets forth."

Just as the glow of many living coals issues a single heat, so from that image one sound declared the love of many souls.

At which I cried: "O everlasting blooms of the eternal bliss, who make one seeming upon my sense of all your many perfumes—

my soul has hungered long: breathe forth at last the words that will appease it. There on earth there is no food with which to break its fast.

I know that if God's justice has constructed its holy mirror in some other realm, your kingdom's view of it is not obstructed.

You know how eagerly I wait to hear; you know the what and wherefore of the doubt I have hungered to resolve for many a year."

Much as a falcon freed of hood and jess stretches its head and neck and beats its wings, preening itself to show its readiness—

so moved the emblem that was all compounded of praises of God's grace; and from it, then, a hymn they know who dwell in bliss resounded.

Then it began to speak: "The One who wheeled the compass round the limits of the world, and spread there what is hidden and what revealed,

could not so stamp his power and quality into his work but what the creating Word would still exceed creation infinitely.

And this explains why the first Prideful Power, highest of creatures, because he would not wait the power of the ripening sun, fell green and sour.

And thus we see that every lesser creature is much too small a vessel to hold the Good that has no end; Itself is Its one measure.

Therefore, you understand, our way of seeing, which must be only one ray of the Mind that permeates all matter and all being,

cannot, by its very nature, be so clear but what its Author's eye sees far beyond the furthest limits that to us appear.

In the eternal justice, consequently, the understanding granted to mankind is lost as the eye is within the sea:

it can make out the bottom near the shore but not on the main deep; and still it is there, though at a depth your eye cannot explore.

There is no light but from that ever fresh and cloudless Halcyon; all else is darkness, the shadow and the poison of the flesh.

By now, much that was hidden from your view by the living Justice of which you used to ask so many questions, has been shown to you.

For you used to say, 'A man is born in sight of Indus' water, and there is none there to speak of Christ, and none to read or write.

And all he wills and does, we must concede, as far as human reason sees, is good; and he does not sin either in word or deed.

He dies unbaptized and cannot receive the saving faith. What justice is it damns him? Is it his fault that he does not believe?'

—But who are you to take the judgment seat and pass on things a thousand miles away, who cannot see the ground before your feet?

The man who would split hairs with me could find no end of grounds for questioning, had he not the Scriptures over him to guide his mind.

O earthbound animals! minds gross as wood! Itself good in Itself, the Primal Will does not move from Itself, the Supreme Good!

Only what sorts with It is just. It sways toward no created good, but of Itself creates all Good by sending forth Its rays."

As a stork that has fed its young flies round and round above the nest, and as the chick it fed raises its head to stare at it, still nest-bound—

so did that blessed image circle there, its great wings moved in flight by many wills, and so did I lift up my head and stare.

Circling, it sang; then said: "As what I sing surpasses your understanding, so God's justice surpasses the power of mortal reasoning."

Those blazing glories of the Holy Ghost stopped, still formed in the sign that spread the honor of Rome across the world, to its last coast,

grew still, then said: "To this high empery none ever rose but through belief in Christ, either before or after his agony.

But see how many now cry out 'Christ! Christ!' who shall be farther from him at the Judgment than many who, on earth, did not know Christ.

Such Christians shall the Ethiopian scorn when the two bands are formed to right and left, one blest to all eternity, one forlorn.

What shall the Persians say to your kings there when the Great Book is opened and they see the sum of their depravities laid bare?

There shall be seen among the works of Albert, that deed the moving pen will soon record by which Bohemia shall become a desert.

There shall be seen the Seine's grief for the sin of that debaser of the currency whose death is waiting for him in a pig's skin.

There shall be seen the pride whose greed confounds the mad Scot and the foolish Englishman who cannot stay within their proper bounds.

There, the debaucheries and the vain show of the Spaniard and the Bohemian who knew nothing of valor, and chose not to know.

And there, the cripple of Jerusalem: a *I* put down to mark the good he did, and then, to mark his villainies, an *M*.

There, the baseness and the greedy rage of the watchdog who patrols the burning island on which Anchises closed his long old age; and to make clear how paltry is his case, his entry will be signs and abbreviations that the record may say much in little space.

And there the filthy deeds shall be set down of his uncle and his brother, each of whom cuckolded a great family and a crown.

There shall be marked for all men to behold Norway's king and Portugal's; and Rascia's, who lost most when he saw Venetian gold.

Oh happy Hungary, had she suffered all without more griefs ahead! Happy Navarre were she to make her peaks a fortress wall!

And every Navarrese may well believe the omen of Nicosìa and Famagosta whose citizens have present cause to grieve

the way their beast, too small for the main pack, keeps to one side but hunts on the same track."

Canto XX

THE SIXTH SPHERE: JUPITER
The Just and Temperate
Rulers
The Eagle

THE EAGLE PAUSES briefly and the spirits of the blest sing a hymn, not as one symbolic entity, but each in its own voice. The hymn ended, the Eagle resumes speaking in its single voice, and identifies as the chief souls of this sphere those lusters that compose its eye. In order they are: DAVID, TRAJAN, HEZEKIAH, CONSTANTINE, WILLIAM OF SICILY, and RIPHEUS.

Dante is astonished to find Trajan and Ripheus in Heaven, both of whom he had thought to be pagans, but the Eagle explains how by the special grace of God Ripheus was converted by a vision of Christ a millennium before His descent into the flesh, and Trajan was returned from Limbo to his mortal body long enough to undergo conversion to Christ and to allow his soul to mount to Heaven.

So once again for Dante's doubts about the virtuous Hindu and God's justice, for who can say how many more God has so chosen to his grace? The Eagle concludes with a praise of God's predestined justice, rejoicing even in the limitation of its own knowledge, resting in the assurance that the unknown consequences of God's will cannot fail to be good.

When the sun, from which the whole world takes its light, sinks from our hemisphere and the day fades from every reach of land, and it is night;

the sky, which earlier it alone had lit, suddenly changes mode and reappears in many lights that take their light from it.

I thought of just that change across night's sill when that emblem of the world and of its leaders had finished speaking through its sacred bill;

for all those living lights now shone on me more brightly than before, and began singing a praise too sweet to hold in memory.

O heavenly love in smiling glory wreathed, how ardently you sounded from those flutes through which none but the holiest impulse breathed.

When then those precious gems of purest ray with which the lamp of the sixth heaven shone let their last angel-harmony fade away,

I seemed to hear a great flume take its course from stone to stone, and murmur down its mountain as if to show the abundance of its source.

And as the sound emerging from a lute is tempered at its neck; and as the breath takes form around the openings of a flute—

just so, allowing no delay to follow, the murmur of the eagle seemed to climb inside its neck, as if the neck were hollow.

There it was given voice, and through the bill the voice emerged as words my heart awaited. And on my heart those words are written still.

"Look closely now into that part of me that in earth's eagles can endure the Sun," the emblem said, "—the part with which I see.

Of all the fires with which I draw my form those rays that make the eye shine in my head are the chief souls of all this blessed swarm.

The soul that makes the pupil luminous was the sweet psalmist of the Holy Ghost who bore the ark of God from house to house:

now, insofar as he himself gave birth to his own psalms, he is repayed in bliss, and by that bliss he knows what they are worth.

Of the five that form my eyebrow's arc, the one whose glory shines the closest to my beak consoled the widow who had lost her son;

now he understands what price men pay who do not follow Christ, for though he learns the sweet life, he has known the bitter way.

The next in line on the circumference of the same upper arch of which I speak, delayed his own death by true penitence;

now he knows that when a worthy prayer delays today's event until tomorrow, the eternal judgment is not altered there.

The third, to give the Shepherd sovereignty, (with good intentions though they bore bad fruit) removed to Greece, bearing the laws and me;

now he knows the evil that began in his good action does not harm his soul although it has destroyed the world of man.

And him you see upon the arc beneath was William of that land that mourns the life of Charles and Frederick, as it mourns his death;

now he knows how heaven's heart inclines to love a just king, as he makes apparent by the radiance with which his being shines.

Who would believe in the erring world down there that Ripheus the Trojan would be sixth among the sacred lusters of this sphere?

Now he knows grace divine to depths of bliss the world's poor understanding cannot grasp. Even *his* eye cannot plumb that abyss."

Like a lark that soars in rapture to the sky, first singing, and then silent, satisfied by the last sweetness of its soul's own cry—

such seemed that seal of the Eternal Bliss that stamped it there, the First Will at whose will whatever is becomes just what it is.

And though my eagerness to know shone clear as colors shining through a clearest glass, I could not bear to wait in silence there;

but from my tongue burst out "How can this be?" forced by the weight of my own inner doubt. —At which those lights flashed in new revelry.

And soon then, not to keep me in suspense, the blessed emblem answered me, its eye flashing a yet more glorious radiance.

"I see that you believe these things are true because I say them. Yet, you do not see how. Thus, though believed, their truth is hidden from you.

You are like one who knows the name of a thing whose quiddity, until it is explained by someone else, defies his understanding.

By every living hope and ardent love that bends the Eternal Will—by these alone the Kingdom of Heaven suffers itself to move.

Not as men bend beneath a conqueror's will. It bends because it wishes to be bent. Conquered, its own beneficence conquers still.

You marvel at the first and the fifth gem here on my brow, finding this realm of angels and gift of Christ made beautiful by them.

They did not leave their bodies, as you believe, as pagans but as Christians, in firm faith in the pierced feet one grieved and one would grieve.

One rose again from Hell—from whose dead slope none may return to Love— into the flesh; and that was the reward of living hope;

of living hope, whose power of love made good the prayers he raised to God to bring him back to life again, that his will might be renewed.

And so the glorious soul for whom he prayed, back in the flesh from which it soon departed, believed in Him who has the power to aid.

Believing, he burst forth with such a fire of the true love, that at his second death he was worthy of a seat in this glad choir.

The other, by that grace whose blessings rise out of so deep a spring that no one ever has plumbed its sources with created eyes,

gave all his love to justice, there on earth, and God, by grace on grace, let him foresee a vision of our redemption shining forth.

So he believed in Christ, and all his days shunning the poisonous stink of pagan creeds, he warned the obstinant to change their ways.

More than a thousand years before the grace of baptism was known, those maids you saw at the right wheel, stood for him in its place.

Predestination! Oh how deep your source is rooted past the reach of every vision that cannot plumb the whole of the First Cause!

Mortals, be slow to judge! Not even we who look on God in Heaven know, as yet, how many He will choose for ecstasy.

And sweet it is to lack this knowledge still, for in this good is our own good refined, willing whatever God Himself may will."

In these words the blest emblem of that sphere gave me these gentle curatives of love with which my clouded vision was made clear.

And as the skillful harpist, string by string, makes every cord attend on a good singer, adding a greater pleasure to the singing;

so, I recall, that as it spoke to me these paradisal words, the holy lights of Trajan and Ripheus in sweet harmony,

as if they blinked their eyes with one accord, made their flames pulse in time with every word.

Canto XXI

ASCENT TO SATURN
THE SEVENTH SPHERE: SATURN
The Contemplative:
Peter Damiano

*BEATRICE AND DANTE ENTER the Sphere of Saturn. BEATRICE DOES NOT
SMILE in her new bliss to announce their arrival, for her radiance would then
be such that Dante's mortal senses would be consumed, as Semele was
consumed by the Godhead of Jupiter. Rather, Beatrice announces that they are
there and commands Dante to look into the crystalline substance of that Heaven
for the vision he will see of the SOULS OF THE CONTEMPLATIVE.*

*Dante turns and beholds a vision of a GOLDEN LADDER on which countless
Splendors arise and descend wheeling like birds in flight. That host of the
blessed descends only as far as a given rung, but one radiance among them
draws closer to Dante and indicates by its radiance that it is eager to bring him
joy. It is the soul of PETER DAMIANO, a Doctor of the Church, renowned for a
severely ascetic life even in high Church office. Peter Damiano explains to
Dante that THE MYSTERY OF PREDESTINATION is beyond the reach of all
but God, and that men should not presume to grasp it. He concludes with a
DENUNCIATION OF PAPAL CORRUPTION, and at his words, all the souls of
Saturn fly down to form a ring around him and thunder forth HEAVEN'S
RIGHTEOUS INDIGNATION at evildoers. So loud is their cry that Dante
cannot make out their words, his senses reeling at that thunderclap of sound.*

My eyes were fixed once more on my lady's face; and with my eyes, my soul,
from which all thought, except of her, had fled without a trace.

She did not smile. "Were I to smile," she said, "You would be turned to ash, as
Semele was when she saw Jupiter in his full Godhead;

because my beauty, which, as it goes higher from step to step of the eternal
palace, burns, as you know, with ever brighter fire;

and if it is not tempered in its brightening, its radiance would consume your mortal powers as a bough is shattered by a bolt of lightning.

We have soared to the Seventh Splendor, which is now beneath the Lion's blazing breast, and rays its influence, joined with his, to the world below.

Now make your eyes the mirror of the vision this mirror will reveal to you, and fix your mind behind your eyes in strict attention."

Could any man conceive what blessed pasture my eyes found in her face when I turned away, at her command, to find another nurture—

then would he know with what a rush of bliss I obeyed my heavenly escort, balancing one side and the other, that joy against this.

Within the crystal that bears round the world the name of its great king in that golden age when evil's flag had not yet been unfurled,

like polished gold ablaze in full sunlight, I saw a ladder rise so far above me it soared beyond the reaches of my sight.

And I saw so many splendors make their way down its bright rungs, I thought that every lamp in all of heaven was pouring forth its ray.

As grackles flock together at first light, obeying a natural impulse to move as one to warm their night-chilled feathers in glad flight;

after which, some go off and do not come back, others return to the points from which they came, and others stay with the flock in its wheeling track;

—just such an impulse seemed to work among those sparkling essences, for they flocked together the instant they had reached a certain rung.

One that came nearest where we stood below then made itself so bright I said to myself: "I well know with what love for me you glow!"

But she from whom I await the how and when of my speech and silence, was still; and despite my yearning I knew it was well to ask no questions then.

She saw in the vision of Him who sees all things what silence held my eager tongue in check, and said to me: "Give your soul's impulse wings!"

"O blessed being hidden in the ray of your own bliss," I said in reverence, "I am not worthy, but for her sake, I pray,

who gives me leave to question, let me know why you, of all this sacred company, have placed yourself so near me, here below;

and tell me why, when every lower sphere sounds the sweet symphony of Paradise in adoration, there is no music here."

"Your sight is mortal. Is not your hearing, too?" he said. "Our song is still for the same reason Beatrice holds back her smile—for love of you.

Only that I might make your spirit gladder by what I say and by the light that robes me, have I come so far down the sacred ladder.

Nor was it greater love that spurred me: here as much—and more—love burns in every soul, as the flaming of these radiances makes clear.

But the high love that makes us prompt to serve the Judge who rules the world, decrees the fate of every soul among us, as you observe."

"O sacred lamp," I said, "I understand that in this court glad love follows the will of Eternal Providence, needing no command; but the further point I cannot grasp is this: why, among all these blisses with whom you dwell, were you alone predestined to this office?"

Before I finished speaking, that lamp of grace like a millstone at full speed, making an axle of its own center, began to spin in place.

And then the Love within the lamp replied: "I feel the ray of God's light focused on me. It strikes down through the ray in which I hide.

Its power, joined to my own, so elevates my soul above itself, that I behold the Primal Source from which it emanates.

My bliss flames only as that ray shines down. As much of glory as I am given to see my flame gives back in glory of its own.

But in all Heaven, the soul granted most light, the Seraph that has God in closest view, could not explain what you have asked to know.

The truth of this is hidden so far down in the abyss of the Eternal Law, it is cut off from all created vision.

Report what I have said when you are back in the mortal world, that no man may presume to move his feet down so profound a track.

On earth the mind is smoke; here, it is fire. How can it do there what it cannot do even when taken into heaven's choir?"

I left that question, his own words having thus prescribed me from it; and, so limited, was content to ask him humbly who he was.

"Not far from your own birthplace, row on row between Italy's two shores, peaks rise so high that on them thunder sounds from far below.

A humpback ridge called Catria rises there. Beneath it stands a holy hermitage once given entirely to meditation and prayer."

So, for the third time now, that soul of grace began to speak, continuing: "I became so rooted in God's service in that place,

I lived on lenten olive-food alone and bore both heat and cold indifferently, rejoicing ever more in contemplation.

Once that cloister sent here, sphere on sphere, harvests of souls. Now all its works are vain as, soon now, righteous punishment shall make clear.

I was Peter Damiano there, and became Peter the Sinner by the Adriatic in the abbey sacred to Our Lady's name.

Little was left me of my mortal course when I was chosen and summoned to wear the hat that seems forever to pass from bad to worse.

Cephas, and the great ark of the Holy Ghost once came among mankind barefoot and gaunt, eating by chance, with charity as their host.

But now your pastors are so bloated and vain they go propped on either side, with a man before and another coming behind to bear the train.

They cover even their mounts with the cloaks they wear so that two beasts move under a single hide. O Heavenly Patience, how long will you forbear!"

As he spoke these words, I saw more ardors yearning downward in circling flight, from rung to rung; and grow more radiant with every turning.

Round him they came to rest, and all burst forth in unison of love: a cry so loud the like of it has not been heard on earth.

Nor could I understand it, for the peal of that ominous thunder made my senses reel.

Canto XXII

THE SEVENTH SPHERE: SATURN
The Contemplative:
St. Benedict
ASCENT TO THE SPHERE OF THE FIXED STARS
THE EIGHTH SPHERE: THE FIXED STARS
Dante Looks Back
at the Universe Below

DANTE'S SENSES STILL REELING, he turns to Beatrice, who reassures him, and prophesies that he will live to see GOD'S VENGEANCE DESCEND ON THE CORRUPTORS OF THE CHURCH. She then calls his attention to the other souls of this sphere. Looking up, Dante sees A HUNDRED RADIANT GLOBES, one of which draws near and identifies itself as the heavenly splendor that had been ST. BENEDICT.

Benedict explains that the Golden Ladder, like the contemplative life, soars to the summit of God's glory, and he laments that so few of his Benedictine monks remain eager to put the world behind them and begin the ascent, for they are lost in the degeneracy of bad days. Yet God has worked greater wonders than would be required to restore the purity of the Church.

So saying, Benedict is gathered into his heavenly choir of radiances, and the whole company ascends to the top of the sky and out of sight.

Beatrice then makes a sign and Dante feels himself making the ASCENT TO THE EIGHTH SPHERE, THE SPHERE OF THE FIXED STARS. But before the souls of that Sphere are revealed to him, Beatrice bids him look back to see how far she has raised him. Dante looks down through the Seven Spheres in their glory, seeing all the heavens at a glance, and the earth as an insignificant speck far below. Then turning from it as from a puny thing, he turns his eyes back to the eyes of Beatrice.

My sense reeled, and as a child in doubt runs always to the one it trusts the most,
I turned to my guide, still shaken by that shout;

and she, like a mother, ever prompt to calm her pale and breathless son with kindly words, the sound of which is his accustomed balm, said: "Do you not know you are in the skies of Heaven itself? that all is holy here? that all things spring from love in Paradise?

Their one cry shakes your senses: you can now see what would have happened to you had they sung, or had I smiled in my new ecstasy.

Had you understood the prayer within their cry you would know now what vengeance they called down, though you shall witness it before you die.

The sword of Heaven is not too soon dyed red, nor yet too late—except as its vengeance seems to those who wait for it in hope or dread.

But look now to the others. Turn as I say and you shall see among this company many great souls of the Eternal Ray."

I did as she commanded. Before my eyes a hundred shining globes entwined their beams, soul adding grace to soul in Paradise.

I stood there between longing and diffidence and fought my longing back, afraid to speak for fear my questioning might give offense.

And the largest and most glowing globe among the wreath of pearls came forward of its own prompting to grant the wish I had not given tongue.

These words came from within it: "Could you see, as I do, with what love our spirits burn to give you joy, your tongue would have been free.

To cause you no delay on the high track to the great goal, I shall address myself to none but the single question you hold back.

The summit of that mountain on whose side Cassino lies, once served an ill-inclined and misted people in their pagan pride.

And I am he who first bore to that slope the holy name of Him who came on earth to bring mankind the truth that is our hope.

Such grace shone down on me that men gave heed through all that countryside and were won over from the seductions of that impious creed.

These other souls were all contemplatives, fired by that warmth of soul that summons up the holy flowers and fruits of blessèd lives.

Here is Romualdus, and Maccarius, too. Here are my brothers who kept within the cloister and, never straying, kept hearts sound and true."

And I to him: "The love you have made clear in speaking as you have, and the good intent I see in all the glories of this sphere, have opened all my confidence: it grows and spreads wide on your warmth, rejoicing in it as does, in the Sun's heat, a full-blown rose.

I therefore beg you, Father: can I rise to such a height of grace that I may see your unveiled image with my mortal eyes?"

And he then: "Brother, this shall be made known in the last sphere. Your wish will be answered there where every other is, including my own.

There, every wish is perfect, ripe, and whole. For there, and there alone, is every part where it has always been; for it has no pole,

not being in space. It is to that very height the golden ladder mounts; and thus you see why it outsoars the last reach of your sight.

The patriarch Jacob saw it, saw it mount to lean on that very sill, that time he dreamed it covered with angels beyond all mortal count.

To climb it now, however, none makes haste to lift his feet from earth. My rule lives on only to fill the parchments it lays waste.

The walls that were retreats in their good hour are dens for beasts now; what were holy cowls are gunny sacks stuffed full of evil flour.

But even compound usury strikes less against God's will and pleasure, than does that fruit whose poison fills the hearts of monks with madness.

For all the goods of the Church, tithes and donations, are for the poor of God, not to make fat the families of monks—and worse relations.

The flesh of mortals is so weak down there that a good beginning is not reason enough to think the seedling tree will live to bear.

Peter began with neither silver nor gold; I, with prayer and fasting. And Brother Francis in humble poverty gathered souls to his fold.

And if you look at the origins of each one, then look again at what it has become, you will see that what was white has changed to dun.

Yet Jordan flowing backward, and the sea parting as God willed, were more wondrous sights than God's help to His stricken church would be."

So did he speak; then faded from my eye into his company, which closed about him, and then, like a whirlwind, spun away on high.

And my sweet lady with a simple sign raised me along that ladder after them, conquering my nature with her power divine.

There never was known down here, where everything rises or falls as natural law determines, a speed to equal the motion of my wing.

Reader, so may I hope once more to stand in that holy Triumph, for which I weep my sins and beat my breast—you could not draw your hand out of a tongue of flame and thrust it back sooner than I sighted and had entered the sign that follows Taurus on Heaven's track.

O glorious constellation! O lamp imbued with great powers, to whose influence I ascribe all my genius, however it may be viewed!

When I drew my first breath of Tuscan air the Sun, the father of all mortal life, was rising in your rays and setting there.

And then when I was granted Heaven's grace to enter the great wheel that gives you motion, I was led upward through your zone of space.

To you devoutly now my prayer is sped: make my soul worthy of the call it hears to the great passage that still lies ahead!

"You are so near the final health of man you will do well to go clear-eyed and keen into that good," my Beatrice began.

"Therefore, before you enter further here look down and see how vast a universe I have put beneath your feet, bright sphere on sphere.

Thus may you come in the fullness of delight to the Triumphant Court that comes in joy through the round ether to your mortal sight."

My eyes went back through the seven spheres below, and I saw this globe, so small, so lost in space, I had to smile at such a sorry show.

Who thinks it the least pebble in the skies I most approve. Only the mind that turns to other things may truly be called wise.

I saw Latona's daughter glowing there without that shadow that had once misled me to think her matter was part dense, part rare.

My eyes looked on your son, Hyperion, nor did they falter. And wheeling close around him, I saw the motion of Maia and Dione.

Next I saw how Jupiter mediates between his father and son, and I understood why the motion of one and the other vacillates.

And all the seven, in a single view, showed me their masses, their velocities, and the distances between each in its purlieu.

And turning there with the eternal Twins, I saw the dusty little threshing ground that makes us ravenous for our mad sins,

saw it from mountain crest to lowest shore. Then I turned my eyes to Beauty's eyes once more.

Canto XXIII

THE EIGHTH SPHERE: THE FIXED STARS
The Triumph of Christ
The Virgin Mary
The Apostles
The Angel Gabriel
St. Peter

BEATRICE STARES expectantly toward that part of the sky where the Sun is at its highest point, and Dante, moved by the joy of her expectation, follows her look. Almost at once there descends from the highest Heaven the radiant substance of the VISION OF CHRIST TRIUMPHANT as it rays forth on the garden of all those souls who have been redeemed through Christ. The splendor too much for his senses, DANTE SWOONS. He is recalled to himself by Beatrice and discovers that, newly strengthened as he has been by the vision of Christ, he is able to look upon her smile of bliss.

Beatrice urges him to look at the Garden of Christ's Triumph, upon the Rose of the VIRGIN MARY and the Lilies of the APOSTLES. Christ, taking mercy on Dante's feeble powers, has withdrawn from direct view and now rays down from above.

Dante fixes his eyes on the brightest splendor (the Virgin Mary) and sees a crown of flame descend to summon her back to the Empyrean. It is the ANGEL GABRIEL. So summoned, Mary ascends to where her son is, and the flames of the souls yearn higher toward her. There, among the souls that remain below, Dante identifies ST. PETER.

As a bird in its sweet canopy of green covers the nest of its beloved young
through all the night when nothing can be seen;

but eager for the loved, lit face of things, and to go hunting for its fledglings'
food in toil so glad that, laboring, she sings; anticipates the day on an open
bough and in a fire of love awaits the sun, her eyes fixed eagerly on the pre-
dawn glow—

just so my lady waited—erect, intense—all her attention toward that part of heaven beneath which the sun's daily pace relents:

and I, observing her blissful expectation, became like one who yearns for more than he has, feeding his hope with sweet anticipation.

But the interval between *when* and *when* was slight—the *when* of my waiting, I say, and the *when* of seeing the sky begin to swell with a new light.

And Beatrice said: "Before you now appears the militia of Christ's triumph, and all the fruit harvested from the turning of the spheres."

I saw her face before me, so imbued with holy fire, her eyes so bright with bliss that I pass on, leaving them unconstrued.

As Trivia in the full moon's sweet serene smiles on high among the eternal nymphs whose light paints every part of Heaven's scene;

I saw, above a thousand thousand lights, one Sun that lit them all, as our own Sun lights all the bodies we see in Heaven's heights; and through that living light I saw revealed the Radiant Substance, blazing forth so bright my vision dazzled and my senses reeled.

Oh my Beatrice, sweet and loving guide! "What blinds you," she said to me, "is the very power nothing withstands, and from which none may hide.

This is the intellect and the sceptered might that opened the golden road from Earth to Heaven, for which mankind had yearned in its long night."

Fire sometimes spreads so wide that it shoots forth from a cloud that can no longer hold it in, and against its nature, hurtles down to earth.

That feast of bliss had swollen my mind so that it broke its bounds and leapt out of itself. And what it then became, it does not know.

"Open your eyes and turn them full on me! You have seen things whose power has made you able to bear the bright smile of my ecstasy!"

As one whose senses have been stricken blind by a forgotten vision comes to himself and racks his wits to call it back to mind—

such was I at that summons, my spirit moved to a thankfulness that shall live on forever within the book where what is past is proved.

If there should sound now all the tongues of song Polyhymnia with her eight sisters nourished, giving their sweetest milk to make them strong,

they could not help me, singing thus, to show a thousandth part of my lady's sacred smile, nor with what glory it made her features glow.

Just so, that Heaven may be figured forth, my consecrated poem must make a leap, as a traveler leaps a crevice there on earth.

My theme is massive, mortal shoulders frail for such a weight. What thoughtful man will blame me for trembling under it for fear I fail?

The seas my ardent prow is plowing here are no place for small craft, nor for a helmsman who will draw back from toil or cringe in fear.

"Why are you so enamored of my face you do not turn your eyes to see the garden that flowers there in the radiance of Christ's grace?

The Rose in which the Word became incarnate is there. There are the lilies by whose odor men found the road that evermore runs straight."

Thus Beatrice. And I, prompt to her guidance in fullest eagerness, raised my feeble lids once more to battle with that radiance.

At times when the sun, through broken clouds, has rayed one perfect beam, I have seen a field of flowers blazing in glory, my own eyes still in shade:

just so, I saw a host of hosts made bright by rays of splendor striking from above, but could not see the source of that pure light.

O Majesty that seals them in such glory! you raised yourself on high, withdrawing there in order that my feeble eyes might see!

The name of that Sweet Flower to which I pray morning and night, seized all my soul and moved it to fix my eyes upon the brightest ray;

and when both my eyes had been allowed to know the luster and magnitude of that chosen star that triumphs there as it triumphed here below,

from Heaven's height a torch of glory came, shaped like a ring or wreath, and spinning round her, it wound and crowned her in its living flame.

The sweetest strain that ever swelled aloud to draw the soul into itself down here, would be as thunder from a shattered cloud,

compared to the melody that then aspired from the bright lyre that crowned the purest gem by which the brightest heaven is ensapphired.

"I am the Angelic Love that wheels around the lofty ecstasy breathed from the womb in which the hostel of Our Wish was found;

so shall I wheel, Lady of Heaven, till you follow your great Son to the highest sphere and, by your presence, make it holier still."

Thus the encircling melody of that flame revealed itself; and all the other lamps within that garden rang out Mary's name.

The royal mantle whose folds are spread abroad round all the spheres, and that most burns and quickens being nearest to the breath and ways of God,

turned its inner shore at such a height above the point at which I then was standing that I could not yet bring it into sight.

I could not, therefore, with my mortal eyes follow the flight of that crowned flame that soared to join her son in the highest Paradise.

And as a newly suckled infant yearns after its mother with its upraised arms, expressing so the love with which it burns;

each of the splendors of that company extended its flame on high in such a way as made its love of Mary plain to me.

Then they remained there, still within my sight, singing *"Regina coeli"* in tones so sweet the memory still fills me with delight.

Oh what treasures cram and overflow those richest coffers of the eternal grace who sowed such good seed in the world below!

Here is true life and relish of the treasure their tears laid up in the Babylonian exile, in which Christ left man gold beyond all measure.

Here sits in triumph under the lofty Son of God and the Virgin Mary in His triumph, and in the company of everyone

crowned from the New or the Old Consistory, the soul that holds the great keys to such glory.

Canto XXIV

THE EIGHTH SPHERE: THE FIXED STARS
The Triumph of Christ
St. Peter
The Examination of Faith

CHRIST AND MARY having ascended to the Empyrean, St. Peter remains as the chief soul of the Garden of Christ's Triumph. Beatrice addresses the souls in Dante's behalf, and they, in their joy, form into a dazzling VERTICAL WHEEL OF SPINNING RADIANCES.

Beatrice then begs St. Peter to conduct an EXAMINATION OF DANTE'S FAITH. St. Peter thereupon questions Dante on the NATURE OF FAITH, THE POSSESSION OF FAITH, THE SOURCES OF FAITH, THE PROOF OF THE TRUTH OF FAITH, MAN'S MEANS OF KNOWING THAT THE MIRACLES OF FAITH ACTUALLY TOOK PLACE, and finally on THE CONTENT OF CHRISTIAN FAITH.

Dante answers eagerly, as would a willing candidate being examined by his learned master. The examination concluded, St. Peter shows his pleasure by dancing three times around Dante.

"O spirits of that chosen company that feeds on the Lamb of God, the flesh of which satisfies hunger to all eternity—

if by God's grace this man is given a foretaste of what falls from your table, before death takes him from time and lays his body waste,

consider the boundless thirst with which he burns; bedew him from your plenty. You drink forever the waters of that spring for which he yearns!"

So spoke Beatrice, and those blissful souls, flaming as bright as comets, formed themselves into a sphere revolving on fixed poles.

As the wheels within a clockwork synchronize so that the innermost, when looked at closely seems to be standing, while the outermost flies;

just so those rings of dancers whirled to show and let me understand their state of bliss, all joining in the round, some fast, some slow.

From one I saw, the loveliest of them all, there grew a radiance of such blessedness that it outshone the hosts of the celestial.

Three times it danced round Beatrice to a strain so heavenly that I have not the power so much as to imagine it again.

Therefore my pen leaps and I do not write; not words nor fantasy can paint the truth: the folds of heaven's draperies are too bright.

"O sacred sister whose prayer is so devout, the ardor of your love enters my bliss within that lovely sphere and calls me out."

—When it had come to rest, that Fire of Love directed its breath to my lady and spoke these words exactly as I have set them down above.

And she: "Eternal Light of the great priest to whom Our Lord brought down and gave the keys to the sublimities of this joyous feast;

at your own pleasure, whatever it may be, test this man on the greater and lesser points of the faith in which you once walked on the sea.

If love and hope and faith are truly his you will discover it, for your eyes are turned where you can see the image of all that is.

But since this realm is peopled from the seed of the true faith, he will the better praise it, could he discuss with you the perfect creed."

As a bachelor arms himself for disquisition in silence till the master sets the terms for defending, not deciding, the proposition;

so did I arm myself for the expression of every proof, preparing while she spoke for such an examiner, and such profession.

"Speak, good Christian, manifest your worth: what is faith?"—At which I raised my eyes to the light from which these words had been breathed forth:

then turned to look at Beatrice, and she urged me with her eyes to let the waters of the spring that welled within my soul pour free.

"May the Grace that grants the grace of this confession to the captain of the first rank," I began, "grant that my thoughts may find worthy expression!"

Continuing: "Father, as it was set down by the pen of your dear brother, who, with you, set Rome on the road that leads to glory's crown,

faith is the *substance* of what we hope to see and the *argument* for what we have not seen. This is its *quiddity*, as it seems to me."

Next I heard: "This is, in fact, the essence. But do you understand why he classifies it first with *substances*, then with argument?"

And I in answer: "The profundities that here reveal themselves so liberally are so concealed, down there, from mortal eyes

they exist in belief alone. On belief the structure of high hope rises. It is *substant*, therefore, or 'standing under' by its very nature.

Starting with this belief, it is evident, we must reason without further visible proofs. And so it partakes, by nature, of *argument*."

I heard: "If all that mortal man may know through mortal teaching were as firmly grasped, sophists would find no listeners there below."

Such was the breath from that Love's Ecstasy, continuing then: "You have assayed this coinage, its weight and metal content, accurately;

now tell me if you have it in your possession." And I then: "Yes. I have. So bright, so round, usage has worn down none of its impression."

After these words the breath once more resounded from the light that shone before me: "This dear gem on which all good and power of good are founded—

whence comes it to you?" And I, "The shower of gold of the Holy Ghost, which pours down endlessly over the sacred Scrolls, both New and Old,

reasons it to such logical certainty that, by comparison, all other reasoning can only seem confused and dull to me."

And I heard: "These propositions, the Old and New that move you to this conclusion, for what reason do you accept them as divinely true?"

And I: "The proof that shows the truth to me is in the works that followed. Never has nature heated and forged such iron in its smithy."

And I was answered: "Tell me how you know there were such works. What seeks to prove itself—it only and nothing more—swears it was so."

"If the whole world became Christian without the aid of the miraculous, that is a miracle a hundred times greater than the rest," I said,

"for poor and hungry, by faith alone upborne, you entered the field and sowed there the good plant that was a vine once, and is now a thorn."

This said, that high and holy choir let ring *"Te Deum laudamus!"* sounding through the spheres such melody as the souls of heaven sing.

And that Baron, who, examining my belief from branch to branch, had drawn me out already to where we were approaching the last leaf,

began again: "The grace whose loving good had pledged itself to your mind, has moved your mouth, up to this point, to open as it should.

I approve what has emerged thus far, but now it is time you should explain *what* you believe, and from what source it comes to you, and how."

"O holy Father, spirit that now can see what faith once held so firmly that you were prompter than younger feet to the tomb in Galilee," my answer ran, "you wish me to expound the *form* of my own promptness to believe, and you ask what reasons for it I have found.

And I reply: I believe in one God, loved, desired by all creation, sole, eternal, who moves the turning Heavens, Himself unmoved.

And for this faith I have the evidences not only of physics and of metaphysics, but of the truth that rains down on my senses

through Moses, the prophets, the psalms, through the Evangel, and through you and what you wrote when the Ardent Spirit made you the foster father of God's People.

And I believe in three Persons; this Trinity, an essence Triune and Single, in whose being *is* and *are* conjoin to eternity.

That this profound and sacred nature is real the teachings of the evangels, in many places, have stamped on the wax of my mind like a living seal.

This is the beginning, the spark shot free that gnaws and widens into living flame, and, like a star in Heaven, shines in me."

As a master who is pleased by what he hears embraces his servant as soon as he has spoken, rejoicing in the happy news he bears;

so, that glorious apostolic blaze at whose command I had spoken heard me out, and blessing me in a glad chant of praise,

danced three times round me there in the eighth great rim, such pleasure had my speaking given him.

Canto XXV

*DANTE, blessed by St. John himself as a reward for his labors and his hope,
declares that if his poem may serve to soften his sentence of exile from Florence,
he will return to his baptismal font at San Giovanni and there place on his own
head the poet's laurel wreath. Such is one of the great hopes of his poem, and on
that note ST. JAMES, the Apostle of Hope, shows himself.*

*Beatrice begs James to conduct the EXAMINATION OF HOPE and she
herself, in answer to the first question, testifies to Dante's POSSESSION OF
HOPE. Dante then replies on THE NATURE OF HOPE, on the CONTENT OF
HIS HOPE, and on the SOURCES OF HOPE.*

*The examination triumphantly concluded, a cry in praise of the grace of hope
rings through Paradise, and thereupon ST. JOHN THE APOSTLE appears.
Dante stares into John's radiance hoping to see the lineaments of his mortal
body. The voice of John, the Apostle of Love* (caritas) *calls to him that what he
seeks is not there, and when Dante looks away he discovers he has been
BLINDED BY THE RADIANCE OF LOVE.*

If ever it comes to pass that the sacred song, to which both heaven and earth so
set their hand that I grew lean with laboring years long,

wins over the cruelty that exiles me from the sweet sheepfold where I slept, a
lamb, and to the raiding wolves an enemy;

with a changed voice and with my fleece full grown I shall return to my
baptismal font, a poet, and there assume the laurel crown;

for there I entered the faith that lets us grow into God's recognition; and for that
faith Peter, as I have said, circled my brow.

Thereafter another radiance came forth from the same sphere out of whose joy had come the first flower of Christ's vicarage on earth.

And my lady, filled with ecstasy and aglow, cried to me: "Look! Look there! It is the baron for whom men throng to Galicia there below!"

At times, on earth, I have seen a mating dove alight by another, and each turn to each, circling and murmuring to express their love;

exactly so, within the eighth great sphere, one glorious great lord greeted the other, praising the diet that regales them there.

Those glories, having greeted and been greeted, turned and stood before me, still and silent, so bright I turned my eyes away defeated.

And Beatrice said, smiling her blessedness: "Illustrious being in whose chronicle is written our celestial court's largesse,

let hope, I pray, be sounded at this height. How often you personified that grace when Jesus gave His chosen three more light!"

"Lift up your head, look up and do not fear, for all that rises from the mortal world must ripen in our rays from sphere to sphere."

So spoke the second flame to comfort me; and I raised my eyes to the mountains that before had borne them down by their weight of majesty.

"Since of His grace Our Lord and Emperor calls and bids you come while still in mortal flesh among His counts in His most secret halls;

that you, the truth of this great court made clear, may make the stronger, in yourself and others, the hope that makes men love the good down there,

say what it is, what power helped you to climb, and how you bear its flowering in your mind." —So spoke the second flame a second time.

And that devout sweet spirit that had led the feathers of my wings in that high flight anticipated my reply, and said:

"Church Militant, as is written in the Sun whose ray lights all our hosts, does not possess a single child richer in hope—not one.

It was for that he was allowed to come from Egypt to behold Jerusalem before his warring years had reached their sum.

The other two points—raised not that you may know but that he may report how great a pleasure hope is to you, when he returns below—

I leave to him. They will not be difficult. Nor will the truth seem boastful. Let him answer and may God's grace appear in the result."

As a pupil who is eager to reply to his professor, knowing his subject well, and quick to show his excellence—such was I.

"Hope," I said, "is the certain expectation of future glory. It is the blessed fruit of grace divine and the good a man has done.

From many stars this light descends to me, but it was first distilled into my heart by the ultimate singer of Ultimate Majesty.

'Let them hope in Thee,' sang the God-praising poet, 'whoso doth know Thy name!' And who can feel a faith as firm as mine is and not know it?

And your epistle sent down once again a fresh dew on his dew, till I was full and overflowed to others your sweet rain."

While I was speaking thus a luminescence trembled within the bosom of that flame, sudden and bright as lightning's incandescence.

"Love that still burns in me," I heard it breathe, "for that grace that followed even to the palm, and till I left the field for happy death,

moves me to speak further: you know the true and lasting joy she brings:

gladden me, therefore, by telling me what Hope holds forth to you."

And I: "From scripture, new and old, descends the symbol, and the symbol points me to it. All those whom God has chosen as His friends—

as Isaiah testifies—they shall be dressed in double raiment in their native land; and that land is this sweet life with the blest.

And your brother, where he writes so ardently of the white robes, sets forth this revelation in great detail for all of us to see."

As soon as I had spoken there rang clear from overhead, "Let them hope in Thee, O Lord!" and the response rang back from all that sphere.

At once within that choir there blazed a ray so bright that if the Crab had such a star one month of winter would be a single day.

And as a joyous maid will rise and go to join the dance, in honor of the bride and not for any reasons of vain show,

so did that radiant splendor, there above, go to the two who danced a joyous reel in fit expression of their burning love.

It joined them in the words and melody; and like a bride, immovable and silent, my lady kept her eyes fixed on their glory.

"This is he who lies upon the breast of Our Pelican; and this is He elected from off the cross to make the great behest."

So spoke my lady, nor, her pose unbroken, did she once let her rapt attention stray, either before or after she had spoken.

As one who stares, squinting against the light, to see the Sun enter a partial eclipse, and in the act of looking loses his sight—

so did I stare at the last flame from that sphere until a voice said, "Why do you blind yourself trying to see what has no true place here?

My body is earth in earth where it shall be one with the rest until our numbers grow to fill the quota of eternity.

Only the Two Lamps that are most aglow rose to their blessed cloister doubly clad. Explain this to your world when you go below."

And when these words were said the flaming wreath broke off the dancing and the sweet accord in which it had combined its three-part breath,

as oars that have been striking through the sea pause all together when a whistle sounds to signal rest or some emergency.

Ah, what a surge of feeling swept my mind when I turned away an instant from such splendor to look at Beatrice, only to find

I could not see her with my dazzled eyes, though I stood near her and in Paradise!

Canto XXVI

JOHN ASSURES DANTE that Beatrice will restore his sight. Dante expresses his willingness to await her will since he knows her to be Love. John, thereupon, begins the EXAMINATION OF LOVE, asking Dante to explain how he came into the POSSESSION OF LOVE, and what drove him to seek it. He then asks Dante to describe the INTENSITY OF LOVE and to discuss the SOURCES OF LOVE.

Dante concludes with a praise of God as the source of Love. At his words all Heaven responds with a paean, and immediately DANTE'S VISION IS RESTORED.

There appears before him a fourth great splendor which Beatrice identifies as the soul of ADAM. Dante begs Adam to speak, and learns from him the DATE OF ADAM'S CREATION, HOW LONG ADAM REMAINED IN EDEN, THE CAUSE OF GOD'S WRATH, and WHAT LANGUAGE ADAM SPOKE IN HIS TIME ON EARTH.

While I stood thus confounded, my light shed, out of the dazzling flame that had consumed it I heard a breath that called to me, and said:

"Until your eyes once more regain their sense of the light you lost in me, it will be well for discourse to provide a recompense.

Speak, therefore, starting with the thing that most summons your soul to it, and be assured your sight is only dazzled and not lost;

for she who guides you through this holy land has, in a single turning of her eyes, the power that lay in Ananias' hand."

"As she wills, late or soon, let remedy come to my eyes," I said, "the gates through which she brought the fire that ever burns in me.

The Good that is this cloister's happiness is the Alpha and Omega of the scripture love reads to me with light and heavy stress."

The same voice that had soothed my fear away when I found suddenly that I could not see called me back to the question. I heard it say:

"Surely a finer sieve must sift this through. You must explain what made you draw your bow at this exalted target—what and who."

And I: "By the arguments of philosophy and by authority that descends from here such Love has clearly stamped its seal upon me.

For the Good, to the extent imperfect sense grasps its goodness, kindles love; the brighter the more we understand its excellence.

To the Essence then in which lies such perfection that every good thing not immediate to It is nothing more than Its own ray's reflection—

to It, above all else, the mind must move once it has seen the truth that is the proof and argument that so compels man's love.

That truth he first made evident to me whose proofs set forth the First Cause and First Love of every sempiternal entity.

It was proved by the True Maker's voice sent forth to Moses when It said, meaning Itself, 'I shall cause you to see a vision of all worth.'

And proved by you in the high proclamation that cries to earth the secrets of this heaven more clearly than any other revelation."

And I heard: "As human reason and Holy Writ in harmony have urged you, keep for God the first, most sovereign passion of your spirit.

But tell me if you feel yet other ties bind you to Him. Say with how many teeth this love consumes you." So in Paradise

Christ's Eagle spoke his sacred purpose whole, concealing nothing; rather, urging me to make a full profession of my soul.

I therefore: "All those teeth with power enough to turn the heart of any man to God have joined in my heart, turning it to Love.

The existence of the world, and my own, too; the death He took on Himself that I might live; and what all believers hope for as I do—

these and the living knowledge mentioned before have saved me from the ocean of false love and placed me by the true, safe on the shore.

The leaves that green the Eternal Garden's grove I love to the degree that each receives the dew and ray of His all-flowering love."

The instant I fell still, my love professed, all Heaven rang with "Holy! Holy! Holy!" my lady joining with the other blest.

As bright light shatters sleep, the man being bid to waken by the visual spirit running to meet the radiance piercing lid by lid,

and the man so roused does not know what he sees, his wits confounded by the sudden waking, till he once more regains his faculties;

so from my eyes, my lady's eyes, whose ray was visible from a thousand miles and more, drove every last impediment away;

in consequence of which I found my sight was clearer than before, and half astonished, I questioned her about a fourth great light

near us, and she: "In that ray's Paradise the first soul from the hand of the First Power turns ever to its maker its glad eyes."

As a bough that bends its crown to the wind's course, and then, after the blow, rises again uplifted by its own internal force;

so did I as she spoke, all tremulous; then calmed again, assured by a desire to speak that burned in me, beginning thus:

"O first and only fruit earth ever saw spring forth full ripe; O primal sire, to whom all brides are equally daughters and daughters-in-law;

speak, I beg, devoutly as I may. You know my wish. To hear you speak the sooner I leave unsaid what there is no need to say."

An animal, were it covered with a shawl and moved beneath it, would reveal its motion by the way in which the cloth would rise and fall;

in the same way, that first soul let me see through the motion of its covering, with what joy it moved in Heaven to bring joy to me.

Then breathed forth: "Without any need to hear what you would say, I know your wish more surely than you know what you take to be most clear.

I see it in the True Mirror, Itself the perfect reflector of all things in Its creation, which nothing in creation can reflect.

You wish to know how many years it is since God created me in the high garden where she prepared you for these stairs to bliss;

and how long my eyes enjoyed the good they prized; and the true reason for the great rejection; and the tongue I spoke, which I myself devised.

Know, my son, that eating from the tree was not itself the cause of such long exile, but only the violation of God's decree.

Longing to join this company, my shade counted four thousand three hundred and two suns where your lady summoned Virgil to your aid.

And circling all its signs, I saw it go nine hundred and thirty times around its track during the time I was a man below.

The tongue I spoke had vanished utterly long before Nimrod's people turned their hands to the work beyond their capability,

for nothing of the mind is beyond change: man's inclination answers to the stars and ranges as the starry courses range.

That man should speak is nature's own behest; but that you speak in this way or in that nature lets you decide as you think best.

Till I went down to the agony of Hell the Supreme Good whose rays send down the joy that wraps me here was known on earth as *EL*;

and then was known as *JAH*; and it must be so, for the usage of mankind is like a leaf that falls from the branch to let another grow.

On the peak that rises highest, my total stay, in innocence and later in disgrace, was from the first bright hour of my first day,

to the hour after the sixth, at which the sun changed quadrant, being then at meridian."

Canto XXVII

THE EIGHTH SPHERE: THE FIXED STARS
Denunciation of Papal Corruption
ASCENT TO THE PRIMUM MOBILE

ST. PETER GROWS RED with righteous indignation and utters a DENUNCIATION OF PAPAL CORRUPTION. All Heaven darkens at the thought of such evil. Peter's charge, of course, is that the papacy has become acquisitive, political, and therefore bloody. Having so catalogued the crimes of the bad Popes, Peter specifically charges Dante to repeat among mankind the wrath that was spoken in Heaven.

The triumphant court soars away and Dante is left with Beatrice who tells him to look down. Dante finds he is standing above a point midway between Jerusalem and Spain, and having seen earth (and all its vaunted pomps) as an insignificant mote in space, Dante once more turns his thoughts upward as Beatrice leads him in the ASCENT TO THE PRIMUM MOBILE, discoursing en route on the NATURE OF TIME (which has its source in the Primum Mobile). The TIME OF EARTH'S CORRUPTION, Beatrice tells Dante, is drawing to a close.

"Glory to the Father, the Son, and the Holy Ghost"—a strain so sweet that I grew drunk with it rang from the full choir of the heavenly host.

I seemed to see the universe alight with a single smile; and thus my drunkenness came on me through my hearing and my sight.

O joy! O blessedness no tongue can speak! O life conjoint of perfect love and peace! O sure wealth that has nothing more to seek!

The four great torches were still burning there, and the one that had descended to me first began to outshine all else in that sphere.

As Jupiter might appear if it and Mars were birds and could exchange their glowing plumes—such it became among the other stars.

The Providence that assigns to Heaven's band the offices and services of each, had imposed silence there on every hand

when I heard: "You need not wonder that I change hue, for as I utter what I have to say you shall see all these beings change theirs, too.

The usurper of the throne given to me, to me, to me, there on the earth that now before the Son of God stands vacant, he

has made a sewer of my sepulcher, a flow of blood and stink at which the treacherous one who fell from here may chuckle there below."

With the same color I have seen clouds turn when opposite the rising or setting sun, I saw the sweet face of all heaven burn.

And as a modest lady whose pure bearing is self-secure, may blush at another's failings, though they be only mentioned in her hearing;

so Beatrice changed complexion at a breath, and such eclipse came over heaven then as when Supreme Might suffered mankind's death.

Then he continued speaking as before, his voice so changed, so charged with indignation that his appearance could not darken more:

"The bride of Christ was not suckled of old on blood of mine, of Linus, and of Cletus to be reared as an instrument for grabbing gold.

It was to win this life of blessedness Sixtus, and Pius, and Calixtus, and Urban let flow the blood and tears of their distress.

We never meant that men of Christian life should sit part on the right, part on the left of our successors, steeled for bloody strife.

Nor that the keys consigned into my hand should fly as emblems from a flag unfurled against the baptized in a Christian land.

Nor that my head should, in a later age, seal privilege sold to liars. The very thought has often made me burn with holy rage!

From here in every pasture, fold, and hill we see wolves dressed as shepherds. O hand of God, mankind's defender, why do you yet lie still?

Gascons and Cahorsines are crouched to drink our very blood. Oh excellent beginning, to what foulest conclusion will you sink?

Yet the high Providence that stood with Rome and Scipio for the glory of the world will once again, and soon, be seen to come.

You, son, who must yet bear around earth's track your mortal weight, open your mouth down there: do not hold back what I have not held back!"

Just as the frozen vaporings sift down out of our earthly atmosphere when the horn of heaven's Goat is burnished by the Sun;

just so, up there, I saw the ether glow with a rising snow of the triumphant vapors who had remained a while with us below.

My eyes followed their traces toward the height, followed until the airy medium closed its vast distance on my upward sight;

at which my lady, seeing me absolved from service to the height, said: "Now look down and see how far the heavens have revolved."

I looked down once again. Since the last time, I had been borne, I saw, a length of arc equal to half the span of the first clime;

so that I saw past Cadiz the mad route Ulysses took; and almost to the shore from which Europa rode the godly brute.

And yet more of this little threshing floor would have been visible but, below my foot, the sun was ahead of me by a sign and more.

My mind, which ever found its Paradise in thinking of my lady, now more than ever burned with desire to look into her eyes.

If nature or art ever contrived a lure to catch the eye and thus possess the mind, whether in living flesh or portraiture,

all charms united could not move a pace toward the divine delight with which I glowed when I looked once more on her smiling face.

In one look then I felt my spirit given a power that plucked it out of Leda's nest and sent it soaring to the swiftest heaven.

From its upper and lower limits to its center it is so uniform, I cannot say what point my lady chose for me to enter.

But she, knowing what yearning burned in me, began thus—with so rapturous a smile God seemed to shine forth from her ecstasy:

"The order of the universe, whose nature holds firm the center and spins all else around it, takes from this heaven its first point of departure.

This heaven does not exist in any place but in God's mind, where burns the love that turns it and the power that rains to it from all of space.

Light and Love contain it in one band as it does all the rest; and such containment only the Cunctitenant can understand.

Its own motion unfactored, all things derive their motions from this heaven as precisely as ten is factored into two and five.

So may you understand how time's taproot is hidden in this sphere's urn, while in the others we see its spreading foliage and its fruit.

O Greed that has drawn down all Adam's blood so deep into its dark that none has strength to raise his eyes above its evil flood!

The will of man comes well to its first flower, but then the rain that sets in endlessly blights the good fruit and leaves it green and sour.

Faith and innocence are found nowhere except in little children; and both have fled before their cheeks have sprouted a first hair.

Still young enough to lisp, one fasts and prays; then, his tongue freed, devours all sorts of food even in Lent, even on fasting days.

Another will love his mother and behave while yet a lisper, who, with his freed speech will be impatient to see her in her grave.

So the fair daughter of Him who leaves us night and brings us morning, changes her complexion, and her white skin turns black in Heaven's sight.

Consider, if you marvel at what I say, how there is none to govern on the earth, whereby the human family goes astray.

But before January falls in spring because of that odd day in each hundred years that all neglect down there, these spheres shall ring

so loud with portents of a season's turn that the long awaited storm will sweep the fleet, blowing the bows around to dead astern

and set the true course straight. Then all shall see first blossom turn to good fruit on the tree."

Canto XXVIII

THE NINTH SPHERE: THE PRIMUM MOBILE
The Angel Hierarchy

DANTE TURNS from Beatrice and beholds a vision of GOD AS A NON-DIMENSIONAL POINT OF LIGHT ringed by NINE GLOWING SPHERES representing the ANGEL HIERARCHY.
   Dante is puzzled because the vision seems to reverse the order of the Universe, the highest rank of the angels being at the center and represented by the smallest sphere. Beatrice explains the mystery to Dante's satisfaction, if not to the reader's, and goes on to catalogue the ORDERS OF THE ANGELS.

When she whose powers imparadise my mind had so denounced and laid bare the whole truth of the present state of miserable mankind;

just as a man before a glass can see a torch that burns behind him, and know it is there before he has seen or thought of it directly;

and turns to see if what the glass has shown is really there; and finds, as closely matched as words to music, the fact to its reflection;

just so, as I recall, did I first stare into the heaven of those precious eyes in which, to trap me, Love had set his snare;

then turned, and turning felt my senses reel as my own were struck by what shines in that heaven when we look closely at its turning wheel.

I saw a Point that radiated light of such intensity that the eye it strikes must close or ever after lose its sight.

The star that seems the smallest, seen from here, would seem a moon, were it placed next to this, as often we see star by star appear.

And at about the distance that a halo surrounds a heavenly radiance that paints it on the densest mist that will yet let it show;

so close around the Point, a ring of fire spun faster than the fastest of the spheres circles creation in its endless gyre.

Another surrounded this, and was surrounded by a third, the third by a fourth, the fourth by a fifth, and by a sixth the fifth, in turn, was bounded.

The seventh followed, already spread so wide that were Juno's messenger to be made complete she could not stretch her arc from side to side.

And so the eighth and the ninth, and each ring spun with an ever slower motion as its number placed it the further out from the first one,

which gave forth the most brilliant incandescence because, I think, being nearest the Scintilla, it drew the fullest share of the true essence.

I was on tenterhooks, as my lady saw. To ease my mind she said: "From that one Point are hung the heavens and all nature's law.

Look at the closest ring: I would have you know it spins so fast by virtue of Love's fire, the ray of which pierces it through and through."

And I to her: "Were the ordering we find in the universe like that of these bright wheels, what I have seen would satisfy my mind.

But in the sensible universe one can see the motions of the spheres become more godlike the nearer they are to the periphery.

If there is food for my soul's appetite in this most glorious and angelic temple whose only boundaries are love and light,

you must explain why it has been so planned that the form and the exemplum are at odds; for by myself I cannot understand."

"It is small wonder such a knot defies your fingers, for since none has ever tried it, the coils have set together like a vise."

So spoke my lady, going on to say: "If you would understand, grasp what I tell you, and around it give your mind's best powers full play.

The physical spheres are graduated in size according to the power that infuses each and fixes it to its station in the skies.

The greater good intends a greater grace. A greater body can hold more of good if all its parts are perfect, as in this case.

This sphere, then, that spins with it as it goes all of the universe, must correspond to the angel sphere that most loves and most knows.

If you will measure not by what appears but by the power inherent in these beings that manifest themselves to you as spheres,

you will observe a marvelous correspondence of greater power to larger, and lesser to smaller, between each Heaven and its Intelligence."

As the airy hemisphere serenes and glows, cloudless and blue into its furthest reach, when from his gentler cheek Boreas blows,

purging and dissolving with that breeze the turbulent vapors, so that heaven smiles with the beauty of its every diocese;

so was it in my mind, once I was given my lady's clear reply; and I saw the truth shining before me like a star in heaven.

And at her last word every angel sphere began to sparkle as iron, when it is melted in a crucible, is seen to do down here.

And every spark spun with its spinning ring: and they were numberless as the sum of grain on the last square of the chessboard of the king.

From choir to choir their hymn of praise rang free to the Fixed Point that holds them in fixed place, as ever was, as evermore shall be.

And she who felt uncertainty bedim my dazzled mind explained: "The first two circles have shown you the Seraphim and Cherubim.

Being led, they chase the reins in their eagerness to resemble the Point the more, and they can the more the more they look upon Its blessedness.

The beings in the next bright wheel you see are titled Thrones of the Eternal Aspect; and they complete the first great trinity.

And know that all these raptures are fulfilled to the degree that each can penetrate the Truth in which all questioning is stilled.

Hence one may see that the most blest condition is based on the act of seeing, not of love, love being the act that follows recognition.

They see as they are worthy. They are made to their degrees by grace and their own good will. And so their ranks proceed from grade to grade.

The second trinity that blossoms here in this eternal springtime of delight whose leaves nocturnal Aries does not sear,

warble 'Hosannah!' everlastingly, and their three melodies sound the three degrees of blessedness that form this trinity.

These are the divinities therein found: Dominations first, then Virtues, then, in order, the ranks of Powers within the widest round.

In the next two dances of this exhaltation whirl Principalities first, then the Archangels. The last contains the Angelic jubilation.

All fix their eyes on high and as their sight ascends their power descends to all below. So are all drawn, as all draw, to God's height.

Dionysius gave himself to contemplation of these same orders with such holy zeal that he named and ranked them just as I have done.

Gregory, later, differed with his conclusions. But hardly had he wakened in this heaven than he was moved to laugh at his own delusions.

And if a truth so hidden was made clear by one still in the weight of mortal dust, you need not wonder: one who saw it here

returned and told him this: this and much more of the bright truth these circles hold in store."

Canto XXIX

THE NINTH SPHERE: PRIMUM MOBILE
The Angel Hierarchy

BEATRICE, gazing on God, sees Dante's unspoken questions and explains to him GOD'S INTENT IN WILLING THE CREATION, THE ETERNITY OF GOD, and the SIMULTANEITY OF CREATION.

She proceeds then to explain the TIME FROM THE CREATION TO THE REVOLT OF THE ANGELS, HOW THE LOVING ANGELS BEGAN THEIR BLISSFUL ART, and that GRACE IS RECEIVED ACCORDING TO THE ARDOR OF LOVE.

She then DENOUNCES FOOLISH TEACHINGS, and concludes by pointing out THE INFINITY AND THE DISTINCTION OF THE ANGELS.

When Latona's twins, one setting in the sign of Aries and the other rising in Libra, are belted by the same horizon's line;

as long then as the zenith's fulcrum bears their perfect balance, till one and other leave their common belt and change their hemispheres,

so long did Beatrice, smiling her delight, stay silent, her eyes fixed on the Fixed Point whose power had overcome me at first sight.

Then she began: "I do not ask, I say what you most wish to hear, for I have seen it where time and space are focused in one ray.

Not to increase Its good—no mil nor dram can add to true perfection, but that reflections of his reflection might declare 'I am'—

in His eternity, beyond time, above all other comprehension, as it pleased Him, new loves were born of the Eternal Love.

Nor did He lie asleep before the Word sounded above these waters; 'before' and 'after' did not exist until His voice was heard.

Pure essence, and pure matter, and the two joined into one were shot forth without flaw, like three bright arrows from a three-string bow.

And as in glass, in amber, or in crystal a ray shines so that nothing intervenes between its coming and being, which is total;

so the threefold effect rayed from its Sire into created being, without beginning and without interval, instantly entire.

Order was the co-created fact of every essence; and at the peak of all, these angel loves created as pure act.

Pure potential held the lowest ground; between, potential-and-act were tied together so tight they nevermore shall be unbound.

Hieronymus wrote to you of the long span of centuries in which such beings existed before the other world was made for man;

but the Scribes of the Holy Ghost clearly declare the true account in many passages, as you will see if you will read with care.

It can, in part, be grasped by intellection, which cannot grant such powers could long exist apart from the functioning of their perfection.

This much will answer where, and when, and how the angels were created; and so are quenched the first three flames of your desire to know.

Nor could you count to ten and ten before some of those angels fell from Heaven to roil the bedrock of the elemental core.

The rest remained here and around their Cause began the art you see, moved by such bliss that their glad revolutions never pause.

It was accursèd pride for which they fell, the pride of that dark principal you saw crushed by the world's whole weight in deepest Hell.

These you see here were humble, undemanding, and prompt in their acknowledgment of the Good that made them capable of such understanding;

whereby their vision was exalted higher by illuminating grace and their own merit, in which their wills are changeless and entire.

Now hear this and, beyond all doubt, believe it: the good of grace is in exact proportion to the ardor of love that opens to receive it.

And now, if you have heeded what I said, you should be able to observe this college and gather much more without further aid.

But since your earthly schoolmen argue still that the angelic nature is composed of understanding, memory, and will,

I will say this much more to help you see the truth that is confounded there below by the equivocations of sophistry:

these beings, since their first bliss in the sight of God's face, in which all things are revealed, have never turned their eyes from their delight.

No angel's eye, it follows, can be caught by a new object; hence, they have no need of memory, as does divided thought.

So men, awake but dreaming, dare to claim, believing it or not, they speak the truth—though the hypocrite's is the greater sin and shame.

You mortals do not walk a single way in your philosophies, but let the thought of being acclaimed as wise lead you astray.

Yet Heaven bears even this with less offense than it must feel when it sees Holy Writ neglected, or perverted of all sense.

They do not count what blood and agony planted it in the world, nor Heaven's pleasure in those who search it in humility.

Each man, to show off, strains at some absurd invented truth; and it is these the preachers make sermons of; and the Gospel is not heard.

One says the Moon reversed its course to throw a shadow on the Sun during Christ's passion so that its light might not shine down below;

others say that the Sun itself withdrew and, therefore, that the Indian and the Spaniard shared the eclipse in common with the Jew.

These fables pour from pulpits in such torrents, spewing to right and left, that in a year they outnumber the Lapi and Bindi in all Florence.

Therefore the ignorant sheep turn home at night from having fed on wind. Nor does the fact that the pastor sees no harm done set things right.

Christ did not say to His first congregation: 'Go and preach twaddle to the waiting world.' He gave them, rather, holy truth's foundation.

That, and that only, was the truth revealed by those who fought and died to plant the faith. They made the Gospel both their sword and shield.

Now preachers make the congregation roar with quips and quirks, and so it laugh enough, their hoods swell, and they ask for nothing more.

But in their tippets there nests such a bird that the people, could they see it, would soon know what faith to place in pardons thus conferred.

Because of these such folly fills the earth that, asking neither proof nor testimonials, men chase whatever promise is held forth.

On such St. Anthony's pig feeds on, unstinted, and others yet more swinish feast and guzzle and pay their way with money never minted.

But we have strayed. Therefore before we climb turn your attention back to the straight path that we may fit our journey to our time.

So many beings are ranked within this nature that the number of their hosts cannot be said nor even imagined by a mortal creature.

Read well what Daniel saw at Heaven's height. You will soon see that when he speaks of 'thousands' every finite number is lost from sight.
To all, the Primal Light sends down Its ray. And every splendor into which it enters receives that radiance in its own way.

Therefore, since the act of loving grows from the act of recognition, the bliss of love blazes in some of these, and in some it glows.

Consider then how lofty and how wide is the excellence of the Eternal Worth which in so many mirrors can divide

Its power and majesty forevermore, Itself remaining One, as It was before."

Made in the USA
Monee, IL
10 May 2023

4cd70db1-79ba-4ccd-ad3c-1e474c0cb125R01